THE
TRENCHES

Parker Bilal is the author of the Makana Investigations series, the third of which, *The Ghost Runner*, was longlisted for the Theakston Old Peculier Crime Novel of the Year Award. *The Divinities*, the first in his Crane & Drake London crime series, was published in 2019. Parker Bilal is the pseudonym of Jamal Mahjoub, the critically acclaimed literary novelist. Born in London, he has lived in a number of places, including the UK, Denmark, Spain and, currently, the Netherlands.

@Parker_Bilal | jamalmahjoub.com

Also by Parker Bilal

Crane and Drake

The Divinities
The Heights

The Makana Series

The Golden Scales
Dogstar Rising
The Ghost Runner
The Burning Gates
City of Jackals
Dark Water

Standalone

Whitehavens

THE TRENCHES

PARKER BILAL

CANONGATE

First published in Great Britain, the USA and Canada in 2022
by Canongate Books Ltd, 14 High Street, Edinburgh EHI ITE

Distributed in the USA by Publishers Group West and in Canada
by Publishers Group Canada

canongate.co.uk

I

British Library Cataloguing-in-Publication Data
A catalogue record for this book is available on
request from the British Library

ISBN 978 1 83885 512 3

Typeset in Centaur MT by Palimpsest Book Production Ltd,
Falkirk, Stirlingshire

Printed and bound in Great Britain by Clays Ltd, Elcograf S.p.A.

'O'er those dead bones they built their city.'

Dante

＊

'The Eighth Circle of Hell is a huge funnel of rock, round which run a series of deep, narrow Trenches called "bolges". *Malbolges* is . . . the image of the City in Corruption: the progressive disintegration of every social relationship, personal and public. All . . . are perverted and falsified, til nothing remains but the descent into the final Abyss where faith and trust are wholly and forever extinguished.'

Dorothy L. Sayers, *Notes on Dante's Divine Comedy*

1

The single wiper scraped back and forth across the glass, making almost no impression against the pummelling rain. Rab Otley squinted through the sheet of water into the darkness, trying to make out any feature that would help him navigate. He'd been out in worse weather than this but not often, and the night was shaping into a real zinger.

The wheelhouse door flew open and a figure appeared. Small and covered in dirty yellow oilskins, you could hardly make out the damp, wispy hairs on the narrow chin.

'Get back up to the bow, Lemmy!' Rab yelled. 'I need your eyes.'

'I think there's something out there,' the boy gulped between gouts of saltwater. He wiped a hand over his wet face and pointed. 'Starboard quarter.'

Keeping one hand on the helm, Rab leaned out through the doorway. It was easier to focus somehow without the water streaming down the glass. He narrowed his eyes and squinted blindly into the blackness. A long minute went by before he saw it. Nothing more than a faint flicker, but his instincts told him that it was something real.

'What do you reckon, skipper?' Lemmy spluttered.

Despite the wind and the rain, Rab could still catch a hint of the sour smell of the boy's breath. He didn't seem to believe much in personal hygiene. The deck of the *Aurora Grey* was heaving up and down. It tilted sharply, forcing them to lean into it. Rab stepped back inside to grab the wheel with both hands.

'What do we do?' Lemmy asked again. Nineteen and fresh out of prison for some juvenile foolishness, he was not a natural fisherman. Rab suspected he didn't even like the sea.

'Let's take a look, shall we?' said Rab.

Inside the shelter of the wheelhouse, Lemmy tugged off his hood. The expression on his face suggested he wasn't convinced about the wisdom of this decision. Rab let out a loud laugh.

'Cheer up, son, this is nothing. Just a little shower.'

The only reason Lemmy was out here was that back in the day – when there were still fish in the sea, as Rab liked to say – Lemmy's father had taught Rab everything he knew. The old man was gone now, or as good as. Dementia. Couldn't remember what day of the week it was, or which side of the pot to piss in. The *Aurora Grey* had passed to Rab, who took the boy on as a favour to the old man. A decision about the wisdom of which he asked himself every day. Rab wasn't the type to complain. He just got on with things. Lemmy would be all right.

The little vessel lurched. Rab grabbed the helm a little

tighter. Through the glass Lemmy glimpsed what looked like a forest of tall, white trees. Straight trunks that were higher than anything he'd ever seen on land. They were bare of branches and leaves and seemed to be made of some weird kind of wood that didn't look as though it belonged on this planet. Trees made of bone. And they were talking to him.

The whisper was a steady beat, indistinguishable at first from the rain but now he could differentiate the two. The rhythmic hiss sounded like a gigantic thresher, the blades scything through the damp air overhead.

'What's that sound?' Lemmy squealed.

Rab ignored him. He was leaning forward over the wheel, trying to see what was ahead of them. They were way off course. The coordinates he had been given had to be wrong. Either that or the GPS naviagator was playing up. He ought to have replaced it months ago, but how was he supposed to afford that?

Suddenly he realised what it was. He threw his arm out and pulled back the throttle.

'Turbines!'

He cursed himself under his breath. Fuck's sake, Rab, what were you thinking?

In this weather they were going to have their work cut out to avoid hitting anything. The deck was heaving like a trampoline as the *Aurora Grey* came to a stop.

'It's not on the charts,' said Lemmy, scrabbling across the board, looking at the map.

'Of course it's not.' Rab thumped the screen of the GPS device bolted to the instrument panel, realising that the wind farm wasn't marked. They would have to find their own way out of this. The small trawler was bobbing angrily. With the engines idling, they were at the mercy of the waves. They couldn't stay here for long.

Lemmy pointed off into the distance.

'What is that?'

Rab leaned forward until his nose was almost touching the glass. The wiper swept back and forth in front of him.

'Are those people?' Lemmy asked, his voice spiralling upwards again.

'Shit!' muttered Rab. He pushed the throttle down and spun the wheel. Lemmy gave a yelp.

'Hey, skipper, wait, what are you doing?'

Rab looked at the boy. No one could say he hadn't given the kid a chance.

'I'm not going in there, lad!' he yelled back. 'We'll hit one of the pylons for sure. End of story.'

Lemmy was horrified. 'But we can't just leave them out here in this. They'll die, for sure.'

'Not my problem, lad.'

'You can't do it, Rab. You just can't.'

There was a long moment in which the only sound was the wind and the rain, the steady thump of the engine. Then Rab swore again.

'Get up to the front, then, and keep a lookout. And clip your harness in!'

Lemmy looked as though he regretted having spoken now. Then he realised that he had no choice. He pulled up his hood and headed out of the wheelhouse. The wind and spray hit him in a full-frontal blow. He staggered sideways until he got his footing, then he leaned into it and moved forward, clinging to the slick gunwale with both hands, hauling himself on. Ahead he could see the fluorescent spray breaking over the rising and falling of the bows. They were making progress again, slowly but enough to make a difference. The *Aurora Grey* was gaining momentum.

Lemmy reached the bow of the little fishing boat and stood there swaying, trying to hold on. He grabbed for the safety lanyard and fumbled, attempting to clip his harness into it. The snap catch was giving him trouble again but after several failed attempts he finally managed, crouching down for protection from a huge wave. When he peered out again he could make out two figures perched on the bottom of the access ladder at the base of the wind turbine dead ahead of them. Lemmy wiped a hand across his eyes to try and clear his vision. Behind him in the wheelhouse, Rab switched on the overhead lights. The powerful beams picked out driving darts of rain. They were closing in steadily. Lemmy shifted across to the starboard side. He could see now that one of the two looked like a child. The other was a woman. How in hell did they wind up out here?

Rab hung his head out of the wheelhouse door and yelled something that Lemmy couldn't catch. Something he was doing wrong, no doubt. The miserable bastard was always on his case. Lemmy tied a line to a life ring that he cast over the side. Rab was yelling something again. Fuck off, Lemmy willed in his mind. Leave me alone. I'm doing the best I can. He found himself praying. Dear God, let me help those people. That poor kid out there. He peered over the bow again and this time he could no longer see the two figures. Were they in the water? He leaned further out over the side, trying to look down. Rab was turning the little searchlight on top of the wheelhouse left and right, sweeping the beam out over the dark, heaving surface, trying to pick up anything else in the water, but there was nothing. No people and no vessel of any kind.

Rab could make out the two figures now. A woman and a small child she was clutching to her. A toddler. No more than a couple of years old. She had one arm wrapped around the maintenance access ladder that led up to the base of the wind turbine towering over them. The water was hitting them, threatening to dislodge them at any moment. Rab realised he was gritting his teeth. He could see Lemmy leaning over the side to haul in the life ring and throw it again. He hoped the idiot had remembered to clip his safety harness in. The deck heaved again. They weren't going to get any closer.

'Jump!' he willed the woman under his breath. She would never hear him. Even if she did, there was no guarantee that she would understand him. Lemmy was shouting, probably the same thing he was thinking. Then, incredibly, Rab saw the woman make a move. She too must have realised this was her only chance and so she plunged straight into the water, managing to get one arm through the life ring, the other still holding her child.

'Fuck!'

Rab spun the helm. Any closer and they risked ramming into the platform under the turbine. There was nothing

6

more he could do except pray the woman had the strength to hold on. He aimed the wheel for the open water ahead of them and pushed the throttle gently forward. All she had to do was hang on for a little while longer. He could see Lemmy hauling the lifeline back in. They were slowly coming free of the wind park. Locking the wheel in place, Rab stepped out of the wheelhouse to make his way forward. Lemmy was shouting something that Rab couldn't make out. Then, to his horror, he saw Lemmy unclip his safety harness.

'What the hell are you doing?' Rab yelled.

'The child,' Lemmy pointed. 'She's not going to make it. She's not strong enough.'

Reaching the bow just as Lemmy jumped over the side, Rab grabbed the lifeline and carried on pulling. There was already a rope ladder hanging down over the side of the *Aurora Grey*. He saw the woman below him.

'Climb up!' Rab yelled to her, gesturing to show what he meant.

He could see Lemmy in the water next to her, holding up the child for the woman to take. By some miracle she had managed to get onto the ladder. She was never going to be able to climb it, especially with the child now under her arm, so Rab began hauling it up, rung by rung, his arms straining with the weight. In his favour was the fact that she was clearly light. The deck heaved and he timed himself to use the swell of the boat, lifting as the deck tilted to starboard and then holding on as it rose up again. Finally he had hold of her arm. She was still clutching the child tightly to her. He pulled them both over the side. They all fell to the deck, but Rab was up straight away, tossing the ladder back down. He leaned over gunwale, yelling into the storm.

'Lemmy! Lemmy!'

2

The rain lashed over the seafront in high waves that broke across the road in sheets. Cal Drake could feel the water dripping off his chin as he walked back to the car. He managed to wrestle the door open against the wind and climb inside without dropping anything.

'Damn!' he muttered, shaking himself off. He set the coffee on the dashboard and the chicken wrap on the seat beside him. He switched on the engine and turned up the heat. Yes, it was bad for the environment, but right now avoiding hypothermia was his primary concern. He managed to extricate his phone from his side pocket and discovered it was so waterlogged it had switched itself off, hopefully not permanently.

Strewn over the seats, front and back as well as the floor, were folders and sheets of paper. Banking transactions, legal documents, property deeds. These were the files that had been taken from the safe of one Barnaby Nathanson, a lawyer who had been murdered nine months ago. The investigation had since been dropped and the case left open-ended. This wasn't actually the reason Drake was here. The fact was that Drake had always had trouble letting go. It didn't matter that he was a private operative now and no longer working for the Met; it was always his instincts that he relied on. Even back then when he was a detective inspector and should have known better.

Looking around at the chaos he was buried in, Drake felt annoyance, along with a faint twinge of guilt. He started tidying up the mess but wound up throwing handfuls onto the back seat before giving up and closing his eyes. After another night out he was seriously lacking in sleep. As the coffee sat cooling on the dashboard, he fell into a deep slumber.

He woke with a start to find an old man peering in at him through the side window. Drake yawned as he reached for the button to lower the glass.

'Can I help you?'

The man said nothing. He was wearing an overcoat and a long scarf, his white hair fluttering in the gentle breeze. Without a word, he turned and started off down the street, his walking stick marking each step with a thump.

The engine was still running, with the heating turned all the way up. With a groan, Drake switched it off and cracked open the door. The sun was out and the wind had dropped. It had been positively stormy overnight, not the perfect time for pulling an all-nighter. It was still chilly as Drake locked the car and zipped up his combat jacket. Down the street on a corner was an old-fashioned caff, the High Tide Café. He pushed the door open and sank into the damp fug of frying bacon and burned toast.

On the table by the window lay a crumpled and well-thumbed tabloid from the previous day. Generally, Drake did his best to steer clear of them. Depressing at the best of times, the nauseating whirl of self-righteous, muck-raking voyeurism and hardcore prejudice were enough to destroy what little faith he had left in humanity. He sometimes wondered what the impact of daily exposure to such vile amorality might be, and it surely wasn't good. He was about to throw the rag onto the next table when something caught his eye. An inset box under the red banner showed a photograph of a young man wearing sunglasses and an expensive suit, the shirt open to the waist. Twenty-six-year-old Silas Barron, it read, the wealthy tycoon worth half a billion, had disappeared. His whereabouts were unknown. Drake tried to recall why that name was familiar to him.

'What'll it be?' The waitress gave the table a quick wipe as she spoke.

'Coffee. Full breakfast. No bacon, or sausages.'

'Veggie breakfast. Gotcha.'

Drake thumbed through the pages until he came to the article itself. It was a double-page spread with pictures of Silas with a variety of celebrities, none of whom Drake recognised. He decided he'd had his fill and put the paper aside as his coffee arrived.

'You almost feel sorry for them,' said the waitress.

Drake looked up at her. 'How's that?'

'I mean, all that money and their lives are still shit.'

Before he had time to think of a comeback she had slid away. Everyone's a philosopher these days, he thought to himself as he chewed his way through sugary beans and soggy toast. The real question on his mind was what was he was doing in this place? Why couldn't he just let it go? It was the past, ancient history. Gone. Just drop it. But somehow he couldn't. More than facts, more than memories, this was a part of him now. Moving on just wasn't an option. Zelda's death was compounded by how she had died, what had been done to her and why. Zelda had been his key witness. He'd promised to protect her, and he'd failed. There was also the death of her son, Darius. Drake had been right there when it had happened. He'd felt the life go out of the boy's body. These were more than just memories. It was more than just another unsolved case. It was personal. To free himself he had to exorcise the demon from his soul.

That's why he was here.

The only thing was that he was making no progress at all. He had tried to convince himself that combing through Nathanson's files would provide a trail that would lead him through the maze to those responsible. But no clear path had become apparent, and all this was beginning to look like a colossal waste of time. Ray would not be happy. He owed her a call, to report in, to at least let her know he was still alive. He'd managed to put that off for the last three days and this was shaping up to be day four of radio silence. He knew that the longer he waited the more pissed off she would be, but somehow he couldn't bring himself to do it.

As he was exiting the café, two men were walking in. One of them bumped shoulders with him.

'Watch where you're going!'

Drake turned. He knew the look. It might have been a genuine accident, but the tone of the man's voice and the little snigger from his friend told him otherwise. They were looking for trouble. Drake considered his options. He was in no doubt that he could take the two of them out without even breaking into a sweat. But that wasn't why he was here. So, instead, he turned and walked away, noting the blue Ford Fiesta they had just parked on double yellow lines. He heard their chuckles behind him.

'Wanker!'

Arriving back at the car, Drake found another surprise waiting for him. A police car was parked in front of his old Vauxhall Astra. A BMW X5, which he identified as an Armed Response Unit. There were two officers standing by his car, one of them peering inside.

'Can I help you?' Drake asked as he came up.

The closest officer turned to face him. A thin, tall man with a wispy beard that gave him a rodent-like appearance.

'Is this your vehicle, sir?'

'What seems to be the problem?'

'We've had a report of suspicious behaviour by a man matching your description.'

Drake remembered the old man who had knocked on his window that morning.

'A little excessive, isn't it?' Drake smiled, nodding at the car. 'Pulling out an ARU for a dodgy punter?'

This brought a frown to the young officer's face. He was about to respond when the second officer stepped from behind the ARU, putting away his phone as he did. A tall, ruddy-faced man with straw-coloured hair that looked as though it had been cut with a lawnmower.

'Well, I never. Cal Drake. As I live and breathe.'

Drake smiled. 'Hello, Andy. Didn't know you were working this patch.'

Andy Felton tapped the epaulettes on the shoulder of his regulation pullover. 'Promotion. When opportunity beckons, you have to follow the calling.'

'You know this gentleman, sir?' the young PC asked, clearly wondering what possible connection there could be between this scruffy character and his chief inspector.

'DI Drake and I served together in Matlock, Constable. One of the best detectives I've ever had the pleasure of working with.'

The PC looked unconvinced but appeared prepared to give Drake the benefit of the doubt. For his part, Drake was a little surprised by the degree of warmth in Felton's introduction. Their time together during Drake's exile to Matlock had not been without difficulty, so far as he could recall.

'I was a DS back then,' Drake corrected him, but Andy wasn't having it.

'The demotion was unfair. If I'd had these back then' – he indicated the pips on his shoulders – 'I'd have restored you to detective inspector in a flash.'

'Kind of you to say so,' nodded Drake.

'So what brings you round our neck of the woods?' Felton asked when the young PC had retired to the vehicle to report on the situation.

'Well, I'm no longer on the force, for one thing,' Drake began.

'Yes, I heard a rumour,' said Andy Felton. 'Can't say it came as a surprise. The way you were treated — and, let's be honest, you're too much of a lone wolf to make it in an institution like the Met.'

'You may have a point.'

'So, what are you doing here?'

Drake nodded down the street. 'I have an old address for someone I'm looking for.'

'You're working a case?'

Drake shrugged. 'It's one of those old itches that won't go away. I need to talk to him.'

'What's his name? Maybe we can help.'

'Grayson Brodie. Old army buddy of mine.'

'The name rings a bell.'

'He's come up in a number of investigations. Nothing ever stuck.'

Felton nodded. 'And you've got your sights on him because . . .?'

Drake knew there was no point trying to pull the wool over Andy's eyes. If he wanted his cooperation, he was going to have to give him something.

'A young woman involved in an organised-crime case I was working on. Zelda. She went missing and disappeared. Her head turned up last year.'

Andy pulled a face. 'I heard about that. Nasty business.'

'Tell me about it.'

'And you think this man, Brodie, had something to do with it?'

'That's the way it looks. Problem is, he's vanished, and for want of a lead I came down here.' Drake jerked a thumb down the street. 'His mother used to run a boarding house at number thirty-three.'

'And you've been here all night?' Felton looked at the car.

'The private sector, all the trimmings,' shrugged Drake. 'Same old Cal. Look, let me do some digging.'

'Sure, that would be helpful, thanks. Oh, and by the way, a couple of jokers almost ran me down in their haste to park on a double yellow.' Felton got the message. 'You might want to send your PC over to have a word. Blue Ford Fiesta.' He gave him the number plate.

'I'll do that.' Felton waved the junior officer over and told him. The ARU sped off eagerly. While they waited for him to come back, Felton leaned in the window as they exchanged contact details.

'It must have been rough out here last night. We had a bit of a storm.'

'Yeah, I did notice. I thought that was normal for these parts.'

'No, it was a little more than that.' Felton gazed out at the sea. 'A fishing boat lost one of its crew members, a young lad.'

'What were they doing out in that weather?'

Felton heaved a sigh. 'These boys get up to all sorts. The fish is scarce and a few of them turn to other tricks to put food on the table. Lot of drugs coming in from the continent. Cocaine, happy pills, you name it, and of course there's money to be made in human trafficking.'

'You think that's what they were up to last night?'

'It's not clear.' Felton shook his head. 'The skipper has

16

contradicted his own testimony. In his first statements to the harbour master he mentioned a woman and a child.'

'He was confused? Hypothermia?'

'"They're safe," he said. "The lad saved them."'

'Meaning?'

'I'm not sure. That's why I'm off to interview the skipper again. Try to get some sense out of this.'

The two men shook hands.

'If you're back up this way, let me know and we'll have you over for dinner.'

'I'll do that,' said Drake. 'Sounds very respectable.'

'Oh, aye, not like the wild old days,' Felton laughed. 'Marriage. You're looking at a tamed beast.'

3

'Thank you for calling. You've reached the offices of Crane and Drake Investigations. None of our operatives are free to take your call. Please leave your name and number and we'll get back to you as soon as possible.'

Crane heard the answering machine go off in the outer office and got up from her desk to go over and shut the door. Heather was off sick and Crane really couldn't be bothered with a temp. They were often more trouble than they were worth. She'd thought she could manage – and had expected Cal to have returned by now from his little jaunt, but so far there had been no sign of him, not even a call to let her know when he would be back. She still might have managed, despite Cal's absence, except for the fact that she now appeared to be trapped in a meeting with potential clients that was turning into a full-blown emotional meltdown.

It had started well. Mr and Mrs Spencer had arrived together and that was saying a lot. They were one of those couples that had ploughed on when they probably should have gone their separate ways years ago. The one thing that still united them was their son, Jason.

'The Foreign Office has been next to useless,' Millie Spencer said as Crane took her seat again behind the desk.

'They don't care. They've washed their hands of the whole affair. It's disgraceful.' Crane allowed Paul Spencer to finish out of courtesy, even though none of this was helpful. She drew in a deep breath and looked at the notepad in front of her.

'Okay, tell me again why you think Jason is back here in this country?'

Mrs Spencer glanced at her husband before speaking. She was in her mid-fifties, blonde hair turning grey. She looked as though she took care of herself. Crane imagined Pilates classes combined with brisk walks and a lot of gardening. She also sensed that being married to Mr Spencer was actually quite hard work. Crane had met him for the first time a little over forty minutes ago but already she had the measure of him. Paul Spencer was one of those men who felt the world had treated him unfairly. He deserved better and, of course, he would never be satisfied with what he had.

'When he was a child, he used to play this game . . .' Millie Spencer began.

'Always playing bloody games.' Mr Spencer threw in a disapproving shake of the head.

'He used to leave messages for me rolled up and tucked into the little bird house down at the end of the garden.' Mrs Spencer was smiling at the memory. 'He was always a . . . an inventive child.'

'Look where that got him,' grunted Mr Spencer.

Mrs Spencer ignored the comment. 'An enquiring mind, is how one of his teachers described it.'

'So, you're saying that you found a message in the bird house and you think it was from Jason?'

'Oh, I know it was him.' Millie Spencer was adamant. 'Nobody else did that. It has to be him.'

'And you agree with this?' Crane turned to Mr Spencer.

'I saw the note,' he began. He seemed to be struggling to commit himself. 'It could well be him. It makes sense. The government has made it clear that people like Jason will be thrown in jail. He doesn't dare approach us openly.'

Crane nodded sympathetically. She lifted the note, now encased in a plastic sleeve, to study the handwriting. The script was neat and childish. The broad, looping letters in blue biro looked as though they had been written by a schoolboy. The sheet of lined paper could have been torn from a copybook. In places the ink had run. She turned it over. On the rear was a series of lines that looked like a rough map. Unlike the lines written on the other side, these were not diluted by water damage.

'When was it, exactly, that you found the note?'

'Three weeks ago tomorrow,' said Mrs Spencer firmly. 'It was the first Tuesday of the month, which is bridge night. That's why I remember.'

'But you didn't actually see Jason?'

'No, of course not. Why do I get the feeling you don't believe me?'

'I just need to be sure of the facts. It strikes me as odd that he would go to the trouble of hiding a note instead of, well . . .' Crane paused. 'Knocking on the door.'

It was Mr Spencer who answered. First with a long sigh that seemed to imply that Crane's question had confirmed his misgivings about coming here in the first place.

'He knows they're watching the place.'

'Who is *they*?' Crane turned her gaze to him.

'The police, Special Branch, what have you.'

'You know this for a fact?'

'Well, it's obvious, isn't it?' Mr Spencer's tone was irritated. 'They know. Of course they know. They're on the lookout for people like Jason. Stands to reason.'

Crane decided not to labour the point. The chances of any of the intelligence or security agencies being interested enough to mount a round-the-clock surveillance operation on the Spencers' house was patently absurd. They simply didn't have the resources. Still, that didn't stop the Spencers from believing it. And if they subscribed to the theory, there was no reason why Jason himself might not have drawn the same conclusion. She turned back to the note.

'You didn't actually see him?'

'No, but . . . there was a woman.'

Crane looked up. 'You saw her?'

'She was standing in the trees,' said Mrs Spencer. 'But I saw her. She was dressed all in black. Her head was covered and . . .'

'What else?'

'She had a child with her. A small child.'

Crane wondered if Mrs Spencer was prone to hallucinations, or perhaps was fond of a drink.

'And you're absolutely sure it's from him?'

'Those are his words!' Mrs Spencer's eyes were pleading. She just wanted to be believed. 'I'd know my son's handwriting anywhere.'

Her husband was studying the arm of the chair he was sitting in. 'It's him. I can feel it. He wants to come in.' His eyes lifted to find Crane's. 'He's done nothing wrong.'

'Well, technically he joined a designated terrorist organisation,' said Crane, tapping her pen on the notepad. 'Islamic State. That's a serious charge.'

'He was confused,' Mr Spencer said. 'His mind . . . He wasn't right.'

'I sympathise, Mr Spencer,' said Crane slowly. 'But whatever Jason's reasons for travelling to Syria, there are going to be consequences.'

'Of course.'

Mrs Spencer was smiling. 'He was always a romantic boy at heart,' she said.

'Oh, for god's sake, woman!' muttered her husband.

'He used to love *Beau Geste* when he was small,' she continued, ignoring him. 'The idea of running off and joining the French Foreign Legion.' She laughed. 'I used to catch him dressed up with a napkin over his head.'

'This wasn't the bloody foreign legion!' Spencer growled.

Crane stepped in, sensing that things were about to go off the deep end.

'We want you to bring our son home,' Mrs Spencer began again.

'We've been over this, Millie,' her husband immediately

corrected her. 'Legally, we can't know his whereabouts.' They had consulted the family solicitor on the subject. He dragged the words out. 'We just want to know if he's in this country.'

Crane tried to point out that the distinction was academic. If their son Jason was alive and in the UK, the real question was what he wanted to do.

'He's a grown man, after all and, as I said,' Crane went on, steering the conversation back, 'there is no clear consensus on how to treat those returning from fighting in Syria. Some countries are advocating leniency, de-radicalisation programmes and so forth. The UK government takes a harder line.'

'Too right,' agreed Mr Spencer. 'My father fought in the war. Younger than Jason, he was. He would be turning in his grave if he knew about this.'

'He probably is anyway,' said Mrs Spencer tartly. 'He was never happy about anything either.'

'Jason's a good lad,' Mr Spencer went on, returning to the subject in hand. 'His head was turned.'

Jason Spencer had left home to attend Norwich University. It was there that he appeared to have found a new course in life.

'It was that woman who turned him,' Mr Spencer went on.

'Which woman?' queried Crane, looking up from her notes.

'Oh, just a woman he met when he was at uni. She turned his head.' Mrs Spencer shrugged as if to say this was just a man thing. 'Selina. That was her name.'

'You are so simple. You're simple-minded,' Mr Spencer chastised her before addressing Crane. 'She's the one. She led him on. She wasn't even at uni. They met online, one of these chat rooms or whatever they call them. She told him his life was superficial, that all he cared about was material things.'

'Well, it's true,' Mrs Spencer interjected. 'Look at us.'

'For god's sake, woman!' Mr Spencer thumped his fist into his thigh. 'She made him give it all up, everything he'd worked for, everything *we'd* worked for.'

'Please,' Crane pleaded with them both. 'I really need to get as much solid information as I can. So it would be helpful if we just stick to the facts.' She delivered this with a smile. Secretly she was cursing Drake for not being there. At times like this, though she hated to admit it, it could be useful to have a man around. People like Mr Spencer responded better.

'The facts are plain.' Mr Spencer leaned forward to tap his index finger on the desk. 'That woman persuaded him to drop out and turn his back on everything: university, career, future prospects, family, even his religion.'

'Are you saying that this woman, Selina, persuaded Jason to convert to Islam?'

Mr Spencer couldn't bring himself to answer that one. Mrs Spencer looked down at her hands before speaking.

'We didn't really think much of it at the time. I mean, it seemed no worse than when he'd come home with his hair dyed blue. Kids go through phases when they're young, don't they?'

'That's what you thought this was?' asked Crane. 'A phase?'

'We thought he'd grow out of it,' said Mrs Spencer. Her voice was wavering now.

'*You* thought he would. I knew we were in trouble,' said Mr Spencer.

'Of course you did,' smiled Mrs Spencer, her voice dripping with irony.

'He came up to London to be with her, that woman, and that was the end of it.'

'Just to be clear' – Crane tried again to establish a timeline – 'when exactly was this?'

'He went to Norwich in September 2013.' Mrs Spencer counted on her fingers. 'So six, nearly seven years ago now. He dropped out after his first year and then moved to London.'

'Were you in regular contact with him at the time?' Crane's gaze shifted from one to the other.

'No.' Mrs Spencer shook her head. 'Not regular. He would call occasionally. He knew we didn't approve.'

'He disapproved of us,' said Mr Spencer. 'Didn't want anything to do with us.'

'You don't know that,' Mrs Spencer retorted.

'He was ashamed of us. Who we are and how we live.' It was Mr Spencer's turn to shake his head. 'I've never heard anything like it. How can you be ashamed of who you are, or where you come from?'

'And when did you know that Jason was thinking of going to Syria?'

'Oh, well, we didn't,' said Mrs Spencer. 'We only found out once he was there.'

'He contacted you?' Crane asked. 'Can I ask how?'

'Facebook,' said Mrs Spencer slowly. She sounded reluctant to divulge the information. 'He knew he could always reach me there.' She reached into her bag and produced a stiff envelope. 'I took some screenshots. I don't know why. I just thought I needed something to hold on to him.'

'You must have been shocked,' said Crane, ignoring Mr Spencer's dismissive sigh.

'At first, I just didn't believe it. I mean, what business did he have being out there?' Mrs Spencer fished a handkerchief from her sleeve and wiped her nose. 'But I could see it was him, with a big beard and wearing Arab clothing.'

'How did he seem?'

Through her tears, Mrs Spencer smiled. 'Happy. He was trying to put a brave face on it.'

'Can't bloody credit it,' muttered Mr Spencer.

'And this was when, exactly?' Crane asked, as she leafed through the prints of Jason's Facebook page. She would look at them more closely later, see if there was any information there she could use.

'This was the middle of May, 2015.'

Crane knew that this coincided with the moment when Daesh, or Islamic State, was at the height of their expansion.

'You said he seemed happy. Did he seem balanced to you?' Crane asked, noticing how the question caused Mr Spencer's hands to ball into fists on his knees. He said nothing.

'He said he'd found what he'd always been looking for.' Mrs Spencer hesitated. 'A lot of what he said didn't make much sense to me. I mean, he was rambling, talking about the Spanish Civil War. What has that got to do with anything? He believed he was part of history.'

'Un-bloody believable!' muttered Mr Spencer under his breath.

'Did Jason give any indication then that he planned to return to this country?'

'Oh, no, not then. I mean, as I said, he seemed to believe in what he was doing.' Mrs Spencer hesitated. 'It was on the later call that he seemed to have changed his tune.'

'When was this?' Crane asked.

'More than a year later.' Millie Spencer glanced at her husband, who was shaking his head again. 'I was alone. It was in the afternoon and I suddenly got this call. Jason looked different.'

'Different how?'

'He was thinner. He'd lost weight.' Mrs Spencer's face clouded over as she tried to recall the details. 'His eyes were dark. You know? Like he was worried. I could see he wasn't sleeping properly. It was dark, the room, I mean. While we were speaking, there was what sounded like an explosion. I asked him what it was and he said nothing. Just exercises.' She paused to collect her thoughts. 'I could see he was scared. I could feel it. I said to him, you don't belong there, Jason. Come home. And he smiled in a kind of strange way. He looked lost. He said, I wish I could. There's nothing in the world I want more.' She looked up at Crane. 'Then the line went dead and he was gone.' Her voice trembled. 'I didn't know what to think. I was terrified.'

Now Crane addressed herself to Mrs Spencer. 'Do you think the woman who you saw in your garden could be the same woman who he met online?'

'I don't know.' Mrs Spencer began to fret. 'It didn't occur to me. She looked so . . . alien.'

Crane went back over her notes, circling places where she needed more information. She asked more questions and took all the details of addresses and numbers, names. She had photocopies of Jason's passport and driving licence. She persuaded a reluctant Mrs Spencer to share her Facebook username and password.

'How much is this going to cost us?' Mr Spencer asked warily.

'We have a standard introductory package that includes a preliminary investigation,' said Crane. 'If we find anything substantial, we'll let you know. Then you can decide if you want to go further.'

'And if you don't – find anything, I mean?' Mr Spencer asked.

'Then that's the end of it.'

'It's not about the money,' Mr Spencer explained. 'He's my son, no matter how I feel about his actions. I'll do whatever needs to be done.'

'I understand that.' Crane took a deep breath. 'It's important not to get your hopes up.'

'If you find him,' Mrs Spencer began, 'do you have to hand him to the police?'

Crane shook her head. 'We're not obliged to do that. We're a private consulting firm.' She looked at them both. 'But if he's in this country, Jason would be advised to turn himself in at some point. I suggest we take this one step at a time.'

Downstairs at the front door she shook hands with them both.

'I'll be in touch as soon as I have something.'

Back at her desk, Crane went over the details again. If Jason Spencer was on a watch list then his passport would have been flagged. That was no guarantee he would be picked up, in this country or anywhere in between. People slipped through holes in the system all the time. But if he was careful he would have tried to travel by some less conventional route. Islamic State was more or less finished. Lots of fighters were trying to get home to the safety of Europe without facing charges. A fake passport was another possibility, but it wasn't clear how easy it would be for him to acquire one, either in Syria, or Turkey, assuming he could get there.

She began by making a couple of calls. First to a contact on the foreign desk at *The Times* who told her that up to nine hundred people were believed to have left the UK to join Daesh – an acronym for Dawla Al Islamiyya fi Iraq wa'al Sham, the Islamic State in Iraq and Syria. Around a fifth of them were estimated to have been killed. Half of the remainder were thought to have returned. Figures were vague. Nobody really knew what was going on. In a sense, the government didn't want to know. It was a thorny subject; what to do with them. There were thousands of people, men, women and children, with European nationality sitting in camps in Kurdistan, their fate unclear.

This was confirmed by her contact at the FCO, Dick Renshaw.

'We're sitting on our hands and that's creating more of a problem. These people are our responsibility, whether we like it or not. We should bring them back and deal with it before it comes back to bite us.'

'Then why not do it?'

There was a lot of political opposition. 'The optics are not good. Nobody wants helping terrorists on their resumé.' Also, Renshaw explained, in legal terms things were very grey. 'Do we go through the whole business of trying them under laws of treason?' Over a hundred people so far had had their British citizenship revoked, despite the fact that this was actually illegal under international law. Nothing was clear. The vagueness of the situation made it the perfect political football – to be kicked in whatever direction current popular sentiment was leaning.

At the end of all this, Crane felt she was only slightly wiser than she had been at the outset. Still, their job was to find Jason first. Facing the consequences would come after that. The most obvious place to start was with Selina, the mystery woman who had entered his life and apparently turned his head, at least according to his parents. The term meant different things to each of them. To the mother it meant love, while Mr Spencer was clearly convinced that Selina had been instrumental in persuading Jason to convert to Islam and travel to Syria. Either way, she had to be worth talking to.

Crane started going back through the press, looking for any reports on anything that might be connected. She came across one that was interesting. A reporter on a local paper, the *Freshney Gazette*, had a story about the skipper of a fishing boat describing rescuing a woman and child at sea. His crewmate was lost in the process. No other outlet made any mention of this story.

Crane sat back with a sigh and stared at the clock on the wall. The day had shot by and still no sign of Cal. What was he playing at? Recently, she had begun to ask herself if bringing him in had been a mistake. He was an excellent investigator whose instincts always seemed to lead him in the right direction but he was also bloody infuriating at times.

4

It was past midnight when Drake arrived back in London. The traffic was smooth and light. He was coming in from the north, which posed him with something of a dilemma. He had tried calling Ray, but by then her phone was off or out of juice, or whatever. Since she was usually something of a night owl, there was a strong possibility that she might be home and just didn't want to talk to him, which was fair enough. He owed her an explanation. The decent thing to do was to drop by and fill her in on what he had been doing these last three days.

The easier course of action was to drive straight down to south London and leave it for tomorrow. But he knew that once he was home he would crack open a bottle of rum, order a takeaway and kick back. Happy just to be able to sleep in his own bed after being scrunched up in the back seat of the car for days. By the time he dozed off it would be the early hours and since he hadn't slept properly for the last two nights he had some catching up to do. All in all this would add up to more than twelve hours' delay to his conversation with Ray.

His conscience took hold of the wheel and swung it, cutting over the white lines to hit the off ramp at speed, hearing the startled protest of an articulated lorry's horn bellowing in his wake. He settled down and drove smoothly through empty streets of orange sodium glow towards west London. Fifteen minutes later found him a stone's throw from Paddington Station, gliding down the cobblestones into Balfour Mews. There were no lights on anywhere in the house except the downstairs living space/kitchen. Drake unlocked the door and let himself in. He switched off the alarm, which told him that Crane was probably asleep upstairs. He took a light swipe at the punch bag as he went by.

The familiar surroundings made him suddenly realise how tired he was. He pulled open the fridge and found a bottle of Corona in the door. When he swung the door shut, he let out a cry. She was standing right there, holding a baseball bat.

'Fuck's sake! Did nobody ever tell you that you can give a man a heart attack doing that?'

Crane set down the bat against the wall in the corner. 'It's been so long since I've seen you I thought it was an intruder.'

Drake moved past her to find an opener in the drawer. 'I feel for the guy, even though he doesn't exist.' He took a swig from the bottle and sat down at the island counter shaking his head.

'I was beginning to wonder.' Crane leaned on the counter. 'Where've you been?'

'Chasing a ghost.'

'Zelda? Again? Come on, Cal. I told you, you have to let it go.'

'I will, just as soon as I find Brodie and settle this once and for all.'

'We are still partners, right?'

'Last time I checked.' Drake took another swig of beer.

'Get some sleep,' Crane said as she started walking back towards the front stairs. 'We can talk tomorrow. We have a new client.'

He managed to take off his boots and find a blanket in a cupboard by the stairs, then he lay down on the long sofa and shut his eyes. The last thing he heard was the sound of the rain clattering onto the cobblestones outside. He was instantly asleep.

When he opened his eyes dawn was just breaking, the rooftops and chimneys of the next building visible through the high windows at the back of the room. An old garage door that could be slid open in the summer to reveal an enclosed little courtyard whose walls were surrounded by plants. A cat was strolling along the top of the high wall. A movement caused it to stop and look in through the window. Drake turned his head. Looking over towards the kitchen area on the other side of the room he saw a woman that he did not recognise. Her long, black hair stretched all the way down to her naked behind. She was drinking orange juice straight from a plastic container. She wiped her mouth as she put it back. As she turned she caught sight of Drake looking at her. Without a word, she turned and walked away and disappeared up the staircase that led up to Ray's bedroom.

Drake shut his eyes and tried to sleep some more. He managed another couple of hours before being woken again by activity in the kitchen. He struggled to sit up and rubbed his eyes to see Crane busy moving around with more energy than he could muster. It made him tired just to watch her throwing fruit into a smoothie blender and grinding coffee beans.

'Somebody's bright-eyed this morning,' he yawned. She looked over at him.

'You look like you've been held hostage for months.'

'That's kind of how it feels.' Drake rubbed his chin and decided he was probably in need of a shower and a shave. 'I met your friend.'

Crane shrugged. 'We've hooked up a couple of times. She's nice, but it's nothing special.' She handed him a mug of coffee that Drake took gratefully. 'Speaking of which, how's your sex life?'

Drake winced. 'Not worth mentioning, I'm afraid.'

'How about Maritza? I thought you had something there.'

'Well, I suppose me being the reason her son was taken hostage put the whole thing in a different light.'

'Yeah,' nodded Crane. 'I can see that.'

Drake sipped his coffee, which was good. He liked to be dismissive of Crane's obsession with grinding beans and all the rest of it, but he couldn't deny the fact that this was a lot better than the instant stuff he tended to subsist on at home.

'How are things holding up here?'

'Oh, you mean, like work?' Crane raised her eyebrows.

'Look, I'm sorry, I should have called, or something.'

'Or something sounds about right.' Crane eased herself up onto one of the high stools. 'I take it you didn't find him.'

'Brodie?' Drake turned the coffee mug round in his hands. 'I'm not even sure what I would do if I did find him.'

'You know it's not your fault Zelda was killed, right?'

'I've tried telling myself that over and over.' Drake shrugged the blanket off as he got to his feet, noticing there was a hole in his left sock that he had not seen before. 'It just doesn't go away.'

'But you're convinced that Brodie is the one who killed her?'

'I can't say, but I've known Brodie a long time. I need to look him in the eye when I ask him.'

It was hard for Drake to understand how a man like Brodie, someone he would have trusted with his life, could have killed Zelda, decapitated her and then lied about his involvement.

'What took you up to Grimsby, of all places?'

'His mother used to run a boarding house up there.' Drake paced to the window and looked out onto the little yard. The rain had started again and water was splashing into little pools between the uneven cobblestones. 'He told me years ago. It was somewhere he could get away from everything.'

'His mother?' Crane frowned. 'Doesn't sound that hard to find.'

'Brodie never knew his mother. He was adopted. When he tracked her down she had already passed away. He bought the house and carried on running it in her name. No direct connection.'

Truth be told, Crane had always found this loyalty between enlisted men hard to grasp. She'd seen it first hand when she was in Iraq and she knew that Brodie and Drake had served over there together. Cal had told her plenty of stories about how Brodie had helped him, saved his life even. A bond was created. That much she understood. But all of these military types had a weird element to them that was difficult to describe. It was as if they recognised something in each other, something they couldn't find in other people.

'You're still convinced he's innocent,' she said. 'Deep down, I mean.'

'Maybe. I want to give him a chance to explain himself.'

'And if you're wrong?'

Drake had asked himself the same question more times than he cared to remember. 'I guess I'll have to deal with that when I get there. Speaking of work, did you read about this rich kid who went missing – Silas Barron?'

'What about him?'

'Maybe we should contact the family and offer our services?'

'Nice idea, but there's probably a queue already waiting to do the same. And besides' – Crane hopped down from the stool – 'we already have a new client.'

It wasn't the answer Drake had been hoping for. His interest in Silas Barron's disappearance was not entirely random. The missing boy's father, Jarvis Barron, was a key name in the paperwork Drake had been obsessing over for months. He was, in other words, central to a case that no longer existed and of which he was no longer a part.

Crane sensed his hesitation. 'Is there a problem?'

'Not at all. Anything interesting?'

'Could be,' said Crane. 'Perhaps it would be good for you, having something new to focus on.'

'You're right, of course.' Drake came over and sat down at the island counter while Crane refilled his mug. She explained about Jason Spencer's parents. When she had finished the whole story it was time for her to make another pot of coffee. Drake had to wait for the grinder to stop before speaking.

'So, we don't actually know that he's back in the country?'

'If he is, then he's keeping a low profile to avoid prosecution.'

'Makes sense,' nodded Drake. 'Listen, I meant it when I said I was sorry.'

She looked at him. 'It's okay,' she said, 'we're cool.'

'So I'm assuming you've already thought this through. Where do we start?'

'I have a few ideas,' said Crane, folding her arms. 'Are you sure you're ready to put your ghosts behind you for this?'

Drake met her gaze. 'I'm ready,' he said quietly.

5

Kelly Marsh was standing in the rain in Freetown when the call came in. In front of her the splintered debris of a scooter lay scattered across the road. A mangled squad car was crumpled against a wall, where it had wound up after the driver lost control, the distinctive yellow and blue Battenberg sides twisted out of shape. She could see streaks of red paint where the scooter had scraped along the side of the response vehicle.

'How bad is it?'

'One of them suffered a severe neck injury. He was airlifted to hospital in a critical condition,' said the young female uniform who was policing the scene.

'Who are they?' Marsh nodded towards the ambulance parked down the street where the two officers who had been in the car were being treated for minor cuts and bruises.

'Warren and Taylor,' the PC said with a shrug. 'I don't know them.'

Marsh didn't know them either. She went over to stand by the rear door of the ambulance.

'Haven't seen you two around here before,' she said.

'We're part of the new task force,' said the shorter one, Warren.

'First I've heard of it,' said Marsh.

'I wouldn't worry about it, love,' said the second. 'Nobody's too worried about a couple of mopes.'

'Detective Sergeant Marsh to you, Constable,' she said. She had learned not to let things like 'love' get to her, but she also knew you had to keep reminding people who you were.

'Sorry, Sarge.'

Marsh no longer jumped at every little slight. You needed to conserve your anger, store it up for the right moment, but here she was surprised by their attitude. They were both in their twenties and cocky with it. They looked similar. Dark hair cut short. Warren had a rounder face. Taylor was taller and leaner. Lads. Grinning to each other about their narrow escape. Didn't seem too bothered about the damage they'd done.

'What's this task force about, then?'

'You should talk to DCI Pryce, Sarge.' Taylor, the slimmer of the two, seemed to feel some pity.

'I will.' Marsh looked to the paramedic who was treating a cut on Warren's face. 'Any news about the kids on the scooter?'

'One's in surgery, the other's in intensive.'

'Thanks,' said Marsh and left them to it. She found her phone and called Chief Superintendent Wheeler to let him know about the situation. She gave him a quick summary. The

Incident Response Vehicle had been in pursuit of a sixteen-year-old kid who was making a pizza delivery. He ran a red light and the IRV had decided to give chase. Against all advice. Chases tended to produce little except damage. So just a couple of keen officers who let their emotions get the better of them. The driver lost control, or so he said. By the looks of things he had rammed the scooter.

'I wasn't informed about a task force, sir.'

'It's Pryce. Orders from on high. He's trying to clean up the area.'

'He should know better than to let a couple of rookies loose in Freetown, shouldn't he?'

Wheeler sighed down the line. 'You know Pryce, likes to do things his own way.'

'That's fine for him, but we're going to be cleaning up after him.'

'Just do the best you can. I'll try to have a word with Pryce, for what it's worth.'

'One of the scooter's occupants is in intensive care. Let's just hope they don't decide to sue.'

As she hung up, Marsh glanced at the crowd that had taken up residence along the police tape that had been strung across the street. This being Freetown, the whole situation could turn volatile at any moment. The onlookers were mostly young, no doubt friends of the two kids who had been making their getaway on the scooter. It wouldn't take long, in her opinion, for them to decide to take matters into their own hands. The graffiti on the walls around them already made plain the general feeling round here towards the police: Cops = Killers was spray-painted on the shutters of the closed-down shop to her left. Even at a distance you could feel their anger. It had been a bad call to chase the kids onto the estate. By nightfall she reckoned there would be roads blocked and tyres set alight, all in time for the evening news.

Marsh's phone began to ring. It was Wheeler again. She couldn't believe he'd had time to talk to Pryce already. It turned out the Chief Superintendent was calling for an entirely different reason.

'Marsh, are you still in Freetown?'

'Yes, sir.'

'Well, hand over command to DS Bishop. I have something more urgent for you.'

'More urgent, sir?' Marsh surveyed the scene in front of her.

'It's a murder and it involves a member of parliament,' Wheeler said crisply. 'That trumps a couple of juvenile delinquents, wouldn't you say?'

'Yes, sir.'

'And we need a woman's touch on this one.'

'Sir?'

Although Marsh would have been happy to labour the point, to which she might have added her doubts about leaving Bishop in charge of this mess, she had no objections to being transferred to a murder case. On the contrary, it was what she had been asking for and nothing was going to persuade her otherwise, though she did grind her teeth a bit. Wheeler, however, appeared to have anticipated her misgivings.

'And before you start getting yourself worked up that you're getting the job because you're a woman, let me set your mind at rest. You've earned this on merit. The fact that you're a woman only underlines why you are the right officer for the job.'

'I think I can live with that, sir,' said Marsh.

'Good, then get over to Liston Road. The officer in charge of the scene is a DS Chiang. He'll hand over to you when you arrive. And Marsh . . .'

'Sir?'

'There's going to be a lot of press attention on this one. That translates into we need it dealt with sharpish.'

'Got you, sir.'

As Marsh signed off, the female uniform came up and showed her an evidence bag containing a small plastic sachet of white powder.

'Is that what I think it is?' she asked.

'Cocaine would be my guess.'

'Where was it?' Marsh asked.

'Underneath the pizza, inside the box.'

'Nice. Order a four seasons and get a ticket to the stars.' The uniform didn't seem to get her attempt at humour. Marsh wondered how the officer had known to look inside the box. The Little Sammy's Pizzeria box had blazing lettering and featured a bloke with an Italian moustache on roller skates. She wondered who Little Sammy was and who he was working for.

'Tell DS Bishop I had to leave,' she said, but before she could finish, Marsh spotted a grey figure coming towards her. Too late. She'd been hoping to avoid the chinless wonder. Bishop had hanging pouches under his bloodshot eyes and was chewing gum like a pro. 'Never mind,' she muttered. 'I'll do it myself.'

Bishop had the usual smug look on his face. She filled him in as briefly as possible. He could find out the rest by himself if he could be bothered.

'Believe it or not, Marsh, I was doing this before you made DS,' he said.

'Just don't set the place on fire while I'm away,' she said.

'Very funny. Off you go, then.'

She hadn't mentioned the political angle to the case she was heading for. That would only have made him jealous. Bishop thought that promotion would come his way because he did all the right things. He played on the squad football team, bought drinks for all the right people. He socialised. It would have been a source of irritation to him that he might be passed over by someone like Marsh, who did none of the above, and was a woman to boot.

Liston Road was in the Old Town area of Clapham, north of the Common. It was a nice enough street, rows of neat Victorian houses with steps up to the front door. The kind of place where clever, young, upwardly mobile couples settled for a time while they plotted their rise to the top.

The house was cordoned off by a squad car on either side and a Scene of Crime van that was parked further down. A smart new black BMW with grille lights was parked at an angle. Some neighbours were standing on their doorsteps wrapped in cardigans but a surprising number of people seemed to take little interest. They crossed the street and went on their way. They glanced through windows and then went back to their game shows or whatever. Nobody wanted to get involved.

The uniform at the bottom of the steps recognised Marsh and waved her inside. Upstairs a crime scene officer was busy dusting the front door for prints. Inside the hallway, Marsh paused to look around her. There was an oil painting of two greyhounds facing a long mirror on the opposite side, next to an antique coat rack. From the moment you stepped into the house you could tell there was something classy about the place, and the people who lived there.

The hallway was cluttered with objects and people. Evidence boxes, UV light cases, medical kits, along with photographers and more crime scene officers. Figures in disposable blue jumpsuits shuffled around one another.

The door to the front living room was on the left. The rear wall had been knocked through to make a wide arch at the back of the room that gave access to a dining room. Beyond that five wide steps led down to an extension built onto the back of the house. This was taken up by an open-plan kitchen. Terracotta tiles on the floor and dazzling black marble on every surface. Marsh took all of this in with a glance before turning her attention back to the body.

The victim was a woman in her thirties. Red hair, hazel eyes that would have been pretty in life. She was slumped across a wide desk pushed into the bay window. The surface was a mess of papers, stacks of books and heaps of folders. The edges of the desk were decorated with a row of multi-coloured Post-It notes tacked onto the wood. Marsh squinted at a couple of these, trying to make out what was written on them, without success. The folders appeared to hold newspaper clippings and photocopied sheets stapled together in bunches. Marsh couldn't tell if the chaos was intentional or had been caused by somebody turning it over looking for something.

There was no doubt about the murder weapon. The weird-looking axe was still lodged in the victim's spine. The metal shaft was curved and painted a bright lime-green colour. Some kind of ergonomically designed tool, was her first thought. The blade resembled a velociraptor's claw. It was a nasty-looking thing, narrow and serrated. The tip was sunk so deeply into the woman's body it must have severed the spine instantly. Marsh leaned over for a better look.

'My guess is carbon fibre,' said a voice behind her. 'For the shaft. The blade is hardened steel.'

She turned to see a tall man standing in the doorway. He was wearing a rather fancy leather coat over a smart suit. His hands were in his pockets. He took one of them out as he stepped forwards.

'DS Chiang,' he said. 'You must be Marsh.'

Marsh shook the proffered hand. The name sounded Chinese, and there was something East Asian about the man's eyes and the straight black hair that hung down across his forehead a little too far. Too cute for his own good. The hand went back into the pocket of the coat as he stepped around her.

'The pathologist is on the way, but I would say death was instantaneous, wouldn't you?'

Marsh might, but she wasn't going to jump to his tune just yet. 'What is that thing?' she asked.

'It's an ice axe,' said Chiang. 'Climbers use them for tackling frozen waterfalls and suchlike.'

'Suchlike.' Marsh nodded, taking a last long look at the tool with its weirdly space-age design. The blade looked as though it was designed to imitate the shape and impact of a claw. It must have gone in like a hot knife into soft butter. She was a little annoyed that Chiang knew so much about these things.

First impressions were important. She'd learned that much from Drake. This was the way the killer had left the scene. Marsh stepped back, took a deep breath and tried to take in the whole room with fresh eyes. Apart from the desk, nothing much appeared to have been disturbed. There was remarkably little blood, considering. The victim's right hand had tipped over a mug of coffee. The liquid had soaked into the papers that were distributed across the desk. She tried to get a look at what was printed there as she spoke over her shoulder without looking.

'What are you then, Special Operations?'

'Parliamentary and Diplomatic Protection. How did you know?' Chiang's eyebrows arched when she turned to him.

'The car outside,' said Marsh. 'The flashy Beemer? That's you, right?' She waited for him to nod before going on. 'So what's the connection? She's your client?'

'Not her,' said Chiang. 'She's not the registered owner.'

'Okay,' said Marsh, waiting for more. When it didn't come she took another look at the victim. 'She's been moved.'

Chiang seemed taken aback by that. He moved round to the other side of the body from Marsh. He studied the positioning of the papers for a moment before nodding his agreement.

'She was pushed to one side.'

'She was in the way,' Marsh went on. 'The killer wanted something off the desk and she was lying on it.'

'Could be,' said Chiang. He seemed to be uncomfortable when he wasn't in complete charge.

Marsh was testing the floorboards. They were old enough in places to squeak. 'Why didn't she hear him coming up behind her?'

Chiang pointed to the set of headphones lying on the floor. 'She was listening to music. With those things on you wouldn't hear an elephant charging at you.'

It was more than feasible. 'So who is it? The VIP who lives here?'

'Zoë Helms.' Chiang waited for a reaction on Marsh's face. 'Rising star of the Conservative Party? Has a seat up in Lincolnshire.'

Marsh knew little about Zoë Helms off the top of her head. She'd seen her on the news and in the papers. Generally speaking she didn't take much of an interest in politics.

'And you're supposed to be protecting her?'

He shook his head. 'She's too low profile for a protection detail. But our job is to step in if there is anything involving a Member of Parliament.'

'To make sure there's no political angle?' asked Marsh.

'Something like that.'

The two of them turned as a slight, bespectacled figure appeared in the doorway. Milo Kowalski blinked as he looked around the room. He came in without saying hello to either of them and took a look at the body.

'It's Leon Trotsky,' he muttered.

Marsh stared at him. 'Come again?'

'Trotsky,' Milo explained, glancing at Chiang. 'He was murdered in Mexico. The assassin, Ramon Mercader, used an ice axe.'

'As I've said before, you're a mine of useless gems,' said Marsh. 'Milo Kowalski meet DS Chiang.'

'Charmed,' said Milo before addressing Marsh. 'The chief pathologist is here.'

'Right,' nodded Marsh. 'We'd better get out of his way, then.'

'I think I'll stay here,' said Chiang. Milo and Marsh exchanged looks.

'Suit yourself,' said Marsh. She led the way into the next room, with Milo trailing behind.

'I thought you were in charge of this?' Milo whispered.

'I am, but the owner of this place happens to be a Member of Parliament, so we're saddled with Inspector Gadget there.'

'Right, PaDP.'

Neither of them had had many dealings with the Parliamentary and Diplomatic Protection department. They knew it had a reputation and saw itself as somewhat above the general level of the average police officer. They had reached the kitchen. One of the overalls waved them over and pointed down a short passage.

'Looks like they got in this way.'

Milo and Marsh followed the crime scene officer along the corridor into a utilities space. On one side a washing machine and dryer were stacked above one another. There was a toilet next to that and the walls of the corridor were lined with cupboards and shelves. Past all of this was an open seating area with French windows on three sides. A pane of glass had been smashed on the left-hand side.

'Wouldn't someone have heard that?' Milo asked.

'It could have been done earlier,' Marsh pointed out. 'Unless you came all the way down here, you wouldn't see it. Plus, she had headphones on. I don't see a device, though.'

'No phone, no laptop either?'

'Not so far as I can tell.'

From the living room above them they could hear Archie Narayan lecturing DS Chiang.

'I don't care how you do things in Whitehall. If you don't get out of my way I shall write you up as obstructing my work. Are we clear?'

It wasn't possible to make out Chiang's response, but they heard him walking out of the room.

'Well, can't say we didn't warn him,' Milo grinned.

'What do we know about this woman, Zoë Helms?'

'I didn't have time to do much research before coming out,' Milo said, fishing his notebook out of the pocket of his anorak. 'Zoë Helms trained as a lawyer. She went into politics about ten years ago and is considered a rising star of the centre right.'

'I don't know what that means,' said Marsh.

'As far as I can tell, it means she keeps switching parties.

Started out in Labour, then a stint in the Lib Dems and now landed in the Conservatives.'

'Like she can't really make up her mind?'

'It's modern politics – hard to tell where one thing ends and another begins.'

While Milo was reading out his notes, Marsh was poking around the utilities space. A large section of wall in the corridor was taken up by a collection of old VHS tapes. She ran her eye over the film titles. A mix of classics that someone had obviously gone to the trouble of collecting before technology took a leap and couldn't quite bring themselves to get rid of. Alongside this was the built-in storage space that contained the washing machine and dryer along with piles of towels, laundry baskets. Next to this hung a heap of ropes, rucksacks and climbing gear, including an ice axe similar to the one embedded in the victim's spine. 'This is where the killer found the murder weapon.'

Milo came back over to join her. 'Better get SOCO down here.'

'Makes it look as though the murder was unplanned,' said Marsh. 'Killer breaks in, looks around for a weapon and heads up the stairs.' Marsh followed the line the killer would have taken. 'Get them to check the walls, all the surfaces here and here. They might have put a hand out to steady themselves. Let's see what Archie has to say.'

'Oh, yippee!' muttered Milo, who always found Archie difficult to deal with.

Back in the front room the chief pathologist was supervising the removal of the body. Two assistants were lifting the dead woman onto a stretcher to take out to their van. The murder weapon had already been removed and was placed in an evidence bag for forensics. There was no sign of DS Chiang.

'So, what have you got for us, doc?' asked Marsh.

'The victim was a young woman. Mid-thirties in age and in good physical shape. Death was delivered by the severance of the spinal cord by a sharp instrument. Echoes of Leon Trotsky.'

Milo couldn't help grinning at this. Archie gave him an odd look. Surprised, no doubt. For once the two of them seemed to be on the same wavelength.

'Someone in the house was a keen mountaineer, I take it?' Archie asked, wincing as he straightened up, one hand to his back.

'Are you all right?'

'Age. Nothing that death can't fix.' Archie flashed her an acid look.

'There's a cupboard full of equipment in the utilities room,' Marsh said.

'So, opportunistic or planned?' he asked.

'Hard to say at this point,' said Marsh. 'The house belongs to Zoë Helms. She's an MP.'

'Ah, the people strike back,' muttered the pathologist. 'Politics poisons everything.'

Marsh was inclined to agree. Politics was never a good sign. It brought in all manner of complications. For the moment, though, she would try to ignore it.

'Nice of Wheeler to give you this one,' said Archie, pulling off his latex gloves with a snap. 'It's going to be touchy. I already met a rather superior member of the specialist squad.'

'That would be DS Chiang,' smiled Marsh, glad that even Archie found the other officer difficult. 'What did you do with him, anyway?'

'He was fidgeting, leaning over my shoulder.' Archie pulled a face. 'I sent him outside. How did they get in?'

'A patio door was forced. She was sitting here. The killer finds the axe in the cupboard downstairs, comes up behind her and whacks her.'

'Motive?'

'Search me, doc. No trace of sexual assault?'

'Not so far. Wait till I get a good look at her.' Archie looked around him with a sigh. 'Something odd about it, though, isn't there?'

Marsh nodded her agreement. 'It looks like a deliberate act of murder. No attempted rape or sexual assault. No sign of robbery.'

'Maybe he just didn't like politicians,' suggested Archie.

'Could it be that? Just a case of mistaken identity?'

'Your job to determine, DS Marsh.'

Marsh sniffed. She agreed there was something off about the whole thing. This was no opportunistic burglar who panicked. She surveyed the surface of the desk.

'We need to get all this stuff bagged and tagged.'

'All of it?' Milo frowned.

'I'd like to know what she was doing,' said Marsh. 'She would have had a telephone, iPad or laptop. No sign of a device. What was she listening to?'

'Could be a bluetooth connection to a home entertainment system,' said Milo helpfully.

'Have a poke around, will you, see what you can find.'

Milo disappeared. That was the good thing about him; give him a task and he was off to run it down in record time.

'I don't envy you this one,' Archie said, as he snapped the locks on his case shut. 'Politics has a habit of complicating everything it touches.'

'And there was me thinking it was my lucky day,' murmured Marsh.

'Don't take it personally.' Archie patted her on the shoulder as he went by. 'Opportunity never comes knocking in exactly the form we'd like it to.'

'True dat.' Marsh leaned over to push the curtain aside. 'What's going on out there?'

A black cab had just pulled up outside the house and a woman in her forties was standing in front of it speaking to DS Chiang. She was wearing what looked like an expensive dark red coat. Under one arm she held a bundle of folders. She dressed like a barrister, was Marsh's first thought.

'Looks like the lady of the house has arrived,' she said, noting that Archie's assistants had already managed to get the body into their van.

'I'm sorry, madam, you can't just walk in there . . .' The uniform at the bottom of the steps was trying to stop her. Marsh cursed under her breath and started out to the front door.

'Of course I can, I live here,' Zoë Helms announced, loudly and clearly.

'What seems to be the problem?' Marsh asked from the top of the steps. Helms had already brushed past the uniform. Marsh waved for him to stand down.

'Are you in charge here?' Helms demanded, facing Marsh.

'I'm DS Marsh, madam. I'm leading the investigation.'

'Right, well, perhaps it would help if you informed your men about who actually lives here.'

'We sent a squad car to fetch you.'

'Yes, well, I wasn't going to wait for that, now, was I?'

Marsh had no idea what this woman was prepared to do. She spotted Chiang coming up the steps behind the politician and tried deflecting her. 'I take it you've spoken to DS Chiang?'

'Yes, and he rather gave me the impression that *he* was in charge,' Helms said. 'You should get your act together. Can I come into my house now?'

'I'm afraid we're still busy with forensic work.'

Helms did a double take. 'You're not proposing that we stand here on the front steps, are you?'

'No, of course not,' stuttered Marsh. 'I'm just saying, you might find it a little disturbing.'

'Thank you. I don't need pampering. The press will be here any minute and I don't want this to be on the front pages tomorrow.'

'Perhaps you should step inside, ma'am.'

'Would you please stop calling me that.' Helms stepped past her and into the house. 'This all seems a bit much for a burglary. What is going on?'

Marsh glanced down at Chiang. She had assumed he would have informed Helms about the body. So much for liaison. Right now the detective was lighting a cigarette while looking up and down the street like all this was nothing to do with him. Typical of Special Operations. Always acting like super-heroes flown in to sort out everyone else's mess. But when you really needed them they were never around.

Marsh followed Helms back inside. Dumping the large handbag and pile of folders she was carrying on the table by the front door, she was already inside the living room by the time Marsh caught up with her.

'What's all this?' Helms asked, looking at the table. 'What happened here? Where's Cathy?'

'Cathy?'

'Cathy Perkins,' Helms said, her voice faltering. 'She lives with me.'

Marsh turned and addressed the two crime scene officers who were still wandering about like lost aliens in their overalls.

'Okay, everyone, could we have the room, please?'

They weren't happy about it, but they understood. Marsh gestured towards the kitchen.

'Perhaps we could talk through here.'

By now it was clear from Helms's face that she realised something serious had happened. Marsh sat her down in the kitchen and explained. Helms buried her face in her hands and sobbed quietly to herself.

'I know this is difficult,' said Marsh after a time. 'But in cases like this we need to move quickly.'

'I understand.' Helms sniffed, reaching for a roll of kitchen paper and tearing off a sheet of it to blow her nose.

'We'll need details about Cathy. Her next of kin, and so forth.'

'Of course, of course.' Helms cast around her for something to say. 'She was the best thing that ever happened to me. I can't, I just can't believe she's gone. How?'

'We can get into the details in a moment. It seems that Ms Perkins, Cathy, was alone at home. She was seated at that table in there.'

'Yes,' sniffed Helms. 'She used it as a desk. It was her space. I have an office upstairs.'

'Did she often work at home?'

'She's a freelance journalist. She was working on a book. She quit the paper about six months ago.' Helms was dabbing at her eyes. 'Why does any of this matter?'

'It's important to understand why this happened. We also need to assess the risk to yourself, to establish whether you might be in danger.'

'Are you saying someone might have mistaken her for me?' Helms looked up. 'I can't believe that.'

'There was some slight resemblance, I believe.'

'From a distance, perhaps, in the dark, with bad eyesight. Cathy and I are a similar size and build, although she's in much better shape than I am. And younger.'

'She was a keen climber, I understand.'

'Yes.' Helms frowned. 'How did you know that?'

'We found a load of equipment.' Marsh nodded towards the utility room.

'That was her thing. A bit of an obsession, really. She tried taking me a couple of times, but I don't have a head for heights like her. Cathy is . . . was.' Helms paused, as if hearing the echo of her own words. 'Fearless. In everything,' she sobbed.

6

Crane sat in the fifteen-year-old Audi TT listening to a top forty show in the rain. She'd inherited the car from her former boss and mentor, Julius Rosen. Rosen had taken Crane in when she was in need of a new direction in life, and a job. Eventually, she took over much of his work as a forensic psychology consultant for the Met, and became a partner, and when Rosen died Crane inherited his side of the practice, as well as the Audi TT. His little middle-aged present to himself, as he used to joke.

She was bored. One thing she had no trouble admitting was how much she disliked surveillance, despite the fact that she hated being bad at anything. Cal was a lot better at this. He seemed to adapt to it, rather like a hibernating creature of some kind. He had even offered to take this shift, but Crane knew it had to be she who made the approach this time. She tapped her finger on the steering wheel. This was her third day sitting in the car park of the supermarket and she was beginning to ask herself if finding Selina Baker, now Selina Bouallem, was going to be as straightforward as she had imagined.

When Jason Spencer moved to London five years ago he hadn't disappeared completely. He stayed in touch with his mother, at least in the beginning. He called her regularly to let her know that he was all right; better than ever, in fact, according to him. He was sharing a flat with a number of other men. He didn't tell her their names. Who they were and what they did, Millie Spencer never learned. Some kind of brotherhood. At least, Jason would refer to them as his 'brothers'. She imagined some kind of sect, which was a little worrying. Her fears rose when he told her he was converting to Islam. On one of the screenshots Mrs Spencer had taken of her son's now defunct Facebook page Crane recognised a building she'd seen before; the old mosque in Birch Lane over by Freetown estate.

'It's as if everything I've believed up to this point is a lie,' he told his mother.

Jason had always been something of a dreamer, ever since he was a small child, but nothing had prepared the Spencers for this, as Mrs Spencer had explained when Crane called her to check the details and to get more background.

'It was as if he hated us, for everything we had given him. Our entire lives, striving to make things better,' she wept. 'It was all for nothing.'

Jason had always had a rebellious streak. His creative side, as his mother liked to put it, which he had inherited from her. He was sensitive, easily disturbed by everything that was happening in the world. Maybe it was their fault, Millie Spencer wondered. They had brought him up in a fairly conventional household. They took an interest in current events, or she did, which meant the war in the Middle East, the invasion of Iraq. She had taken Jason on several marches. Mr Spencer was having none of it, but she was there, with Jason, marching through the streets of London in 2003. It was exciting to be part of something like that, she had told Crane. Not that it changed anything. Nearly twenty years later and the world hadn't become a better place. In many respects it had become worse. As a teenager, Jason had been involved in forming a protest group at school. He even started a campaign calling for Blair to be tried for war crimes. Mrs Spencer could remember feeling quite proud of him for taking a stand like that. His father wasn't that impressed, of course. Said it was nothing to do with them what was going on thousands of miles away in a country they had never heard of until then, for people who couldn't even speak the same language. But Jason was not deterred.

Crane found herself going back over her conversations with the Spencers. It still didn't quite add up to the whole story of why Jason had been moved to take an interest in Islam, eventually converting. Which was why she was here. One of the missing links was Selina, the woman he had met online, the one who had apparently convinced him to change his life and move to London.

The emerging picture was that of an earnest young man who believed that he could make a difference. Jason must have been one of those kids who was born with a conscience, putting his parents to shame, always looking for a cause, convinced that his choices would set him on the side of what was morally right. Crane had been a bit like that when she was young, burning for one thing or another, trying to put the world to rights. Jason's mother had given Crane a video clip the boy had posted on his Facebook page – which had since been taken down. In it, Jason rambled on about financial fascism, the Bilderberg Group, political corruption and much more. It sounded as though he had waded deep into the territory of conspiracy theories.

'It was the perfect storm,' Mrs Spencer had said, stifling a sob. 'He even changed his name, as if Jason wasn't good enough. As if everything in the world, all his life, had conspired to lead him to this place.'

Where it led him in the first instance was to Selina. They had met on a student chat forum online. Somehow she had made him give it all up: his education, his career, even his family. For what? What had she tapped into in his vulnerable mind? Loneliness, perhaps, or a sense of there being nothing of real substance in his life. Either way, Crane was curious to meet the woman.

To her surprise it seemed that Paul Spencer had not entirely turned his back on his son. He had actually done some detective work of his own. Monthly bank statements continued to be delivered to the family home. Jason had forgotten to cancel his cards or change his address when he moved from home. Initially, from these it appeared he was making regular withdrawals of cash from his account at one of two cash machines in Clapham. Soon after Jason moved to London Mr Spencer had decided to confront his son in an effort to try and persuade him to come home. He'd staked out the cash machine and had even managed to photograph Jason in the company of a woman dressed in black from head to toe. Selina. Crane had those pictures on her phone. Jason must have left his bank card with Selina, because regular withdrawals were still being made, but from another ATM, this one located outside a supermarket on Lavender Hill. The one Crane had been staking out.

It was Saturday morning and the centre was crowded with shoppers. Little children jumped up and down, tugging their mothers' arms. Men lumbered along grumbling behind their distracted wives. The volume of disjointed traffic stopping and starting, moving in and out of the car park, was sizeable enough to be a concern. Every few minutes a car would pull up and the driver would start signalling, using a variety of hand gestures to try and harry Crane out of her spot. She was getting a little tired of shaking her head in response. Now she just stared at them until they got the message. She wasn't cooperating. They glared back and seemed to take affront, as if her being there was an infringement of their right to find somewhere to park. It was a busy day. What did they expect?

Crane was ruminating over all of this when she spotted Selina through the side window. She was coming from the road behind Crane, walking towards the supermarket along a covered pedestrian walkway that led straight between the parked cars. She was wearing a black ebaya that came down to her ankles. Her face was circled by a tightly wrapped hijab, but Crane was sure it was her. Pale and unhappy, the plumpness of her glum face was accentuated by the headscarf. She was shoving a stroller ahead of her with quick, brusque movements.

Crane got out of the car, ignoring an angry man in a Toyota who gesticulated as if she had led him on in some way. Then she was on the walkway, following behind woman and stroller. When she reached the supermarket, Selina turned left and went towards the ATM by the entrance. Crane held back while the other woman waited impatiently in line before extracting cash from the machine. It was a chance to observe her. She seemed edgy; certainly she was irritated by the child, snapping at its attempts to extricate itself from the stroller and ignoring its subsequent whining.

After that, mother and child went into the supermarket. Crane picked up a basket and trailed along behind them. Shopping was clearly not a task that Selina enjoyed. She seemed to find it a distraction from the more important business of speaking on her phone. She made her way round with the device clamped to her ear, tucked into her head scarf to leave her hands free as she wandered up and down the aisles, dropping items at random into the basket propped on top of the stroller. The child, now released from its restraints, stumbled along behind her, pausing to pull items onto the floor. His mother carried on, seemingly oblivious. It offered Crane the chance to intervene. She lifted the child up from the packet of cat food it was trying to gnaw its way into.

'No, I don't think you want to do that,' said Crane.

The mother came storming back down the aisle. 'Let me call you right back,' she snapped into her phone as she approached. 'What are you doing with my child?' she demanded.

Crane, straightening up with a smile, said, 'He was about to get a mouthful of kibble. Not sure that was such a good idea.'

Selina was outraged. 'You can't just go around picking other people's kids up.'

'I was only trying to help.'

'Well, mind your own business,' Selina retorted. 'I can take care of my own child, thank you very much.'

'I didn't mean to suggest you couldn't.' Crane shrugged. 'I know how difficult it can be.'

'Do you? Really?' Selina pushed Crane aside as she scooped the child up and carried him over to the stroller, the little boy kicking and screaming in protest.

Crane withdrew and went outside to wait. She saw them struggling along, Selina now trying to manoeuvre the pushchair weighted down with wriggling child and several carrier bags heavy with groceries.

'You again?' Selina asked when Crane appeared in front of her.

'Look, I feel bad about what happened. Let me give you a lift.' She gestured at her car, then before Selina could respond she bobbed down to smile at the kid. 'Mashallah, he's a handsome boy.'

'You're not some kind of stalker, right?'

'No.' Crane laughed. 'Not a stalker, I promise.'

The other woman stared at her, unsure what to make of all this. The child kicked out again, this time finding purchase on one of the supports and sending the back of the pushchair tilting up. Crane's quick reflexes allowed her to grab it before it tipped over. Selina was wrestling with two large shopping bags and couldn't have righted it alone.

'Stop it!' she yelled at the child. 'Do you hear what I'm saying?'

The question was redundant. The little boy was beyond listening. He was hysterical.

'It's really not a problem,' said Crane. She could see that Selina's resistance was waning. Together they managed child, shopping and stroller, and loaded them into the car. Even then, Selina stood looking at Crane over the roof as if expecting some trick.

'Why are you doing this?' Selina asked, as they were driving away.

'Does there have to be a reason?' Crane flicked on the wipers as the rain started again. Fat, heavy drops plumped onto the windscreen. 'Helping a sister in need.'

'What's your name?'

'Rayhana,' said Crane. 'Ray.'

Selina considered this, the child now sitting quietly in the back watching them.

'So, you're a Muslim?'

Crane nodded. 'I was raised a Muslim by my mother, yes.'

'Where's she from?'

'Iran. Was. She was from Iran.'

The other woman nodded as some kind of recognition of Crane's loss. Mentioning her mother was a potential risk since Selina, as an apparently conservative Sunni, might have a dim view of the Iranian Shia. Crane was counting on it being sufficient to create some kind of bond between them.

'I'm not practising,' she added.

Selina seemed to take this as fair enough, not offensive, despite the fact she was done up from head to toe in garments declaring the strictness of her faith.

'Which way?' asked Crane.

'Turn right at the lights.'

They drove in silence, disturbed only by the occasional comment from the child, who seemed to have settled down now. Selina gestured again and they turned into a side road. A few moments later they pulled up alongside a small terraced house. The front garden had been paved over and was now a catch-all tip for objects that appeared to have spilled out from within. Crane spotted a standing lamp, a couple of broken chairs and a vacuum cleaner that had been partially dismantled, along with rubbish bins, a rusty pram and cardboard boxes filled with damp newspapers and plastic soft drink bottles. The front door opened as they approached and a small woman appeared in the doorway. She was very young, not much more than sixteen, and heavily pregnant. She looked up and down the street while pulling a scarf up over her head.

'Sister, where you been?' she whined.

Crane heard Selina give a tut of annoyance, ignoring the question. As she helped unload her things from the car, Crane scribbled her number down on the back of a flyer someone had pressed on her at the supermarket.

'Listen, if you need help shopping another day, you can just give me a call. I'm often free.' Selina looked at her.

'Why would I want that? I don't even know you.'

'We all need someone to talk to some time,' shrugged Crane, as she helped her set the stroller down.

Selina stared at her, then turned and walked straight into the house without another word.

'Who's that?' Crane heard the younger woman ask, frowning at her.

'Nobody,' said Selina. The door slammed shut behind them.

7

There was a hungry crowd in the Alamo that afternoon. It was a Saturday and people arrived bearing a week-load of steam to blow off. Crane found Drake perched at the end of the bar, trying to keep his head down. Behind the counter, Doc Wyatt was fending off orders while trying to sort out an issue with the television reception amid loud complaints from customers who were trying to watch the match on the huge screen that took up a chunk of one wall.

'Is it always like this?' Crane asked, as she slipped onto the stool next to him.

'Saturday crowd. It's like they just got out of jail,' muttered Drake. 'Or the zoo.'

'You're in a fine mood,' said Crane, catching Doc Wyatt's eye and ordering a tonic and another lager for Drake.

'How did it go?'

'Ah, I'm not sure.' Crane was less than happy with how things had gone with Selina. When the drinks arrived she suggested grabbing a table in the corner, so they could hear each other. Drake followed along. 'I'm not sure this approach is going to work. I made contact, but I'm going to have to be more forceful next time. She's cautious.'

'Isn't that a good thing?'

'It might be,' conceded Crane. 'I got the feeling she was pretty fed up.'

'Small child, no job, maybe that's normal.'

'It was more than that, almost as if she's tired of the whole gig.'

'She's a convert, right?'

Crane nodded. 'She used to be Selina Baker. Grew up in Southend. Father an insurance salesman, mother a teacher.'

'What happened? They were too busy to give her the attention she needed?'

'Maybe she just wanted to be different?'

'So, what about this husband of hers?'

'The house is registered to Magid Bouallem. Born in Algeria, came over here as a student in 1998 and never went back. He's a good fifteen years older than her. In 2004 he married a woman named Barbara Grisham, and gained citizenship before the marriage was dissolved.'

'A marriage of convenience?'

'Could be. I haven't interviewed Grisham but her social media activity tells me she believes in a lot of causes.'

Drake nodded. 'Trying to do the right thing.' He glanced away as a cheer went up. The television screen had come back to life and the football was restored.

'Also, Bouallem was quite different back then. Looks like he went through some changes.'

'Post 9/11?'

'His religious activism started around then. Before that he was by all accounts a well-integrated, drinking, smoking, Western-living man.'

'Amen to that.' Drake raised his glass. Crane narrowed her eyes at him but said nothing. There were still things about Cal that she didn't entirely know or understand. In time, perhaps it would all become apparent, but she wasn't too sure of that. And most of the time it didn't matter. Right now she was keen to finish her story.

'For a while Bouallem was a person of interest. His name was flagged on the counter-terrorism list. He's calmed down a little in recent years, but he still seems to get a kick out of preaching hardcore Salafism to impressionable young men.'

'So, he's gone silent. Doesn't mean he's no longer active.'

'Exactly. It looks like he's been careful not to draw too much attention to himself. Now he runs a cultural centre over in Stockwell, for young men who have lost their way.'

'All this you got through Stewart Mason, I take it?'

'He has his moments,' said Crane.

Mason was Crane's former boss in the security services. She had worked on assignments in Iraq and Afghanistan, the details of which she rarely discussed. But Drake had never taken to him. There was something about Stewart Mason that he didn't trust.

'What did he want in return?'

'Just to be kept informed if anything useful came up.'

'Right. Why does he think we work for the National Crime Agency, or wherever he is these days?'

'He doesn't,' said Crane. It felt odd to be standing up for Mason. God knows he'd let her down enough times. But somehow she couldn't bring herself to cut herself off completely. 'He just likes to keep his options open, and he's a useful contact to have.' She sighed. 'Look, we have to be realistic. You may not like him but he can put a lot of good work our way. We shouldn't turn our noses up at it.'

'Then what would we be? A secret arm of the government?'

'You used to work for the government not so long ago.'

'That was then, and at least it was above board. Don't kid yourself, Ray. This would be the stuff they want kept off the books. Nothing that could be traced back to them.'

'We don't have to do anything we don't like the sound of.'

'Assuming we'll be able to tell the difference.' Since departing the Met, Drake had been asking himself how he had managed for all those years and what exactly he had thought he was defending. Did he ever really believe in all of that? 'Back to the case in hand. What's your angle on Selina?'

'I'm not sure. I sense some tension in the household.' Crane described the younger woman who had come to the door when they arrived.

'So, what are you thinking, a second wife?'

'Could be,' conceded Crane. 'That might go some way to explaining why Selina is so unhappy.' She broke off as the shadow of a lanky figure fell over the table.

'You goin' to introduce your lady friend, or what?' The newcomer wore a white shirt under a tan leather jacket with big straps on the shoulders like it was 1999.

'Wynstan, this is Ray, my partner.'

'Charmed, I'm sure. So, you his regular?'

'She's not my . . .' Drake started to explain and then gave up. 'What's on your mind, Wynstan?'

'Well, funny you should axe.' He slid onto a low stool that made his long legs come up to somewhere around his ears. 'We got a slight problem on we hands.'

'We?' Crane asked.

Wynstan glanced at her before addressing Drake. 'Couple of me boys got taken down by a candy car.'

'I'm not in the force any longer, you know that, right?'

'Tjah, right.' Wynstan sounded his irritation. 'Don't tell me you can't pull no strings. What you drinkin'?'

'Who is this guy?' Crane asked, while Wynstan was at the bar.

'Local character. I knew him back in the day. Let's hear what he has to say.'

Wynstan was a man of few words, so he spelled it out quickly, explaining how two of his boys had been knocked off their scooter.

'These were couriers, right?'

'They on the clock,' Wynstan shrugged.

'What were they carrying?'

'Nuttin,' Wynstan puffed. 'A little weed. A little blow. Small stuff.'

'Not the first time someone's made a move on your turf, is it?'

'You missin' the point.' Wynstan sucked his teeth. 'There was me thinkin' you got brains.'

'Tell me why it's important.'

'There's a new kid on the block, and this one is connected. He's got strings that pull some high and mighty bells.'

'Who is he?'

'Small sprat. Goes by the name of Berat Aslan. Wants to play with the big fish.'

'Why haven't I heard of him?'

'Used to work for Balushi. Fetch this, take that. Now he's breakin' out on his own.' Wynstan gave a grunt of disbelief. 'Aslan the talking lion.'

Drake glanced at Crane. She didn't need reminding who the Karachi gangster was. A year ago she had found herself cornered in a meat locker with one of Balushi's henchman, Khan.

'So he's connected. He's got someone covering him?'

'Exactly.' Wynstan stabbed the table with his forefinger. 'Find him and you've got your culprit.'

'Like I told you,' Drake said. 'I'm out of the game. I'm a private citizen, like you.'

'Right,' Wynstan grinned. 'That'll be the day.'

'Why do you want us to look into it?' Crane was intrigued. Wynstan turned. He looked as though he'd forgotten her. He started to smile but then wisely decided to play it straight.

'Better the devil you know. Isn't that what they say? The game is changing. Old-style gangsters being replaced by new. This new breed don't care if they burn the whole house down with it.' He rocked his head from side to side.

'Who are these people?' Crane asked.

'They're the ones what rule de world,' Wynstan said. 'The ones who want to build it all back up again.' He jabbed a finger at the window. 'You see all this change out there? The new buildings? That shopping mall, what they call it now?'

'The Bathhouse,' Drake supplied.

'That's what I'm talking about. Property development is where the money is. But mark my word, if they win, this place is going to turn nasty.'

8

D rake promised Wynstan they would make some calls and see what they could do. When they were alone again it was Drake's turn to talk. From his Facebook page it was clear Jason had had contact with the mosque on Birch Lane. It was a place Drake knew. Although he'd veered away from religion years ago, there had been a time when he'd found some sense of purpose in faith. In his younger days, as a troubled teenager, Islam had given him a way of seeing himself in a society that he felt he belonged to but was alienated from. It gave him a sense of worth, a belief in the idea of being part of something that was bigger than any one country, especially this one that didn't seem to want him. There was power in connecting to a community that extended all across the world. Islam also provided spiritual comfort, a sense of order and purpose to life. It didn't last. In time, he had found himself rebelling against the constraints of religion, the hypocrisy as he saw it, of a system of belief that promised reward in return for obedience. Drake had never been good at following rules. So he opted out, traded the Quran in for a gun and a uniform and for almost a decade the army was his home.

The Birch Lane *masjid* had been central to his life in that period. Nearly two years ago the Magnolia Quays case had brought Drake back to his old stomping ground in Freetown following an arson attack on the mosque. He'd been brought full circle, facing his younger self and questioning some of the decisions he had taken in life. It was this element of doubt, the question of faith itself, that he had decided to use with Imam Ahmad.

Freetown was changing. The old swimming baths that Drake remembered as a child had been turned into a fancy shopping mall. It was to be the centrepiece of the wave of change that was sweeping south from the river. To the north and east of the estate old establishments were sinking into the ground, replaced by pop-up fashion stores, eco-food shops and gourmet coffee bars with hardwood floors and baristas sporting nose rings and fashionable tattoos. This mall was going to be an outpost, a temple of rebirth built in the hope it would attract more affluent people to the area. It wasn't quite finished. Plastered across what would be the front entrance was a huge poster declaring the official opening day was coming soon! January 25th, to be exact. Above this they were putting the finishing touches to the swirly red neon letters that spelled out the name Freetown Arena. He'd thought it was going to be called The Bathhouse but he could see now how this was even more perfect. The shabby old estate would be replaced by a shining new temple dedicated to consumerism. The estate itself was being emptied out, as the buildings were shut down for renovation and then sold in their new refurbished form. The walkways were dotted with boarded-up windows and doors.

Drake suspected that the old residents would not exactly be welcomed here. Even as he processed this thought he saw a couple of private security guards, gorillas in Mickey Mouse uniforms, standing on the steps eyeing a shabby figure shuffling from foot to foot. Drake had never seen him before but he recognised the type. Dirty, unwashed hoodie. Greasy jeans. Grubby fingernails and shifty eyes. Right now he was looking particularly uncomfortable because he was on the receiving end of a lecture from Imam Ahmad, who was standing in front of him.

'You have to fight it, brother. Allah will help you, but you must try with all your heart.'

'Inshallah,' murmured the kid, though turning towards Mecca seemed like the last thing in the world he would try. Still, there was an uncomfortable mixture of embarrassment and gratitude in his voice. Maybe this was all it took, to be seen not as a dealer at the bottom of the food chain but as someone for whom all hope had not yet been extinguished.

'Inshallah,' repeated Imam Ahmad. He turned to move on when he caught sight of Drake. The look in his eyes said it all; another lost cause. With a sigh he walked on as Drake fell in alongside him.

'You never give up on them, do you?'

'If I were to give up, who would they have?' Imam Ahmad asked. 'I'm surprised to see you around here again. Were you looking for me?'

Drake nodded and the two of them walked together in silence back across the estate towards the *masjid* on Birch Lane. The old place was looking the worse for wear. It had never really recovered from the arson attack. The fire had been connected to the case Drake had been working on at the time, when he was still a detective at the old Raven Hill station – itself destined for the scrapheap in the not too distant future. Some of the bricks around the entrance were still blackened. Drake wondered if they were short of funds, or if there was a degree of wilfulness involved, to put their persecution on display. The imam himself showed signs of his own suffering in that ordeal. The left side of his face was criss-crossed with scar tissue. The ear was deformed. He made no effort to hide this when he sat with Drake in his office.

'You used to come here when you were young,' Imam Ahmad began. 'Like many young men in this country, you lost your way.'

'Sometimes the answers are not to be found in prayers and holy books.'

'Answers do not always come easily. One has to work on them.'

'You may well be right,' conceded Drake. 'I didn't come here to talk about my problems.'

The imam was in his early sixties and might have looked younger without the white beard and heavy spectacles. Exuding age and wisdom seemed to be tied to his vocation.

'Always it is about work, never about the spirit, the really important things in life.'

'Maybe you have a point,' said Drake. 'I spend my life trying to make a difference.' He paused. 'In this life. The next world will have to wait.'

'You may have the best intentions, my son, but none of us can live without spiritual understanding.'

'Maybe.' Drake pulled up the picture of Jason Spencer on his phone and passed it across. 'Have you ever seen this man?'

Imam Ahmad glanced at the picture briefly. 'What makes you come to me?'

'He had a picture of this mosque on his Facebook page.'

'Coincidence perhaps? A tourist of some kind?' Imam Ahmad handed the phone back. 'If it is true you are no longer working for the police, then why are you looking for this man?'

'His parents are worried about him. They think he went out to Syria to join Daesh.'

Imam Ahmad gave a sigh of dismay. 'People think of us only in terms of violence.'

'It's the times we live in.'

The imam shook his head. 'It's more than that, and you know it. We are not welcome in this country.'

'It might help if some of us stopped setting off bombs.'

'The ailment that drives young people to turn to violence is not created by Islam.'

'They turn to it because it promises a cure.'

'We try to teach them that violence is not a cure for anything. This is what I tell them.' The older man turned his head to display his deformed ear, the scar tissue left by the burns. 'I did not create this violence, but I must live with its consequences.'

'We all must.' Drake was eager to get back to the purpose of his visit. 'You're sure you've never seen him?'

'Our door is always open. People come in out of curiosity and leave without a word if they do not find what they are looking for.'

'I understand. You're not responsible for them.'

'That's not what I'm saying.'

'Then what?'

'There are others. People who pray on such lost souls.' The imam blew out his cheeks. 'Do you know how many people come to me asking to enter the house of Islam?' The chair creaked as he leaned back. 'To most of them it is a fashion, like getting a tattoo, or having your ears pierced. It is interesting for a time and then' – he made a sweeping gesture with his hand – 'it is forgotten, replaced by something else. You were like that.'

'I believed at the time. I was honestly looking for answers.'

'Perhaps, but our lord will be the judge of that.' The imam studied him closely. 'You believe this boy went to Syria?'

'It looks that way. What we're not sure about is whether he came back. There are people, networks.'

'I have never encouraged anyone to go and fight for Daesh, or arranged their passage. As far as I am concerned, they are criminals, abusing the word of Allah and the trust of the faithful.'

'But you can see why someone might be drawn to that life, to believing in a state ruled by the laws of the time of the Prophet.'

'I see it, but I don't believe it,' said Imam Ahmad. 'All law is a matter of interpretation. Islam begins with Allah's compassion. Where is the compassion in what they do?'

'He was looking for something,' Drake reflected, thinking of what had led him to the army. 'Is it possible that he met someone here, someone who might have helped him?'

'Led him astray, you mean.' The imam was shaking his head. 'Not anyone from our *masjid*.'

'I'm only interested in finding him. I'm not looking for someone to blame.'

'You, perhaps.' Imam Ahmad tilted his head to one side. 'But others might see it differently.'

Framed on the wall behind the imam's head was a Special Achievement Award from the Mayor of London's office for the imam's contribution to the community, alongside a picture of him shaking hands with a scruffy man with blonde hair.

'You're looking at this the wrong way round,' said Drake. 'If this blows back on you, everything you've built here will be in jeopardy, believe me. You know how the system works. If Jason was recruited by someone inside your community, it'll come back to hit you in the face.'

The imam looked Drake in the eye, his right hand tapping on the arm of his chair. 'Let me ask some of the others. Perhaps they have seen or heard something.'

Doc Wyatt appeared at the table, breaking into Drake's narration of the morning's events. He was wearing one of his colourful shirts as usual, red with yellow and green hot air balloons dotted over it. He wore it open over a Lenny Kravitz T-shirt. He gestured at their glasses.

'Another round?'

'Not for me, thanks,' said Crane. Drake just nodded his head.

'Thanks, Doc.'

'No problem. Is this a social visit, or you here for the local trouble?'

'You mean those kids?' Drake asked. 'Wynstan was asking about that.'

'They were his boys,' Doc Wyatt said. 'Say what you like about him, but he's one of our own. These new crews, they are something else.'

'So they're really moving in?' said Drake.

'And they ain't takin' no prisoners, if you get my drift,' said Doc Wyatt gravely. 'Tearing up the streets at night. People are scared.'

'Sounds serious,' said Crane.

'Local politics.' Drake looked across at the group of men sitting in the far corner. At the centre of them was the slim, wooden-faced figure of Wynstan Smyth. He raised his glass in salute and Drake nodded back.

'Your old patch,' said Crane.

'Yeah.'

They were drug dealers whichever way you spun it, but Drake knew that Wynstan was more than that. In an area where residents had little time for the authorities, and even less for the police, Wynstan and his men provided some kind of social order. People went to him when they needed a favour and he was known to be generous to those who were struggling. He had contacts in the local council offices who could get your case pushed through in record time. Not exactly Robin Hood, but he had respect around here. In return, he carried on with his business interests, the drugs and the clubs, and there were few who would rat on him to the police.

'People like to think nothing changes,' said Drake. 'But it's not true. Things change all the time. It's just that mostly we don't notice. Then one day we look in the mirror and wonder where that stranger came from.'

Crane laughed. 'You're in fine fettle.'

'Yeah, sorry. But if this was about bent coppers protecting one of the other crews, I should check in with Kelly, see how she's doing.'

Crane tapped a fingernail on the table. 'Have you given any further thought to the idea of handing her those documents from Nathanson's safe?'

'I told you, when I'm done with studying them.'

'Come on, Cal, that's an excuse and you know it. Besides, all due respect, but what do you know about financial transactions?'

'Fair enough. I just feel there's something there.'

'Just remember, Kelly trusts you and you don't want to lose that.'

There was something about the idea of handing over the papers he had lifted from the lawyer's safe which felt to Drake too much like giving up.

'You're right. I promise I'll make a decision soon.'

9

Back in his flat that evening, Drake gave up on his supper. Frozen lasagne, snatched recklessly from a nondescript supermarket on his way home and heated up insufficiently with equal haste only compounded his bad choice. He made a game attempt at interesting himself, stabbing the fork through layers of pasta the consistency of cardboard before tossing it aside in disgust.

Urged on by his conversation with Crane and a nagging conscience, he set about having one last crack at Barnaby Nathanson's files. At some point, soon, he would have to surrender them to Kelly Marsh, and probably would have done so already except for a stubborn refusal to admit defeat. So long as there was even the faintest chance that somewhere among this heap of folders there was the key that would help him unlock why Zelda had been so brutally killed, he would try to hang on to them.

Drake was unable to explain rationally why Zelda's death

was still important to him. He didn't need Crane's professional expertise to know it was some expression of guilt. It wasn't just that the whole affair had been so catastrophic for him personally, for his career, it was about doing right by her. He'd given Zelda his word. Not that such things counted for much these days, but he knew that until he brought her killers to justice he would feel her loss as an open wound. Zelda had trusted him. And in the end that's what it boiled down to.

He considered the idea of having another drink and then decided against it. He knew he had one shot at this and it involved him having a clear head. Instead he made himself a mug of instant coffee that tasted worse than it looked. He stared at the mucky liquid and remembered the coffee Crane had made at her place. If he carried on in her company for much longer, he would be in serious danger of becoming a hipster.

He started by clearing the coffee table in the living room. This was completely buried under a rather embarrassing accumulation of newspapers, dirty plates, cups, glasses, beer cans, receipts and letters from the tax office that had been sitting there for months, along with a set of keys he thought he'd lost forever. There was a whole stack of other items, some of which he couldn't even identify. He swept the whole lot, minus the keys, into a black plastic bin liner and set it by the front door for chucking out. He couldn't remember ever having seen the table this clean before and realised it wasn't a bad-looking piece of furniture.

He felt better after that and set about sorting out the folders and the papers they contained into some kind of order. It was quite a mess. Nathanson clearly knew the material inside out. He had only kept a specific set of files in his home safe, probably in case he needed them at short notice. Drake was convinced Nathanson had been blackmailing one of his clients. Nathanson had a cocaine habit, which might explain, at least in part, how he had become involved with people like Donny Apostolis and Goran Malevich, both of whom were running their own organised-crime groups. When Operation Hemlock had kicked off, targeting Malevich, Drake had found an unlikely ally in Donny Apostolis.

As he spread the papers out on the table, Drake once again realised that he was out of his depth. This was complex numbers stuff and he probably needed a trained accountant to make sense of it. He tried to sort out the references to the shell company Novo Elysium but was surprised to find so few references. He went to the kitchen to make more coffee. He'd barely touched the first cup, but if it was unpalatable when warm, it was even more disgusting cold. It could only be drunk when it was scalding hot.

'Maybe I'm doing something wrong,' he muttered to himself, staring at the mug of coffee but thinking about the task in hand. Leaving the kettle still whining its way to the boil, Drake went back to the living room and sifted his way through the documents. At some point, he thought he might be getting somewhere. It looked as though Nathanson had manipulated the Swift codes. Drake went online to check his own account. Normally, these consisted of a series of four letters designating the bank, followed by two letters for the country code and two for the location. Sometimes a branch code would be added at the end, but these were often left as XXX. The problem was that none of the codes in Nathanson's spreadsheets seemed to make sense. After spending almost an hour staring at the codes, Drake gave up and sat back.

There were times when Drake missed the easy access to resources that he had enjoyed during his time in the Met. Right now, for example, he could have used Milo's technical skills. The only problem with that, of course, was that Drake wasn't supposed to be in possession of these documents. Officially, they had disappeared from Nathanson's safe in his flat in Pimlico on the night he was murdered. Removing material from a crime scene was a criminal offence. The fact that Drake hadn't killed the solicitor himself was neither here nor there. He had the folders and he had not declared them.

He decided it was finally time for a drink and went into the kitchen to search for a glass. He found one that was reasonably clean and poured himself a good measure of rum. He drank it slowly, standing by the window looking out at the lights over the city. His conscience told him that sooner or later he was going to have to come clean, that perhaps now was a good time to call Kelly Marsh. He looked at his watch. It was nine thirty on a Saturday evening and it seemed more than likely that she would be out and not have time to answer her phone.

He was wrong, she answered on the third ring.

'Chief?'

'Hey, Kelly.' Drake found it touching that she still addressed him the way she did when he was her boss back at Raven Hill. He knew it was more an affectionate term than an indication of subordination. Kelly had already proved herself more than capable as a detective sergeant and Drake suspected that she would go far in a very short time.

'Still raking it in on the free market?'

Drake had to laugh. 'It has its moments, but I have to admit there are times I miss the rough and tumble of everyday operations.'

'Never thought I'd hear you say that,' said Marsh.

'Me neither. I didn't think I'd catch you at home on a Saturday night.'

'Ah,' Marsh sighed. 'It's been a tough week.'

'I heard about the trouble over in Freetown.'

'Yeah,' said Marsh thoughtfully. 'A couple of teenage couriers were run off their bikes. Not sure what to make of it. Could be just a couple of overzealous rookies, or it could be more.'

'I heard about that. Who was in the IRV?'

'Warren and Taylor. You don't know them. I don't know them. Cocky and young. Both suspended. Turns out they've been moonlighting for a private outfit. Anyway, it's all in Bishop's capable hands now, so not my problem.' Drake heard a long sigh from the other end. 'I have other fish to fry.'

'Tell me about it.'

Marsh filled him in swiftly on the Helms case.

'I should be over the moon for drawing a big one, but the truth is I'm terrified.' Down the line Drake heard the sound of a can of what he assumed was beer being opened. He backtracked to the kitchen to retrieve the bottle of rum. 'It's not even referred to as the Perkins case, even though she's the victim. This is the Zoë Helms case, as far as everyone is concerned.'

'So, killer breaks in through the rear of the house, sees the victim at the desk and assumes it's his intended target,' Drake went on, summarising what he'd just been told.

'That's the way it looks.'

'Where was the murder weapon?'

'In a utilities cupboard in the rear annexe.'

'And this was an axe, you said?'

'The high-tech kind,' said Marsh. 'Used by mountaineers for climbing icefalls. Very sharp and strong. Cut straight through the spinal cord. She died instantly.'

'So, the killer knew where the murder weapon was, or were they improvising?'

He heard Marsh take a long sip of her drink. 'Hard to say. I mean, you'd be taking a chance going in and not having a weapon with you.' He could tell from her voice that she'd already had a few.

'If that was their intention. The killer could have had knowledge of the house.'

'It's pretty cold to use an axe like that. I mean . . .' Marsh fell silent as the image of Cathy Perkins' body came back to her. 'Not a nice way to go.'

'They could have panicked. If it was a break-in that went sideways. Anything taken?'

'The only things missing appear to be Perkins' laptop and phone.'

'Nothing else? No valuables?' Drake mused. 'Either they grabbed the nearest things and scarpered, or . . .'

'They took what they came for.'

'Okay, so you're assuming Perkins was the target?'

'Well, that's the second problem. Since Helms officially lives there, that makes her the obvious target, and that brings an added fun factor to the equation. Seeing as she's an MP, I'm sharing the glory with Specialist Ops.' Marsh explained about DS Chiang and the Parliamentary and Diplomatic Protection department.

'I'm guessing that doesn't make your life any easier.'

'This Chiang guy is a weird one. I looked him up. Earned his stripes in vice, working the Triads in Gerrard Street.'

Drake had been pouring himself another drink. At this, he set the bottle down on the coffee table. 'How long ago was this? Pryce was working Chinatown at some point.'

'Yeah, well I wouldn't take that as a recommendation,' said Marsh. 'Pryce is a dick.'

'You'll hear no arguments from me on that score. Anyway, go on.'

'According to DS Chiang, Helms gets hate mail and death threats on a daily basis. Part and parcel of going into politics when you happen to be a woman.'

'And you think he might be missing something?' In the background he could hear the muted sound of voices and imagined she'd been spending the evening sitting in front of the television with a takeout. Much like himself, except Drake didn't own a television, hadn't done in years.

Marsh said, 'If Helms wasn't the intended target, she would still make the perfect cover.'

'All eyes would be on Helms, and nobody would be looking into Perkins.'

'It would be the perfect deflection.'

'It's a possibility, but you're going to have to tread softly, Kelly. Helms is high profile. Nobody is going to take the chance of looking elsewhere unless there is clear evidence. You need something solid to back up a claim like that.'

'I know,' sighed Marsh. 'But so far all I know about Cathy Perkins is that she was a journalist.'

In the time they had worked together Drake had never had cause to distrust Kelly Marsh's instincts. There was no reason to start now. He trusted her. If she was in doubt about whether Helms was the intended victim, there might well be something to it.

'Any idea what Perkins was working on?'

'Not really, and without her phone and laptop we're in the dark,' said Marsh. 'We're trying to find out more, but apparently she was secretive.' He heard her take another slug of beer. 'This is a big chance for me, Cal. If I fuck this up Wheeler won't give me another one.'

'Have a little faith, Kelly. You wouldn't be where you are now if you didn't trust your instincts.'

Marsh grumbled what might have been a begrudging agreement, not entirely convincing.

'Don't shut down any line of inquiry until you are sure you can eliminate it. You can't let personal feelings outrule your head, Kelly.'

'I know, I know. I just . . .'

'And don't let yourself get spooked by this fly boy from Specialist Ops,' said Drake. 'Dig into Perkins. Find out about her background. Former partners, etc. Someone must know something about her work. If nothing comes up then move ahead with Helms. You don't need me to tell you all this, Kelly.'

'I know,' sighed Marsh. 'Sometimes it just helps to hear it spoken out loud.'

'You'll be fine,' said Drake. 'Wheeler put you in charge because he thinks you're up to it.'

'Maybe that's what's worrying me. I've never handled anything this high profile.'

'Like I said, Kelly, you'll be fine. Don't let this Chiang guy spook you.'

'I suppose you're right,' admitted Marsh. 'Anyway, tell me about you, what are you up to?'

'Ah, well, nothing so exciting,' said Drake. 'A missing persons case.'

As he spoke, he reached under the cushion behind him on the sofa and found his stash of dope. Putting the phone on speaker, he set it on the table and began rolling a joint. Recently this was the only thing that seemed to untangle the knot of nerves that was trapped in his spine. The old night-mares had started to return, the ones that took him back to Iraq, the ones that left him crashing to the earth in a helicopter, waking up bathed in sweat with the smell of burning flesh in his nostrils.

'I was actually thinking about the Barnaby Nathanson case,' Drake said as casually as he could, running his tongue along the cigarette paper. There was a pause on the line which told him he'd made a mistake.

'You know that's still a sore point, right?'

'I know. I know.'

'You've been holding out on me.'

'I just need a little time.'

'I understand,' said Marsh, 'but you know that we might have got a lot further if we'd been able to get hold of all those documents that were stashed in his safe . . .'

'This is personal, Kelly. You know that.'

'You think Nathanson's death is connected to Zelda.'

'I think the whole thing is connected.' Drake paused to light up. He took a long drag. 'Zelda had information that got her killed. She knew something.'

'Come on, Cal, if we've been over this once we've done it a thousand times.'

'Just bear with me here, Kelly. Nathanson was running a trust, which means he had control over his clients' money.'

'How does that help you?'

'I think he was blackmailing one or more of them.' Drake paused. 'The truth is I'm not sure about any of this.'

'Jesus. Listen to yourself, Cal! You're not making any sense.'

'Maybe you're right.' Drake breathed out slowly. 'Listen, forget it. If there's anything I can help with, you know how to reach me.'

'Thanks, Cal, I'll keep it in mind.'

Drake tapped his phone off. Suddenly the pile of printouts in front of him looked like an insurmountable summit. He decided the joint wasn't helping so he stubbed it out and leaned back to stare at the ceiling. If Nathanson had been running a trust for more than one client, what would they do after his death? They would presumably have to find someone to replace him. How else would they keep track of their money? After a time, he sat up and started going through the papers again. There was something there. He could feel it. All he had to do was find it.

10

For the best part of a week Crane kept an eye on the terraced house where Selina lived. Surveillance was probably the least attractive part of any investigation as far as she was concerned. All of this was new to her. In some ways it felt like a natural progression from the work she'd done for the intelligence services, both here and abroad, which had always involved some degree of inquiry. Whether it was tracking down potential jihadi recruits in Bradford, or helping to sort out fact from fiction in the testimony of an informer in Kabul, her work for the Met had proved a challenge. It was no small thing to help piece together the mindset of a serial killer. But such cases came along far too infrequently to satisfy her restless intellect.

It soon became clear that Selina had no discernible job. Her only routine appeared to be taking the child to a nearby crèche every morning. Usually she returned straight home, but not always. Sometimes she would take a detour. Crane followed her up to Clapham Common, where she watched her wandering aimlessly round the streets, peering through the windows of estate agents and thrift shops, generally wasting time. There was a café on the high street where Selina would stop to drink coffee and eat a muffin or a brownie. A sad kind of place that looked as though it ought to have closed down years ago. Occupied for the most part by pensioners wearing transparent plastic bonnets to protect their hair from the rain, or teenagers in uniform who were skipping school. Another favourite haunt was the local library, still open by some miracle. Here Selina would hunch over her phone in a corner pretending to read the local newspaper, which, in Crane's view, held nothing but horror stories and outrageous tales that one couldn't make up for love or money.

It all added up to a portrait of a lonely and unhappy woman. Crane suspected that her domestic situation had something to do with it. The other woman who had come to the door of the house that first day was clearly much younger than Selina and also very pregnant. She did not resemble either Selina or Magid, which ruled out her being someone's sister and suggested she was a second wife. No more than sixteen or seventeen at a pinch. At that distance, and with the headscarf, it was hard to tell, but Crane would have put money on it. All of which begged a few questions. Magid Bouallem was a hefty man pushing fifty, his Salafist leanings made manifest by the unkempt beard. Hard to see the appeal. Not rich, but he had a house and a British pass-port, which may have been more than enough to transform him into an attractive prospect. He never left the house in anything but skullcap and long black djellaba, usually over loose-fitting tracksuit pants and large, white trainers. It wasn't clear what he did. Crane devoted a morning to following him, discovering a circuit of mosques and prayer centres across south and west London that he drove to in a battered old Honda Civic. At each place he would stumble up, clutching a crumpled Sports Direct bag, to be greeted with handshakes and embraces by the men hanging around the entrance. He seemed to elicit respect wherever he went. Crane wondered what was in the bag. On the Friday he left the house early, Crane guessed he would be spending the day at the mosque. She decided that perhaps this was a good time to approach Selina again. The sun was out as she trailed behind Selina pushing the stroller towards a bench on the common, where she fiddled with her phone, looking up from time to time to address the child who had climbed out of the pushchair and was busy throwing crisps to the rather insolent pack of crows hopping around them. She didn't look up until Crane sat down next to her.

'Hello again.'

The younger woman squinted at Crane for a moment before placing her. The expression on her face turned from surprise to confusion before congealing into anger.

'Where did you spring from?'

Crane ignored the question.

'Are you following me?' Selina began to gather up her things and get ready to go. The child had other ideas. He lay on the ground and started to scream. Selina slumped back on the bench and clamped her hands over her ears. The child was so

97

surprised by this that he sat up and stared at her, half-chewed crisps spilling from his open mouth.

'I can't do this any more!' Selina wept.

'Can't be easy, being relegated to second place by a teenager.'

'What's it to you?' Selina sniffed, searching for a tissue in her bag. 'And why are you sticking your nose in my business?'

'I'm trying to help.'

'Help? Help who? Me?'

'Maybe, at some point. But more immediately I am concerned about Jason.'

'I don't know what you're talking about.' Selina turned back to her child.

'Jason.' Crane held up her phone, displaying his Facebook page, a picture of Selina with him clearly visible. 'His parents are worried about him.'

The little boy crushed himself up against his mother's thigh, peering up at Crane.

'What are you? Special Branch?'

'Not exactly.' Crane tilted her head. 'They think he might have come back to this country.'

'From Syria?' Selina did a double take. 'Why would they think that?'

'A handwritten message was delivered to their home. They think he's in hiding.'

'I haven't heard from him, if that's why you're here.' Selina stared at the ground.

'Tell me about Magid. He seems to have a taste for young girls. Is that how he found you?'

'You don't know anything about me,' Selina snapped, starting to get to her feet before slumping down again and turning on Crane. 'Are you one of those dykes who gets off trying to convert straight women?'

'Why?' Crane looked her in the eye. 'Are you one of those straight women who's always dreamed of being converted?'

Selina drew back with a look of disgust, but she stayed put. Slowly, her expression changed.

'Why can't people just leave me alone?' she cried.

'Tell me about Jason Spencer.' Crane gave her a sideways look. 'You met him a few years ago. Online. You brought him in, remember? Found him a place to stay with some like-minded individuals.'

'Just go away, will you?' Selina stood abruptly, grabbing the child and the stroller and starting to move. Crane stepped in front of her.

'This is not going away, Selina. I've seen the messages. I've seen all of it.'

'I told you, this has nothing to do with me,' Selina whined.

'I think it does.'

'You can't prove anything.'

'You don't understand. I'm not trying to get you into trouble. I'm just trying to find Jason. That's all.'

Selina let go of the child's hand. He looked up at them, aware that something weird was happening. Weird enough to silence him.

'Let's just walk for a bit,' suggested Crane. 'Can we do that?'

Reluctantly, Selina took a step and then another. The child, forgotten, came along slowly behind them. They turned right along the path and started round the little park again.

'Tell me about yourself,' Crane said. 'How did you get into all this?'

'I don't know,' said Selina, shaking her head. 'It was a bit of a lark. I was just your average Essex girl. Boring. Nothing out of the ordinary. I wanted to be special, I suppose. Different.' She gestured at her clothes. 'You dress like this and people take a step back. I mean, they laugh at first, but when they see you're serious, they get scared. They don't know how to deal with it.'

'So, this was your little rebellion.'

'Something like that.'

'You left home, moved up to London.'

'Yeah.' Selina nodded. 'It just progressed. I went on marches, protesting this and that. War, asylum seekers. I was a sister.' She paused. 'It was good. Radical. Felt like we were going to change things. People just think about themselves. They don't see what they are doing.'

'And Magid – was that part of your rebellion against society?'

'Oh, god!' Selina moaned. 'I suppose so. I don't know what I was thinking.' She paused for a moment. 'It was different, old-fashioned, you know? Like one of those things on the telly.'

Crane frowned, not sure where this was going. Selina explained.

'You know, like costume dramas? On the BBC?'

Crane nodded. 'Jane Austen.'

'Yeah, whatever. Anyway, I met Magid's sister. She was really kind to me. Then she suggested I meet her brother. It was all very formal. We sat around drinking endless cups of tea and not looking at one another. It was romantic, not like all the boys I'd known who just want to shove a hand up your skirt.' Selina glanced up at Crane to see if she was following. 'I just wanted to get away from it all. The boring old life I had. I wanted something new, something different. Fuck was I thinking?'

She fell silent and they walked on, reaching the end of one path and turning right.

'How long ago was all this?'

'Seven or eight years ago.'

'Before you met Jason, then?'

'Yeah, well, that was . . .' Selina broke off with a weary sigh. 'Look, I was fed up. I'd just had the baby. I felt like shit. I dunno. I was just angry. I wanted someone to pay.'

'Pay for what?'

'I dunno,' Selina shrugged. 'Everything. The mess I was in.' She picked at a thread on the sleeve of her black garment. 'Some of the other women did it, tried to recruit people, get them to convert. It was a bit of a lark, you know? To see if I could do it?'

Crane nodded. Two unhappy people. Isn't that how trouble always begins? Jason was just starting at university and feeling unhappy. Nothing odd about that. Plenty of people found themselves suddenly out of their depth in a new town surrounded by strangers. Crane could recall that during her first months in college there were lots of social clubs and activities vying for your interest. Most of them were an excuse to get plastered and sleep with someone whose name you couldn't remember the next day. Didn't want to remember.

'I saw him on Facebook. I thought he looked sweet. So I messaged him and we got talking.'

'So you were friends. Why go the extra mile and convert him?' Crane asked.

'I told you. I was angry, I wanted the world to pay. And I was more radical than I am now.' The novelty had been wearing thin. 'Besides, he was just so sad. He had all these questions, you know, about life and meaning and all the rest of it.'

'You were leading him on.'

'He was so unhappy. So desperate. He just wanted something to believe in.'

'And that's what you gave him?'

Selina nodded, still looking at the ground. 'Part of me didn't think he would go through with it, the other half wanted to see what happened if he did. Then suddenly he was there and I had to arrange everything.'

'So where did he stay?'

'There's a flat connected to Magid's centre. They use it for people, usually asylum seekers who have nowhere to go.'

'Must have been an eye opener for Jason.'

'It was all part of the deal. There are no borders in Islam. He got that.' She looked round at Crane. 'You can say what you like about me, but Jason found something he was looking for.'

'Did you persuade him to go to Syria?'

Selina shook her head. 'He didn't need persuading. He wanted to go.'

'Tell yourself that if you like,' Crane said. 'He was just a kid. A little confused. He had no idea what he was letting himself in for.'

'Maybe, in some ways, but he knew.' Selina hesitated. 'He saw what was out there. That's part of the reason he went. The bombings, the gassings by Assad. He knew how bad it was. For what it's worth, I never wanted him to go. I just never thought he would go through with it. He didn't seem the type.'

'Then how did he get that into his head?'

'Just, you know. The people that he was staying with. Men. All trying to sound tough. They sit together and watch these videos. They gee each other up.'

Crane was silent for a moment. 'I get the feeling you were expecting more from him,' she said, suddenly understanding. 'Both of you thought this would lead to something. Was that what you were hoping?'

'I dunno.' Selina brushed a hand over her child's head. 'I was unhappy. I suppose I built something up in my head. A fairy tale. That he would come and take me away from all this.' She put an arm around her boy and hugged him to her.

'And when that didn't happen, Jason left for Syria.' Crane waited for Selina's nod. 'And Magid, do you really want to leave him?'

'What's the point? I mean, really, where would I go? He'd find me and bring me back.'

'You wouldn't be the first woman to need protection from an abusive husband.'

'Oh, come on.' Selina gave a harsh laugh. 'He's not abusive, he's just a dick.'

'Tell me about the other woman I saw at the house.'

'Oh, God!' Selina rolled her eyes. 'Ayesha. Fresh off the boat. Doesn't speak English. Doesn't question anything he says. It has its upsides. He leaves me alone. That makes it a little bearable. Well, as soon as she has her baby it will.' She folded her arms. 'I have to go.'

'Let me help you,' said Crane, turning towards her.

Selina squinted up at the blue sky. She took a moment, weighing up her options. How much she trusted this woman to the life she had now.

'I don't need your help, okay?' she said finally. 'I can take care of myself.' The child gave a start as he was bundled unceremoniously into the pushchair. 'Just . . . stay away from me.' Without a backward glance Selina marched off, pushing the stroller ahead of her. Crane watched her walk away, wondering if she'd gone too far.

With a sigh, she wondered if Drake was making any progress.

11

The Cave of the Companions was the rather grand name painted in an uneven hand across a sheet of plywood hanging over the entrance of what had once been a set of council offices in Stockwell. They'd long since been deprived of funds, forced to shut down and turned over to the private sector to fend for themselves. This explained why the stately old red-brick building was currently occupied by a jumbled list of charities and voluntary organisations, some of them fly-by-night, others more seasoned. Almost anyone applying for space was likely to be granted it. Nobody really knew what the Cave represented. Some kind of crossroads between a prayer room and a cultural centre. They had a series of rooms at the back of the building through a set of heavy double doors on squeaky hinges.

Jason Spencer would have needed help to arrange passage out to Syria. You didn't just get on a plane and swan out there like you were going to Ibiza. You needed connections to get you across the border. A network capable of helping you out of Turkey and into Syria, and somebody along the line to introduce you to the right people, so that Islamic State wouldn't just put a bullet in you and leave you by the side of the road somewhere.

There was a good chance that if Jason returned to London he would reach out to the same people who got him out there in the first place, meaning Magid Bouallem and his pals – the Companions. When Jason Spencer had first arrived in London, it was here that he had converted. He had stayed in a flat a few streets away with three others, all of them associated with this centre.

Calling yourself the companions of the Prophet was taking liberties, as far as Drake was concerned, and that fitted with his first impressions of Magid Bouallem. He was a big man, physically, and seemed to equate this with the idea that he actually added up to something more than a fat man who traded in piety. The difference between Bouallem and someone like, say, Imam Ahmad was infinite. Drake's old imam was reserved and humble. Bouallem was full of himself. Swaggering about, puffing his chest out, playing the wise guy, as if he knew something nobody else did.

For the first few days Drake made sure he turned up at the Cave around mealtimes. Food was served in the big, open prayer room to anyone who was in need. They all sat on the carpet and dipped into an array of dishes that were set before them. The food was simple, prepared by a couple of volunteers who worked downstairs in the centre's old kitchens. Drake was curious about where the funding came from. He'd been unable to find out much from official records. Cash donations was the answer he was given whenever he asked. It was hard to believe that a couple of chumps handing out stickers and rattling collection boxes in people's faces could bring in enough. Drake suspected Bouallem had another benefactor. He was always wandering about clutching a carrier bag, from which he produced an endless stream of money that he handed to staff members to cover costs.

Just through the doors the same artist who had painted the sign appeared to have gone to work again. A mural covered the wall from floor to ceiling with a depiction of the Companions of the Cave. A group of young men hide from persecution in a cave and sleep there for three hundred years, a legend also known as 'the Cave of the Sleepers'. A place of shelter for the persecuted. It seemed appropriate.

The artist in question materialised at Drake's side. His name was Edriss.

'You are new here.'

He was a slight figure. Bowed forwards, his hair receding. It made him look older than his years. Soft spoken.

'I used to go to the *masjid* on Birch Lane.'

'Imam Ahmad,' Edriss nodded. 'He is a good man. But tell me, how did you find this place?'

Drake was about to tell him when Magid Bouallem appeared beside them. Bouncing on his toes like an overgrown infant, a cheap parka pulled over his shiny black djellaba. The ever-present carrier bag in his hand.

'Our brother who is always hungry,' he chuckled, patting

Drake on the shoulder. 'We have to watch this one, Edriss, or he will eat us out of house and home.'

The chuckling was reciprocated by the band of followers who always seemed to trail along in his wake. Bouallem was a larger-than-life figure. There was something cartoonish and simple about him that clearly appealed to people. There was also something disturbing about the way the others fell in line with his bullying. The group moved on, leaving Drake alone with Edriss again.

'A brother told me I might find a place to stay here.'

'What brother?'

'He called himself Abu Hamra. Before that he was Jason.'

'I don't know anyone by that name.'

But Drake had seen a flicker of recognition cross the other man's face.

'He told me he used to come here. He said the centre had a flat. Is that true?'

Edriss frowned. 'When did he tell you this?'

It was Drake's turn to be evasive. 'It was a while back. You've never met him? You're sure?'

'That's what I said.' Edriss looked off down the hallway after the others.

'Well, if you hear anything I'd be grateful.'

'Go in peace, brother.'

On his way back across town on the top deck of a bus, then switching to the Tube, taking a roundabout course to shake off anyone who might be following him, Drake had plenty of time to reflect on his progress. Bouallem's comments prompted him not to stay for the evening meal. He didn't want to appear too desperate. He was also wary of crowding Edriss. He might have stuck his neck out by asking about Jason so early on, but Drake's intuition told him that Edriss was not as hardcore as the others and might offer a way into the group. They were a familiar lot. He had frequented several mosques during his time as a believer. The ones he had seen so far on his few visits fitted the general mould. They embraced a combination of hit-and-miss, catch-all theories. The kind that circulate on the further reaches of the internet where they can be picked up by those seeking to find some purpose to inject into their listless existences. Wayward souls, fallen angels, casualties who had lost track of their place in the world. The confused and the plain ignorant, unable to summon the imagination or the effort required to make a go of life. Drake had seen that look in his own eyes once upon a time and so he recognised it easily. He'd found his path, dedicating himself to putting the world right in his own small way. And here he was again, threading his way through the flock, trying to sort the sheep from the wolves.

He was now more convinced than ever that there was something going on with the Companions of the Cave, as they so grandly styled themselves. To begin with, it seemed there was more to Magid Bouallem than just an outsized ego that got its kicks from providing charity for the faithful out of the goodness of his heart. Was it just a money-making scheme for him? If that was the case, then arranging trips to Syria might be a useful tool. Either way, it was still too early for Drake to say. He needed to get closer and that would take time.

It took him almost two hours to get back to Battersea. Cautious and hindered by the usual inexplicable delays and missing trains, he stepped into carriages and then off at the last minute, doubled back on himself, cut through a betting shop that he knew had a back entrance. It was early to think such tactics necessary, but he needed to get into the habit. His years as an undercover agent started to come back to him and for a time he was lost in remembering the period he spent trying to infiltrate Goran Malevitch's organisation. Sometimes it felt as though Malevitch's particular brand of evil would dog him forever.

By the time Drake reached the Ithaka the front lights were off, a sign they were getting ready to close. He was encouraged by the fact that there were still a few tables occupied. Tired and hungry, he slipped quietly into his usual place at the back, underneath the yellowing black-and-white photographs of Demis Roussos and Nana Mouskouri. Kostas and Eleni were nowhere in sight. Instead, the place was being run by the divorced niece whose name escaped him. He could still remember when, not so long ago, she had been a clueless waitress mixing up orders and getting flustered. Nowadays she could run the place singlehandedly like a pro, slapping the coffee machine on while preparing meals from the counter and ringing up sales on the cash register. She looked better too. The influence of the ever cheerful Kostas and Eleni, no doubt. She seemed happier, quite different to the rather grey, nervous figure she had been when she first appeared. There was still a seriousness to her which Drake put down to whatever it was that had brought her to London in the first place. He recalled talk of some kind of domestic crisis, a messy break-up or divorce. He didn't know the details. Eleni would roll her eyes and shake her head whenever the subject came up, but now Drake found himself curious for more details.

A shadow fell over his table.

'May I?'

The man was of average height, but he had bulked himself out with weight training and steroids. There was a touch of the Italian about him but the voice was pure London. On his way in, Drake had clocked the group sitting in the front by the window. A handful of Donny's goons. Drake knew them well enough to give them a nod as he went by, but he had since forgotten all about them.

'Dino, right?'

'Right.' He seemed touched that Drake would remember.

Drake wiped his mouth with a napkin and sat back. 'You run a couple of gyms.'

'Fitness centres,' corrected Dino. 'Yeah, we're doin all right. Got five of 'em now. It's an expanding sector.' He said the words carefully, as if wary of them tripping him up.

'I'll bet it is.'

Dino talked like he was running a multinational enterprise. Drake had always had him pegged as a knuckle-dragging muscle man, but maybe he'd been taking business classes. Dino rested a hand on the chair opposite, ready to pull it out.

'I wanted to have a word. You mind?'

'If you don't mind me eating.'

'No, please, go ahead.' Dino pulled out the chair and sat down.

111

'So what's this about?' Drake asked, digging his fork back into the plate.

'It's about Donny. Some of us are worried about him.'

'Worried, how?'

Dino winced, as if he was in pain. 'As you know, he's been a little obsessed with his business.'

'He's overworked?' Drake was failing to see why this was his concern.

'It's the legal side. He has a lot of investments, some very fine places.'

Drake knew that Donny Apostolis had been eager to start distancing himself from the more dodgy sides of his little empire. The London property market was the obvious one. Organised crime rolled into town and pushed their money through property investments at a rate of knots, buying and selling so fast you couldn't tell who owned what, which was the general idea. The government's efforts to deregulate the sector and make the country more attractive to investors had succeeded spectacularly, for some. Scrutiny had been dialled back to less than zero. Everybody loved England, especially the crooks.

'The problem is,' Dino went on, 'in his line of business it doesn't pay to look weak.'

It surprised Drake that Dino was talking like a financial advisor, not a bouncer. Either he had underestimated Dino, or things had changed.

'So, people are trying to move in on him? That's what you're saying? Nothing new about that, is there?'

Dino looked grave. 'Some big sharks out there. They don't miss a trick.'

'I appreciate the honesty.' Drake put down his fork and reached for his beer. 'But frankly, I'm not sure why you're telling me all this. Donny can take care of himself.'

'He respects you.' Dino conceded the weight of this statement with a tilt of his head. 'I mean, you know Donny. He may not show it, but he means it.'

The conversation was interrupted by the waitress, who arrived bearing a coffee and a small glass of brandy.

'Thanks, Amaia,' said Dino, smiling up at her.

Drake would have put her age at somewhere in the mid-thirties. Her eyes flickered towards him, but he couldn't think of anything he needed, so she was gone.

'I still don't see how Donny thinks I can help him,' said Drake. He had never been in any doubt that Donny's interest in him stemmed from his having been an officer of the Metropolitan Police. That could always come in useful. 'Especially since I'm no longer on the force.'

'Sure, I get that, but it doesn't change things. There are very few people Donny listens to.' Dino leaned forward until his pumped-up chest was almost touching the table. 'Just between the two of us,' he whispered, 'he's getting a little paranoid. Thinks people are out to get him. He's jumping at shadows.' Dino's eyebrows lifted in a petition for sympathy.

'I'm sorry to hear that, but I still don't see where I come in.'

'Donny is reaching out to you,' Dino said, finally spelling it out. 'He wants to talk. You know how he is. Too proud to ask for help.'

'Fair enough, let's talk,' shrugged Drake. 'Now that you're here, let me ask you something.'

'Sure.' Dino paused, slurping up his espresso. 'What do you need?'

'Grayson Brodie.'

'Brodie?' Dino gave a loud sniff. 'You don't need to worry about him.'

'How so?'

'You just don't,' Dino said, looking Drake in the eye.

'That sounds definitive.'

'It's taken care of,' Dino shrugged. 'He's not coming back.'

Drake watched the big man make his way back to his friends. They pulled on their coats and headed for the door. He would have liked to have asked more, but maybe that was one reason to see Donny again.

12

The wipers brushed aside a sheet of water, allowing Kelly Marsh a glimpse of DS Mark Chiang sheltering from the rain in the stone arch of the entrance. He was smoking a cigarette. Something about that long leather coat made Marsh wonder if the DS had ever flirted with fascism. Which would be odd for a man who was at least half Chinese, but nowadays, who knew? Perhaps it was just some kind of retro fashion statement. Maybe he fancied himself as a 1980s New Romantic.

The security man on the gate signalled the all clear and waved her forward, indicating a parking space off to the right. Marsh grabbed her raincoat from the back seat and held it over her head as she ran over. She was aware of DS Chiang's passing interest in the front of her blouse, now rendered semi-transparent by the rain.

'Ready?' she asked, shaking off her coat in the shelter of the doorway. She'd dressed in her newest and smartest charcoal grey suit but somehow still felt shabby next to Chiang's neatly buttoned elegance. She wondered just what proportion of his salary went on clothes. Or maybe he just had money. Tossing his cigarette into the rain, he turned and led the way inside. They filed through another security check, where he flashed his badge, then led the way along a panelled corridor. Marsh had never been inside Westminster before and she was doing her best not to look impressed.

'She's waiting for us in the Strangers' Dining Room,' Chiang said over his shoulder. He didn't slow his pace to wait for Marsh or engage in small talk, something she was quietly grateful for.

'Strangers?'

'It's where members take outside guests.'

'Doesn't she have an office?'

Chiang shrugged. 'She thinks it's better like this. More neutral.'

Marsh thought it a little odd, but what did she know? Everything seemed to be telling her that she was entering a world that was alien to her.

The dining room had a thick burgundy carpet and stately wooden panelling on the walls. It was deserted save for a couple of waitresses in tired uniforms who were busy setting tables and paid them no attention. Zoë Helms was seated at a table over by the high windows that reached up almost to the ornate carved ceiling. The politician looked neat and composed, rather different from the last time Marsh had seen her. She was dressed in a midnight blue suit that looked deceptively simple and was clearly expensive. How expensive, Marsh did not want to know. The two detectives stood by the table respectfully and waited for Helms to finish a phone call before signalling for them to sit down.

'Thank you for agreeing to this,' Helms began. 'I can't begin to explain what a busy time this is. So much is happening.'

Marsh exchanged a glance with Chiang. She wanted to ask why the politician was working at all. Zoë Helms seemed to read her mind.

'I know what you're thinking,' she said, resting both hands on the pile of folders in front of her. 'After such a terrible experience, most people would be expected to take some time off. I'm afraid I'm not most people. I would go to pieces if I was at home right now. I need to keep busy. Does that make any sense?' She addressed the question to Marsh. Chiang looked on wordlessly, probably wondering why he was being ignored.

'It's a natural response,' Marsh said, pausing. 'Just how close were you and the victim?'

Helms turned away to stare out of the window. 'Cathy and I met nearly two years ago at one of those functions where you meet dozens of people and by the time you are home you've forgotten their names. In her case the opposite happened. We exchanged half a dozen words, but I just couldn't get her out of my head. Still, we were both busy with our careers and our paths didn't cross again until about a year ago. This time it just clicked.' Zoë Helms studied the backs of her hands. 'People use expressions like whirlwind romance and falling head over heels, and I'm afraid it was just that. We ticked every cliché in the book.'

'So, she moved in with you right away?'

Chiang appeared to have decided to take a back seat. Either way, he let Marsh ask all the questions. The only indication of any impatience was a light tapping of his forefinger on the tablecloth.

'Not right away, no. We yoyoed back and forth, but we were both busy and it was inconvenient not being home every night, particularly for me. So, when Cathy decided to write her book, it seemed like the perfect moment. She could move in with me. She was the domesticated one. I'm terrible about that sort of thing, but Cathy was organised, thorough. She made things work.' Helms broke off and looked away again. For a moment, Marsh thought she was going to let it all out and burst into tears. There was a long moment followed by a loud sniff, and then she was back.

'It all sounds perfect,' Marsh said, partly to give Helms time to recover. 'So there were no loose ends to tie up. No partners, children, messy break-ups?'

'I know where you're going with this,' said Helms. 'You're thinking of motive, possible suspects?' She looked at Chiang. 'I thought it was a burglary gone wrong. Someone panicked.'

Marsh broke in before Chiang could reply. 'That is still the most likely explanation, yes, but in order to be sure we need to eliminate all other scenarios. A woman in your position attracts more than her fair share of threats.'

'Of course,' said Helms crisply. 'It comes with the territory. Mark has all the details.'

'DS Chiang has promised to share the online threats you've received. Mostly right-wing nut jobs, as I understand.'

'Mostly,' said Chiang. He hadn't actually said he would share the threats they had logged. 'There's a good selection. You'll have the material by end of day.'

'As soon as we have that we can start working through to draw up a list of people who might have an axe to grind.' Marsh bit her tongue. 'Sorry, that wasn't meant . . .'

'It's okay, detective. I'm not squeamish.' Helms waved the apology aside. 'But Mark and his team have already vetted all of the hate mail I get, unless I'm mistaken.'

'We have,' nodded Chiang. 'We follow up on the most extreme or persistent cases. There's a lot of traffic, as you can imagine. It's impossible to track it all. We have to filter it.'

'But there have been no serious, credible death threats recently?'

Chiang was shaking his head, but Helms had more to add. 'In the current political climate everything has become poisonous. It magnifies the hate level. Tempers are running high.'

'We have to recalibrate for that,' nodded Chiang. 'But on the whole, I'd say we're pretty efficient at weeding out the real threats from the general nastiness.'

Helms smiled her agreement. 'They do an excellent job. *You* do an excellent job.'

'We try to do our best,' said Chiang.

What struck Marsh was how the two seemed to have coordinated their act. Either there was a natural consensus, or something else was going on. She flipped through pages in her notebook as if looking for something.

'I still have a few questions about Ms Perkins herself.' She could feel the way they were both looking at her. 'And this is

119

really just to rule out all the alternatives, but is there a chance she might have been the intended victim?'

Zoë Helms looked sceptical. 'I suppose it's possible. I mean, Cathy could get up people's noses, but that someone would go so far as to murder her, if that's what you're saying . . .?' She left the question hanging.

'We have no evidence of any specific threat,' Chiang confirmed. Marsh ignored him.

'She was an investigative journalist. Isn't it possible she got on the wrong side of someone?'

'Far be it from me to tell you how to conduct your investigation,' said Helms. 'But to be quite frank, well . . .' She allowed herself a smile. 'Cathy would be the first to admit she just wasn't that kind of reporter.'

'What kind of reporter is that?' Marsh asked.

'Woodward and Bernstein. Bringing down the government. Controversial. Scandalous. That is what you are hinting at?'

'Maybe she simply upset someone?'

'If she did, I certainly heard nothing about it,' Helms shrugged, gathering up a pair of leather gloves lying on the table. 'She took her work seriously. That's the reason she was at my place. I said she could stay there until she got the book finished.'

'Cathy's laptop and phone are missing. Do you have any idea what her book was about?'

'Sorry, Cathy was rather secretive.'

'She didn't tell you anything? Didn't you find that strange?'

'She was always afraid of being scooped by a rival, or whatever the term is.'

'You mean another journalist, a colleague?'

'Another writer. I understood it was a novel, a satire about modern political life. She has – or had – a great sense of humour.' Helms looked down at the table. 'Cathy always had a wonderful sense of life.'

'Nice one,' murmured Chiang, as they headed for the door. 'Thanks for the support.'

'Why didn't you tell me you were going to raise all that stuff about Perkins?'

'I didn't know I had to clear everything with you first,' said Marsh. 'I'm pretty sure I don't.'

'That's not what I'm saying, and you know it.'

'What are you saying, then?'

'I'm saying it would help if we were on the same page when we went in to interview her.'

Marsh rounded on him. 'Look, DS Chiang.'

'Mark.'

'Okay, Mark. Look, I'm not here to step on your toes, but I've made no secret of the fact that I'm not happy just dismissing every other possibility until we've eliminated them properly.'

'Okay, then what would satisfy you that this was about Helms?'

'I want to know why they took that laptop and I want to know what this book Perkins was working on was about.'

'All you had to do was ask,' snapped Chiang.

As she drove away, Marsh was thinking that perhaps she should have played it a little smoother with him. She didn't want Chiang to start making moves to get her removed from the case, which she was pretty sure he probably could.

Back at Raven Hill, Milo was eager for details. 'So, what did you make of her?'

'Zoë Helms? I don't know. Politicians, what can you say?' Marsh's immediate concern was finding where someone had hidden the sweetener. She opened and closed cupboards in the little kitchenette without luck. Either someone had decided to take it home with them or it had run empty and nobody had bothered to replace it. Maybe she should just accept the inevitable and go without. She took a sip of coffee and decided she could live with it.

'I hear you,' said Milo, who was flicking rubber bands at the large Lego Batman on his desk. 'I mean, who sets out to make a career in politics?'

'It used to be people who wanted to change the world,' Marsh said over her shoulder. 'Nowadays they just seem to be out to line their pockets.' She sat back. 'To be honest, I was a little disappointed. I mean, here's a woman who's made a career for herself in what is basically a boys' club. I expected more from her.'

'Doesn't make a difference,' Milo shrugged as he swivelled his chair round to face her. 'They're all the same, whether they wear skirts or not.'

'Yeah, so much for emancipation, eh?'

'How about Mr Chang?'

'Chiang,' Marsh corrected. 'He set me straight on that once already. I'm not going to give him the chance to do it again.'

'What's his story?'

'What's to tell? He slipped out of running gangs and pimps in Chinatown and landed a cushy job in Westminster. Even gets to carry a gun.'

'Something about a man with a gun,' murmured Milo.

'You keep talking like that and you'll find yourself voted gay of the month.'

'I was thinking about you.'

'Perish the thought. He's about as far from my type as you can get.' Even as she spoke, Marsh wondered if she was right. Mark Chiang might not have shown any real interest in her, but he wasn't exactly the kind who advertised his feelings. 'Did he send through the social media stuff?'

'Yeah, I've been working through it.' Milo spun back towards his computer screens – there were three in all, two large ones and a laptop he carried with him everywhere. 'So far it's just the usual nasty stuff. Men describing in graphic terms what they'd like to do to her. Makes you wonder.'

'About men, you mean?' Marsh was shaking her head. 'Never underestimate the depravity of the male mind.'

'That's so depressing.'

'Cut it out, Milo, you're sounding sensitive again. Anything concrete in there?'

'A couple of death threats, but DS Chiang's squad have already followed up on those.'

'Don't take everything he tells you for granted.'

Milo's brow furrowed. 'What does that mean?'

'Just that he seemed awfully close to Helms. I wonder how much influence she has over him.'

'We're talking what, *The Bodyguard*?'

'I wouldn't go that far,' said Marsh, her nose wrinkling in distaste. 'I'm just saying, I'm not sure he's a hundred per cent objective. He's inside the politics of it.'

'So what's your next move?'

'Cathy Perkins. The more they push the political angle, the more I want to know what Perkins was up to. We never found any kind of external disc belonging to her at the flat?'

'Negative.'

'How about any printed matter? Anything to give us an idea of what she was working on. Helms mentioned something about the book being a novel.'

'There's a box full of stuff that you're welcome to go through. Looks like research material. No laptop, smartphone, iPad or suchlike.' Milo indicated a plastic evidence box. 'That's just from the desk where she was found.'

'People don't get murdered for writing novels,' Marsh murmured to herself while sifting through the contents. 'At least none that I've read are worth dying for.'

'That's not the same thing,' said Milo.

'So what's the alternative? A short-sighted killer or a junkie looking for something to sell?' She pulled out a VHS cassette. A 1947 film entitled *Black Narcissus*. Sounded like some kind of weird porn fantasy. No case. 'I can't believe that's what it was.'

'Maybe you just don't want to believe it?'

Marsh tossed the video cassette back into the box. 'Don't get above your station, Detective Constable Kowalski.'

'Always seems like a waste, to lose your life over a stupid iPhone.'

'You'd have to be pretty desperate to kill someone for one of those, but it wouldn't be the first time.' Marsh gave up looking through the box of files and clippings that seemed to cover a range of things in no particular order. She sat back. 'How do we find out what she was working on? What about the cloud? Could she have kept a copy of whatever it was on there?'

'It's possible. Not sure we can access it, but I can try.' Milo looked up Cathy Perkins' email accounts and started searching. Marsh sipped her coffee and thought about how much more sense it made to cut sugar out of her diet altogether. Then she set the mug down and flipped on her computer.

'Helms said Perkins used to work at a paper.'

'*The Guardian.*' Milo spoke over his shoulder without taking his eyes off the screen in front of him. 'What are you thinking?'

'I'm thinking that maybe she had some friends. Might be worth a shot. What?'

Milo was tapping his foot nervously. 'I just, you know. Are you sure about this?'

'What do you mean?'

'Don't take this the wrong way,' Milo said. 'But you're sticking your neck out on this one.'

'Then I'd better not fuck it up,' Marsh muttered under her breath.

13

The Spencers had done well for themselves. Their home was the biggest in the street, right at the bottom end of a neat horseshoe. The leafy estate was on the outskirts of town, built maybe thirty years ago, maybe a little more. Everything was very tidy and discreet. Before she rolled up to the front door, Crane took a moment to have a look around the village of Horkstow. The local church was a sombre building constructed by the Knights Templar back in the twelfth century, according to the information plaque outside. It was dedicated to Saint Maurice, an Egyptian, Crane discovered via Wikipedia, who was depicted as an African until the sixteenth century, when the slave trade transformed perceptions and being black was no longer viewed as benignly as it had once been.

By the time she was being shown into the living room, Crane felt the day had already proved itself not to be an entire waste of time. The cluttered interior made her conscious of her boots and motorcycle jacket. Alongside the ornate fireplace,

126

the carriage clock on the mantlepiece and the blown glass figures arrayed on every surface she felt clumsy and awkward, although Mrs Spencer did not seem to mind.

'It's too early for any concrete results, I'm afraid,' Crane began, so as not to get Mrs Spencer's hopes up. She had already said that on the phone, but decided it was worth repeating. She didn't want her getting emotional at the idea that no progress had been made. 'I thought it would be helpful to come up and take a look at where this message was placed.'

'Yes, of course, I understand.' Mrs Spencer was wearing a fluffy pink cardigan and looked as though she'd been to the hairdresser's that morning. Maybe she dressed that way every day, or maybe she had nothing much to do with her time. The tea set was silver and as ornate as something you might see on the *Antiques Roadshow*. 'Milk?'

'No, thanks.' Crane could feel herself growing itchy. This kind of place usually made her want to rage and maybe smash a few ornaments. Something about it made her think of her father, and that was never good. The quaint illusion of it all. She felt as if cracks would appear in the facade if she breathed too heavily.

'Actually, I'm glad you came today.' Mrs Spencer was holding the teapot as she dropped her voice. 'I think I saw her again. The woman, the one I told you about.'

'Today?'

'No, it was yesterday evening. At least, I think it was the same one.' The smile faltered as she lowered the pot down.

'You think it was her? Did she have a child with her?'

'I-I'm not sure now.' Mrs Spencer looked genuinely confused. 'Perhaps I imagined her.'

Crane shifted in her seat. 'Has this ever happened before?'

'Well, you know how it is. I'm always worried about losing my marbles. Paul says I'm forgetful, but he never has anything nice to say.' She lifted her cup and then seemed to lose her thread. 'Do you really ride that thing all over the place? Isn't it dangerous?'

It took a moment for Crane to realise that she was talking about the Triumph Bonneville.

'It's a machine,' she said. 'If you treat it with respect, it will respect you back.'

'I see,' nodded Mrs Spencer, although it wasn't clear she did. Crane felt obliged to elaborate.

'You have to be careful. You learn never to trust other people.'

'I suppose in your line of business that makes sense,' said Mrs Spencer.

Crane had meant other road users, but she could see how it might apply to other parts of her life. She would be the first to admit that she had trust issues. Cal had reminded her of the fact enough times for her to know that it could become a problem between them. Like her, Cal had an instinctive sense of whether or not he trusted people. Unlike her, it made him withdraw. He didn't let you in. It was something she had to work on. Now she got to her feet and went over to the windows looking out on the back garden.

'Tell me again about this woman,' Crane said. 'How many times have you seen her?'

'Oh, only the once, and then again.' Mrs Spencer came over to join her. 'Out there in the trees, but sometimes it's difficult to see. There are shadows.'

'You said she was dressed all in black last time.'

'Yes, exactly. Like one of those things you said, the way they do over there.'

'An ebaya? A full-length garment. All in black? And she was holding a child.'

'A small child, yes.' Mrs Spencer had one hand clutched to her mouth. 'It was so bizarre. It was almost like something out of the Bible. A miracle.' She looked up to see if Crane understood. 'When it happened again, I thought I'd imagined it. I really did,' she added softly.

The garden was fairly big. A long strip of well-manicured lawn was broken in the middle by an opening with shrubs and rose bushes. At the far end was a grove of trees.

'What's beyond those trees?'

'Oh, well, it just keeps going. If you go far enough you come to a road,' said Mrs Spencer, as if uncertain what the question meant. 'But it's basically just woods.'

'And no fence?'

'We've never needed one.'

Crane had the sense of Mrs Spencer being something of a free spirit.

'Tell me about the messages in the bird house.'

'Ah,' Mrs Spencer nodded, focussing her mind. 'Well, it began when Jason was small. He would leave little notes for me. It was our secret place.'

'How old would he have been then?'

'Oh, seven or eight.'

'And how long did it last?'

'Oh, probably far longer than was healthy,' Mrs Spencer laughed. 'In some ways, Jason always remained that little boy.'

Crane wondered how this might have affected his choices later in life.

'Was Mr Spencer aware of this?'

'You make it sound as if we did something wrong.' Mrs Spencer looked concerned. 'Of course, Paul knew we had our little secrets.'

'And he didn't mind?'

'Well, maybe he did, but there is a special bond between a mother and her son. Do you have children? No, I don't suppose you have time.'

Crane ignored the comment. 'Sometimes one parent can feel threatened by their partner having a closer relationship to their child than they do.'

'That sounds terribly complicated. This was simply something we did.'

'I understand.' Crane abandoned the thread and returned to her original tack. 'I know you've told me this already, but walk me through it again please. Tell me exactly how you found it.'

'The note? I can show you.' Mrs Spencer reached for the handle on the patio doors and led the way out. Feeling the chill, she wrapped her arms around herself. 'It's still damp from last night,' she said, meaning the grass.

They started down the garden. After a few paces, Crane turned to look back at the house. From this angle it appeared completely secluded, with no visible neighbours on either side.

It was solitary and easy to approach without being seen. To her right a hedgerow separated the Spencers' property from open fields. As they reached the end of the strip of lawn the grass sprouted in wild clumps that gave way to the wooded area a good fifteen paces away. Crane followed Mrs Spencer along the narrow path that furrowed through untended nettles, dock leaves and raspberry bushes. The bird house nailed to a pine tree was hidden from sight. If you didn't know it was there you wouldn't find it. It looked homemade, but robust, the wood dark with age.

'My father made it for me when I was a child. I kept it and brought it here when we moved.'

Crane smiled understandingly. She was only half listening, her eyes searching the trees, trying to see beyond. The moss gave the trunks a blurred, grey appearance.

'Tell me again, how you found it,' she said.

Mrs Spencer looked back towards the house. 'It was just an ordinary day. Paul had gone off to do something and I came out to do some pruning. I had my gardening things and I was kneeling, right over there,' she pointed. 'I don't know what made me turn. It was almost as if I could feel a presence.'

A presence. Mrs Spencer's grasp of reality seemed to be heavily influenced by her imaginative faculties. Crane went along with it.

'You sensed Jason was there behind you?' she said.

'Yes, that's it.' Her voice trembled. 'That's why it felt like . . . like a miracle when I saw the note, rolled up and stuffed into the opening on the bird house, just like we used to do. I couldn't believe it.'

Crane moved slightly to her left. From the house the bird-house would have been concealed, at least partially, by one of the pear trees in the garden.

'Why would he do that?' Crane said, repeating the question she had been asking herself since their first meeting. 'I mean, why not simply come up to the door? I understand the concern about the law, but surely, he's your son. He would know you were worried.'

'I know, I know. It makes no sense,' fretted Mrs Spencer. 'It's so unfair.' She frowned. 'We all make mistakes, don't we? But, after all, he's our son. This is his country.'

That, thought Crane, was open to debate. In today's climate there were no grey areas. You are either with us or against us seemed to be the current thinking. Jason had walked out into no-man's-land and was trying to find his way back across the lines. Only now he was perceived by some as the enemy.

'I'm going to walk further in,' said Crane. 'You can go back to the house.'

'Whatever for?' Mrs Spencer seemed taken aback.

'Just to have a look around. It'll be fine.' Crane smiled reassuringly. 'I'll speak to you later.'

Begrudgingly, Mrs Spencer turned and headed back across the lawn towards the house. Crane felt relieved. It was easier to think when she was alone. She took a moment to get her bearings. The woods thickened towards the east. Beyond the birdhouse the path was swallowed up by undergrowth. Crane tried to imagine someone who knew the lay of the land. She carried on, following natural breaks, openings and gaps in the trees. Already, after about five minutes, she felt as though she was deep inside a forest, as her route took her away from the house. The path had pretty much vanished. She looked back and could just make out the gabled roof through the trees. She wasn't worried. Crane had a natural sense of direction and knew she was unlikely to get lost. It was silent now, but for the sound of the occasional bird. In the distance somewhere, a woodpecker was tapping a lonely Morse code message into a tree.

A greyness floated around the birch trees ahead of her and Crane felt as though she were surrounded by ghosts. Faces from her past lurking in the vague shadows. Killers she had interviewed. Men who cut up their victims, strangled their wives, their mothers. At the centre of their eyes they all had the same empty, hollow spot. The place where their souls should have been.

Jason had played here as a child. He would have been able to find his way through these trees with his eyes closed, in the dark. Mrs Spencer had pointed vaguely as she mentioned a road and this was what Crane hoped to find. If he had wanted to approach the house without being seen, Jason might have parked up somewhere and made his way through the woods to deliver his message in secret. Crane was still troubled by the fact that he would go to such lengths just to leave a message rather than see his parents. Why would he hide? To be so close after all these years, he must surely have felt the urge to see his mother. Not just to put her mind at rest, but simply to throw himself into her arms, to come home. If he could reach the bird house without being seen then he would have been able to reach the kitchen door, for example. So why hadn't he done that? Was there something else, other than fear of being picked up by the authorities, that prevented him from walking that final stretch?

Crane smelled woodsmoke. It could have been a house, but from what Mrs Spencer had told her she was pretty sure nobody was supposed to be living in this direction. She stopped to listen. After a while she heard a thump of metal, which confirmed that there were people nearby. It took her the next ten minutes, moving first in one direction and then another, before she pinned down what she was looking for.

The collection of rough shelters stood in a clearing. Sheets of PVC plastic hung over lengths of washing line strung between trees. Stained, ripped mattresses with the stuffing coming out of them and flattened cardboard boxes had been shaped into the walls of a flimsy stockade. There was one real tent that looked like an old army surplus thing that had come out of a dump. The heavy canvas was ripped and patched with duct tape. The rest were sheets of plastic draped over drooping lines. The source of the smoke was a small campfire on which a couple of blackened pots rested.

The only person in sight was a man with a beard. His face was grubby with what looked like weeks of accumulated grime. He was trying to repair an old pop-up toaster. The thump she had heard was him striking the side of it with a monkey wrench. Catching sight of her, he slowly put down the toaster, but tightened his grip on the wrench. Crane held up a hand.

'It's okay.' She waited for a response. There was none. 'Speak English? Francais? Español? Arabic?'

To this last, the man gave a cautious nod. Crane saw a woman poke her head out from within the tent and then withdraw from sight.

'*Maat khaf*,' Crane said, showing her hands again. *Don't be afraid.*

'Bolis?' asked the man.

'Not police.' Crane shook her head as she stepped forward. The man stood up. He held the wrench, which was big and heavy-looking, against his chest. 'Syrian? Where are you from?'

'Haleb,' said the man. Aleppo.

'How long have you been here?'

The man held up a finger.

'A week?'

'A month,' he said.

'How many are you?' Crane asked, looking around. The woman was hovering, just inside the entrance to the tent, her eyes wide with terror. Mrs Spencer's mind was not as wayward as Crane had feared. The chances were that someone had approached the house through the woods and Mrs Spencer had seen them. The presence she had felt was real.

Crane swiped her phone and held up the picture of Jason for the man to see.

'How about this man. Have you seen him?'

The man licked his lips. He didn't like questions.

'Bolis?' the man repeated.

'No, I told you, I'm not police. I just need to find this man.'

The man didn't know what Crane really wanted but something in his eyes told her that he'd stopped trusting people a long time ago. All that was left after that was fear, and anger at the world that had put him here. She turned and stepped towards the tent, hearing the woman inside scurrying backwards. He took a step towards her. Crane stood her ground. He stayed where he was. She could hear the woman inside the tent breathing heavily, pretending not to be there, as if the old canvas was an invisibility cape. Crane listened for a time and knew she would get no more out of them at this time.

14

The Golden Scales appeared largely unchanged since the last time they'd met there. Drake was in two minds, in the mood to try something different but not finding it. When he had been stationed at Raven Hill, it had been a regular haunt. The colourful posters for popstars and festivals he'd never heard of were the only visible nod to decoration. Stripped down to the bare minimum, it promised quick and easy food and little else. He was studying the menu, to the visible annoyance of the diminutive woman behind the counter, who stood tapping her little order pad impatiently on the Formica.

'Maybe the sweet and sour?' he wondered aloud.

She cocked her head. 'You asking or ordering?'

'I'm trying to decide.' Drake considered smiling, but then thought better of it. He knew from experience that she wasn't interested in his efforts at being sociable. She decided to take his query as a request. The game was up. He knew there was no point in arguing.

'Chicken or pork?'

'Chicken.'

The business of ordering more or less taken care of, Drake retreated to one of the high stools by the narrow counter in the window. It was strewn with crumpled newspapers like a cat litter box, mostly of the local variety. As he sifted through, sorting them into a pile on one side, he was reminded of the café in Grimsby and his search for Brodie. Reaching for his phone, he called Andy Felton to ask if anything had come up on the boarding house. Felton sounded like he was stressed.

'Sorry, this is not a good time.' There was a long pause. Drake could hear people shouting in the background and what sounded like horses. 'Look, Cal, don't take this the wrong way, but maybe you should just move on.'

'Sorry?' Drake wondered if he had misheard.

'I'm just saying, I mean, this whole thing with your witness, that was how long ago – five, six years? Maybe it's time.'

Maybe it was. They agreed to speak at some later point and Drake sat there looking at his phone until the door next to him opened and Kelly Marsh appeared.

In contrast to Drake's experience, the welcome Marsh got from the woman behind the counter was positively ecstatic.

'Where you been? Why you no come here no more?' the woman chastised her before moving round the counter to give Marsh a hug.

'Sorry, I've just been so busy. I haven't had a moment.'

'You want special?'

'Yes, please,' said Marsh. 'I'm starving.'

'Don't you worry,' the woman winked. 'I make sure it extra special for you.'

'How do you do that?' Drake asked, as Marsh settled onto the stool next to him. 'I've been coming here for years and she still treats me like I murdered her favourite puppy.'

'Must be your manner, chief. You just give out this aura.'

'What aura?'

'I don't know,' shrugged Marsh. 'A sense of menace.'

'You're not cheering me up.' Drake separated a set of chopsticks with a snap. 'So, how's the case going?'

'That's what I wanted to talk about. I'm still not happy going along with Chiang's theory.' Marsh filled him in on her visit to Westminster to meet Zoë Helms.

'She's a politician,' said Drake. 'They tend to see themselves at the centre of the universe.'

'I need something concrete to make my case.'

'I get that you're on thin ice.' Drake tapped his chopsticks on the counter. 'Wheeler will have pulled some strings to clear you getting this case.'

'Pryce is the senior on all murder investigations these days.'

Drake was aware that Pryce had been promoted to run a section of the Murder Investigation Unit, overseeing teams that worked all over the south and south-west of the city. Wheeler was Marsh's direct supervisor, but in murder cases Pryce would have had to sign off on taking the lead on the investigation. Perhaps he had assumed that DS Chiang would keep her in line.

'Did you get any more about what Perkins was working on?'

Marsh rubbed her chin. 'All I've got is that she was writing a book.'

'What kind of book?'

'Not clear on that score. Helms claims it was a novel, some kind of satire on Westminster.'

'Hardly sounds like a reason to kill her. Maybe that was a line she was selling Helms.'

'You think she was playing her?' Marsh considered the idea. 'It's possible. Helms is pretty sure of herself.'

'You said the killer took her laptop and phone. Could she have left a hard copy somewhere?'

'Not so far as we can make out. Apparently she was wary of making hard copies.'

'I thought writers often printed things out . . .'

'Not this one. I spoke to one of Cathy Perkins' old colleagues at *The Guardian*.'

It had been an interesting conversation. Stella Wright claimed to be an old friend of Cathy Perkins. She said she was surprised on first hearing the two had got together because they seemed quite unsuited. In her opinion, Helms was too conservative for Perkins.

'In the beginning I think it was just a lark, you know, picking up a high-flying MP. But Cathy was never one to compromise, on anything. If something was wrong, she wouldn't keep quiet about it.'

'Then wasn't it strange that she moved in with Helms?'

'That could have been Cathy just being Cathy.'

'Meaning what exactly?'

'She wanted to write her book and she needed somewhere to stay. She sublet her place and moved in with Zoë – everybody wins.'

'What specifically do you think Cathy would have objected to in what Helms was doing?'

'Well, she had her name attached to a few things that frankly Cathy would never have accepted.'

'Such as?'

'Well, austerity cuts for one,' said Wright.

She was a large, no-nonsense blonde in her late thirties. They sat on the terrace of a café on the concourse at Euston station. Marsh immediately connected with her. Wright was genuine, which in turn told Marsh something else about Cathy Perkins. 'It was more than that. Recently, stuff was coming out about Helms being involved in some kind of arms deal with the Saudis.'

'Why is that important?'

'Yemen? The war that everybody is conveniently forgetting.'

'Right,' said Marsh, not wanting to appear stupid. She had heard of the war, of course, read about it in the paper, watched the images on the news. It just seemed so far away and, truth be told, she had no real understanding what it was about, or even where Yemen was to begin with. 'So Cathy knew about this, about Helms's involvement in this deal?'

'She knew.' Wright fiddled with her vape pen. 'That's why she was getting ready to leave her.'

'Cathy was going to break up with Helms?'

'I'm just surprised it hadn't happened already.' Stella Wright paused, pushing a hand through her messy hair. 'I never trusted her, to be honest. I mean, I think she saw Cathy as a useful prop.'

'That's a bit harsh, isn't it?'

Wright's look seemed to imply that Marsh had a lot to learn, particularly in the area of relationships.

'Cathy was a reminder of her younger self,' and that's me being generous. Hard-nosed. Dedicated. Unwilling to compromise. Maybe that's how Helms liked to think of herself. But politics is a funny business. It can make even the most resolute idealist find themselves compromised.'

Marsh nodded. 'Tell me about the arms deal. You say Helms was involved. How exactly?'

'I'm not sure of all the details. Cathy was the expert. I think it was investments mostly, through her husband.'

'I thought they were divorced.'

'They were, but they remained close. These investments dated back to before the divorce.'

'Helms told me Cathy was working on a novel. What you're telling me sounds a lot more serious.'

Stella Wright was laughing. 'Cathy would never write a novel. No, this was serious investigative journalism.'

'Woodward and Bernstein?' said Marsh, remembering Zoë Helms citing the two prize-winning journalists.

'If you like. She always dreamed of getting recognition for her work. This was going to be it.'

'Have you seen the book?'

'No. Cathy was secretive. We're all afraid someone is going to steal our scoop.'

'Did she leave a copy for safety anywhere?'

'Never.' Wright shook her head. 'Cathy's work on security firms and cybercrime made her pretty paranoid about hackers, people breaking into your system and stealing stuff online.'

'How did she get around that?'

'She kept making copies.'

'You mean, physical copies?' Marsh asked. 'Not in the cloud?'

'Definitely not. No, these were thumb drives, USB memory sticks. She would hide them in the most ridiculous places.'

The door behind them opened, cutting off Marsh's narrative. Three teenagers in school uniforms, jostling one another. When the woman appeared behind the counter, they sobered up and gave their orders.

'You said you found nothing at the crime scene?' Drake asked, returning to the subject at hand.

'Nothing. We looked everywhere. Forensics have been through Perkins' personal files. Milo has managed to access her online accounts and storage space, but nothing.'

'Let's go back to Helms,' said Drake. 'Little risky for a politician, isn't it, to be in a relationship like that with a journalist?'

Marsh rolled her eyes. 'Come on, Cal, nowadays nobody cares. In fact, there's a certain cachet to being in a same-sex relationship. Makes you look edgy, modern.'

'Thanks for the tip, but I was thinking more of the political side. Helms could have been compromised.'

'It sounds that way,' said Marsh, pausing. 'I have to say, from what I've seen of Helms so far she's a strange one. Politically, she's switched horses more often than the Pony Express. She worked through all the parties to finally wind up with the

Conservatives. She seems to be more about who can take her further rather than any serious political conviction.'

'Maybe that's what politics is these days.'

'You may be right.'

'What about this arms deal?' Drake looked up as his food arrived. A carrier bag dumped on the counter next to him without a word. The woman disappeared again silently. 'Must be something I said,' he muttered.

'The question is whether Helms benefited in some way from approving the deal.'

'And that would be through what – investments, shares?'

'Something like that. According to Stella Wright, her investments were linked to her ex, a solicitor by the name of Alex Hatton. Worked for a big company based in Mayfair. Clayton Navarro.'

The name must have registered on Drake's face because Marsh was staring at him.

'What did I say?'

'Nothing,' said Drake, as he spooned sauce onto his fried rice. 'Who is he?'

'Some kind of hedge-fund investor. I really need to get hold of a copy of whatever she was working on. Wright mentioned an old colleague of Cathy's, something of a mentor. I'm trying to find him, but he's a bit of a recluse so far as I can make out.'

'Keep an open mind. It's not a hundred per cent sure that's why Perkins was killed.'

'The thing is,' Marsh continued, 'if she made money out of an arms deal that she helped vote through parliament, it would not make her look good.'

'You'll need something solid if you're going to convince Pryce.'

'Good point,' she conceded.

The conversation was suspended by the arrival of Marsh's food. This time the woman took her time, setting down three foil containers along with a fresh napkin and disposable cutlery.

'Today's special,' she announced with a big smile. 'Enjoy!'

'Thank you!' said Marsh. 'This looks wonderful.'

'I must be doing something wrong.'

'It's a woman thing.'

'Hmm.' Drake chewed a mouthful of sweet and sour chicken thoughtfully before speaking.

'Let's get back to the thesis that Helms discovered Cathy Perkins was using her and, to rub salt into the wound, was planning to write about her involvement in the arms deal.'

'You're suggesting that Helms is behind the murder?'

'I know – it would be a stretch,' agreed Marsh. 'Maybe it wasn't like that. I mean, imagine you invite this woman into your home and everything is fine. Then you realise she's writing a book that will not only make you look bad, it could sabotage your political career.'

'Wouldn't she just throw her out?'

'That wouldn't spike the story.'

'It's still a stretch. I'm not saying it couldn't happen, but Helms is a politician. Generally speaking, they are not good at getting their hands dirty. How would she arrange something like that? Remember, this is someone she was involved with.'

Marsh put down her spoon. 'You're right. It's too much of a stretch.' She glanced at her watch and began repacking her food, sealing the foil containers and replacing them in the plastic bag. 'I've got to get back. Can't leave Milo alone for too long. He gets panicky. Thanks for the chat. It helps to be able to speak my thoughts aloud.'

'You'll be fine. Just don't get ahead of yourself.'

'Right.' Marsh picked up her food and stopped. 'There's no way this was a break-in gone wrong. I don't care what Pryce and his poodle say about it.'

'Go easy on Chiang, Kelly. Pryce will have you off the case if he thinks you're trying to cut out his man.'

Drake sat there in silence after the door closed behind Marsh. He put down his chopsticks with a sigh. Once again he felt a pang of guilt for not having told Marsh that Clayton Navarro was the legal firm Barnaby Nathanson had worked for. Perhaps it didn't mean that much. London was, he supposed, a fairly small place when it came to solicitors and financial shenanigans. Everyone knew everyone. To tell Kelly would have meant coming clean on how he had come by the documents taken from Nathanson's safe. He would hand the files over to Kelly when the time was right. In the meantime, he was curious about Donny's involvement. Maybe it was time to pay him a visit.

'You don't like?' The woman appeared at his elbow.

'No, it's great. I just have to go back to work.' Drake got to his feet.

'You take with you.' It wasn't a question.

'Sure. Good idea.' His smile was wasted.

15

Selina was late. By the time she arrived, Crane had been treated to the entire life story and opinions of the proprietor of the Sinan Café, or at least it felt that way. Sinan himself was harmless in his own fashion. A tiny, bald man who hailed originally from Istanbul. He was named after a very famous architect, he said proudly. The man who built all the bridges in the Ottoman empire, nodded Crane. That delighted him. He was almost jumping up and down with joy. She had even visited the Selimiye Mosque in Edirne, believed to be his masterpiece, but she kept that to herself, letting the proud man offer her the benefit of his worldly knowledge. He'd met his wife here in London forty years ago, Sinan explained, bringing her another coffee, on the house, to keep his audience captive. He spoke English well but with an acquired accent that cut off the endings of words. In Crane, he seemed to sense a kindred spirit.

'People nowadays they never speak. Like a proper conversation, yeah? Too busy with their little phones, innit? If you speak to them, right? They think there's something wrong with you.'

When Selina finally pushed open the café door, Sinan was discreet enough not to say anything, though the way his eyes slid away told Crane he disapproved of the whole orthodox number, the black ebaya and headscarf. Customers came in all shapes and sizes after all. He retreated tactically behind the counter and went about his business, while Selina sat down alongside Crane, avoiding her gaze.

'How are you doing?' Crane asked. When the other woman lifted her chin, Crane saw the swelling on the left side of her face. She had tried to cover the bruise rather ineffectively with make-up. 'What happened?'

'I made the mistake of complaining. It's my own fault. I mean, that bitch really gets on my nerves.' Selina glanced up at Crane, to check on her complicity – one sister telling on another, unsure how it was going to be taken – before going on. 'And at night.' Her mouth twisted in distaste. 'Well, she . . . makes a lot of noise. I have to hear them together.'

'I thought she was pregnant.'

'It doesn't seem to make a difference. They're like animals.' Selina put her gloved hands over her ears like a 1950s Hollywood diva. 'I can't stand it any more.'

'Listen to me.' Crane reached out to touch the other woman's arm. 'It's not your fault. Tell me how I can help.'

'I don't know.' Selina looked ready to scream. 'Could you kill them both for me?' It wasn't entirely clear that she was joking.

'How long is it since you've seen your parents?' Crane asked.

'My mum and dad? Please. They don't want to know. I think they just died of shame when they saw me dressed like this. Mum especially.' Selina hardly looked up as the tea she'd asked for arrived. Sinan had seen the bruise. His gaze lingered on Crane with the kind of reverence you might show a saint. She gave him a smile of encouragement as he slipped silently away again. 'I have a sister. Angie.'

'Why don't you contact her?'

'What's the point?' asked Selina, with a sigh of despair.

'It seems to me you need somebody,' Crane said quietly. 'Everybody needs family sometimes.'

Selina worried at a thread on her sleeve for a time before giving up. 'You said Jason's family were worried about him?'

'They are,' Crane nodded. 'They're really worried about him.'

'I think he's dead.' The bluntness of the words cast a shadow over the younger woman's face. 'I think I killed him.'

'By sending him over there, you mean? I thought you said he wanted to go?'

'I did. I know, I know. It's just . . .'

'And you don't know that for certain.'

'No. Not for certain,' Selina conceded. 'It's just what happens, isn't it?'

'Some of them come back.'

'He's dead,' insisted Selina. 'I can feel it. And it's my fault.'

'Would you like something to eat?' Crane signalled to Sinan, who was watching from behind the high counter, following the unfolding drama. He hurried out, wiping his hands on the apron he was wearing and suggested a blueberry muffin, to which Selina blankly nodded.

'I don't know how I got myself into this mess. I mean, it was all just a lark and then suddenly all this serious shit started happening. I was good in school. I could have made something of myself. I was just, you know, too busy getting into scraps.'

'I understand,' said Crane, and she did. She'd had her own rebellion, against her father, whom she hated, but couldn't get rid of. Against a society that wanted to put her in a box and pretend she didn't exist.

'Last time you mentioned a place where Jason had stayed. A flat.'

'It's a safe house. That's what you call it, right? Anyway, it's actually just an old council flat, over in Freetown.'

'It's run by your husband, Magid?'

'Well, him and the goons around him.'

'Who are they?'

'Just a bunch of idiots who think they are fighting the fight.' Selina was spooning sugar into her tea like there was a shortage coming.

'You think they're the ones who helped Jason get over to Syria?'

'I think so. They're all these frustrated young men. A bunch of losers. I should never have talked him into it.'

'Where does the money come from?'

'I don't know. People in the Gulf, rich oil sheikhs. Magid goes out and comes home with a sack full of cash. He thinks if he carries it around in that stupid bag no one will guess what's in it.'

As she watched Selina picking at the muffin, Crane realised she was surprised at how much resentment the young woman felt towards people who, up until recently, she had sympathised with. It added to the sense that she had never really been convinced about this radicalisation track. Now she was wondering how she had, in her own words, got herself into this mess.

'Did you ever speak to these men?'

'We're not allowed to.' She licked a finger to pick up a crumb from her plate. 'Magid goes ballistic if he even thinks you looked at another man. You know, there's a chapter in the Quran about women.'

'Surat al-Nisa,' supplied Crane.

'You'd think there would be some kind of equality.' Selina was shaking her head. 'But we're just property, to be ruled by men. I spend all my time with the other women. It's so boring. Most of the time they just talk about nothing at all. Their stupid children and where to buy cheap things. It drives me mad.'

'Tell me about Jason's trip. How did he get out to Syria? Was that Magid?'

'No, he keeps his hands clean, always afraid the law will come and get him. Chance would be a fine thing.' Selina smiled. 'My mum used to say that. Look at me, turning into her now.'

'If it wasn't Magid, then who?'

'One of the morons. Probably Adeeb. He's the thickest of the lot, but thinks he knows everything.' Selina fell quiet as an impish Sinan set a plate of shortbread in front of them.

'On the house. Enjoy!' he beamed.

'Adeeb is up to no good.' Selina leaned over and dropped

151

her voice. 'He's in tight with a lowlife drug dealer named Aslan. You know, like the lion?'

Crane wondered if she was being played. 'I thought you said you didn't talk to anyone?'

'I pick up a lot.' Selina gave a quick grin as she helped herself to a piece of shortbread. 'If you keep your mouth shut they forget you're there. They think women are part of the furniture.' She stopped herself. 'You're not going to take any of this to the cops, right?'

'All I'm interested in is finding Jason.'

'Like I said, he's probably dead.'

'Let's assume he's not. If he came back to this country, he would have done it under the radar, to avoid prosecution. Otherwise he'd be in the system.'

'How do you mean?'

'I mean, he might have called on the same contacts that got him out to Syria in the first place. He doesn't know anyone else, right?'

'How does that help me?' Selina bit into another piece of shortbread.

'Listen to me, Selina.' Crane leaned across. 'Sooner or later this is going to surface and when that happens you want to be sure that you and your son are protected.'

Selina listened in silence. 'I don't owe them anything, him anything. Specially now.' She looked up. 'What do you need from me?'

An hour later Crane found herself back at Balfour Mews. The big front door slid open to reveal her partner sitting at the kitchen counter eating what looked like a Chinese takeaway. Crane trundled the Triumph Bonneville Black in from the rain, setting it on its stand as the door rolled shut behind her. Drake had something going on the stereo and the long room reverberated to the sound of a drum solo competing with a trumpet.

'Let me guess,' she said, as she came up to him. 'Dizzy Gillespie. "A Night in Tunisia".'

'Art Blakey. Close.'

'I never had you pegged as a jazz head,' Crane said, as she went behind the counter.

'I'm not. I just find it helps me relax.'

'You know you have an office upstairs, right?' Crane retrieved a bottle of tequila and two shot glasses from one of the overhead cupboards.

'Yeah.' Drake pulled a face. 'Something about that room . . .'

'Ghosts?' Crane found a lime in the fridge and deftly sliced it into quarters. 'I didn't know you were superstitious.'

'I'm not. I'm just, you know . . .' Drake wondered why conversations with Ray often felt like you were playing a game of chess. 'Isn't this a bit early for you?'

'Just had a meeting with Selina.'

'That bad?'

'Magid hit her.' Crane poured the tequila into two shot glasses. 'That just makes me so angry.'

'I hear you.'

They both lifted their glasses and drank. Crane refilled the glasses.

'Is she more willing to cooperate?'

'Too early to say. She's in two minds, about everything. What's this?'

Crane leaned over and reached for the newspaper clipping Drake been reading.

'Story about a fishing boat that got into trouble up in Grimsby. Isn't that near where the Spencers live?'

'It's close,' Crane nodded, as she read the story.

'There's a suggestion of a people-smuggling ring.'

'You think it might be connected?'

'You said there were people in the woods there, by the Spencers' house?'

'Yeah, that was pretty dismal. Any news from your old pal?'

'Andy Felton? Well, he's a busy man.'

'Right,' said Crane. 'And the rest of it?' She motioned at the folder of printouts and documents.

'Just my ongoing research.'

'A-ha.' She bit into a chunk of lime and felt the sharp acidity on her tongue. The conversation with Selina had depressed her. Something about that woman's attitude, or just her situation, left Crane despairing. 'So, how are you getting on?'

Drake pushed aside the remains of his meal and leaned his elbows on the counter to give her a summary. He tried to put a positive spin on it, but Crane, as usual, saw right through him.

'Sounds like it's not really happening.'

'It's slow moving,' shrugged Drake. 'Like a glacier. Trying to get a feel for this group. I've spun a story about getting out of prison recently. I have to say, this is an odd bunch.'

'What makes you say that?'

'Well, I've been seeing the same faces around, at the kitchen and the mosque, but it's like a collection of misfits.'

'What about Magid?'

'He's the clown. Likes to play himself up as everyone's big brother, but my feeling is he's got an eye on the money side of things.'

'Selina mentioned something about that.'

'Anyway, I went back to Imam Ahmad to see what he could tell me about Bouallem. According to him he has contacts in the Gulf. Abu Dhabi, Dubai, Riyadh. He's bringing in a lot of money.'

'Private sponsors who want to spread the zealous word. That chimes with what Selina said.'

'So, that's his thing. He carries bundles of cash around with him in an old sports carrier bag. Dishes it out here and there, playing the boss man.'

'You think he's financing people to travel to Syria?'

'My guess is he throws money at anyone who asks. He's a weekend warrior. Wants to be in the thick of it but doesn't really have the courage to do anything himself. Will Selina help us?'

'She wants out,' Crane nodded. 'She's no longer his favourite. He has a new wife, younger and pregnant.'

'Did she mention any names?'

'Have you come across someone called Adeeb?'

'Oh, yeah, full of himself. A lot of swagger and brains to match.'

'Well, according to Selina he has something going with a dealer named Aslan.'

'Berat Aslan? The guy Wynstan was talking about.'

Crane sighed. 'Do you really think this will bring us any closer to finding Jason?'

'Hard to say,' said Drake. 'My feeling is that something is going on. Whether it's trafficking or another racket, I can't say, but they're paranoid and nervous for a reason. I need them to trust me.'

Crane studied him. 'If you're sure about it. I mean, we could find another way.'

'It's okay. I only need to find a way into their network, which might lead to Aslan. Maybe he's the lynchpin.'

Crane knew that Drake had worked undercover before. It required a set of skills that not many people had. To be utterly convincing you had to believe in your cover and you could never let your guard down. Your story had to be watertight, with no holes other than those you intended.

'So, what's the problem?'

Drake frowned. 'What makes you think there's a problem?'

'Psychological profiling is what I do, remember? Also, I've known you for long enough to tell when you are fully engaged with something and when' – she waved a hand towards the folder of documents lying on the counter – 'when your mind is elsewhere.'

'I had a meeting with Kelly. She's caught a murder investigation and she was asking my advice.'

'And?'

'There's a connection to Clayton Navarro, the firm where Nathanson used to work.'

'You've been down this road so many times,' said Crane, rolling her eyes.

'I know, but this is different.'

'Have you ever considered that your obsession with Zelda's death might be turning into just that, an obsession?'

'I don't need your psychotherapy advice, Ray.' Drake quickly held up a hand in apology. 'Look, let me just run this by you, okay?'

It had only been nine months since Zelda's decapitated head had turned up on a Tube train in Clapham and Crane knew how much, although he hadn't shown it, Drake was affected by this. The head had been stored in the walk-in freezer of a Halal meat processing plant. That was when Crane had had her run-in with Hamid Balushi's thug, Khan, whom Drake had believed was responsible for Zelda's death.

Crane took a slow, deep breath. 'We're going to need more lime.' She pulled open the fridge, while Drake shuffled through the documents.

'Okay, so banking is not exactly my area of expertise, and I can't claim to have got to the bottom of this, but there seems to be a common link between some of these accounts.' Drake indicated the list of Swift codes he had drawn up in his notebook. 'Nathanson modified the codes in his records so that they don't actually tell you anything unless you know what to do with them.' He pointed out where letters had been added in order to confuse anyone trying to find out where the money had been sent.

'So where do the breadcrumbs lead?'

'That's where I'm a little lost. The only holding company I can really pinpoint is Novo Elysium, and that's because I know Donny had business with them.'

Crane pointed at the spreadsheet. 'So what are all these other companies?'

'They're all interconnected. Barnaby Nathanson was good at what he did. That much I can say. They fold into one another, splinter into consortiums, move their registration to another country. The names change. He uses anagrams.' Drake threw up his hands. 'I mean, who does that?'

'I know I'm going to regret saying this, but maybe I know someone who can help.'

'Your financial creep? I thought he was in Germany.'

'He is, but they have email in Frankfurt. I can scan this stuff and get it over to him.'

Drake had to admit this made sense, even though he didn't like the idea of giving the material to an outsider, especially one that he didn't know. Crane sensed his reluctance.

'If it's a way of getting you out of this rut, I think we should try it.'

'This is the guy who jumped you, right? You really trust him?'

'Oh, yes. He's scared of me.' Crane leaned back and reached for the bottle again. 'I have enough to ruin his life several times over.'

Crane had first encountered Jindal Amrit on a date that went badly sideways. After that she had done some digging and found a disturbing pattern of abuse involving a string of women whom he had intimidated over the years. Like most bullies, Jindal folded once she threatened to expose him. It could be said that it was unethical of her not to report him, but Crane was convinced that she could make him pay in other ways. She had a handle on him and she used it whenever he proved useful. Right now he was making payments every month to a series of women's shelters and organisations. He had his uses.

'You have to promise me that if this pays off you'll put this whole case behind you.' The bottle hovered over Drake's glass until he nodded his agreement. 'Good, that's settled then. Now, tell me, how does this connect with Kelly's case?'

Drake outlined the details of the Cathy Perkins murder, as he understood it.

'And you think the murder might be tied in to Zoë Helms's financial history?'

'Nathanson was running offshore accounts for a number of dodgy clients.'

'Including your friend Donny.'

'I think Donny's connection could be the way in. At least I know something about his operations.' Drake sighed. 'I need to be sure about this. Taking those documents from Nathanson's flat was against the law and I don't want Kelly getting caught up in my misdemeanours.'

'Perhaps you should have thought of that before you stole the papers . . .' Crane held up a hand. 'Okay, that was unfair. What do you have to link Helms and Nathanson?'

'Her ex-husband used to work for Clayton Navarro.'

'This could just be another wild goose chase.'

'I have a feeling there's something there. I think this is what Cathy Perkins was working on.'

'Okay, here's a suggestion' – Crane lifted a finger – 'I know you don't like him, but how about speaking to Stewart Mason?'

'I don't want to bring the National Crime Agency in at this stage. That could make things difficult for Kelly.'

'Stewart can be discreet. You wouldn't be bringing the NCA into it. We could just have a chat, see what he thinks.'

Drake knew Crane had worked for Mason in the past, before he joined the National Crime Agency, back when he was flitting between the more shadowy sections of the intelligence services, but Drake had never really understood Crane's trust in him.

'Let's try your dodgy stockbroker first.'

'Okay. But only on the condition that if he comes up with nothing then you promise to drop it.'

'Scout's honour.'

'Don't forget, we're trying to run a business here. Speaking of which, what's your next move?'

'On Jason?' Drake scratched his chin. 'I think I'm going to grow this beard some more and then go back and see the brothers.'

'I'm not sure that's what I'd call a plan,' said Crane, reaching for the bottle. 'But it'll have to do.'

16

Kelly Marsh stayed on late at Raven Hill. Not for the first time, her conversation with Cal had left her wondering what he was not telling her. She decided to go back and refresh her memory, and so keyed up the files on Goran Malevich, Zelda and the Magnolia Quays double murder. It wasn't that she thought there was any connection between Cathy Perkins and Drake's checkered past at the Met, but there was a chance that he had picked up on something that he wasn't telling her – yet.

To begin with, Drake had gone over the line. He'd been stretching the rules when he persuaded Zelda, real name Esma Danin, to provide evidence against Goran Malevich, head of a Serbian gang. To be fair, Drake had been under-cover for six months, trying to build a case and getting nowhere. He had managed to find a way into the organisa-tion but Goran kept everything around him airtight. Drake had begun to suspect that someone on the investigation was tipping Goran off. That was what prompted him to take Zelda off the books and hide her away in a room in Brighton without telling anyone. Breaking the regulations is all well and good, until you get caught. When Zelda subsequently disappeared, Drake was forced to come clean. It wasn't enough. When her decapitated body washed ashore a week or so later, Drake found himself facing an internal inquiry into his conduct.

With Zelda's death, the investigation they were building against Malevich evaporated. Since he had already stuck his neck out, Drake was the one who took the fall. This, Marsh knew, was largely down to the man who had been leading the undercover operation, then DI Vernon Pryce. There was no love lost between the two, even back then. Pryce implied that Drake was dirty. He accused him of having broken with procedure because he was on the payroll of Donny Apostolis, one of Malevich's rivals and the man who stood to gain the most by his death. Pryce couldn't prove it, but he didn't have to; the damage was done and Drake was never able to completely shake off the charge. All the hard work and expense that had gone into Operation Hemlock had been washed down the drain. Things were further complicated when Malevich was gunned down shortly afterwards in broad daylight, in a car park in Brighton. Pryce pushed for Drake to be drummed out of the Met. Superintendent Wheeler weighed in on Drake's side. Instead of being forced to resign, Drake was demoted to DS and transferred out of town to serve out six months in Matlock.

Typical, thought Marsh. Banish the man to the far north until the whole thing blows over. Some old-fashioned idea of penance. All of this was years ago. Quite why it was still rumbling on was a mystery to Marsh. She read on in silence, going back over events that had happened before her time. She was familiar with the case, of course, but now she found herself picking up on details she had missed before.

Marsh knew from her conversations with Drake that there had always been conflict between him and Pryce. In his view, Pryce had been promoted too soon to a position of authority that he wasn't ready for. His conclusion was that Pryce was the dirty one. Marsh took this with a pinch of salt. It wouldn't be surprising for him to have a negative view of the man. Drake's version of the story was that Pryce was incompetent and he had made a number of bad decisions that not only jeopardised the operation but also put people's lives in danger, including Cal's.

With both Pryce and Drake pointing fingers at one another, it was a stalemate. It was easy to see why Drake was obsessed with all of this. The case had effectively stopped his career in its tracks. Sure, he came back to work at Raven Hill but he was toxic, and he knew it was only a matter of time before the axe fell. The writing was on the wall and nothing was going to bring him back from the dead. The thing about obsessions is that they don't just go away because you want them to. They stick around until they are good and ready to leave. And this one appeared to be showing no signs of abating.

The surfacing of Zelda's severed head nine months ago had brought everything hurtling back into focus. It was clear that Goran Malevich's death had been not so much the end of something as the beginning of a new phase in the evolution of the underworld. Donny Apostolis was not the only player in organised crime, he was just the most visible; there were others whose shadows had started moving across the walls.

Just going back through all this material was exhausting. It felt like an interminable task. At some point, feeling the stiffness in her shoulders from sitting still for too long, Marsh got up to fetch herself another cup of coffee from the kitchenette on the second floor of Raven Hill. On her way back to her desk she met Milo coming in from the stairwell.

'I thought you'd gone home hours ago,' she said.

'I could say the same to you,' Milo said. 'I just finished my yoga class. I forgot something, had to come back.' He picked up a book lying on his desk and turned to head for the door. 'Watch yourself, the Prince of Darkness is on the prowl.'

Their nickname for Pryce, or one of them. Milo, who knew these things, said that the DCI's name always reminded him of Vincent Price, whom he was shocked to learn Marsh had not heard of. 'Like in all those old Hammer House of Horror flicks? They show them late at night when they think everyone's drunk enough to enjoy them.'

Marsh had an idea she knew the films he was talking about, but she didn't remember the actor in question. Nevertheless, the label stuck and from then on the DCI's name never came up without Milo making some oblique reference to movie history.

'By the way . . .' Milo halted. 'How did it go with the chief?'

'You know what he's like, always keeps his cards close to his chest.'

The door swung open, narrowly missing Milo's face, and DCI Pryce appeared. He was in full uniform and carrying a briefcase in one hand.

'DS Marsh?'

'Sir?'

'Putting in the hours, I see. Have you spoken to DS Chiang?'

'Not recently, sir.'

'I can't emphasise how important it is for you to remain in close contact over this case. I know he's been trying to reach you.'

This last struck Marsh as odd. Chiang had her details. He could have called or emailed her anytime. Pryce made it sound like she was avoiding Chiang.

'Give him a call, will you?'

'Now, sir? I was about to log off for the night.'

Pryce squinted at her. 'DS Marsh, Superintendent Wheeler led me to believe you were keen and deserved this opportunity.'

'I do, sir. It's just that . . .' Marsh bit her tongue. She knew she had already said too much.

'Is there a problem between you and DS Chiang, something I ought to know?'

'No sir, not at all. We just don't seem to be quite on the same page.'

Pryce glanced at Milo, who remained where he was. 'Enlighten me.'

Marsh swallowed. 'Well, firstly, I don't think we should dismiss the idea that Cathy Perkins was the intended victim.'

'Helms is a leading politician, Marsh. Perkins was a second-rate hack. Why would anyone want to kill her?'

'It might have something to do with what she was working on.'

'Which was what?'

'That's the point. I haven't been able to get the exact details, but I believe she was writing a book, some kind of in-depth investigation.'

Pryce heaved a sigh, shifting his case from one hand to the other. 'So, we're talking what here, some kind of deep-state conspiracy?'

'I'm not sure I would go that far. I just think we should look into it.'

'Okay, listen to me very carefully, Marsh. DS Chiang has been generous with you on this one. He's an experienced officer. I've worked with him myself. I know I can trust his instincts. Frankly, he should have been handed this case from the outset, but that's not how things work nowadays, so this is what's called an opportunity, for you. And they don't come along every day.'

'I appreciate that, sir.'

'Good, because we're talking about an attempt to kill one of our elected politicians. I don't need to tell you how much media scrutiny comes with this case. You need to get on top of things as fast as possible. Call Mark Chiang and get your act together.'

There didn't seem to be much more to say to that. Marsh went back to her desk.

'What was that all about?' Milo whispered, coming over to join her.

'Don't get me started.' She checked her phone to see if she'd missed something. Nothing. She called DS Chiang.

'Marsh here, I understand you've been trying to reach me?'

'That's right. There's been a breakthrough.'

'What kind of a breakthrough?' Marsh leaned back in her chair.

'Forensics found something in the downstairs bathroom at Helms's house. It seems the killer decided to take a leak. He left the seat up. He was wearing gloves, of course, but apparently his aim was off. They managed to retrieve a DNA sample and we've got a match.'

'How sure are we that it's the killer's?'

'According to Helms no men have been in the house since the cleaner's visit last Wednesday.'

'Okay, sounds good,' said Marsh. 'Who's the match?'

'A known offender, Rachid Mourad.' Marsh could hear him reading from a file. 'Small-time burglar with a pervy sideline in preying on women. He picks one and gets obsessive. Likes to break in and jerk off in their sheets, steal their underwear.'

'Sounds like an unlikely profile for a mad axe killer.'

'Maybe, but it still fits with the idea of a break-in gone wrong. Makes sense that he would target a place he knows. Maybe he had a little burglary planned and things went sideways.'

'Convenient,' muttered Marsh to herself, but not softly enough.

'Did you hear what I said? We have evidence that ties him to the scene.'

'That doesn't really square with this being political.'

'Agreed.' Chiang took a moment. 'Look, this guy is a wacko, whichever way you slice it. You know what these types are like, always pushing the boundary. This time he went too far. We need to bring him in for questioning.'

There was no way to argue with that. Marsh wasn't happy, and she didn't like the way Chiang seemed to be twisting things this way and that. Either Helms was the target or this was a burglary. You couldn't have it both ways. All in all this guy Mourad didn't seem to fit the picture. Or rather, it was too neat. Mourad's fondness for women's underwear only muddied the waters further.

'You've spoken to Helms about this?' Marsh asked. She was scratching lines with her pencil on the page of her notepad. It was like something itching in her mind that she couldn't get out.

'I did,' confirmed Chiang. 'No way that Mourad was in the house for a legitimate purpose.'

'No connection to the staff? Cleaner, housekeeper, or whatever?'

She heard him chuckle. A rather haughty sound. 'Not sure what kind of a life she lives, Marsh, it's pretty low key. She has a cleaner twice a week and a caterer who comes in to cook when she has guests. Both of them are women. We've already spoken to them and none of them know Mourad.'

'How about maintenance, plumbers and so on?'

There was another chuckle. 'Give it up, will you, Marsh? Mourad was in there without the knowledge of the owner or any of the staff.'

'Okay, fine.' Marsh tossed the pencil down on the pad.

'Sounds like you've got the whole thing tied up. What do you need from me?'

'Well, seeing as you are lead on this investigation, I thought you might like to tag along.'

Marsh sat up. 'You've got him?'

'He's working part time in an amusement arcade over in Canada Water.'

'With his record?'

'Wonders will never cease,' said Chiang. 'There's a fast turnover in these places. They probably haven't got round to checking his references yet.'

'You sure you've got enough to stick?'

'The DNA is enough to hold him. Let's see what happens when we lean on him.' Chiang paused. 'So, we're getting ready to leave. You want to meet us there?'

'Wait for me, right?'

'Don't worry about it,' Chiang laughed. 'Officially, you're still the SIO on this.'

Marsh didn't like the fact that Chiang had stolen the lead on her. That bothered her almost as much as the fact that she had heard nothing about samples taken from the toilet at Helms's house. She didn't punch the phone to call forensics until she was in the car with the siren on.

'Why wasn't I informed about these DNA samples taken from the crime scene?'

The person she got was new and had no idea about anything. Everyone else had gone home.

'I'll have to look into it,' he said, as if he had a hundred and one other things to do. 'Can you call back?'

'No, I can't. I'll wait.'

As she cut over Westminster Bridge and turned onto the Embankment, Marsh could hear him shifting things around on his desk. She knew there was only a skeleton crew on overnight. If anything urgent came in, a team was on standby, but for routine administrative matters nobody was on hand. He finally came back on the line.

'As far as I can tell, all analysis was sent over to the PoDP. They use a private lab.'

'Are you serious? How can they do that?'

'Er . . . I don't actually know.'

Realising she wasn't going to get any more out of him, Marsh cut short the call. Traffic was heavy and despite the lights and siren she wasn't sure she was going to get over to Rotherhithe in time. Her anger caused her to drive a little more aggressively than usual but she managed to arrive in one piece.

The Funderdome arcade was built inside a huge warehouse close to the old docks. It looked like someone had given the place a quick facelift and shoved a lot of flashing lights and beeping machines in there. Despite it being a weekday night the car park was full; people were thronging through the front entrance. Marsh found Chiang and his team in the north-west corner of the car park as agreed. It was clear they had come prepared. They had a Transit van with a dozen officers clad in black body armour and a blueprint of the building spread out between them.

'Overdoing it a little, aren't we?' she said, peering round the faces of the group gathered at the rear of the van.

'I'm not taking any chances,' Chiang said, tightening the Velcro tabs on his anti-stab vest. Then he handed out pictures of the suspect, Rashid Mourad. Marsh took one. Mourad had long, dishevelled hair and the unfocussed stare of a person suffering from some kind of mental distress. The image added to Marsh's doubts about whether this could be the perp they were after. Chiang was unconcerned, busy checking the Glock he had tucked into his belt. 'He murdered one person and he's quite capable of trying again.'

Marsh led him aside. 'Maybe it makes sense to wait for him to come out. It's probably crowded in there.'

'No way. I'm not holding off any longer.'

'I thought I was in charge,' Marsh pointed out.

'Of the investigation, sure.' Chiang nodded. 'But *this* is my area. We're a protection unit and more prepared for dealing with dangerous, possibly armed suspects.'

'There's no indication he's armed.'

'We're not taking that chance. If he killed that woman he's capable of extreme violence.' Chiang straightened up and signalled to his second in command. 'We're ready to move in. Stay behind me,' he said to Marsh.

She didn't bother replying. She was too angry.

'Hold on,' she said. 'Before we go charging in there, maybe we should try and do this quietly.'

Mark Chiang looked at her, aware that the rest of the team was watching them. Technically, she was still the SIO on this. She could pull rank on him.

'Okay,' he conceded with a loud sniff. 'What did you have in mind?'

'How many exits are there apart from the front entrance?'

'Five,' came the answer from a man to her left.

'We need to cover those. If he makes a break for it, we'll catch him on the way out.'

Chiang wasn't happy, but he could see the logic of not charging into a crowded place like this. He broke the team up, assigning three men to each side of the building. It was still going to be thin, but it was better than nothing. That left them with three men at the main entrance, which, it seemed to Marsh, was the least likely path for any fleeing suspect to take, but she wasn't going to argue.

'We go in first. Your team holds back. There are a lot of people in there and we don't want to start a panic.'

'All right,' said Chiang tersely. 'We'll do it your way.' Meaning that if it all went sideways the blame would fall squarely on her shoulders. Marsh felt she could live with that.

Inside, the huge industrial space was cramped with aisles full of one-armed bandits and fruit machines. The noise was deafening. There were rows of beeping electronic roulette wheels and video games with speeding cars and fighter jet consoles. It was literally a machine room for generating cash. All of it screeching and wailing, sirens and flashing lights. It was disorienting. Marsh was glad at least that she had got DS Chiang to go along with her plan, but she was really not sure how this was going to work out.

They made their way across the huge space, dodging crowds of exuberant young people. Clearly a lot of drinking was going on. The smell of stale beer hung in the air. Plastic cups splintered underfoot. There were families too, with small children who should have had school the next day. Did nobody care about such things any more, Marsh wondered? There was an air of desperation here, as if the end of the world had been announced. Everyone just trying to drown out the sound of real life for a little while longer.

'This way,' Chiang indicated off to the north-east corner, where Marsh caught sight of a spark in the air. Mourad was working on the bumper cars. And there he was, exactly where he was supposed to be. A lean, even scrawny figure, wearing baggy, shapeless jeans and a long-sleeved sweatshirt that hung loosely over rounded shoulders. As luck would have it, just as they were approaching the cars came to a stop. Mourad was leaning over a couple of young girls. Marsh estimated their age at around twelve and nine. He appeared to be making sure the safety belt was properly fastened, but he was taking his time. His hands were out of sight inside the bucket of the bumper car. The girls were squirming around as he moved, trying to avoid him touching them. They were laughing as if this was a game, but Marsh could see from the intense look on Mourad's face that this was more than that to him.

'For god's sake!' she muttered.

'Seems to be enjoying his work,' observed Chiang.

'A little too much for his own good.' Marsh wondered where the girls' parents were. It took a moment to locate them on the far side. They were engaged in conversation and absorbed with their phones.

As he straightened up, Mourad tossed lank, greasy strands of hair out of his face and his eyes met Marsh's. She could see the guilt written there as plainly as could be. And he knew it. In that moment he made them as police officers. Hopping casually off the side, Mourad pushed his way through the jumble of dodgem cars facing all different ways. Kids and adults alike were already twisting the steering wheels from side to side in anticipation of the moment when the power came on.

Marsh hopped up over the perimeter step and onto the rink, with Chiang right behind her, as Mourad slipped into the control booth on the other side. He was staring down at something, avoiding looking at her, but she knew he had seen her and he could tell that they were coming for him. When Marsh and Chiang were halfway across the floor area, the bell sounded and everything about them came to life.

The cars lurched into motion, clunking forward as the power came on. Over the sound of the screeching music playing overhead and the whine of the cars, Marsh heard Chiang swear loudly as someone rammed into him. She looked round to see him clutching his knee and pointing.

'He's getting away!'

Marsh turned back to see Mourad come out of the control booth and step onto a ladder that led upwards. It seemed like a crazy idea. The top of the bumper car ride was covered by metal netting through which electric power flowed. Sparks leaped as the vertical arms running up from each of the cars scraped along, picking up the current.

'He can't get over there,' Marsh said aloud, but almost to herself. She jumped sideways as a car whirred by, then she saw that Mourad was going for the narrow maintenance gangway that ran over the top of the net. He was almost directly over-head now at the centre of the ride. He turned and began running. At the point where the ride almost touched the wall of the building a ladder ran upwards from the floor to a metal door under the roof. It must have provided access to some kind of maintenance gallery. Lifts, electrics, heating. Who knows. She had no idea where it led. All she knew was that once Mourad went through that door there was a good chance they wouldn't see him again.

All the while this was going through her head, she was trying to make her way over to that side of the rink, doing her best to avoid being hit by the lumbering cars that lurched about with no logic or sense to them. They spun around in circles and veered this way and that. Out of the corner of her eye she saw Chiang leap onto the side of one car and grab the wheel from the children in it, attempting to get across that way.

Marsh looked up to watch helplessly as Mourad pounded along overhead, the wooden boards bouncing loosely under-neath him as he ran. Marsh was standing on the lip of the rink looking up. She saw his feet in a pair of grubby trainers with their laces undone. He was having trouble coordinating his movements but still, he would have been able to jump the gap to reach the maintenance ladder if he hadn't hesitated at the last moment. As if his nerve failed him, he pulled back and overcompensated. Then it was over. One foot slipped and he spun down, sprawling out across the flat net. There was a terrible sound as the current went through him. She heard him scream as his body was enveloped in a whiteness so bright it was almost blue. The air was filled with the smell of it, the cries of horror all around her as the acrid burn of electricity and burned flesh turned the air sour.

17

Drake stopped in at the Ithaka for breakfast. He had a feeling it was going to be a long day and although he would be loathe to admit it, he took some comfort from the place. It was the closest thing to what might be called home these days. The concept of family was not one that he had ever really known. As a child he had grown up with a dysfunctional mother whose regular descents into drug- and later drink-fuelled oblivion left him in the hands of social services. His life then followed an irregular course through a string of care homes and foster parents. In time he graduated to correctional centres. Time would also no doubt have eventually led him to prison and a life of crime, but fate intervened. Or perhaps it was more than that. Either way, one rainy afternoon in the middle of October he found himself standing outside a mosque in East London and that set him off on a course. He found faith and for a while it gave him what he needed. A sense of purpose, but also of belonging. Drake didn't really believe in fate, or anything in fact, but he was convinced that things sometimes happened for a reason and that often we didn't stop for long enough to register that, or to understand the implications. Faith had now receded into the distance. Deep down he would, if pressed, confess to being a spiritual person by nature. The problem he'd always had was finding something to believe in that actually made sense in this world. In this respect, he and Crane were quite different. She took a much more intellectual view of things. Although fond of the time she spent growing up in Tehran with her mother's family, she saw Islam, any religion really, as a form of patriarchal order to which she refused to submit.

Kostas and Eleni were still away, leaving Amaia, who was, perhaps, the central reason Drake found himself making his way over to his customary table at the back of the room. He watched her deal with the clientele in the brisk, no-nonsense manner that he had grown to like. She didn't go in for fiddly small talk; it made a change from the ever talkative Eleni and Kostas.

'What can I get you?' she asked, holding up her order pad and pen as she waited.

'Eggs?'

'Eggs? How would you like them?'

'I don't know. What do you suggest?'

'How about scrambled?'

'Sounds good.'

'Scrambled.' She jotted it down. 'And maybe a cheese pastry?'

'Perfect.' She was about to turn away when he spoke again.

'Sorry, your name?'

'My name?' She looked puzzled. 'What about it?'

'I just wondered, is it Greek?'

'No. Spanish.'

'Right. I thought you came from Athens.'

'On my mother's side, yes. But my father is from Spain.'

The way she told it made it all sound obvious and Drake decided he'd asked enough foolish questions for one day. Instead he turned his attention to the newspaper that had been lying on the table. The front page was taken up with a story about a dramatic chase at a fun fair that had resulted in the death of a suspect. Rashid Mourad was believed to have made a botched attempt on the life of the politician Zoë Helms. In the blurry photograph of the scene outside the Funderdome warehouse in Rotherhithe he thought he could make out the familiar figure of Kelly Marsh. An unexpected turn of events. It sounded as though that was the end of her investigation. He considered calling her, but then his food arrived and for next few minutes he sat and ate. An email from Crane told him that her broker in Frankfurt was studying Nathanson's financial records. Amaia returned to refresh his coffee and ask how the food was.

'Excellent, just what I needed.'

'That's good,' she smiled. She looked as though she were about to say something else, but then changed her mind. Drake, feeling guilty about being too intrusive, left a large tip on the table.

The rest of the morning found Drake going through what had become his daily routine, using public transport to plot a zigzag course that sent him bouncing in every possible direction across London before depositing him at Stockwell Underground station. Having spent long months undercover, Drake understood the importance of being patient and thorough. He changed carriages, waited on platforms, went up and down escalators, got on and off buses, always double-checking the people around him.

The centre was quiet when he arrived. Only one of the brothers, a man who called himself Slimany, sat cross-legged in the prayer room. He wore glasses and had a mousy appearance, accentuated by a wispy beard. There was something studious about him. Drake slipped off his shoes and stepped into the prayer room. With a brief nod to the other man, he went over to the far side and sat down on the carpet by the low bookshelf that ran underneath the window. From his pocket he produced the string of prayer beads that he had inherited, in a manner of speaking, from his father. He chose a book of the Hadith and opened it on his lap. He sat there, reading while counting the beads through his fingers, and waited.

'I see you are a fan of al-Bukhari.'

'I find him to be the most reliable source,' said Drake, looking up.

Slimany nodded, sitting down without being invited. He stared at Drake for a long moment before leaning forwards. Even though they were alone in the room he lowered his voice.

'I hear things about you.'

'What kind of things?'

'Driss says that you have fought. That you are a jihadi. A real one, not like all of these would-be warriors.'

Drake saw the half smile on the other man's face. 'I have fought, but not in the way you think.'

'Tell me what it is like.' Slimany's eyes were gleaming.

Drake closed the book in his lap. 'It's not something that you want to remember.'

'I wish I could fight.' He clenched the beads in his fist.

'No, you don't. You just think you would.'

'You're calling me a coward?'

'Bravery has nothing to do with it,' Drake said quietly. 'When you're out there, it's the last place on earth you want to be.'

'Then why did you do it?'

'I had no choice.'

'That's how I feel also. I want to fight, to become a martyr.'

'There's no war worth dying for.'

'How can you say that?' He seemed offended. 'Jihad is worth dying for.'

'It wasn't like that for me,' said Drake.

'I don't understand.'

'I was in the British Army.'

There was a moment's silence. Slimany's expression hardened. 'Then you are a kaffir, an unbeliever.' The awe turned first to anger and then confusion. 'Why are you here?'

'Maybe because of what I did.' Drake shrugged.

'I understand. You want to make things right.'

'Something like that.'

'You should,' said Slimany. 'Make it right.' He seemed to be in two minds. Drake decided to push him a little.

'If you're so keen on fighting, why are you still here?'

'It's not that easy.' Slimany was drawing patterns on the

carpet between them. 'A few years ago, maybe, but now . . .' He looked up. 'I have a wife and child now. Another one coming in the autumn. Why did you come to this place?'

'I heard that the people here have contacts.' Drake paused to let his words sink in. 'They can help you get out there.'

'Who told you that?' Slimany pushed his glasses back up his nose.

'A guy I knew, he made it. He went to Syria.'

'When was this?'

'A few years ago,' said Drake. 'Probably before your time.'

'What was his name?'

'What was whose name?'

Slimany's face froze as a new voice boomed over them. A large, clumsy figure sat down heavily, thumping Slimany on the shoulder as he did so. He wore a loose tracksuit, scruffy beard and a woollen skullcap. Drake had seen him a couple of times, but, unlike Slimany, Adeeb was not exactly welcoming. He seemed to view Drake with distrust.

'What were you two lovebirds whispering about?' The question was aimed at Slimany, but Adeeb was looking at Drake.

'We . . . we were talking about ji-had,' Slimany stuttered.

'Is that right? Your mysterious past.'

'Nothing mysterious about it,' said Drake.

'Yeah? Funny that, because you never actually tell us what you did.'

'What would you like to know?'

'Everything? What you're doing here, for example?'

'Why?'

'Why what?'

'What business is it of yours?' Drake smiled at him. 'I don't need your permission to be here.'

'You what?' Adeeb's heavy accent slipped. He looked as if nobody ever talked to him like that.

'Why don't you leave him alone,' Slimany said, his voice thin and reedy. Adeeb didn't even look at him, his eyes staying fixed on Drake.

'Leave him alone? This is not a game, Slimany. Jihad is not a game.'

'How do you know what jihad is?' Slimany asked, emboldened perhaps by Drake's presence. 'You never fought in a war. He has.'

'What are you talking about?' Adeeb sneered. 'I know it takes courage. Who says he fought?'

Drake put the book away and got to his feet.

'Hey wait! Hey, I'm talking to you!'

Drake ignored him. He reached the doorway and was bending down for his shoes when Adeeb grabbed his arm.

'How do we know you're not an informer?'

'Take your hand off me.'

'I asked you a question.' Instead of removing his hand, Adeeb pulled Drake around and pushed him against the wall.

'Are you sure you want to do this?' Drake asked.

'Leave him alone,' Slimany said from behind Adeeb.

'You should listen to him,' Drake said quietly.

'I'll decide that,' said Adeeb.

'What's going on here?' asked Magid Bouallem. 'There is no fighting here, brothers. This is a place of worship.'

Adeeb pushed past him and disappeared down the

corridor. Bouallem looked at Drake, then he nodded towards his office.

'We need to talk.'

The room resembled less an office space than a jumbled storeroom that time had forgotten. An old metal filing cabinet had piles of old newspapers and letters falling off it. Cardboard boxes containing flyers and papers were heaped in unstable stacks everywhere you looked. A bookcase in one corner had fallen off the wall and was now slumped sideways. Bouallem squeezed between wall and desk to wedge himself behind the computer, an old and grubby vintage of twenty years or more.

'So, Calil, tell me what is this about?'

'I don't know,' shrugged Drake. 'Adeeb doesn't seem to like me.'

'He's not the only one. Others do not trust you. Tell me why that is.' Bouallem sat back and rested his elbows on the arms of his chair, linking his hands together across his belly. He was happiest playing the all-wise father figure, even though he wasn't that much older than most of the people who staffed the Cave. His bulk added to his presence, along with the thick beard and the black turban.

'It's not easy for me,' said Drake. 'I have trouble trusting people I don't know.'

'Let me tell you something, Calil.' Bouallem allowed himself a little smile. 'I consider myself a good judge of character and I feel that you have a lot to offer.'

'Maybe, but I feel I'm not getting anywhere here. I'd prefer to write it off as a bad job and move on.'

184

'That would be a shame.' Bouallem leaned forwards to rest his hands on the table. 'What would you like to happen?'

'I don't know. I feel you're keeping me on the outside.'

'You're impatient.' Bouallem smiled. 'Adeeb thinks the police are everywhere.'

'Why's he worried about that?'

'Who knows? People worry. When you first came here, you told me what you were looking for. Do you remember?'

Drake nodded, staring at the floor.

'Justice. You said you wanted justice. All your life you have been dealing with hatred.'

'It's true,' Drake consented. 'All my life I've been the object of scorn. I'm tired of that. I want respect.'

'You want revenge.' Bouallem stroked his beard.

'Maybe. Is that so bad?'

'No, of course not. We have been dealing with Christian oppression for centuries. Nothing has changed since the crusades, a thousand years ago. They say it is politics. They say it is human rights. Where are human rights in this country?'

Drake made no attempt to reply, sensing that it was better to let the other man talk.

'You must give yourself time,' Bouallem said. 'Allow things to take their natural course. Then, inshallah, you will arrive at the place where you want to be.'

'Inshallah,' said Drake.

'I see so many wounded souls,' Bouallem said with a heavy sigh. 'I imagine you were like them once. Kids who find themselves caught in the middle. They try their best to fit in, to be accepted in this country.' He was shaking his head. 'But they never will. So when they come to me, it is only natural. They find their spiritual home here.' He gestured magnanimously around. 'It is a matter of culture. The English will never accept people like us.'

'Actually, I heard about this place from a convert.'

'Really?' Bouallem tilted his head to one side. 'What was the name of this man?'

'Abu Hamra. Before that his name was Jason.'

'Edriss told me you mentioned that name. Why Abu Hamra?'

'On account of his red hair,' Drake explained.

'And you and this man . . .?'

'We planned to travel to Syria together. Only I got picked up.' Drake wore a disgusted look on his face. 'It was the usual shit. Trumped-up charges. Typical.'

'You went to prison.'

'I spent three months inside. By then I'd lost track of him. I heard that he made it out there.'

'That's why you came here, because you want to go and fight?'

Drake leaned forward intently. 'It's all I dream of.' He placed a hand flat on the table. 'Look, I know that you don't really know me. I'm new here, but I came here because I believe you're the only person who can help me.'

Bouallem sat back in his chair and rubbed his knuckles, watching Drake.

'You are not like the others.'

'I never said I was.'

'Most of them, they come here, they talk, but they do nothing. You are different.'

'That's what I've been trying to tell you.'

Bouallem nodded slowly. 'What you are asking is not easy.'

'But you have the contacts, right?'

'Maybe.' Bouallem wagged a finger at Drake. 'You could get me into a lot of trouble.'

Drake frowned. 'Why would I do that?'

'Because nowadays you can trust nobody. You understand? You have no friends. You should remember that.' Bouallem stared fiercely at Drake as he spoke. 'You cannot trust anyone.'

'I know I can trust Jason, Abu Hamra.'

'Your red-haired friend. I thought you said he was out there.'

'I heard he was back. In this country.'

'That's why you came to me?' Bouallem frowned. 'Because you are trying to find your friend?'

'He's my ticket to Syria. I want to go and fight.'

'Why are you in such a rush? You think there's nothing to fight for in this country?'

Drake sensed that Bouallem was growing suspicious again. 'Here? I'm not talking about blowing myself up. I want to rebuild the caliphate. They need fighters now.'

'That dream is over. I'm afraid you missed your chance while you were in prison.' Bouallem stood up. The conversation was over. Bouallem opened the door for him. Drake held back.

'I can pay, if that's an issue.'

'It's not about money.' Bouallem shook his head. 'A word of advice. Be careful who you speak to of these things.'

18

Crane found Andy Felton waiting for her at the High Tide Café. He was dressed discreetly in a standard issue navy blue police sweater. He had a mug of tea in front of him and was chatting to the waitress. Clearly he was familiar to both staff and several of the regulars in the café. Crane was aware of the eyes of everyone in the place following her as she came through the door. A small community recognises a stranger in their midst the moment they appear. For his part, Andy Felton was instantly smitten and turned on all the charm.

'Cal didn't tell me what to expect,' he said with a broad smile.

'Sounds like you know him well.'

'Cal? Sure.' Andy Felton waved over the waitress and waited while Crane ordered coffee and a grilled cheese sandwich. 'He's a bit of a one-off, a maverick, if you like. We worked together over in Matlock. He was something of an anomaly over there. Nobody really knew what to make of him.'

'I'd say that's a fairly common reaction.'

'Don't get me wrong, he proved himself to be more than competent.' Felton shifted in his seat, turning his mug around in his hands. 'We had a fairly nasty case while he was there. A serial killer the likes of which none of us had seen before. I was glad of his help, frankly. I mean, we didn't always see eye to eye, I have to admit. I outranked him, but he was clearly the more experienced.'

'He was banished,' Crane nodded. 'Matlock was some part of his demotion.'

'Yes, it took us a while to get that out of him. Still, he never showed any resentment or bad feeling towards us. He just put his back into it.' Felton was shaking his head. 'I was sad to hear that he'd left the force.'

'I don't think it was an easy decision.'

'Politics,' sighed Felton. 'It's put paid to the careers of more than one good man, and woman,' he added, remembering who he was talking to.

While Crane ate her lunch, Felton gave her a breakdown of the situation.

'We've had our eyes on a number of skippers over the last eighteen months or so. We're pretty sure they've been up to no good. Can't blame 'em really. I mean, the fishing community has been hard hit. Of course, there's nothing new about smuggling. It goes together with the sea, and it's been going on for as long as you care to look. But the economic downturn, the lack of fish in the sea basically, has made it all the more difficult to make an honest living out of it.'

Crane nodded. 'So they turn to other means.'

'I don't want to tar them all with the same brush. There are a few bad 'uns, but most of them just carry on as best they can, until they can't.'

The conversation continued outside as they walked in sunshine back to Felton's dark green Range Rover. It smelled of wet dog and Crane spotted a saddle in the back.

'Three daughters and they're all mad about ponies. What can you do?'

'I used to ride when I was little,' Crane said, the saddle bringing childhood memories back.

'I'll bet you were good at it too,' Felton smiled. Crane couldn't decide if he was being creepy or sweet, and decided to give him the benefit of the doubt. She tended to be too quick off the mark.

'I did okay. Even won a few trophies.'

'Well, it's all my girls live for.'

Which sounded fair enough. They reached the harbour and parked facing the water. The sun was out and the sea was a shining silver and bronze shield. Andy Felton gave a satisfied sigh.

'You can say what you like about this town, but this view more than makes up for it.'

'I'm sure,' Crane said, straightening up in her seat. 'Tell me about the *Aurora Grey*.'

'She's a good-sized fishing trawler. Getting on. The skipper is a man named Rab Otley. He's in his forties, family man. The sea is all he knows. Been in the game since he was a kid. His father before him. Rab did well. Inherited the boat from the previous skipper when he retired.' Felton shifted in his seat. 'But it's not been easy these last few years. Less fish in the sea, and what is there tends to be scooped by the bigger trawlers. They come from all over, you know. Russia, China, you name it.'

'Sounds like you feel sympathy for them.'

'The locals?' Felton dragged his gaze away from the sea to look at her. 'I do. But only up to a certain point.' He let a long breath out of his lungs slowly. 'Cocaine. It's huge. I mean, they are shipping it into ports like Rotterdam by the tonne. So much of it that the authorities can't deal with it. They catch one container and another two drive by them while they're checking it.'

Crane was aware that the volume of cocaine in circulation had increased in the last few years. The price had dropped as the number of users had grown exponentially. It was now the drug of choice for people who were looking for something different while still carrying the cachet of being a classy substance. A party drug that kept you going, countered the effects of drink and increased your sex drive. What more could you ask for?

'So that's what he was doing, this Rab Otley?'

'Say what you like about booze, and I know it kills more people than any drug, but at least it comes in a bottle with a label that certifies what it contains.' Felton shook his head. 'These kids, smart, with jobs and good prospects, have no idea what they're snorting.'

'You get casualties?'

'It comes and goes. A bad batch gets through and they fall like flies.' A shudder went through Felton. 'Anyway, the point is that dealing with drugs brings you in contact with some dark people, and I'm not talking about the colour of their skin.'

Crane let the comment pass. 'Somebody was lost at sea.'

'Young lad named Lemmy. He'd had his ups and downs, but Rab gave him a second chance working on the boat.'

'How did he go overboard?'

'Well, that's the thing. Otley doesn't want to go into it. He's told the story a couple of times, to the coastguard and to us, but there are inconsistencies.'

'Such as?'

'They were out in rough weather. In a sector that is not a fishing area. It's a wind park.'

'He was off course?'

'My money is on a meeting. You get one number wrong in a six figure grid reference and you'll be miles off course.'

'You think he was meeting a drug shipment?'

'Your guess is as good as mine.' Felton tapped the steering wheel in front of him. 'Human smuggling is not common in these parts. There are narrower sections of the channel where it's easier.'

'You think that's what this was about?'

'The remains of an inflatable washed up about five miles south of here.'

'What happened to the occupants?'

Felton lifted his hands from the wheel. 'So far, no trace of them.'

'What did Otley say?'

'Not much that makes a lot of sense. He claims it was coincidence they were in that sector. In his first statement he said that the boy, Lemmy, died trying to help a woman and a child they spotted clinging to one of the new wind turbine anchors out there.'

'A woman and a child?'

Felton nodded. 'Cal said you were looking for a man.'

'That's right. Jason Spencer. His parents hired us. They believe Jason is back in the country.'

'What's the connection between Spencer and this woman?'

'Jason's parents received a message from their son, a hand-written note. A woman matching her description was seen nearby.'

'And what makes you certain this is that same woman?'

'I'm not certain, but this incident happened just before the message was delivered, as far as I can make out. I'm also assuming that Jason would have chosen to come into the country by an unconventional route, to avoid being picked up.'

'Why send the woman? Why not go home himself?'

'Perhaps he's being overly cautious.' Crane shrugged. 'The truth is, we don't know what he's thinking.'

'The woman was brought ashore alone, with a child. No sign of Jason.'

'You said there were no others picked up from the wreck of the dinghy. That doesn't mean nobody else made it ashore.'

'A lot of maybes in all of that,' said Felton, 'but I can understand your thinking.'

'Either way, it's a line of investigation that has to be eliminated. Is there a chance I could speak to Otley?'

'You could try. He's pretty upset about losing the kid.'

'Sounds like you have your work cut out.'

'It's all a little insane,' said Felton. 'I mean, we do what we can, but the coastguard is underfunded. They hardly have workable vessels and can't afford to launch unless there's an emergency. Plus, the whole wind farm business is creating its own problems.' Felton made a gesture of helplessness. 'We just don't have the resources, the manpower to follow up on all of these cases. That's part of the reason I agreed to meet you.'

'I appreciate that.'

'Well, I know Cal would do the same for me if this was the other way round, but I have to tell you that in my humble opinion you're chasing shadows.' Felton pursed his lips. 'These are just your average refugees, running away from god knows what horrors.'

'Do you think Otley was out there to pick them up?'

'I don't know,' sighed Felton. 'It doesn't sound like him, but he's already changed his story a couple of times. He only made mention of the woman in his first statement. After that he said Lemmy fell overboard while pulling in nets, which I don't believe, certainly not in that weather.'

'Perhaps he's afraid of someone?'

'Possibly. In any case, he's definitely hiding something.' Felton paused. 'You said Jason Spencer would try to get into this country this way? I thought he was British.'

'He is, or was. I'm not sure what his legal status is right now.'

'I see,' said Felton slowly. 'So he was out there fighting in Syria? On the wrong side?' Crane nodded. 'The more I hear about this, the less I like it.'

'That's why I've been a little economical with the facts. Sorry.'

'It's okay. I understand. For what it's worth I actually think we need to give them a chance. Certainly, we should listen to what they have to say, if only to prevent others from going out there.'

'I'm not sure your colleagues would see it the same way.'

'Probably not, but my personal feeling is the ones coming home are not the ones we need to worry about. It's the ones who didn't have the courage to go out there, but still think they know what it's about.'

'Maybe you're right.' Crane sighed and stared out at the sea.

'It's a fucked-up world, whichever way you look at it.'

'But someone has to live in it, right?'

'Yeah.' Felton gave a hollow laugh.

'If I wanted to find this woman, where would you suggest I start?'

'Assuming she's still in town, there's a shelter for women called the Nest.'

'Okay, that sounds good,' said Crane. 'And where do I find this skipper?'

'Rab Otley? At the bottom of a glass somewhere.'

19

Magnolia Quays had come a long way since Drake had last set eyes on it. The entrance to the complex was now barred by a high gate of black railings. A uniformed security guard lifted a phone to call someone before waving him through. Another one pulled open the lobby door for him. As he crossed the marble floor, Drake remembered the first time he'd set eyes on the place. One dark winter morning nearly two years ago when there had been nothing more than a concrete skeleton frame standing. In the spot where the turnaround fountain now stood there had been a patch of muddy ground, and a large hole that had been excavated to make space for an underground car park. Two bodies had been lying down there, pulverised by a truck load of gravel dumped on top of them. It was a macabre sight and one that remained a vivid memory.

Looking back now, Drake saw that moment as the beginning of something much bigger. Crane was right; not so much a case as an obsession. A haunting that seemed destined to remain unsolved. Quite why Zelda's death bothered Drake so much he couldn't really say. Just another fallen soldier. But her death was an open wound that would not heal. It kept on getting worse until the stench became unbearable. And part of him knew he would never be completely rid of it.

She had come back to haunt, literally from the depths of the earth, her head in a plastic bag left on the carriage of a Tube train. Eventually, the finger came to point at his old army buddy and mentor Grayson Brodie. The man who, more than anyone else, had helped him stay out of harm's way when he was stationed in Iraq. Drake owed him a debt, but beyond that fact he not only respected and trusted Brodie, he also liked him. They were friends of a sort, as much as Brodie had any friends. In the service they had watched each other's backs, and they had managed to stay close even when Drake was a murder detective and Brodie was, well, working the other side of the street. Brodie had been spotted down in Brighton just before Zelda disappeared. He'd never said a word about it to Drake, which made it even more damning. All this explained why Drake had been obsessed these past months with trying to find Brodie. Without success. Brodie had vanished, and if Dino was to be believed, he wasn't coming back. Drake still wanted to know why Zelda had been killed and perhaps the answer lay here, in this strange edifice that had risen from the dead ground.

As he stood waiting for the lift to take him up to the top floor, Drake thought it was somehow fitting that the trail should bring him full circle to Donny Apostolis. His shadow seemed to fall over everything. When Drake had gone under-cover to infiltrate Goran Malevich's organisation, he was forced to take Donny into his confidence. Donny was a rival, so he had no real objections, but he had recognised Drake early on and knew he was a cop. It put Drake in a difficult position, even more so when Pryce later started throwing accusations. For a time, in any case, Drake's safety had depended on Donny. And although Drake was fairly certain Donny hadn't engineered Goran's death, he had definitely benefited from it. He was sure that Donny knew more about it than he had so far been willing to share. There was somebody else pulling the strings and somehow they all led back to Donny.

The penthouse was a sight to see. Straight out of the lift onto a cloud of white marble glinting with flecks of black mica. Curved high windows wrapped themselves around two sides of the vast living space, with art deco frames that gave onto the solid oak floorboards of the terrace that ran around the outside. The afternoon sun bounced between glass and steel. The living room was littered with expensive designer sofas and armchairs that looked as though nobody had ever so much as breathed on them.

Drake stood in the middle of the room, where he had been left by a barefoot Filipina maid, who had disappeared without a word.

'Well, well, as I live and breathe, Sherlock-fucking-Drake.' Donny laughed himself all the way over to the drinks cabinet built into the wall. It was all mirrors and smoked glass and looked like it belonged in Las Vegas with flashing lights and a chrome arm attached. Donny was in his usual get-up.

Grey sweat pants and a pink shirt opened down the front to reveal a clutch of gold nestling in his chest hair. 'What can I get you?'

'I'm all right, thanks.'

'What, you stopped drinking?' Donny wagged a finger. 'Come on, you're not on duty any more. You're your own boss now.' With a dismissive wave he turned to throw ice cubes into a couple of glasses and then drown them in Metaxa from a large bottle.

'Dino said you wanted to see me.'

'Dino?' snorted Donny. 'I own horses with a higher IQ than that one.'

'What's this all about, Donny?'

'What do you think of the place? Be honest. Not bad, eh? My wife took the kids back to Greece. She says she doesn't belong in this country any more. *Gamoto!* The kids hate it. So I moved in here. I said, why not, I own the damn building, I should at least enjoy it.'

'Is that why you wanted to see me, to show me the building?'

'Let's get some air.' Donny tilted his head towards the balcony doors. 'Come on.'

Drake obliged, stepping out onto the deck. It was not too wide, but it was long and followed the elegant curve of the building, which allowed for quite a view up and down the river.

'Not bad, eh?' said Donny.

Drake had to admit he was right, although he himself wouldn't have known what to do with all that space. He'd have spent all his time getting from one place to another. 'So what's this all about, Donny? What are you doing hiding away here?'

'Who says I'm hiding?' Donny looked offended.

'You didn't bring me all this way to admire the view.'

'That's right, Sherlock.' Donny wagged a finger before leading the way back inside. He located a remote control and pointed it at the flat screen on the wall. Nothing happened at first. He carried on pushing buttons until an image appeared showing people celebrating, waving union flags, their faces painted red, white and blue.

'What's the matter with this thing? Fanny! Fanny!'

The woman reappeared in the doorway. She immediately saw what was happening and came over to grab the remote from him.

'What you doin?' she demanded angrily.

'I can't get it to work.'

With ill-disguised irritation the woman moved across to the sideboard to find another remote. She pressed a few buttons and the image on the screen changed to a still from a news report.

'You fuck it up good nes tine!' she said as she left the room.

'Crazy bitch!' muttered Donny. 'I can't believe I actually pay her.'

He had the second remote now and was cueing up the video playback. Drake took a moment to study the grainy images. The camera was panning across the scene of a traffic accident. A scooter lay on its side in the street. Drake recognised the grey buildings in the background as the Freetown estate where, a million years ago it seemed, he had once lived. The top box on the back of the scooter had come loose in the crash and had opened, spilling its contents on the ground. Drake watched the replay of the Scene of Crime Officers gathering up the pizza boxes into evidence bags. He recalled Kelly describing the incident.

'The kid was a courier,' said Drake, sipping his brandy.

'You know about this?' Donny threw an angry glare at him.

'I heard something.'

'The fuckin plods what run him down, right? Little Sammy's Pizza. You know whose merchandise that is? Mine!'

'So they're muscling in on your territory,' Drake shrugged. 'Isn't that business as usual?'

'No, no.' Donny was shaking his head. 'You don't understand. This is Sal Ziyade. He's been trying to get rid of me for years.' He lowered his voice. 'Now he's got this punk working for him, Aslan the Lion, they call him. More like Aslan the Pussy.'

'Why do you care? I thought you'd stopped with all the small-time stuff.'

'You're missing the point, Sherlock.' Donny scowled. 'It's symbolic. They're sending a message. This is just the start.'

'Tell me about Aslan. What's his part in all this?'

'He's street-level soldier. Worked his way up from beating up old ladies at bus stops.'

'What about the two officers who ran them off the road?'

'They're on Ziyade's payroll.'

'Can you prove it?'

'You want receipts?' Donny dismissed the idea with a sneer. 'Ziyade's out to get me, won't be happy till I'm buried in the ground.'

'You sound worried.'

'I'm trying to wrap it up, right?' He was digging in the drinks cabinet again, sending ice cubes skittering along the shiny floor. 'But I have obligations, people who depend on me.'

The flat was cluttered with bizarre objects. Art, maybe, but a weird collection of random items that seemed to have no coherence to it, from the full suit of armour that stood by the front door to the plump, pink cherubs floating down the corridor ceiling. Selected no doubt by some distant relative who had set themselves up as an interior designer. There were paintings on the wall that looked like somebody's poor idea of what Picasso did. Donny couldn't seem to make up his mind about what he wanted. Drake shook his head at the second offer of a drink but then found another glass being thrust into his hand anyway.

'You know me, you know how hard I've been trying to go legit, right? I'm serious about that. But it's always the same. Just as I think I'm out, they pull me back in.'

The line from *The Godfather* made Drake wonder if this was all just another of Donny's theatrical performances. Maybe he no longer knew the difference between real life and the fantasies he had in his head.

'Okay, so why am I here?'

Donny put a finger to his lips and nodded towards the terrace. Stepping past the screen, he set down the remote and gestured towards the open doors. Drake was intrigued.

'You think the place is bugged?'

'I don't like to take chances,' Donny said. He spread his arms and filled his lungs with air. 'Smell that. Isn't that great? I feel like I've crawled out of a sewer and now I'm up in the clouds.'

'Very poetic,' murmured Drake.

Donny leaned on the glass railing. 'I'm serious about changing my life. You believe that?'

'What I believe is neither here nor there, Donny.'

'Okay, so Dino told me you asked about Brodie, your old army buddy.'

'What about him?'

'You don't need to worry about him any more.'

'That's what Dino said, but he wouldn't elaborate.'

'Listen to you with the big words.' Donny chuckled, then his face hardened. 'It's family business.'

'Meaning?'

'Brodie got involved. He made it personal. I had to do something.' Donny was staring at Drake.

'And this was connected with Ziyade?'

'You could say so.' Donny lifted his hands defensively. 'I couldn't just turn a blind eye.'

'What did you do to Brodie?'

Donny shrugged, suddenly coy. 'It's being taken care of.'

Drake wasn't sure he liked the sound of that. Brodie had, after all, saved his life.

'Why the long face? I'm doing you a favour.'

'People say that when they really mean they're doing themselves a favour.'

'I thought you wanted Brodie because he took care of your girlfriend, Zelda.'

'I don't know that for sure. That's why I need to talk to him.'

'Why do you have to be such a ball breaker?' Donny prodded a forefinger at Drake. 'I'm telling you that you can save yourself the trouble.'

'I still want to know if he killed her and why.'

'Look, I did you a favour.' Donny took a belt out of his glass. 'You should be grateful.'

'So, you're telling me he's dead?'

'Once my men find him that will be it. End of story.'

Drake looked into his glass. 'I take it this is your way of telling me you want a favour in return.'

'Why do you think I'm always after something?'

'Maybe because I know you.'

'Well, I would never ask you to do something you didn't want to do. Look, relax, I'm trying to help.' Donny gestured at the view in front of them. 'Take a good look. You want the bigger picture? It's right there in front of you,' he said, gesturing at the view. From here you could look up and down the river. Off to the east the buildings of the City looked like gigantic headstones stranded by a colossus on a distant shore. Donny leaned on the glass balustrade.

'I'm not sure I follow,' said Drake.

'Land, investments, banks. Everything comes down to that. There's a direct line between that stuff and what we just saw on the telly. The kids on scooters delivering coke? The coppers who are paid to run them over? It's all part of the bigger picture.'

Donny leaned against the railing and looked Drake in the eye. 'You spent years trying to pin something on Goran. When he was gone you tried to get me,' he said, shaking his head. 'But you barely scratched the surface. It goes a lot deeper.'

'Why are you telling me this now?'

'Because I'm out of the game. I'm serious. I've spent my life playing fucking tiddlywinks when the big money is over there.' Donny nodded towards the east and the City.

'How does Zelda's death fit into all this?'

'I'm telling you. There's a straight line from her into this whole money machine.' Donny gestured again at the view. He seemed slightly erratic and Drake wondered if this was down to the amount of Metaxa he'd put away. 'Just take a look at Sal Ziyade, that's all I'm saying. If you're looking for someone to pin her death on, then he's your man.'

Underneath the frenetic energy, Drake had the sense that Donny was actually weary, tired of the game, the constant battle to stay on top of things.

'That would give you one less problem to worry about.'

'Uhh.' Donny gave a non-committal shrug. 'I'm just saying. You do something for me, and you get something in return. I mean, you should be thanking me. No more Brodie.'

'I need more than hearsay to take this to the Met.'

'Listen to me, Cal. I'm too old for a gang war. I want to enjoy my old age without having to look over my fucking shoulder all the time.'

'Even if I did want to help you, I'm no longer on the force. There's a limit to what I can do.'

'Don't play coy with me. You're perfectly placed. Outside the law but still on the inside track.' He made a gesture with his hands, like a horse running. 'You can still pull a few strings, present them with the facts.'

'Why don't you go to them yourself?'

205

'Come on, you know what they're like. Woodentops. Rules, regulations. To start with they never trust people like me. They'll think I'm trying to pull a fast one.'

'I still need more.'

'What's the matter? You're too good for my money? Let me ask you, all those rich bastards who own this city, who built their fortune on slave labour in China or Bangladesh or some other shithole, the peanuts they pay in taxes is what funds the Met, right?'

'What's your point?'

'My point is that this is no time to be finding your conscience. Come on, I've already done you a favour. A token of my good intentions.'

'I don't want Brodie dead. I want him to face justice.'

'Listen to you,' Donny grinned. 'Justice? You're a regular boy wonder. What justice? I'm talking about doing right by the girl. That's what you want, right?' Picking up Drake's glass, Donny disappeared back inside.

Drake looked at the view. Dealing with Donny was like wrestling with an anaconda. Just when you thought you'd got a good hold of it, you discovered its tail was round your throat.

'Sal Ziyade. Tell me more about him.'

'He's as slippery as a greased pole,' Donny said as he came back out, handing Drake a fresh drink. 'He doesn't even live here most of the time.'

'Then where?'

'Berlin. South of France. Spain. Beirut. He's all over the place.'

'He has business in all those places?'

'Cousins. He has them all over. In the Balkans, in Turkey, even in Africa, bringing in coke to Senegal and shipping it north to Europe. Everywhere I turn, he's there, putting the squeeze on me.'

'And you think proving he ordered Zelda's death will get him off your back?'

'If the case is strong enough.'

'I'm not trying to be funny, but why don't you take care of this in your own way?'

'Have you even been listening to me? I don't want a war. I want my children to grow up respectable. I don't want their friends to be pointing fingers at them. Why are you smiling?'

'No reason, I just never thought you cared about what others think of you.'

'This is not about me, it's about my girls.'

'I thought all the kids in these fancy schools you send them to had parents who were in the Russian mafia and so on.'

'Some of them, but not the ones that matter.'

'Right.'

'Look, you have to understand, Sal Ziyade is a smooth bastard.' Donny rattled the ice in his glass. 'He pops into town, takes care of business and then vanishes again. Like a vampire, innit? Now you see him, now you don't.'

'Let's get back to the facts. Firstly, why would he have had Zelda killed?'

'Because she had stuff on him.'

'What kind of stuff?'

'Personal stuff, about the people he was in with. Politicians. People who protect him.' Donny tapped the side of his head.

'She was a smart girl. Picked things up quickly. Never spoke out of turn.'

'She was working for you,' Drake said, as the penny finally dropped. 'She was passing you information about Goran.'

Donny shrugged. 'Goran was a real bastard. Thought you could solve anything by breaking a few legs. He actually enjoyed using violence. Gave him a kick, that's why people were scared of him.' Donny was staring off into the distance as he spoke. 'But he didn't have vision. Never saw what was out there, which was why he was destined to remain small time. Ziyade is not like that.'

In the years that Drake had known him he'd never seen Donny this worried. He'd never known him to be scared either, but this could be a first.

'Ziyade went after the weakest link in Goran's network. A sleaze by the name of Hamid Balushi. Slum landlord. Goran used him for his dirty work, running safe houses for illegals, smuggling rings. Children. He kept himself at arm's length from all that.'

Drake recalled the first time he'd heard the name Balushi. It was the day Zelda took him to a place she knew, to prove that she was telling the truth. It was a flat run by Balushi. She didn't want to do it, but it was worth it. She'd told him it wouldn't hit Goran directly, but Drake needed something tangible and this would prove to the brass that the undercover operation was working. The children were hidden in a cavity behind the wall. The stench was still there with Drake, lodged somewhere deep inside, somewhere it would never ever completely vanish. He wondered now if Zelda had been playing him too, her loyalty to Donny the stronger bond.

'Where's Balushi now?' Drake asked.

'Where do you think? After that whole mess last year with the police all over his operation he had to get out. I think he's in Canada. Married a niece or something, you know how these people are.'

'So Ziyade ordered the hit on Goran? Convenient for you.'

Donny held his arms wide. 'We all made good. It was in our best interests to work things out. Keep the balance.'

'So what's changed?'

'I told you, Ziyade has plans. He gets itchy and starts to turn. In that sense he's like a wild animal in a cage.'

'Why has Ziyade never really come to light?'

'Friends in high places.' Donny grunted. 'Somehow I was never very good at that. He's a member of a gentleman's club up in St James. He plays golf with dukes and lords. People like Jarvis Barron.'

'The media giant? The one whose son is missing?'

'I can't stand them.' Donny's nose screwed up in distaste. 'Ziyade's trying to make his way.'

'Meaning?'

'Influence. He wants to get to the top. That's why he has all these politicians in his pocket.'

'What politicians?'

A grin stretched across Donny's face. 'So you are interested?'

'I'm just trying to get a feel for all this.'

'Don't worry. I can give you names, places.'

'Okay, let's hear some.'

'Not so fast, Boy Wonder. In time.' Donny paused to take a long sip from his drink.

'Where do I find this Ziyade?'

'He's around,' Donny shrugged. 'There's a shisha bar up in Knightsbridge. There's a chain of them that belong to Ziyade. A good front for his drug business. But you don't really want to find him, if you know what I mean.'

'So how does this work?'

'It's simple,' said Donny, suppressing a smile. 'I pass you the pieces and you, and your friends at the Met, put it together.'

'And that's it?'

'I told you. You get Ziyade off my back and I'll be happy. I'm serious about going legit and I don't want anything that ties me to the old life. From now on it'll all be clean and above board. A regular businessman.' Donny made a magnanimous gesture with his arm. Emperor of all he surveyed. 'Look around. I've already given you the first piece.'

'How's that?'

'Where we are standing. This place. The whole building and everything that goes with it. Start there and you won't go wrong.'

20

C rane realised she needed more time and decided she would have to stay in Grimsby overnight. Andy Felton found her a small bed and breakfast on the seafront at Cleethorpes and then insisted on taking her to dinner.

'Don't you have a family to go home to?' she asked, worried about where this was heading.

'The advantages of being divorced. Nights off.'

Divorced wasn't a good sign and there was a certain glint in his eye that told her she might have trouble with him later. In the end he proved the perfect gentleman. They ate at a gastropub run by a couple of ex-policemen. The food was good and the portions so enormous Crane had to leave a third of her risotto on the plate. Afterwards Felton walked her back to her lodgings.

'You and Cal are an item, I take it?'

'Everyone assumes that,' said Crane. 'We're too different, or too much alike. I can't decide which.'

'He's a good detective. The kind of officer the Met needs more of, frankly.'

'He doesn't seem to think so.'

'The thing about Cal — what makes him a good detective — is that once he's got his teeth into something he never gives in.'

'You're thinking of this business with Brodie. The reason he came up here?'

'He needs to learn to let things go.' Felton was shaking his head. 'I've seen what it can do to people, good coppers, losing it over that one case they can never close.'

Outside the entrance Felton held out his hand.

'It's been a pleasure.'

She held on for a moment longer. 'If you really want to help, perhaps you could tell me where to find Rab Otley?'

Andy Felton laughed. 'I can see why Cal and you work well together. Neither of you knows how to give up.'

'What would be the point of that?'

'Okay, I'll tell you what, I'll pick you up tomorrow at nine sharp.'

'Actually, I'd rather speak to him alone, if you don't mind.'

If Felton was put out by that, he didn't show it. 'I understand. I'll make a few calls and let you know.' He hesitated. 'But if you change your mind, you know how to reach me.'

'Thanks,' she said, adding a smile. Maybe he wasn't so bad after all.

Crane was woken the next morning by the cry of seagulls. It took her a moment to realise where she was. She'd been a little reluctant to stay the night but now she was glad she'd done so. In the overnight holdall she always kept in the car she found her running clothes and shoes. As she jogged off along the seafront she was still trying to understand whether they were right in thinking that Jason Spencer was back in the country. The message left in the birdhouse might have been delivered by a friend, a stranger, or simply someone he had met on his travels. The more she thought about it, the more Crane wondered if they were clutching at straws.

In her mind she went back over what they knew about Jason's trajectory. Dropping out of university suddenly, and with no explanation, to disappear in search of a mysterious woman in London. That must have hurt his parents, especially his father. Then he went a step further into the unknown and headed off for Syria. The Spencers had concluded that the woman, Selina, had turned his head. But after talking to her, Crane was more inclined to believe her version of the story, that Jason had seen in Selina a kindred spirit. Another rebel looking for a cause and a way towards doing something remarkable. He'd grown up in the shadow of war, shoehorned by a well-meaning mother into protesting against the invasion of Iraq. Crane had seen a picture on the mantelpiece of Jason and his mother on an anti-war march. Good people who want to do the right thing. So the boy grows up, sees that the fundamental imbalance of the world will never be changed by well-meaning civilians walking for hours in damp cagoules. No, he decides he's going to make his mark. He's going to make a difference by weighing in on the other side. Entries on his Facebook page made it clear that he saw this as a way of righting the wrongs of history and overturning the traces of European imperialism. He bought into the idea of Islamic State as a modern utopia. One of the first, and most media savvy, things they did was dismantle the border between Iraq and Syria, a line in the sand drawn by British and French administrators. It appealed to the imagination of tens of thousands of young people all over the world. Jason was one of them.

Crane herself had debriefed ex-servicemen who had travelled to join the Kurdish militias in northern Syria. Some of them just wanted adventure, but others saw the conflict as comparable to the civil war in Spain in the 1930s, when the international brigades had gathered to confront fascism. Jason Spencer had simply gone the other way.

Crane leaned on the low stone wall to catch her breath. She watched the foaming white lines of breaking waves chasing one another in towards the shore. She did some stretching, ignored the wolf whistles from a passing white van, and then turned and crossed the street.

Some part of this whole story made no sense. Why would Jason return to this country and not come forward? And if he wasn't here, then where was he? It all came down to the note tucked into the birdhouse. The Spencers were convinced it was genuine, but what was the point of it? To reassure them that he was alive? To give them hope? To guide them to him somehow. It seemed to raise more questions than it answered. The best lead they had was the go-between, the woman who had delivered the message. But who was she? More important was the question of where she was now?

She ate breakfast alone in the front room of the house. The landlady was from Malta originally and insisted on entertaining Crane with her entire life story. How her father had always dreamed of coming to this country and when he finally made it he found he missed home so much that he returned there within a few years, leaving behind his wife and three children.

'But this is home,' said the woman with a smile. She was in her sixties and this house was a little safe haven from the world at large. It was also a statement of belonging. It ran through everything in that front room, from the crocheted Union Jack cushion on the sofa to the pictures of horses on the walls and the painting of a tea clipper toiling in heavy seas with its sails billowing in high wind.

'Malta – isn't that where the Templars came from?' The woman oozed loneliness, causing Crane to feel some need to reach out. She regretted it almost instantly, when she found herself on the receiving end of a confused account of the island's history, with no detail spared. She was saved when a noisy family entered, demanding attention, and Crane could slip out of the room unnoticed.

It was still too early for the pubs, so her first stop was the shelter Felton had mentioned. The Nest was based in a rundown grey building on the outskirts of town. It appeared to have once housed council offices. The name plaques and identifying signs had been removed, leaving anemic patches in the concrete. All that remained of its former purpose was a metal plaque set into the ground at the foot of the front steps, marking the opening of the building thirty-odd years back. More recent declarations were visible in the form of makeshift banners hanging across the windows of the upper floors: Refugees Welcome! End Austerity! Banish the Tories!

Inside, Crane wandered along corridors and up staircases, past abandoned offices that had been turned into improvised living quarters, before meeting a man coming out of a toilet carrying a saucepan full of water. Wordlessly, he pointed her in the direction of the next floor, where she met Max. Tall, stooping, with shoulder-length hair that needed washing and no surname, Max was a frustrating person to talk to. First impressions made him seem elusive and uncooperative about the work they did.

'I'm not sure I can help you,' he began. 'Everyone who comes to us has the right to anonymity.'

'I'm not trying to hurt anyone,' Crane said. 'I'm looking for someone who might need help.'

'Well, sure. We all want to help. That's what we're here for.' He rubbed his nose before revising his attitude. 'Look, the fact is that we are under threat. The council wants to evict us from here.'

'On what basis?'

'They claim we're helping illegals. That's really unpopular with local voters.'

'I understand.'

'Do you?' Max folded his arms defensively. 'We're providing humanitarian assistance, which is something nobody, certainly the local council, is interested in doing.'

Crane looked up and down the room they were in. It was an open-plan office that had been cut up with improvised dividers that came up to shoulder height. Across the top she could see a number of women, many of them eyeing her nervously.

'So these women are not all illegals?'

'We don't use that term,' said Max, scratching his shoulder under the ragged pullover he was wearing. 'Illegal by whose definition? People are people.'

'Sure,' nodded Crane. His righteousness was beginning to get on her nerves.

'They are all victims of abuse or deemed at risk in some way.'

The skin around his nails was badly chewed. Max was clearly a nervous person by nature. He seemed to be ill-suited to the job he had chosen. He was, she surmised, driven more by an ideologic sense of purpose than any natural affinity for the task at hand.

'We don't cooperate with law enforcement agencies, except in emergencies.'

'Look, I'm not here to stir things up,' she explained as gently as she could. 'I'm a private investigator. I don't answer to the authorities.'

He seemed unsure whether to believe her or not. 'I'm not sure how I can help you.'

'A woman and child were brought here by a fishing boat skipper about a month ago.'

'Why are you interested in this person?'

'I think she can help me.' Crane explained about Jason Spencer and his worried parents. Max nodded in an annoyingly vague fashion. Crane couldn't tell if he was trying to be difficult, or if he was genuinely in doubt about how to handle this.

'Why this woman in particular?'

'A message was delivered to the family, by a woman in black with a small child.'

'When was this?'

'Around the time a woman matching the same description was brought here.'

'What are the chances it's the same one?'

'Seems like too much of a coincidence, wouldn't you say?'

Max looked at her, but said nothing.

'Do you mind if I talk to some of them?'

'You can try,' said Max. 'Most of them speak a couple of words of English, not much more.'

'How about Arabic? Farsi?'

'Oh, well . . .' Max sniffed. 'If you speak all of those. Do you?'

'A little.' Crane held up her right forefinger and thumb.

'Then be my guest,' he said, before spinning on his heel and marching away.

Crane turned to face the room. She walked slowly through, smiling at anyone who met her gaze and noticing how the women tended to move away from her, like fish sensing the approach of a predator. An old woman standing by a window did not respond when Crane tried various languages on her. She just stood there staring at the sky. Crane was familiar with the symptoms of trauma. After what these people had been through it was hardly surprising. Some had fled the war in Syria. Many had suffered violence and hardship along the way, and no doubt many had lost relatives to the war, the sea, or left behind in camps. Sons and daughters, husbands, parents. In these circumstances it was quite logical for them to be in a state of shock. A young woman sitting on a foam mattress on the floor was rocking back and forth, weeping softly to herself. Crane crouched down beside her.

'*Ana ismi Ray,*' she said quietly. '*Ismik ay?*'

Crane stretched out a hand to touch her shoulder, but the woman wrenched herself away and started screaming. Crane got up. As she moved away a small, hard-faced woman stepped into her path.

'What you want here?' she asked in English.

'I'm looking for someone.'

'What someone?' The frown deepened.

'A woman with a small child.'

'There are many.' She shrugged.

'This one arrived a few weeks ago.'

'What you want with her?'

'I'm not here to hurt anyone,' said Crane, but the woman wasn't listening.

'You go now.' She pointed towards the door.

A few of the others had come forward to gather behind the woman. Their faces all told the same story. They wanted help for their case, not questions about others. Crane nodded. When she reached the end of the corridor Max was leaning in the doorway of his office.

'No luck, then?' He wasn't actually smiling, but his smugness was evident.

Crane looked back at the room. 'I might come back. If they get to know me a little, it might help.'

'I'm only here two days a week. I'll leave a note for the others.'

'Where are you the rest of the time?'

'We have another shelter down in London.'

Crane made a note of the details. 'I meant what I said. I'm not interested in getting anyone into trouble. I'm just trying to find someone.'

'So you said.' He nodded, clearly unconvinced.

'Thanks, anyway.'

He was gone before she'd finished speaking.

She was on the staircase when she heard a hissing sound. She looked up to see a young girl, no more than sixteen, leaning over the railings waving her back.

'You help me? I tell you about woman.'

'Do you know her?'

'You help me?' Her eyes pleaded.

'I can't promise anything.' Crane shrugged. The girl chewed at her lower lip.

'She came here, late at night. Her clothes all wet. The baby was crying.'

'Do you know her name? Where she came from?'

A shake of the head.

'Where is she now?'

'She run away.' Her eyes darted left and right, then she made her fingers into legs walking. 'London.'

'How long ago?'

More fingers. 'Three, four weeks . . .?'

'Why? Why did she run away?'

'They came.'

'Who came?'

Tears spilled from her eyes, running down her round cheeks.

She pressed a scrap of paper into Crane's hand.

'You help me, yes?'

'Yes,' said Crane, but the girl had already disappeared soundlessly into the shadows.

The sign over the door of the Blue Marlin was a picture of said fish, leaping out of the sea on the hook of a fishing line held by a bearded man who bore more than a passing resemblance to Ernest Hemingway. It seemed an apt image, somehow, for a town where fishing was swiftly passing into the realm of legend.

The interior was neat and tidy and almost completely empty. A woman running a vacuum cleaner across the green tartan carpet did not look up from her work. A solitary man sat alone on a bar stool with his back to the door.

'Rab Otley?'

'Who wants to know?'

The reek of stale alcohol coming off him was enough to turn Crane's stomach but she managed not to show it. She held out a hand.

'My name's Ray Crane.'

'Journalist, is it?' Otley squinted sideways at her.

'I'm not a journalist. I think the woman you saved might help me to find someone.'

'Who told you I saved anyone?'

Crane slid onto the bar stool alongside him.

'It was in the papers. The early reports.' She paused. 'Before you changed your story.'

He drained the last dregs of beer before lifting the glass in

221

the air. 'You're poking your nose where it's got no business,' he said out of the corner of his mouth.

'Look, I'm not here to stir things up.' Crane fell silent as the bartender appeared.

'Same again, Rab?'

'I'll get it,' said Crane. 'Whatever you're having.'

Otley rapped his knuckles on the counter. 'No one pays for my drinks,' he growled.

Crane and the bartender exchanged glances, but neither said anything. The barman slid away.

'Why did you change your story?'

'Ah,' Otley sighed. 'I was confused.' A pause as the recollection of that night came back. 'It was rough out there.'

'Must have been hard losing your friend.'

Otley nodded, but said nothing. His eyebrows slanted upwards as a new pint was set down.

'You changed your story because you didn't want to get into trouble,' said Crane. 'I get that. You didn't want them to know about the woman. Why is that? Who are you afraid of?'

'Who said I was afraid?'

'Is that why you changed your story?'

Otley stared into the bottom of his glass.

'It wasn't just her.'

'How do you mean?'

'She wasn't the only one out there,' Otley mumbled, licking his lips.

'She had a child with her.'

222

'No, I don't mean that.' Otley was staring into space. 'They come through here every ten days or so. They vary it.'

'Traffickers?'

Otley was silent for a long time. 'There are sailors in my family going back centuries,' he began, setting down his glass for a moment. 'Not fishermen. Mariners. Tea clippers, slave ships. Whatever. That was the way of the world. For better or worse, that's our story. The sea is in our blood.'

'You weren't out there looking for fish.'

'No fish worth catching any more. What there is, people don't want to eat. My dad's generation, they saw the best of it. Good times.' Otley reached for his glass again only to find it was empty. 'There aren't enough fish out there to make a living.'

'So you bring in other things.'

A slight nod. 'Got to put bread on the table. Not that it makes any difference now. She took the kids with her. Fucked off somewhere. Lemmy . . .' The voice cracked. 'Poor dumb Lemmy.'

'You were out there to meet someone, something. A shipment. People?'

'Not people. I don't do that.'

'Drugs then.'

'If people want to spend their money on that crap . . .' Otley gave a shrug.

'So it wasn't people?'

'I just said that.'

'Who's bringing people in, then? Is it the same ones who are bringing in the drugs?'

'Did you say you were going to buy me a drink?'

'If you've no objections.'

Otley held his empty glass up to the light. Crane waved at the bartender, who was fiddling with his phone.

'Do you drink when you're on the boat?'

'Never.' Otley looked insulted. 'Quickest way to a watery grave.'

'Where did she go, when you brought her ashore? What happened to her?'

Otley hesitated. A part of him new the game was up. He just wanted this to be over. 'There's a shelter. My wife . . . ex-wife, she works there sometimes. I thought . . .'

'You thought she would know what to do.' Crane paused, giving him time. 'You know, Rab, whoever did this, whoever was bringing those people in, they're the ones who killed Lemmy.'

'Same again?' asked the barman. Otley was still silent, staring at Crane. The barman picked up the empty glass and disappeared.

'That's why I'm here, Rab,' said Crane, her voice dropping to a whisper. She thought she saw something in there behind the anguish and pain in his beaten eyes. 'I'm here to help.'

'He unclipped his harness, silly bugger. I don't know how many times I warned him.'

'It takes courage to do what he did. He was trying to help them.'

The bartender set down a fresh pint and Otley stared at it, not reaching for it like the last time.

'He had a good heart.'

'I believe you.' Crane got to her feet. 'One last thing.' She placed Jason's letter on the counter, still encased in its plastic sleeve.

'What's this?'

Crane turned the letter over to reveal the rough map.

'Did you draw that?'

Otley squinted at the paper and then shook his head.

'Sorry, not guilty.'

It was a long shot. Crane set a business card next to the glass.

'You don't owe them anything. They're never coming back to do business. You're damaged goods. You might even lose your licence. You owe it to Lemmy to set things straight.'

'What would you know about it?'

'I know that you won't find your conscience at the bottom of that glass.'

21

'P lease don't do that.'

Kelly Marsh instantly stopped tapping her foot on the floor. It was a nervous reaction. She wasn't happy about being here. She wasn't happy about a lot of things, but what she mainly was uncomfortable about was having to go over her immediate superiors and contact the super himself. Breaking the chain of command was always a risky move, whichever way you played it, but as Marsh saw it her options were severely limited at this point.

Superintendent Dryden Wheeler resumed his reading. He'd spoken without lifting his eyes from the page in front of him. It took him another ten minutes to finish the file. When he was done he removed his glasses and set them on the desk in front of him.

'You do realise the risk you are taking by bringing this to me, don't you?'

'Yes, sir.'

Wheeler decided to spell it out for her anyway. 'If I find no justification for you jumping the line of command I have to report you, which, I'm sure I don't have to tell you, would have a detrimental impact on your record.'

'I understand that, sir.'

'Good, because I'm having trouble comprehending exactly what leads you to believe you have anything like a compelling argument here.'

'Gut instinct, sir.'

Wheeler winced. 'As you well know, DS Marsh – or should know – gut instinct is low down on the totem pole of police procedure. Frankly, you would have had more luck going with female intuition.'

'Yes, sir.' Marsh swallowed. 'My point is that I believe there is more here than meets the eye.'

'That much I have grasped. This is your opportunity to persuade me of the facts.' Wheeler sat back and folded his hands together.

'I realise that this doesn't look good,' she began.

Dryden Wheeler cut her off. 'I don't want to hear excuses, Marsh. I want to know why I should take your side and reject DS Chiang's case, which provides compelling evidence that the man who killed Cathy Perkins is dead.'

Marsh cleared her throat. 'Sir, as I see it, DS Chiang was following the leads as he saw them. I believe his mistake was in assuming that Zoë Helms was the target.' She was aware that she was repeating herself, that her words were falling over each other. She took a deep breath and tried to clear her mind. 'That's his job, sir. The safety of Ms Helms is his first priority, so naturally he assumed she was the intended victim.'

'And you believe otherwise.'

'Yes, sir, I do.'

'DS Chiang has DNA evidence that puts the suspect in the Helms house. Mourad has, or had, a record of stalking women.' Wheeler tapped a forefinger on the desk. 'Seems pretty convincing to me.'

'Yes, sir, I would have to agree with that, on the surface,' conceded Marsh. 'But that's exactly the problem.'

'Now you've lost me.'

'Bear with me, sir.' Marsh edged forward in her chair. 'Rachid Mourad had a history of stalking prominent women. In 2008 he was convicted of harassing a participant in a reality show. He broke into her house and stole items of underwear. In 2014 a similar case was brought against him by a television sports presenter, Katy Gardiner. That case was later dropped.'

Wheeler frowned. 'And you think this is what he was doing in the Helms house?'

'He's not killer material, sir. In my honest opinion,' she added.

'Anyone can panic. You should know that.'

'Yes, sir. I just don't believe that is the case here.'

'I will remind you, Marsh, that you went over DCI Pryce's head to bring this to me.'

'Yes, sir. I'm aware of that.'

'Whatever action I feel is merited, I have to run it by Pryce, which means it could easily backfire against you. This case was a chance for you to dip your toe in the water, not to drown in the stuff. You remember what I said at the beginning?'

'Yes, sir,' said Marsh. 'A woman's touch.'

'Exactly. Trampling all over the case in heavy boots is not what I had in mind.'

'No, sir.'

With a sigh, Superintendent Wheeler slumped back in his chair and contemplated her.

'I'm still going to need more than this. What about the other side of the argument? Tell me why anyone would target Cathy Perkins?'

Marsh took another deep breath to steady herself. 'She was an investigative journalist. She worked for a number of papers, including *The Guardian*. At the time of her death she was working on a book.'

'I see nothing about a book here.' Wheeler flicked through the papers in front of him in search of answers.

'No, sir, I got that from speaking to one of her former colleagues.' Marsh cleared her throat. 'We found nothing at the crime scene. No laptop or manuscript.'

'In other words, you have no idea what this book is about, or even if there is a book.'

'We're pretty sure she was working on something big.' Even Marsh could hear how hollow her argument sounded. 'We're still trying to ascertain the nature of the work. The laptop she was working on was taken. It's possible she might have kept a copy in the cloud. So far nothing has turned up.'

'Which means you have nothing.' Wheeler sighed. 'Yet you've come to me with this . . . idea. You believe she was killed because of a book you have not seen nor have any idea what it contained. Would that be a fair assessment?' The tone of his voice left no room to doubt just what he thought.

'Sir, I agree it sounds thin, but——'

Wheeler's hand lifted to cut her off. 'You do realise you're in danger of veering into the realm of conspiracy theory?'

'I'm not sure I would put it that way, sir.'

'No? Then how would you put it?'

'Cathy Perkins was hardcore. She was on to something, something big. If she was going after someone, she had to have a solid reason.'

'And who was she going after? Do we at least know that?'

Marsh swallowed. 'I believe she was trying to tie political corruption to organised crime,' she ventured. In for a penny . . .

'That's about as vague as you can get,' observed Wheeler. He was silent for a moment, staring at Marsh. 'DCI Pryce is backing DS Chiang on this.'

'I know, sir.'

'He thinks you're still under Cal's influence. I told him that wasn't the case, that I believe you're a fine officer with a bright future ahead of you.'

'Yes, sir. I appreciate that, sir.'

'I'd like to keep it that way.' Wheeler's finger tapped out a steady beat on the desk, a strange echo of her feet earlier. 'You've bought yourself till the end of the week to come up with something more substantial and we'll look at it again. I can't stretch it any further than that.'

'Yes, sir.'

'Follow up on any loose ends. Try to get hold of Perkins' work. But if, by the end of that time, there's nothing there, I need you to drop it. Is that clear?'

'Absolutely.' Marsh got to her feet. 'And thank you, sir.'

'And try not to step on DS Chiang's toes. He won't thank you for throwing a spanner in the works, and that goes for DCI Pryce as well.'

'Understood.'

'And Marsh . . . I don't want to hear that Cal is mixed up in this in any way.'

'No, sir. Point taken.'

22

Magid Bouallem leaned forwards, rocking over his crossed legs. 'Speak, brother,' he said softly. 'Unburden yourself. Your heart will feel lighter.'

Drake lifted his eyes from the carpet to take in the circle of faces around him. None of the others worried him too much. They were all rather lame. Followers rather than leaders. This seemed to be the way Magid liked to keep things. The exception was Adeeb, who scowled at him from across the prayer room. Drake knew he was the one to keep an eye on. This shura council had been Bouallem's idea, a way of clearing the air. Drake wasn't convinced it would work, but he thought it a good way to introduce himself to the others who frequented the centre.

'Brother Calil has come to us to make peace with himself.'

'Thank you, brother Magid, and thank you all for taking the time.' Drake did his best to sound grateful. There were a few nods from the moderates, but also some long looks. They would hear what he had to say out of respect for Bouallem, but that was as much as he would get.

They were an assortment of oddballs and kids. The younger ones had that fever in their eyes, looking for somewhere to turn their energies, for something to burn. The others were misfits. Men who had fucked up their lives one way or another and were trying to find the centre again. They came from all over. Driss and Slimany he had made progress with. There were a couple of Moroccans, a Tunisian who looked like a professor, an older man with grey dreadlocks who hailed from Martinique. Drake ran his eyes round the group and came to rest them on Driss.

'Brothers, as some of you already know, I've done things I'm not proud of.'

'None of us is perfect, except Allah.' Bouallem stroked his beard sagely. 'We've all done things.'

'Not like this.' Drake glanced at Slimany, as he bowed his head at the carpet. The others were silent. They had no idea what he meant, so they were happy to wait and hear.

'Let us speak frankly.' Bouallem held his arms wide. 'We have no secrets from each other.' He looked around the others before turning his gaze back on Drake. 'You have lain with unbelievers?'

'I have,' Drake said. 'But that's not it.'

'That's not a crime,' shouted a grinning Adeeb from across the room. Bouallem raised a hand to silence him while he continued his interrogation.

'You have allowed alcohol to pass your lips?'

'Again, yes, but . . .'

Magid Bouallem was shaking his head and smiling at Drake's foolishness. 'None of these things is worth worrying about. We are all tempted.' His gaze passed over the others and there were several obedient nods in response. 'Alhamdoulillah, we manage to resist temptation.'

There was a low murmur of 'Alhamdoulillah' from all around.

'Prayer brings forgiveness,' Bouallem went on. 'Following the way of the Prophet, may Allah bestow his blessings upon him. You speak of things that are haram, but we all face this challenge in this country. Living among the kuffar brings its own challenges.' Drake bowed his head as the other man went on. 'Every day our children risk losing their way. They are trapped between the ways of his world and the beauty of the world to come. It's not easy for them to choose. Everything is right in front of them, there for the taking. Sex, drugs, alcohol.' He paused. 'In that sense you have a gift. You know what it is like to lose your way.'

'I've killed people,' Drake insisted quietly.

'Of course,' Bouallem affirmed. 'You lost your way, you can help our children not to.'

'I've killed Muslims.'

There was a murmur of shock and commiseration, murmurs of 'Ya Allah!'

'That's why I'm here.' Drake looked around the group again, this time letting his eyes come to rest on Adeeb. 'I want to make up for my errors.'

Zaki, the mild-mannered accountant, tossed in his penny's worth. 'We are losing the battle for our children. The kuffar are winning.'

'The brother makes a point.' Bouallem nodded his approval. 'We can never let our guard down. The unbelievers are winning minds and hearts.'

'I lost my way.' Drake continued his confession, sticking to his own story. 'I broke the law and then I thought that I could make things right by joining the army.'

A hiss of disapproval rippled through the circle. Drake wondered if he was overdoing it. 'I joined the crusade of the unbelievers.'

Drake looked around the room. There was an embarrassed silence. Nobody would meet his eye. Except Adeeb, who seemed to be enjoying the moment, a sly smirk on his face. Drake understood the others. They were dealing with something they had never encountered before. For many of them war was an abstract concept, far away and more readily associated with video games and the gruesome online clips they passed around between them. It was all distant and theoretical. Most of them had their sights set on making a life for themselves in this country. They might pay lip service to the idea of jihad, but they didn't want it to upset their chances.

As they broke up outside in the street, Zaki squeezed Drake's shoulder.

'That was a brave thing you did in there. I lost a brother fighting for the Iraqi Army. Nothing is as simple as it seems. We all have regrets.'

As he made to walk on, Drake found his path blocked by Adeeb. He was easily the most aggressive person in the group and if Drake were asked to make a bet he would have put money on Adeeb having done time.

'You don't fool us,' Adeeb said.

'How do you mean?' Drake feigned innocence.

Adeeb leaned in closer. 'I mean, maybe you can pull the wool over Imam Magid's eyes, but you don't fool me.'

Beyond him, Drake spotted Slimany and one of the others standing at a distance watching them.

'What are you saying, that Imam is a fool?'

'I didn't say that,' Adeeb snapped angrily.

Drake shrugged. 'Sounded that way to me. Disrespectful.'

'You're twisting my words.' Adeeb's eyes darted from side to side. There was something about him that was ready to explode. 'Just remember, we're watching you.'

Drake watched him go. It might have been all bluff, but he suspected that Adeeb's confidence came from somewhere. He knew something and Drake was curious to know what that was.

23

Every time they met it seemed to Crane that Selina was growing more agitated. They sat together in the car park facing the supermarket. She had come alone and Crane wondered if she was simply using their meetings as an excuse to get out of the house.

'Where's your son?'

'I left him with her.'

Her being the second wife. Crane wondered whether this would have repercussions at some point. The younger wife using the child as an excuse to complain to Bouallem, maybe to try and get Selina thrown out of their happy family.

'I can't stand it any longer. If there was a way to kill him, I'd do it.' Selina looked over at Crane. 'I've looked up rat poison.'

'That would be a bad idea. And besides, they don't put strychnine in rat poison any more.'

That took a moment to sink in.

'So what are you saying, that it's not poisonous?'

'For rats yes, but not for humans.'

'Sure, but like in the right amount it would work, right?'

'You'd have to feed him a ton of the stuff and then he might notice.'

Selina chewed on that for a while. The sun came out suddenly. It was a windy day and ink blue clouds swept back and forth like curtains twitching on a rail.

'I have a friend,' Crane started. 'She's a legal advisor on the Crown Prosecution Service.' She stopped, seeing the blank look that came over Selina. 'I mean, if you're serious about wanting to get him out of your life.'

Selina stared straight ahead of her. 'You're talking about snitching?'

'I'm talking about cooperating with the authorities, yes.' Crane paused. 'Your involvement with Jason . . .'

'What about it?'

'Well, I'm just saying. As far as the law is concerned—' She didn't have time to finish her sentence.

'I didn't do anything wrong,' blurted Selina.

'I know, I know.' Crane tried to calm her. 'I believe you, but facts can be twisted round. I mean, you encouraged him to go to Syria, so, strictly speaking, according to the law, you're partly responsible for him joining Daesh.'

'I didn't have to encourage him,' Selina protested. 'He wanted to go.'

'Sure. I get that. I'm just telling you how a jury might look at it.'

'A jury? I'm not on trial.'

'If Jason is back in this country, and if he is caught or turns himself in, then he will have to tell them the whole story. How he got to Syria, who his contacts were and how he got them. You're a part of that, whether you like it or not.'

Selina looked down at her gloved hands sitting in her lap. Crane watched her. She said nothing and after a moment or two her shoulders began to shake. She was crying. Big fat tears fell onto her gloves, staining the black acrylic fabric with shiny darkness.

'I never wanted anyone to get hurt. I just wanted to please Magid.' She clenched her fist and choked a sob. 'I was so naive.'

'You were young,' said Crane. 'He took advantage of that. And now.'

'Now that he's tired of me he's moved on to a younger model.' Selina sniffed. 'She wants us to be friends. Sisters, she calls us. I'd like to kill her. She's just a child.'

'How do you mean?'

'I mean, she's barely fifteen.'

'That's illegal. How did he manage that?'

'How do you think?' Selina rolled her eyes at the question. 'He married her somewhere you can pay to get things done.'

'You're sure about this. I mean, about her age?'

'Of course I'm sure.'

'Well, if you're serious maybe we can use this.'

'No, I don't want to get her into trouble. I may hate her guts, but she doesn't deserve to be sent home. What would happen to her? Divorced and with a baby at fifteen? What kind of life is that?'

'Look, you have to make your mind up about what you want to do here. If you decide to speak out, you can change your life. And who knows, maybe you can help this girl too.'

Selina was shaking her head. 'I don't know.'

'You want to do something good, right? I mean, that is what you want, isn't it?'

Selina was still looking down so that Crane could not see her face. From time to time she gave a loud sniff.

'Maybe this is a way of setting things right, for yourself, for Jason. And maybe, just maybe, this way you get yourself free of your husband.'

Selina stared at Crane for a long time without answering.

'Okay, what do I have to do?'

24

A big sign now hung over the main entrance of the old bathhouse: Official opening! Jan 25th! Don't Miss it! Crossing the street, Drake spotted a couple of rentacops in their grey DKGS security uniforms. These two looked like they belonged on a football terrace. Forties, overweight with shaven heads and tattoos visible on their forearms. They gave him the once-over but did nothing. Inside, Drake found Crane sitting on the first-floor gallery in a healthy eating place with huge, bright pictures of fruit beaded with water. She was sipping a drink the colour of beetroot while surveying the lower level of the mall over the iron railings.

'Don't tell me what that is,' he said as he sat down. 'I'd rather not know.'

'Hey, don't knock it till you've tried it. Might change your life. Speaking of which,' Crane gestured at their surroundings, 'funny to think how this used to be.'

'The kind of fun I could do without.' Drake could still

recall hanging by his fingertips from these very railings. Back then there had been a long drop below that would have left him at the bottom of the old and very empty pool. He'd have been lucky to have survived without breaking his spine if Crane hadn't hauled him up.

'How did your meeting with Donny go?'

'He's talking about getting out, going straight. Meanwhile he's holed up in his penthouse thinking he's being bugged and talking about Sal Ziyade.'

'Should I know that name?'

'Lebanese. An upmarket rival of Donny's. From what I could dig up he's heavily into property investments, including Magnolia Quays.' Drake sighed. 'Oh, and you'll be glad to hear, Donny claims he's taken care of Brodie for me.'

Crane squinted over her straw. 'Taken care of?'

'I couldn't get him to be more specific. The worst of it is, he thinks I owe him one in return.'

'Right. That could be tricky.'

'Still, there's no doubt he's worried. He thinks Ziyade is moving in on his territory and that he has some players in the Met in his pocket.'

'I thought everyone was talking about this Berat Aslan?'

'Low-hanging fruit. A street-level operator. Someone higher up the food chain is using him to stir things up.'

'This connects with those kids on the scooter?'

'Exactly.' Drake squinted into the distance. 'According to Donny, Warren and Taylor are on Ziyade's payroll.'

'Which means what?' Crane swirled the purple liquid around her glass.

'It could mean that the whole ring is being protected by bent coppers.' Drake's mind was taking him off, leading him through unmarked doors, down into places he wasn't sure made any sense. 'How about you?'

'I heard back from Jindal in Frankfurt. He's looked through all your papers.' She held up an envelope. 'He sent a report.'

'Anything interesting?'

'You need to read it. I don't know enough about it to make sense of what's in there.'

'Okay, I'll do that.' Drake tucked the envelope into his jacket. 'And thanks.'

'Glad to help, if it helps you to move on. Any progress at the mosque?'

'Cultural centre, they call it, and no, nothing yet. It's still possible that someone there helped arrange Jason's journey to Syria, but I couldn't say who, and there's no evidence they're in touch with him now. They're being cautious. They don't trust me yet. An operation like this can take months.'

'Is there anybody who sticks out?'

'Adeeb. He's the one who likes acting tough. The rest of them either don't know anything or they are keeping out of it. Too early to tell.'

'And how are you doing?' Crane turned to him. 'I mean, all this must bring back memories.'

'Being undercover?' Drake rubbed his chin. 'It does.'

'How are you coping?'

'I'll be fine.' Drake sighed. 'In a way it takes me further back, to when I was a kid.'

'Do you remember what you were looking for back then?'

'Peace.' Drake thought for a second. 'A way of looking at the world, of living, that was not about anger and hatred.'

'Is that why you joined the army?'

'Perhaps. I needed discipline, order. Some kind of system of routine that would stop me wasting my life.' Drake gave a sigh. 'It feels like several lifetimes ago.'

'I'll bet.'

Drake, uncomfortable talking about himself, felt the need to change the subject. 'What did you make of Andy Felton?'

It was Crane's turn to laugh. 'Decent sort, I suppose. I'm not sure how far I'd trust him.'

'He's a sly one. Always had an eye for the ladies.'

'You'll have to tell me about your adventures together one day, up in Matlock.'

'Sure, when you have a few hours to spare.'

'I found a shelter where the woman might have stayed, but everyone there is afraid.'

'You spoke to the skipper?'

'Rab Otley.' Crane nodded. 'Seems she was in a dinghy that got into trouble. Otley was out there to pick up a shipment of drugs. The inflatable went down and the woman and child were the only survivors.'

'So Otley can lead us to the traffickers?'

'Not directly. Otley took her to a shelter in town. He told me it was because his ex used to work there, but I think he knows the shelter is linked to the traffickers.'

'He was handing her back.'

'Sounds like that to me. He changed his story to cover it up.'

'Are we any closer to establishing that this is the same woman who delivered the message to the Spencers' house?'

'It's still not a hundred per cent, but the message in the birdhouse was delivered the day after she was recovered from the sea. She went straight there. How did she find it? She had a map. There was a rough map drawn on the back of the letter, after she had been rescued from the sea. I asked Otley about it, but he claimed it wasn't him.'

'You believe him?'

'No reason not to. It could have been anyone. Someone on the street, or at the centre.'

'Okay, let's assume for the moment it *was* her. Where's Jason? Was he on the same boat? Did he make it ashore?'

'We don't know, is the answer to that. The coastguard recovered the remains of an inflatable dinghy five miles down the coast. No sign of anyone in it. Felton texted me that a couple of bodies have washed up, but none of them match Jason's description.'

'He might have sent her on ahead,' Drake suggested, following his thoughts. 'He could still be over in a camp in Calais or somewhere.'

'That's definitely a possibility.'

'What about this camp in the woods – did you go back?'

'I went the next day and it was deserted. I must have scared them off.'

'So what's our next move?'

'My feeling is that all these things are wired together. It's a system. Follow the threads and they'll lead back to the source.'

'So where would this woman go?'

'Put yourself in her shoes. She doesn't know this country. She probably doesn't speak the language very well. The people she was travelling with have drowned. I spoke to a girl at the shelter who said that someone had come looking for the woman.'

'The gang that brought her in?'

'Possibly,' said Crane. 'What if the traffickers are using the centre, places like it, as part of their network, a system to pass people along?'

'Could work,' Drake conceded. 'Using the shelters would be hiding in plain sight.'

'And getting government support to cover it.'

'Devious,' said Drake. 'But no reason why it wouldn't work.'

'The guy running the place in Grimsby mentioned another place in London. They have a branch in Shepherd's Bush.'

25

Drake, unable to face eating at home alone, decided impulsively to take advantage of the Ithaka still being open. Not entirely impulsive. In the event, as he arrived Amaia was busy closing down. She was generous enough to heat him up a plate of moussaka, and went back to clearing out the display cabinet and wiping down the glass while he ate.

'Still not back, then?'

She looked up, as if she had forgotten he was even there.

'Eleni and Kostas?'

'Oh, yes,' Amaia nodded. 'They decided to take advantage of the good weather and went to the islands to visit friends in the Peloponnese.'

'Good for them.'

'It's what I miss most,' she smiled. 'The sunlight. The sea.'

'This time of year, sure, I understand.'

She noticed that he had finished eating and put down her cleaning spray and paper towels and came over to collect his plate. It felt a little awkward to him, though he couldn't say why. It was her job, after all. Somehow it felt wrong.

'I was thinking,' he began.

'Yes?' She stopped in mid-stride, halfway back towards the counter.

'Maybe . . . er, maybe you'd like to go for a drink some time.'

'A drink? With you?'

'Yeah, you know, at a pub.'

Her face twisted in distaste. 'I don't really go to pubs,' she said, shaking her head.

'Okay, sure, then maybe somewhere else?'

She thought about this for a moment, still holding his plate in her hands. Then she gave a nod.

'Okay.'

Back in his flat, Drake pulled out Jindal's financial report and went through it carefully. It was fairly detailed but also frustratingly inconclusive. Drake wondered if this was some kind of financial advisor's trait – never spell things out too clearly. He dug through the spreadsheets that now covered the coffee table in the living room. They spilled onto the floor, trailing around between the chairs. He sat down and began rearranging them, piecing together the threads using Jindal's report as his roadmap. There was so much detail it was easy to get swamped, but the general gist of it supported Drake's theory that Nathanson had been using knowledge of his clients' financial affairs to do a bit of blackmail.

Jindal had honed in on one particular batch of records that were over ten years old and dated back to Nathanson's time at Clayton Navarro. Drake had also thought it strange that the lawyer would hang on to such old records. Drake ran a finger down a list of account numbers in the report, some of which he had already managed to connect to certain names. The biggest of these was Jarvis Barron. Drake knew little about Barron other than that he was a larger-than-life figure whose origins in Eastern Europe somewhere had been shrouded by years of building himself a firm seat in the English establishment. He owned vast swathes of land up and down the country. Abroad he had golf courses, stud farms, health spas, but his real interest was the media. His companies included radio and television channels, as well as a sizeable chunk of publishing. There used to be some kind of law against creating monopolies, Drake reminded himself. Whatever happened to that?

Jindal had managed to unravel Nathanson's system, to some extent. He had pieced together a number of connections between firms that might or might not be traced back to Barron. The problem with shell companies was that while you could follow their expansion or evolution, it was difficult to pin down exactly who owned what. Drake took some satisfaction in the fact that even a trained expert like Jindal had found Nathanson's system baffling. The report made a couple of links but the overall picture was still far from clear. Barron owned property all around the world, in China, the United States, Latin America and the Caribbean, along with a fair-sized chunk of London. When Howard Thwaite had gone bust just over a year ago, it was bought up by a firm called Tampoco Fortuna, which in turn was tied to Novo Elysium through a third company. After an hour or so, Drake felt he was still going round in circles. At least, Jindal did manage to link a number of prime property sites, including Magnolia Quays and the Freetown Arena, to what appeared to be an old sugar plantation in Costa Rica – Angula Aguada.

Drake sat back. The report was a disappointment in many ways – no smoking gun – but it did give him hope that he might be on the right track. Donny had talked about Ziyade cultivating friends in Whitehall. It had never become clear who had killed Nathanson but Drake now reconsidered the question. If Ziyade had been engineering a takeover of Donny's little empire, then he would have needed to get hold of Nathanson's records. Donny had latched onto Barnaby Nathanson when he was a shabby lawyer with a coke problem. He provided drugs for Nathanson's services and eventually the accountant's problem led to him being let go by Clayton Navarro, which was fine by Donny. It meant Nathanson could devote more time to him, finding ways to siphon his money through various offshore accounts into something legit.

But Donny wasn't Nathanson's only client. There were others hidden inside these spreadsheets. And now Drake was working with the idea that Sal Ziyade might be one of them. Whoever murdered Nathanson in his bathtub had done so to clean up.

Barnaby Nathanson had been good at what he did, but he wasn't infallible. He was hasty, perhaps overworked, and frazzled from too much coke. Perhaps the system was not so much brilliant as simply confused.

Drake imagined he was beginning to see patterns. Scanning through one sheet after another, picking out sequences. Numbers that were close enough in amount and also by date. It was like suddenly spotting a line running through a wheat field. Sums of money being transferred between five different accounts. The dates almost consecutive. He drew lines trying to connect. Then the pattern broke and the line seemed to vanish before his eyes, like some kind of sleight of hand.

Slumping back with a sigh, Drake threw the pencil down. He didn't possess anything as fancy as a noticeboard, he just stuck notes onto the wallpaper with drawing pins. Stretching his back as he got up, he went over to stand and stare at the information once more. What he saw was a cascade of names, people, places, dates. The problem was how they all connected to one another. Looking at the left-hand side, he began to rearrange the index cards according to the lineage he had just come across. Novo Elysium was connected to the Kratos Corporation. In between them were half a dozen more obscure accounts. Some of them only appeared once, before vanishing forever. Drake had the sense that he was only staring into a kaleidoscope; turn it one way and you saw one pattern, turn it another and you saw something completely different. The more Drake looked at the figures, the more it seemed they pointed to something that he already knew.

His mind took him back to that morning two years earlier when he had stood on the edge of the huge excavation at the Magnolia Quays site and looked down into the hole. Howard Thwaite's wife and the second victim, Tei Hideo, an ornithologist, had been killed in a twisted act of revenge. The double murder had revealed deep inconsistencies in the construction company's finances. Subsequently, Thwaite was forced to sell his share to Donny Apostolis.

The two bodies had been buried under a mound of industrial gravel from a dumper truck. The delivery firm, Dobson Creek, had been bought and sold half a dozen times since then. It was absorbed into Ypres Development Holdings, which itself went bust less than three months later. Drake had the impression these companies were like dominos, just being shuffled around. The financial and legal transactions of these firms had been in the hands of Clayton Navarro, a high-end company of lawyers. Barnaby Nathanson had been running the offshore accounts of a number of people and he took their business with him when he left.

Drake went back to Jindal's report. Nathanson's clients included business people, ordinary investors, hedge funds. One company provided shelter for half a dozen others and so on and so forth. They were registered all over the world. On the surface there was no connection between them. One thread had been teased out. Dobson Creek was part-owned by some of the same people who owned Keelhaul Water. Finally, he stumbled onto what looked like a connection: a small security firm had been registered twice, under two different names. Hellebard Holdings and Kronnos Security, which Drake recalled had been running things at the Magnolia Quays site. In turn, Kronnos had been absorbed into 4GS Holdings, which also owned Hellebard. 4GS then became Department K Global Security – DKGS, as it was now known – which operated all over the world. They now also owned a sizeable investment in Hawkestone, the private military contractors. Clayton Navarro, the Kratos Corporation, Dobson Creek, Kingsland Road, Dalston, Ypres Development Holdings. DKGS provided the security for all of them.

Drake finally gave up and fetched himself a beer from the kitchen. Opening the can, he lay back on the sofa and stared at the ceiling. He had been hoping that Jindal's report would provide the silver bullet, something that would help him to tie the whole thing together. It wasn't. Or if it was, he couldn't see it. He closed his eyes.

In his dream he was in a hole in the ground. He was trying to scramble up a mound of rubble but could not reach the top. It was endless and just kept getting higher. The harder he tried, the more quickly it grew, until he knew he was going to suffocate.

He awoke in the cold, grey light of dawn, with the buzz of his phone next to him.

'Were you asleep?'

'Kelly? What time is it?'

'Your friend Donny took a dive off his balcony. Thought you'd want to take a look.'

Drake sat up, rubbing a hand over his eyes.

'How bad is it?'

'The doctors say he's going to live, but it's touch and go.'

'I'm on my way.'

'You know where?'

'Magnolia Quays. Where else?'

253

26

There was something surreal about seeing the place again at that hour of the morning. It made his dream seem all the more strange. Kelly being there, just as she had been nearly two years ago now, only added to the weirdness.

The DKGS security guards were off to one side. The uniforms were keeping them out of the way, which made sense. There were so many of these cowboy outfits around these days, ready to pin a badge on the first person who answered an ad. References rarely checked out. It was a hard slot to fill and the positions often attracted the kind of people who didn't really want to do much more than swing their dicks around shopping precincts and sit around lobbies making life difficult for anyone who showed up. It was a reflection on human nature that Drake found too depressing to contemplate at this time. Only this wasn't any old firm. The grey uniforms had a dark blue insignia patch on the sleeve with a red lightning flash across the diagonal. Drake gave them the once-over as he went by. He wanted to remember their faces.

Marsh had left word, so they let him through. In the event, the uniform on the door of the flat recognised him with a nod. The interior was much as Drake recalled from his last visit, except that there were now signs of a struggle. A fancy table lamp was lying in the middle of the floor, its cracked tangerine shade spread in starburst fragments. One of the sliding windows was cracked; the glass had splintered but not shattered.

Drake stepped out onto the terrace to find Marsh telling a Crime Scene Officer what to photograph. Glancing round, she said something to the officer and then turned to lead Drake away.

'I'm assuming you didn't call me for old time's sake?'

'We asked the maid about visitors. She remembered you.'

'Well, at least I made an impression.'

Marsh shrugged. 'She couldn't remember your name, so we ran the security footage.'

'When did it happen?'

'The maid came in early this morning, saw the mess, looked over the side and saw him lying down there.'

'Anything on the CCTV?'

'Everything after you was wiped. Also . . .' Marsh hesitated. 'You're seen arriving, but not leaving.'

'This is not your way of telling me I'm a suspect, I hope?'

'I'm keeping an open mind, but if I know Pryce he'll be all over this like beans on soggy toast. Now's the time for you to tell me what you know.'

'What's to tell?' Drake edged closer to the railing and peered over. Down below on the mudflats there were a dozen or so people trying to manouevre a stretcher. 'There's no chance he took a dive by himself?'

'Did he seem depressed when you saw him?'

'Maybe a little more than usual,' said Drake, 'but Donny's not the type.'

'You know better than I do how often people say that.'

'True.'

'But in this case we do have signs of a struggle.' Marsh nodded towards the room behind them.

'Prints?'

'We've found a few on the railings.' She indicated the traces of aluminium powder on the steel bar. 'Including yours, I would imagine. But too soon for a match.'

'You're not actually asking if I pushed him over?'

'Course not, but like I said, I'm not the only person on this. The last thing I need right now is to find out you were involved in this in some way.'

'I hear you.'

The wind blew her hair across her face. Marsh pushed it out of her eyes. 'So was this just a social visit?'

'Donny said he was trying to go legit.' Drake turned his back to the railing and the wind. 'He was concerned that his rivals were after him.'

'So, why would he turn to you?'

'He seemed to think we could help each other.'

'You're going to have to explain that one,' said Marsh. In the stark, early morning light she looked older to Drake, more mature. In command. She was shaping up to be a good detective. Something that had never really been in doubt to his mind, but it was still good to see it.

'He wasn't making a lot of sense,' Drake began, recalling the conversation and his own confusion at the time. What had Donny been trying to tell him? 'He felt people were after him.'

'Your average paranoia, or something real?'

'I can't really say.'

'Okay, but when Pryce gets here he's going to want an explanation, and I don't think he's going to swallow the idea you were counselling Donny for his paranoia.'

'No, I get that.' Drake felt the cold wind blowing in off the river. It looked a long way down.

'If he's really trying to go legit, how much is he willing to give us?'

'Difficult to say, especially now.'

'If he was serious about it, he could be a major asset.'

'Well, we can ask him just as soon as he wakes up.' Drake glanced over his shoulder to see if there was anyone within earshot. 'Where are you with Cathy Perkins?'

'It's not looking good. Wheeler's given me an ultimatum.' Marsh lowered her voice, glancing towards the interior, where the forensics team were busy. 'I've got till the end of the week. After that, I have to give it up. Mourad takes the rap and Perkins goes down as a casualty of an attack on Helms.'

'Can you prove Perkins was the intended victim?'

'Not until I find out what she was trying to write about.'

'Wheeler was always there for me, but there's a reason he chose the command track rather than continue in investigation.'

'I think he's feeling the pressure. Pryce is moving up the ladder.'

'Right,' agreed Drake, 'and with retirement coming up soon Wheeler doesn't want to mess it up.'

'Well, he seems happy to go along with pinning Perkins death on Massoud,' muttered Marsh.

'Look, Kelly, maybe there's a connection.'

She frowned at him. 'With Cathy Perkins? How?'

'I'm just saying, you should let me help you.'

The wrinkle at the centre of her forehead deepened. 'What is it you're not telling me?'

'This may not be the best place,' Drake said, nodding at their surroundings.

Marsh tapped a hand on the railings.

'I don't have a lot of time on my hands, Cal.'

'Fair enough.'

'You said Donny was worried about enemies?'

'One in particular, Sal Ziyade.'

'Should I know who that is?' frowned Marsh.

'Lebanese-Egyptian background, started out in gambling, ran hotel casinos in Beirut, Cairo and a couple in France. Also has his hand in the drug trade.'

'Nice.' Thrusting her hands into her pockets, Marsh stared out over the river.

'What he's really interested in now is restaurants and property. He owns a stake in this place, and I get the feeling he's trying to expand. I think Ziyade has been playing the long game.'

'Is this part of what you wanted to talk about?'

'Some of it, yes. I think he's connected to that business over in Freetown.'

'The kids on the scooter?'

'The cops who ran them off the road, I think they might have been on Ziyade's payroll.'

'Do you think Ziyade had Donny thrown off here?'

'Seems like a good bet to me,' said Drake. 'By the way, could you do me a favour?'

'Is it that time already?'

Drake passed her a slip of paper.

'What's this?'

'Group of men I'm getting close to over Stockwell way. Maybe you could run it by CTU and see if anything comes up. This one in particular.'

'Adeeb Akbar.'

'Might be an alias, but if anything shows I'll be interested.'

'What are you getting into, Cal?'

'This is just a missing persons case, nothing more.'

'Shit!' muttered Marsh, lowering her eyes. 'Heads up.'

Drake turned to see Pryce standing in the doorway behind him. He'd put on weight in the last few months. No doubt down to the good living that came with promotion, running the Murder Investigation Unit out of Scotland Yard.

'What is this man doing here, DS Marsh?'

'Sir, Mr Drake is providing testimony.' Marsh straightened up to face the DCI as she spoke. She knew such things mattered to Pryce. 'He was one of the last people to see the victim before the accident. Thought he might be able to shed some light on the matter.'

'Very commendable, but it's still a crime scene,' said Pryce as he came closer. 'You shouldn't be here, Cal. Not unless you've come to make a confession.'

'A little out of your jurisdiction, aren't you, Vernon? There's no murder here.'

'Attempted is good enough for me.' Pryce looked Drake up and down. 'It's astonishing how many coppers succumb to the temptations of a life of crime. In your case, only a matter of time, I suppose, for you to wind up on the wrong side.'

'I take it you're speaking from experience.'

'Very funny.' Pryce thrust his face into Drake's. 'If you're mixed up in this, rest assured, you will be charged.'

'As DS Marsh explained, I'm here as a witness,' said Drake. 'I came to help apprehend the guilty party.'

'Pull the other one,' sneered Pryce. 'Now get out before I have you arrested for tampering with a crime scene.'

Marsh walked him to the door, under the vigilant gaze of Pryce, who remained on the terrace. As he was about to step out, Drake dropped his voice.

'The missing CCTV footage.'

'What about it?'

'Might be worth taking a closer look at the outfit running home security.'

'You know something you're not telling me?' Marsh searched Drake's eyes.

'Just a passing thought. If I come up with anything else I'll let you know.'

'You'd better.' Marsh tossed her head. 'In case you hadn't noticed, you don't have too many friends left around here.'

27

Crane was sitting in the Bush Theatre café when Rab Otley called. She didn't recognise the number, but the sound of seagulls cawing in the background told her instinctively who it was.

'I've been thinking,' Otley said, after a lengthy silence. 'I feel I owe it to Lemmy to set this straight.'

It was the middle of the day, which immediately threw up a couple of questions. Had Otley started drinking yet? From the tone of his voice, Crane would have said not. Did that signify that he was trying to turn his life around? He sounded like a man with something to get off his chest. So Crane became confessor.

'People round here have been struggling for years. The fishing is all we've ever had, but it's gone now. No two ways about it.'

It felt slightly surreal to Crane, listening to him here of all places. The people occupying the sofas and tables around her in the café were a mix of the young and the middle-aged. The hopeful and the affluent. The distant crash of the sea sounded like ice splintering rocks.

'How did they contact you?'

'Couple of them just appeared one morning down in the harbour. Never laid eyes on 'em before. They just came up and started talking. It was a one-off thing. Not regular. Just every now and then. They like to break up the routes. Never the same place twice in a row.'

'You would go out to pick up a shipment.'

'Sounded all right to me. Nothing too complicated, just the occasional detour to meet another vessel. And no mention of people.'

'Did you get any idea who they were?' Crane offered a pointed smile to the white-haired woman to her left who seemed to be taking an interest in her conversation.

'Not really. The contacts out there were all sorts. Panamanian trawlers. Russian fish factories. Liberian container ships. You name it. Your man there is some bloke who barely speaks English. It's all sign language. The stuff comes over in water-tight plastic barrels. It goes straight down in the hold. When we get back to port someone is waiting to take it off us.'

'No checks?'

'Nah, nothing like that. Everyone knows everyone. Like family. We're all struggling.'

'So you deliver the goods and they pay you.'

'Cash in hand. Hard times. The money came in very handy, I can tell you.'

'I believe you.' Crane tried to ignore the woman. 'You never brought in people?'

'I wouldn't have nothing to do with that. Human trafficking, that's as evil as it gets. Some of the others did, mind.'

'Do you think they might know something?'

There was a long silence. 'These are not people you mess with. They'll cut your tongue out as soon as shake your hand.'

'I'm not asking you to stick your neck out.'

'I can try, I suppose. No promises, mind.'

'That's okay. All of this is helpful.'

Crane had given up caring about the looks she was getting. She could glare too. Which she did.

'That night . . . when you went out with Lemmy.'

The white-haired woman got up to move away. The man next to her, presumably her husband, looked put out, but followed dutifully after her, asking loudly what the problem was. The woman lowered her head to whisper. The man stared over his shoulder at Crane as if he hadn't noticed her there.

'It wasn't supposed to be that way.' Crane heard Otley sigh. 'I knew it was a bad idea. A small boat in that weather? Crazy. I thought they'd at least have someone on board who knew what they were doing.'

'So you thought it was the usual thing, then, a drugs shipment?'

'I should have known better. You can't trust people like that.'

'Still, you went out, despite the bad weather?'

'What else was I going to do? Ach, it wasn't all that bad. If the coordinates had been right we'd have been back in time to miss the worst of it. But they had that wrong too.'

'The wind farm.'

'Not on the charts. They build those things and then it takes months to get them onto the navigation systems. You have to pay for an upgrade and all that shite.'

'That's when you lost Lemmy.'

Otley fell momentarily silent. His voice trembled when it returned.

'They shouldn't have been there. We shouldn't have been there.'

'But you saved that woman and her child.'

'There's that.' Otley was silent for a long moment.

'You took them to the centre where your ex worked.'

'It was the least I could do. I thought . . . I thought, after all that, something should come of it.'

'Is that the only reason you took them there?'

'What?'

'You've never heard of a connection between the Nest and the traffickers?'

There was a long silence. 'I'm trying to do the right thing,' he said, finally.

'I believe you,' said Crane. 'Lemmy would have been proud of you.'

'I hope so.' Crane heard a loud sniff. There remained in her mind a question of whether Rab Otley could have known, and returning the woman and child was paying back some form of debt. She decided she was not going to get more out of this conversation. Rab Otley seemed to have drawn the same conclusion.

'Look, I have to go now. I hope it helps.'

'I'm going to find her,' said Crane. 'But any help you can

give me is welcome.' She spotted Drake wandering about the entrance area picking up leaflets. He hadn't seen her yet.

'I'll have a word with some of the boys. I'm not promising anything.'

'That's fine. I'll wait to hear from you.'

'Whatever I do, it won't bring him back. I'll live with that for the rest of my days.'

He sounded resigned, rather than despairing, so maybe that was something.

After she hung up, Crane went out into the entrance hall where Drake was frowning at the lengthy list of coffee types marked up in chalk on the blackboard over the bar.

'Why do they always make this so complicated?' he muttered as she came up.

'He'll have a double espresso,' Crane said to the woman behind the counter. 'You can drink it on the way.'

Crane filled him in on Otley's call as they walked.

'Have you given any thought to the idea of contacting Stewart Mason?'

'You know how I feel about him, Ray. I just don't trust the man.'

'That's just your general hatred of authority,' Crane laughed.

'Or it could mean that I just don't trust him.'

'You might have to revise that opinion. He's been hinting at the idea of the NCA contracting us to do delicate work.'

Drake pulled up to look at her. 'What kind of delicate work?'

'Stuff that they don't want their fingerprints on. Off the books.'

'I don't like the sound of that.'

'It would be good money. The way things are going we might have no choice.'

Drake turned to look at her. 'I'm not sure I'm ready to start working for the government again.'

'This would be different. Outside the strictures of the Met, with a good deal of freedom.'

'Still.'

'Well, it's just an idea right now. I told him we'd think about it,' said Crane. 'We don't have to burn every bridge we come to ahead of ourselves.'

'I hate planning ahead.' Drake had finished his coffee and was looking for somewhere to put the cup. 'You ever notice how there are less bins nowadays?'

'I can't say I have.'

'Well, it's true. Must be some kind of austerity measure.' Drake crushed the cup in his hand and considered putting it in his pocket. 'Did you hear about Donny?'

'What about him?'

'Took a dive off his balcony early this morning.'

It was Crane's turn to stop in her tracks. 'He fell, or someone dropped him over the side?'

'It's not clear.' Drake balanced his empty cup on a low wall they were passing. Crane fixed him with a glare until he picked it up again and finally tucked it away in his jacket pocket. 'Donny's not the jumping type. This was enemy action.'

'Why would anyone try that?'

'Looks like a turf war kicking off.'

'Well, don't let yourself get sidetracked. Remember we're working for the Spencers.'

'How could I forget? I've got you to remind me.'

They came to a halt outside a terraced house that had fallen on hard times. The windows were grubby and the frames in need of paint. The front steps were chipped and uneven. The plaster had flecked away, taking part of the number 127 with it. They climbed the steps to the front door, which had a small painted sign on it that read simply 'The Nest'.

'And you think she would have come straight here?'

'She had nowhere else to go. She was afraid they would come for her. She would have picked up a leaflet with the address. It would give her a start.'

'Leading her straight back into their arms,' murmured Drake. 'Clever.'

Drake leaned on the bell. They heard it ringing somewhere within, but no one came to the door.

'Looks like nobody's home,' said Drake. He pressed his face against the stained-glass panel next to the door and tried to peer through.

'Can I help you?'

They both turned to see a man in his twenties standing behind them. He was wearing jeans and an old parka that looked too big for him. In his hands he was juggling a bag from a bakery and a cup of coffee while fishing a large set of keys from his pocket.

'We're not open yet,' he said as he came up the stairs. Holding the bag in his teeth, he began to unlock the door.

'Are you the person in charge?'

The man looked at Crane and frowned. He took the bag from his mouth.

'Police, is it?'

'No, mate.' Drake stepped in to help him with the keys. 'I'm Cal and this is Ray. We're looking for a woman who we think is in some trouble.'

The young man gave a hollow laugh. 'Tell me about it, that's all this place deals with.'

Inside, Crane and Drake waited while Frodo, as he said his name was, went about switching things on. They stood in the big dayroom that took up one side of the ground floor. There was a long Formica table with a kitchenette at the back. The front half was a living room, with a couple of sofas and armchairs facing a television set in one corner.

Frodo came back and sat down at the end of the table. While he busied himself with tearing open the paper bag and tucking into his croissants, he glanced up to study his visitors. Behind the glasses he wore, there was a keenly intelligent set of eyes.

'Who did you say you were looking for?' he asked between bites. Crumbs fell from the corner of his mouth onto the table.

'A woman with a small child, just over a year old,' said Crane.

'You have a name?'

'If we had a name we would have told you,' said Drake.

Frodo stared at him. 'Are you sure you're not a cop?'

'Why, don't you like cops?'

Frodo chewed, mouth hanging open, not sure what to make of this.

'Is that really your name, Frodo?'

The young man stared at Drake. 'It's Freddy, okay, but no one calls me that.'

'Do you get a lot of people coming around asking about women with children?' Crane asked.

'It happens,' shrugged Frodo. 'That's what this place is for. It's a shelter. Women come here because they have nowhere else to go.' He was defensive, trying to look casual, but there was something there and both Crane and Drake felt it.

'How did you get into this?' Crane asked.

'How do you mean?' Frodo's jaw slowed.

'I mean, a young man like you. Must be plenty of jobs out there yet you took an interest in helping women.'

'It's not a crime, is it?' Frodo sniffed.

'Nobody's accusing you of anything,' Drake chipped in from the window sill where he was perched. 'We're just chatting.'

Frodo didn't look convinced. 'My mother. She used to work here.'

'Right, so you took over for her,' said Crane.

'Something like that. She was ill.' Frodo sipped his coffee. 'This woman, why are you interested in her?'

'We believe she may be in some trouble.'

'And what makes you think you'll find her here?'

'She was at the Nest in Grimsby. You have much to do with them?'

'Nah, not really.' Frodo shrugged, reaching for the remaining half a croissant. 'Owned by the same charity.'

'We think the traffickers who brought her in might be on her track.'

'Traffickers?' Frodo put down his cup. 'You mean, human smugglers?' He looked at them over his croissant. 'Seriously, do I look like a trafficker to you?'

'To be honest, I'm not sure what you look like,' said Drake.

Frodo started to get to his feet. 'Look, I have work to do. If you want to ask more questions, maybe you should bring a real cop with you next time.'

'Only one more thing,' Crane went on. 'You said this place and the one in Grimsby belong to a charity. Have you got a name, a contact?'

'Sure.' Frodo crumpled up the paper bag, sweeping the crumbs onto it from the table. 'Just leave your details and I can send them.'

'But this woman, she was here?' asked Drake. Frodo nodded. 'What was her name?'

'Her name?' Frodo shrugged. 'I don't . . .' he began, then appeared to grow tired of the whole charade. 'Nahda. Her name is Nahda.'

28

Max Stafford-Bryce lived in a Victorian red-brick house in Hampstead. The house looked as if it had shrunk into itself. The walls curved softly towards the earth. The wooden fixtures were green with mould. Even the recessed doorway, with its gabled eaves surrounded by ivy, looked as though it was caving inwards.

The man who answered the door was in his sixties. Hefty, red-faced and wearing a scruffy, greying beard. The white shirt looked as though he'd slept in it for a week and was hanging out of his cords on one side. The eyes that peered out from behind a pair of wire spectacles glinted with sharp wit. He was expecting them and stood aside to gesture at the staircase behind him.

'Upstairs. Straight ahead.'

Following his instructions, Drake and Marsh reached the landing. The stairs twisted round on themselves and continued upwards, but ahead of them a doorway led into a dark room.

The only light entered through a window facing the wide desk. It too was trimmed by ivy on the outside, reducing the open space and lending the room an impression of being buried inside the trunk of a very large tree. It was cluttered with books and heaps of papers stacked on every surface, including the floor. Files, folders, boxes.

'You'd better sit down. That way there's room for all of us.'

The only place to sit, other than the chair in front of the desk, was a narrow sofa that was clearly an antique. Marsh and Drake found themselves squashed a little too closely together for comfort.

'Thanks for seeing us,' began Marsh. 'You're a hard man to track down.'

Stafford-Bryce didn't appear to be listening. He was staring at Drake.

'We've met before,' he said, settling himself into the swivel chair at the desk and leaning forwards. 'You were in charge of a murder investigation up in Matlock about four years ago?'

Drake's wilderness years, as he sometimes referred to them, when he'd been assigned to the small Derbyshire town as atonement for the Goran Malevich mess. His time there had coincided with one of the biggest serial killer investigations in the country. Drake had a vague recollection of the large journalist. He'd had slightly more hair back then.

'You were the crime correspondent following us around.'

'Security editor, actually. I took a personal interest in the case.'

'You were related to one of the victims, if I remember correctly.'

'Distantly, on my mother's side.' Stafford-Bryce scratched his head nervously. 'So, what's this all about? You mentioned Cathy Perkins.'

'I understand you knew her quite well,' said Marsh.

'We worked together for a time,' nodded Stafford-Bryce. 'I was heartbroken to hear of her death.'

'My condolences,' said Marsh. 'Was she like a protégé?'

'Well, that's probably overstating it a little.' Stafford-Bryce gave a nervous laugh. 'But I had a lot of time for Cathy. I suppose it's instinct. You recognise in someone else the same drive that you felt when you were starting out.'

'You're saying she had what it takes,' said Drake.

'Yes,' agreed Stafford-Bryce, looking at him. 'Definitely.'

Drake recalled he'd had a similar reaction when he met Marsh, although he would have been hard pressed to admit such a thing.

'She was dogged. Once she got her teeth into something she would keep at it and never let go until she'd got to the bottom of it. But I'm not sure how I can help.' Stafford-Bryce leaned back in his chair. It looked frail and creaked alarmingly under his substantial weight, but he didn't seem to notice. 'I thought the case was closed. The man who killed her died in an accident?'

Marsh cleared her throat. 'There are still a few loose ends that need to be tied up.'

'I see.' Stafford-Bryce looked distracted. He picked up a lighter from the desk and then put it down again. 'What kind of loose ends?'

'We're trying to find out what Cathy was working on,' said Marsh. 'Did she ever confide in you?'

'Confide?'

'About her work?'

'Not really. She . . .' Stafford-Bryce broke off. 'Look, the truth is we lost touch over the years. After I left the paper. You know.'

'About that,' said Drake, cutting off Marsh. 'Why did you leave the paper?'

'Usual story, I was getting a little long in the tooth and when they start looking where to make cuts . . .' He didn't finish the sentence. 'It's cheaper to hire some kid who's grateful for any kind of job than keep an old dog like me around. It's the way of things nowadays.'

'So no bitterness, then?' said Drake.

Stafford-Bryce laughed. A cold, cynical rasp. 'It's too late for that.'

'Just to get back to Cathy,' said Marsh, giving Drake a leery look. 'We understand she was working on a book.'

'Only in broad terms.' Stafford-Bryce reached again for the Zippo lighter that was lying on the desk and began snapping the lid open and shut. The nervous tic of a man who has recently given up smoking. 'She was writing about the collapse of the political system in this country.'

'That sounds rather vague,' smiled Marsh. 'Can you be more specific?'

'Politicians no longer wield any real power. Privatisation, fast-growing populations, the collapse of industry. What you are left with is a ship that has no engine, no direction and no purpose. It's basically an empty, hollowed-out hulk, but someone has to be on the bridge.'

'The politicians,' provided Drake.

'Exactly. So, what can they do? Try to keep her afloat by bringing in as many investors as possible, and that means lowering your standards, getting your hands dirty.'

'Corruption, in other words,' said Marsh.

Stafford-Bryce nodded.

'We are in the process of committing a monumental act of national folly. How did it happen? How did a bunch of privileged public schoolkids manage to persuade the electorate that they represent the best interests of the people?' He looked back and forth between them. 'The media. Control the media and you control everything.'

Drake and Marsh exchanged glances. Marsh had been warned by Stella Wright that Stafford-Bryce was something of a conspiracy theorist. 'He sees bogeymen under the bed,' she'd said. It sounded like she was not a million miles off the mark.

'So, you haven't actually seen what she was working on?' Marsh asked, trying to get back on track.

'No, I haven't.' The lighter stopped clicking. 'Hold on, are you saying you haven't got it?'

'Her laptop and phone were taken,' Marsh explained. 'And so far we have been unable to find anything stored online.'

'She didn't trust any of that.' Stafford-Bryce allowed himself a self-satisfied grin. 'I may have influenced her on that score, but working on defence cases can do that to you.'

'Big Brother?' asked Drake.

'They are more vigilant than you think,' said the other man with humourless gravity. 'It was a burglary that went wrong, right?'

'One of the problems we're facing,' said Marsh, 'is deciding if Cathy was the intended target.'

Stafford-Bryce leaned forwards, his interest suddenly piqued. 'You're saying she was silenced.'

'We're not saying that for certain,' Marsh corrected, 'because we don't know.'

'That's why you're here, to find out if something she was working on got her killed.'

Stafford-Bryce was on his feet now, forgetting the smallness of the room. He stepped over to the bookshelves by the door and stood for a moment with his back to them.

'They murdered her,' he said quietly.

'We don't know that for sure,' insisted Marsh, but Stafford-Bryce was beyond listening. He turned round to face them.

'It's obvious,' he said, returning to his chair. 'There is no other explanation. This, this whole thing with a burglary, it's the obvious cover-up.'

Again, Marsh and Drake exchanged looks. He was heading off the deep end and taking them with him.

'You say you don't know exactly what she was working on,' prompted Drake.

'I know what she was working on. I know the broad outlines.'

'Can you be more specific?' Marsh hesitated. 'Did it have something to do with Zoë Helms?'

'Helms is typical of the new breed. No real moral or ethical principles. All she cares about is staying in office. I warned

Cathy not to get involved with her, but of course she didn't listen.'

'She no longer trusted you?' Marsh ventured.

'Something like that. Maybe she thought I was jealous,' Stafford-Bryce snorted.

'Which you weren't?' Drake asked.

'No. I mean, I cared about her. I wanted her to succeed.' The lighter began clicking again. 'I warned her that her work would be compromised by the relationship.'

'You don't like Ms Helms?' Marsh observed.

'That's not the point.'

'What is the point?' Drake asked.

'Nobody gives a damn about Zoë Helms. Her kind are dime-a-dozen, rent-a-suit, walk-on entitled pundits who think they are morally superior to the rest of us.' Stafford-Bryce gave a loud sigh. 'Mussolini defined fascism as the moment when you cannot separate corporate and political power. That's a fair description of what we have today, wouldn't you say?'

'And Helms is part of that?' Marsh asked.

'Helms is typical. She did everything that was expected of her. Good school, then university. Mediocre results. Gets a job as a solicitor. Marries a more successful solicitor. Gets into politics.' Stafford-Bryce paused. 'That's where she really reveals her ambition. She switches allegiances and parties at the drop of a hat. All she wants is to get to the top.'

'The top being?' Marsh was curious.

'A cabinet post, maybe even prime minister.'

'You think she has a chance?'

'Nowadays?' Stafford-Bryce snorted. 'It's like musical chairs up there.' The lighter was clicking like an angry insect looking for something to strike.

Drake reached into his pocket. He held out a folded sheet of paper.

'Do any of those names mean anything to you?'

Stafford Bryce scanned the sheet before shaking his head and handing it back.

'Sorry.'

Marsh gave Drake a long look. She closed her notebook and got to her feet.

'Well, that gives us something to go on. If you think of anything else, please get in touch.'

Stafford-Bryce walked them to the front door. He stood, gripping the wooden doorframe.

'Cathy was careful, always worried about losing material, being robbed. She backed everything up. She kept flash drives in all kinds of places. Posting them to herself, or to friends abroad. Keeping them in circulation.'

'Old school,' murmured Marsh.

'Exactly,' nodded the journalist. 'It's just a matter of working out what she did with them.'

'So where did that come from?' Marsh asked when they were back in her car. 'That list of names?'

'Oh, just something that came up in my research.'

'Don't give me that. I'm not that stupid. You've got Nathanson's papers, the ones from his safe.'

'I'm on your side, Kelly. I'm trying to help you.'

'Then hand over those papers.'

'I can't, not yet.'

'Why not?'

'Because if I'm wrong, then it harms nobody but me.'

'And if you're right?' Marsh asked, one hand on the ignition.

'Then we're all in trouble.'

29

'They named me Wynstan after me grandad, you know? How it was done back then. He was named after the big man.'

'Churchill?'

Wynstan sucked his teeth. 'Wicked ting to make a boy carry a name like dat.'

He was wearing a suit today, grey with a thin, brown cross-hatch and matching fawn shoes. Wynstan liked to drive himself, didn't trust most of the people who worked for him on that. Not hard to see why. Two of his goons were in the back chewing matchsticks. One of them had sunken eyes and a pronounced forehead that made him look like a poster boy for Neanderthal Man. The other resembled a miniature version of Dwayne 'The Rock' Johnson, right down to the Maori tattoo that rose up his neck out of his blue satin bomber jacket.

The car was a black Daimler limousine. About thirty years since it rolled off the production line but still in perfect condition, gleaming chrome and spotless bodywork. It looked like a hearse. Drake was wondering why anyone would drive such a monster but Wynstan had an answer ready.

'Commands respect. The mayor of London use ta drive one a deeze.'

Respect was right. Everyone knew he was coming. And mayor sounded about right too, not of the city but of Freetown. Drake remembered Wynstan's father, a scary man with a pockmarked face who would turn up on your doorstep if there was a death in the family or someone lost their job. He'd bring money and groceries in a cardboard box to tide you over.

Farida Byrnes was in her forties. She was putting on weight around the middle but her face had retained a youthfulness that meant she could easily have passed for ten years younger. Her hair was a loose afro and she was already in her blue nurse's uniform.

'When I finished my training I decided I wanted to be a librarian. I loved books.' She spoke with her back to them, buttering toast and calling to her son to come and fetch his breakfast. The boy ducked in and out of the room with only a quick furtive glance at the visitors.

'When they shut down the library I went back to nursing. That was ten years ago. Ever since then all they been doing is closing down hospitals.' Her head was rocking from side to side. 'You can't run a country into the ground and not pay the price.'

'Dat the god's truth,' said Wynstan. He sat respectfully at the kitchen table alongside Drake, who was still wondering what this was all about, why he was here. The two goons had stayed with the car, though not to guard it. Wynstan could have left the car open with the keys in the ignition and nobody would have dared breathe on it.

'Our loss is their profit,' Farida was saying. 'Half the flats round here are empty. Nobody can afford it no more. They trying to push us out. Cutting services, so the kids have nowhere to go. They just hang around on the streets. So prices drop and then someone steps in and buys the whole lot, turns it into fancy places with doormen.'

Through all of this she was busy setting out mugs of tea, sugar and milk for her guests. Wynstan was grinning.

'That's why you're here. I wanted you to hear it from the horse's mouth.'

Farida cocked an eye at him. 'Who're you calling a horse?'

'Sorry! My bad!' Wynstan cracked up.

'It's easier dealing with you now that you're a private eye,' he said when they were back in the car. 'But you need to see this. People are struggling.'

'Who's buying up the flats?'

'Punks think they can get into the property game. They use different names, collectives, associations, housing funds. They get creative that way.'

'All of this impacts your business.'

'That's my point.' Wynstan snapped his fingers. 'I'm not trying to paint myself as a pillar of the community or anything like that, but we count for something and that's going to be gone if we don't make a stand.'

'This is your way of telling me you're going into politics?'

Wynstan looked over, sticking his chin out, modelling his profile. 'You think that's a crazy idea?'

'I've heard worse.'

'Listen to me, mon. Everything is politics. Ya caan get away from it. From the colour of the skin you was born in to the kind of cereal you eat for breakfast. It's all politics.'

Drake heard an amen from one of the goons in the back seat. No doubt they had heard this speech before and were well versed.

'You heard about Donny?'

Wynstan sucked his teeth. 'Man, that's what I'm talking about.'

'You have any idea who might have done it?'

'It's dog eat dog.' Drake waited for further elaboration. 'He tried to play them at their own game.'

'What game is that?'

'Going big time. Raising the stakes. Cleaning up.' Wynstan shook his head. 'Lot a people don' like dat. Makes them all itchy.'

It wasn't going to get any more specific. Drake asked Wynstan to drop him off well away from the Cave. He didn't want anyone seeing him rolling up to the door in this thing.

'Stay chill, mon,' said Wynstan, leaning over. 'And get rid of the beard. You look like some kind of brother. Or maybe you're trying to become a hipster.'

Laughter echoed out of the window as the Daimler sped away, drowned out by the horns on 'Ghost Town' as it was turned up loud before fading into the distance.

'Some kind of brother, indeed,' Drake muttered to himself as he walked towards the entrance.

The business of tracking down Jason Spencer had become something of a distraction. It wasn't that Drake didn't care about the case, just that his mind was now focussed on Nathanson, Donny and Sal Ziyade. He knew, however, just how important this case was, not only to Crane but to their business generally. They'd been struggling to stay afloat. The downside of the private sector. You need to make a profit. Crane had hinted that they were basically being kept above water by the bank covering them with a loan secured on the property.

'We can't afford to lose any business, or we might have no choice about working for Stewart Mason.'

The sector was surprisingly crowded these days, and not just with pop-up stalls. There were large outfits weighing down the books of insurance companies and legal firms. Firms that ran solid security operations and investigations were just something they offered in case someone wanted one of their employees vetted. The strength of Crane and Drake Investigations rested on their independence, and their experience, although nowadays that was a tough line to sell. Everyone's an expert, or so they claim, and like everything else, either everybody knows your name, or nobody does.

So here he was, back on familiar turf, trying to persuade Akbar and the brothers to trust him. In an effort to demonstrate how keen he was, Drake volunteered for whatever needed doing. He wanted to give the impression of a man just out of prison with nothing much else to do with his life. He stayed on late, washing dishes in the kitchen, cleaning the prayer room, doing odd jobs, helping out wherever he could. It wasn't hard to find something to do. None of the faithful seemed to be particularly bothered about loose doorknobs or windows that refused to open.

Which is why that afternoon he found himself standing on a stepladder in the hallway changing a lightbulb when he overheard an argument coming from the prayer room. Adeeb and Magid Bouallem were alone in there. It wasn't that he had his ear pressed against the door or anything. He couldn't avoid hearing them.

'You're a coward!' Adeeb yelled.

Drake couldn't make out Bouallem's response. From the tone, it sounded as though he was trying to placate the other man, who was clearly having none of it.

'You talk and talk, that's all you do,' shouted Adeeb. 'It's not enough. We need to act.'

'I built this place. You should show some respect.'

'I'm tired of hearing your excuses.'

'You must be careful. Everything we have built here could be ruined.'

'Oh yes, and what is it you think you have built here? A place for us to come and cry together like old women? Is that how you think an Islamic state is built? We have to be worthy.'

'Worthy? Really?' Bouallem's voice dripped with anger. 'When you came to me you were fresh out of prison. You have spent your life going from one criminal offence to another and now you want to lecture me about what to do? Is that what you want, to bring us all down? You think they are not watching our every move?'

'Nobody is watching.' Adeeb gave a harsh laugh. 'The kuffar are too slow, too stupid to know what we are doing.'

'Don't be so arrogant. You're gonna get us all in trouble.'

'Just wait and see. The world will know us.' On that note Adeeb stalked out of the prayer room, almost crashing into the stepladder as he went by. Muttering a curse under his breath, he glanced up briefly at Drake as he headed for the door.

'Why are you here all the time?' Bouallem asked when he came out. He seemed annoyed that Drake had overheard them arguing. 'Don't you have other things to do?'

'Sorry.' Drake began to come down the ladder. 'I was just trying to help.'

Bouallem waved a hand in apology. 'It's all right, Calil. This is a difficult time for some of the brothers.'

'Brother Adeeb seemed upset.'

'He's young and reckless, like a small child who takes no responsibility for his actions.' Bouallem exhaled slowly. 'I know things have not been easy for you . . . with some of the brothers . . .'

'It doesn't bother me,' shrugged Drake. 'I didn't expect them to accept me right away.'

'It is wrong. We must stick together.' The burly man touched a hand to his own chest. 'I believe you have a lot to contribute to our little community.'

'Thank you,' said Drake quietly. 'I wish I could do more.'

'I understand. Like your friend.'

'I wanted to join our brothers in Syria and fight. I thought . . .'

'You thought that if you gave your life for Islam it would make up for what you did in Iraq.'

'Something like that.'

'Listen to me, Calil. There are other ways of paying your debt.' Bouallem examined Drake's face. 'Your friend, the one who led you here.'

'Abu Hamra? You remember him?'

'Vaguely.' Bouallem shrugged, as if it was hard to keep track. 'He went to Syria, you said?'

'Yes. He was going to fight for Daesh.' Drake looked away. 'He told me that if I came here, you could help me to get out there.'

'I understand,' said Bouallem, resting a hand on Drake's shoulder. 'You have the true spirit. I can see that. I'm sure you would be a great fighter.'

'Inshallah.'

'Inshallah, indeed. But it's not so easy.'

'You mean, because of Adeeb?' Drake hesitated. 'I know he doesn't trust me.'

'Brother Adeeb is hot-blooded. He strikes before he thinks.'

'I'm not afraid of him.'

'If you are serious about going to fight, you must convince Adeeb to trust you.'

'I don't want to speak out of turn.' Drake studied the rag he was holding.

'Speak freely, brother Calil.'

'I've seen men like Adeeb before.'

'Brother Adeeb is young and reckless. I've told him as much.' Bouallem stared at Drake. 'If he does not mend his ways, he will bring trouble down on us.'

'He's dangerous, and he's not afraid of you.'

Bouallem frowned. 'What are you saying?'

'I'm saying, maybe I can help. You need someone on your side. Someone who can stand up to him.'

The big, clumsy figure seemed to freeze. He studied Drake's face, as if searching for something.

'Why are you telling me these things?'

'I'm saying we can help each other.' Drake tossed the rag he was holding so that Bouallem had to catch it. 'If you help me then I can help you.'

Bouallem considered the rag. 'I will speak to brother Adeeb,' he said quietly. 'Let's see if we can't find a better use for your talents.'

30

The clip was from a news and current affairs debate programme that had been broadcast five months ago. Zoë Helms was up against a member of the audience. A young man in a check shirt with ginger hair that looked as though he'd cut it himself. He looked reasonable, but almost as he began speaking an aggressive undertone made itself plain.

'Why do you keep asking for compromise when you've given no signs of compromise yourself? You refuse to accept the results of the referendum and continue to claim that you're working in the interests of the people. That's a lie. You and others like you are traitors.' The word brought an audible gasp from the people around him in the audience along with a few groans. 'You should be ashamed. You don't believe in democracy. You don't believe in our country.'

Zoë Helms waited for the flurry of applause and consternation to die down.

'I wish I could explain to you why what you are suggesting is not practical. Our job in parliament is to create the laws that govern this country. We were elected by the people to do that. Now, what you voted for was an idea.' Helms paused, ignoring the jeers, allowing them to die down. 'An abstract notion that meant different things to different people. Our job was how to take that abstract notion and make it into something that is real. A set of laws and agreements that can be enacted. That is the reality and I really think that after three years of debating this subject you and people like you need to accept that we don't live in a magical world where wishes are made real at the wave of a wand.' By now she had to raise her voice over the clamour. To her credit, she soldiered on. 'We live in a real world where our actions have consequences. I am charged with serving the best interests of my constituents – the people who put me in Westminster. It's easy for you to sit there and tell me you disagree with the way I am doing things, that's your right and I would defend that, but I have to answer for my actions.'

'And you will,' the young man shouted back. 'There will be consequences!'

Kelly Marsh tapped the keyboard and the playback stopped. She sat back and stared at the frozen image of Zoë Helms that filled the screen.

'There will be consequences,' she repeated out loud.

It was the third time she had played this clip in the last half hour. There was something about it that bothered her, a niggling doubt that she could not put to rest. What if she was wrong? What if Helms had been the target after all? She had been working on the assumption that the difference between Cathy Perkins and Zoë Helms was that they were not on the same political page. Helms had shifted all over the political spectrum, from her early liberal days to winding up a Tory. At best she was somewhere in the hazy middle. Did any of that matter any more? To Marsh, it seemed that all they did, all any of them did, was just try to stay afloat.

She tossed the biro she had been chewing onto the desk and sat up to start going through the lists in front of her. Every participant in the programme had to fill out a form before they took part. So the name of the young man should have been easy to find. But the BBC were refusing to cooperate willingly and at this point Marsh lacked the authority to apply leverage. Essentially, she was on her own. So they had been forced to resort to other methods. Facial recognition had proven inconclusive.

Marsh shuffled through the stack of papers to find a print of the audience taken from the footage. She drew a circle around the young man. There was something about him. But that was nothing more than her instincts talking. So, effectively, a dead end.

Behind her, Milo cleared his throat.

'Where are you going with this, boss?'

She swivelled her chair round to look at him.

'Don't you think it's odd?' she asked.

'What's odd?'

They had two workstations back to back over in one corner. The rest of the investigation team was scattered around the upper floor of Raven Hill police station. The number of staff had thinned out in recent months. New faces came and went with alarming regularity, but Milo and Kelly had managed to keep a hold of their little corner.

'Zoë Helms. I can't work out which side she's on, politically.'

'As much as there are clear sides any more, sure,' said Milo.

'I've been working on the assumption that Perkins' book would expose Helms.'

'Aren't both things possible? I mean, maybe they weren't that far apart on most issues.'

Marsh had spent days dredging through all the material she had dug up on Helms. She had gone back to her time at Cambridge, when she had first become active politically, organising rallies and marches. It was at university that she had met Alex Hatton. They were married just after they graduated and moved to London together. Both of them had studied law. The marriage lasted ten years until Alex left Zoë for his secretary. So far, so original. There was a Conservative seat going in some corner of Norfolk. Helms had run for it and won. In those days she had supported the war in Iraq, taking the line that it was worth any price to free the Iraqi people from the tyranny of Saddam. Marsh wasn't really up on the ins and outs of the Iraq war, other than she knew that war was generally bad for everyone except the politicians who made the decisions and kept themselves out of harm's way. Cathy Perkins took a different line. Marsh had clicked through a range of published pieces, all of them vehement denouncements of the war and those who defended it – politicians and, as she put it, 'pseudo-liberal intellectuals'. Perkins had started out as an activist for the Socialist Workers Party while still a teenager in Sheffield and had been arrested on a number of protests. She joined the Stop the War coalition and had signed a petition for Tony Blair and Jack Straw to be tried as war criminals. Hard to imagine two more different people getting together. The television debate showed Helms had moderated her position, which was around the time when she and Perkins had started their relationship. Somehow the two women had arrived at the point where they were on the same side. Or were they? Had Cathy Perkins been playing Helms, getting inside her head, and her bed, to research her book?

Marsh held up the printout from the television audience with the circled head on it. 'Can we cross-check this guy against known far-right organisations?'

'You sure?'

'Why not?' Marsh lifted her eyebrows. 'It looks like a set-up.'

'Well, just . . .'

'Spit it out, Milo'

'This investigation is still open, right?'

Marsh rounded on him. 'Why would you ask that?'

'No reason.' Milo cleared his throat and reached for a wine gum on his desk, trying to look casual. 'I thought it ended with the guy in the fun fair becoming toast?'

'It's a follow-up, Milo. Just dotting the i's and crossing the t's. Coffee?' she asked brightly.

'No, please.' Milo grimaced. 'I can't take any more of that stuff.' He started to turn back to his screens and then paused. 'Unless you're offering to go and fetch us a decent brew.'

'Organic, fair trade, soy milk latte?' Marsh teased, getting to her feet. 'Forget it. I don't have the time.'

As she headed over to the kitchenette, Marsh checked her messages. One from Drake asking her to trace a number plate, which reminded her of his query about Adeeb Akbar. She had delayed that one for the simple reason that sometimes she got the impression he thought she still worked for him. And also, she was still annoyed about that business with Stafford-Bryce and the list Drake had magically produced from up his sleeve. She knew that he had a tendency to keep things to himself, but this was bordering on the reckless. She needed all the help she could get and she needed it now. Something else was nagging at her, something Drake had said at Donny's flat. The kettle was old and noisy and starting to whistle. As it went through its routine, she tried to remember what it was she had been thinking of.

She returned to her station, coffee forgotten. The thing Drake had mentioned as he was leaving, about the in-house security at Magnolia Quays. She sifted back through the material on her desk, looking for references to Department K Global Security. The logo summoned the image of the men in grey clustered around the entrance to the building. All looking self-important, even though they were considerably less impressive than they imagined. She resisted the temptation to call Drake and ask what exactly he had been hinting at, preferring to see how far she could get by herself. It didn't take long to run down a couple of articles online that gave her an outline of the history beyond the little potted summary on the company website.

DKGS had started out back in the eighties as a logistics company in Malaga. *Kronnos Pro Seguridad.* They had begun safeguarding goods vehicles and expanded from there, first across Spain and then Europe. Nowadays, as the name suggested, they had gone global, with operations all around the world. A blog by a Lithuanian activist argued that the original company had links to fascism back in Franco's day. He even compared the original Kronnos logo – a winged horse with two red flashes cutting diagonally across it – to that of the Falangists. The current DKGS insignia was a simplified version of this. There were no photos of any of their operatives online, which was not surprising. Marsh picked up the phone and called their head office in Feltham. After some wrangling they promised to send over the information as soon as possible. Marsh remembered her coffee and went back to the kitchenette to finish making it. She was just pouring the water into a mug when Milo appeared holding up a waxed cup of the real stuff.

'I couldn't let you drink that poison.'

'Thanks,' she said. She hadn't even noticed him leaving.

'So, how are you getting on?'

Marsh quickly outlined what she had learned. Milo leaned over her desk to squint at the screen.

'Isn't that the same firm that does the security at Zoë Helm's house?'

'Are you sure?' Marsh began scrabbling through the paperwork, wondering why she hadn't picked up on that. Could it be that simple? She pulled up the sheet with details of Zoë Helms's household and there it was. DKGS was the company responsible for the house's security system. She sat back.

'That's it,' she said.

'What's it?' Milo asked. 'You should drink your coffee before it gets cold.'

Marsh reached for the coffee cup, her mind elsewhere. She put the cup down.

'The sports presenter who accused Mourad of breaking into her house. What was her name?'

'You mean the one whose knickers were stolen?' Milo slid back across to his desk and had the answer in a couple of deft clicks. 'Katy Gardiner.'

'Do you have the file on her report?'

'I'm looking at it. What d'you want to know?'

'Did she have a home alarm system?'

Milo scrolled down through the report. 'Yes.'

'Installed by, let me guess . . . DKGS?'

'You're psychic.'

Marsh swung round towards him. 'That's how Mourad's DNA got there.'

'Okay . . .' Milo scanned her face. 'I'm not following.'

'We've never been able to explain how Mourad's DNA wound up in Helms's bathroom.'

'Assuming he's not the killer, you mean.'

'Obviously.' Marsh scowled. 'I thought we'd established that.'

'You've established that.'

'Are you on my side, or what?'

'Sorry, just playing devil's advocate. That's what Wheeler is going to say.'

He had a point. Marsh went back. 'Okay, fair enough. Assuming Mourad was not the killer leaves open the question

296

of how his DNA got into that downstairs toilet at Helms's place.'

'Sounds better,' nodded Milo, as he sipped his coffee. 'It's getting cold,' he reminded her.

Marsh wasn't interested in coffee, but she picked up the cup anyway.

'So, the link is the security firm. They would have had access to both sites.'

'Hold on, you're saying they contaminated the crime scene on purpose? Why would they do something like that?' Milo scrunched up his nose. 'Also . . . these events were years apart. Would they keep his DNA?'

'Maybe they had a sample on record.'

'On record?' Milo was no longer convinced his partner hadn't gone off the deep end.

'What if he worked for them?'

Milo stared at her. 'I have to say, I think you're well up the conspiracy tree now.'

'Your faith is touching,' Marsh said, turning back to her screen. Milo scooted over to join her as she clicked open her email. 'DKGS promised they would send me a list of their personnel records.'

Milo scanned the same document that she had just opened. He was faster than her.

'Mourad's not on it.'

'Fuck!' Marsh slammed her fist down on the table.

'Too bad, you almost had me convinced,' said Milo, sliding back across to his own side of the workspace.

Marsh sat there in silence. She was annoyed at convincing

herself that the answer would be easy. How many times had she told herself that easy was never an option?

Taking a deep breath and a mouthful of lukewarm coffee, she returned to the DKGS files and began to flick slowly through the faces and the names. She knew she had missed something. Mourad could have worked there under a different name. The list was current. It only went back three years. The Gardiner case happened in 2014. Even if he had been working for them, Mourad wouldn't still be there after a scandal like that. The accompanying email made clear that this was all they had available. The rest was in storage on a different system. To go back further would entail all kinds of difficulties. Blah, blah. Some kind of bullshit technical smokescreen. She clicked open another document in the mail which was a warning about the legal consequences of disclosing the identities of DKGS employees whose lives and safety could be put in danger by such action, etc., etc. More bullshit. Security companies were by nature protective of their data, but Marsh felt like getting a court order to throw at them, just for the hell of it. She reached the end of the list and was about to click back to the start again when another thought occurred.

'What if it was someone else?'

'Sorry?' Milo looked round, but Marsh waved him off.

'Give me a minute. I have an idea.'

Marsh went to the beginning of the personnel list and began going back through it again, slowly. The man in the photograph had a different haircut. He was younger and rounder in the face. It was the dead eyes that gave him away. Marsh scrabbled around her desk until she found the printed snapshot taken from the television studio audience. The eyes were small and cold. Dead. It was the same man. Marsh folded her arms and thought about her next move. She scribbled the name down and handed it over to Milo, asking him to run a check. Then she reached for the phone. DS Mark Chiang was surprised to get her call.

'I assume this is some form of apology.'

'In your dreams,' replied Marsh. 'I wanted to give you a chance to save your own bacon.'

He gave a light chuckle. 'Points for audacity. I'll give you that. Now explain.'

Marsh took a deep breath. 'Okay, I know that officially we have cleared the case, but . . .'

'Let me guess,' Chiang said slowly. 'You're still not convinced that it was Mourad.'

'Officially, I'm on board. Unofficially, nowhere near.'

Marsh heard an exasperated sigh.

'What will it take to convince you?'

'Just hear me out. I just didn't buy into the idea of Helms being the target.'

'Well, you made that clear enough, though why anyone would want to kill a second-rate journalist working for a rag is beyond me.'

'Well, let's examine your theory. The reason you had your sights set on Mourad is because he fit the bill as a creep who preys on women.'

'Kelly, where are you going with this?'

'Mourad's DNA places him in Helms's home.'

'So far, so good.'

Over her shoulder Marsh saw Milo shaking his head in despair. He started a rolling motion with his index finger. She took the hint.

'Look, I just wanted to run this by you . . . to get your thoughts.'

Milo gave her a thumbs-up. Chiang had more years under his belt than she did and Marsh didn't need to be told that men tended to get a little worked up if they weren't shown the right kind of respect. No skin off her back. A little generosity could go a long way. Chiang, at least, was still listening.

'Go on.'

'What if Mourad's DNA was planted by someone.'

'Okay, next you're going to tell me Martians planned the whole thing.'

'Helms had a run-in on a television debate, *Question Time*. The man who got into it with her was a young man who just happens to have worked for DKGS, the same company that ran security on Katy Gardiner's flat.'

'Who?'

'Mourad was convicted of breaking into her home. DKGS keep their own log of DNA samples from cases they have worked.'

'Is that even legal?'

'It's a grey area. They claim it helps them to do their job.'

'Okay.' There was a long pause. 'So, you're saying someone from DKGS could have set Mourad up? Why?'

'Well, to begin with, it worked. The case was effectively shut with Mourad's death.'

There was another pause. Chiang was trying to figure out if he could possibly pass on this, or if he was obliged to act. Marsh waited. If she was wrong, Chiang would have to go straight to Pryce and that would be the end of it, the end of her. Finally, his voice came back on.

'Who's the mope?'

'Ivan Hedley,' Marsh read from Milo's note. 'We ran a quick scan and found he's linked on social media to a number of far-right chat forums.'

'Okay, you've got my attention.' Chiang was quiet, beginning to calculate what this might mean. 'We should at least talk to him.'

'That's what I was hoping you would say.'

She flashed Milo a big smile. He punched the air.

31

The one thing you could say about Dino was that he was as loyal as a sick puppy. Sitting outside the room in the ICU where Donny was being kept, Drake wondered if the name was a nod to the original Dino, Dean Martin. Some kind of homage, or did Dino actually think he bore a resemblance to Dean Martin? Maybe in a dark basement after you'd downed a few pints of limoncello, but otherwise, not so much.

Drake didn't like hospitals. Dino was moved to at least give a grudging nod when he saw him.

'Good of you to come,' he said, shaking hands as if they were distant relatives paying their respects. He gestured formally at the orange plastic seat next to him, as if inviting Drake into his private salon. They sat against the wall, drawing their feet sharply in as a stretcher squeaked by.

'How's he doing?'

'The doctors say it's fifty-fifty. They won't really know till he comes out of the coma.' Dino's thick eyebrows rose to form an arch in the middle. Drake half expected tears. 'If I ever get my hands on whoever did this . . .'

'Any ideas?'

Dino rocked his head from side to side. 'Donny was worried about a few things.'

'He mentioned Sal Ziyade.' Drake waited for confirmation. 'You think he's making a move on Donny's business?'

'People talk.' Dino sniffed loudly. 'Rumours. I mean, who can say? Personally, I don't think he was behind this.'

'You don't think, or you know for a fact?'

'It's not his style.' He craned his thick neck round to peer back at the figure in the bed. 'Not like this.'

'Right.' Drake exhaled slowly. 'So what would be his style?'

'How should I know?' Dino frowned. 'What are you saying?'

'I'm not saying anything. You're the one who said you knew his style.'

'I just said I didn't think it was him.'

'Ziyade would be the obvious place to start. I mean, there's no love lost between them, right?'

'None at all, but they were working things out. Donny said so.'

'Maybe this is Ziyade's way of working things out.' Drake jerked a thumb over his shoulder.

Dino's downturned mouth said he wasn't buying it. 'I don't believe it, and besides, Sal Ziyade is family.'

This was news to Drake. 'He's related to Donny?'

'By way of his brother Stavros, remember him? He's older than Donny. He married Gina Ziyade, against everyone's advice.'

'Gina Ziyade being . . .?'

'Sal's younger sister. She's a real piece of work.' Dino was grinding his teeth as he spoke. 'If Ziyade was behind this, I'll make him pay.'

'Maybe this is a good moment to step back and reflect.'

'What the fuck does that mean?'

'I'm just saying, I'm not sure Donny would want you to go off all half-cocked.'

While Dino mulled this over, Drake took a long look through the window of the ICU. The bed was surrounded by a battery of instruments keeping the patient alive, monitors registering his vital signs. Donny was hooked up to wires, tubes and an oxygen mask. His life force was mapped out in peaks and troughs on an electronic scanner. It was hard to tell from here what his chances were. Dino was coming to the end of his train of thought.

'He reached out,' he said finally, squeezing the words between his teeth like orange pips.

'Sal Ziyade?'

A slight nod. 'Said he doesn't want a war. Says this is bad for business.'

'Uh huh, but you don't believe him?'

Dino shrugged, staring at the floor.

'Why would he say he doesn't want a war and then toss Donny off the balcony?' Drake's question produced another noncommittal shrug. 'Sends a pretty strong message.'

'That's a declaration of war, right there, innit?'

'So, who else could it be?'

'There are people coming up all the time.' Dino shrugged. 'You don't see them coming.'

'People like Berat Aslan?'

Dino's eyes narrowed. 'You know him?'

'I've heard he's getting restless.'

'People talk.' Dino shrugged again.

'Have you spoken to Ziyade's people?'

'Me?' Dino made it sound as if there were a dozen other candidates in the room. 'That's not my business. I work for Donny.'

'You said he reached out.'

Thoughts seemed to clunk around in Dino's head, trying to sort themselves out into some kind of coherent order. It was a tough position. Usually Donny did all the thinking. Dino just did what he was told. This whole thinking things out thing was new to him.

'Donny's been around a while. There must be others after his crown, aside from Ziyade, I mean?'

'There are plenty,' Dino nodded confidently. 'You can't afford to look weak. They come after you if they smell blood.'

'Are you saying Donny was looking weak?'

'Not weak, no.' Dino's head shook vigorously. 'Well, I mean, he's had a lot on his mind recently, all these worries with his wife and kids . . .'

'Sure. He's been wanting to get out.'

Dino looked glum. 'People weren't too happy about that, to be honest.'

'His people? Anyone specific?'

'No, you know, I'm just talking generally.'

'Sure.'

Drake glanced back again at the figure in the bed. Fifty-fifty meant that the doctors had no idea if he was going to make it or not. It was a coin toss. And even if he did there was no way of knowing if he would be able to walk, string a sentence together.

'Donny's old school,' Dino was saying.

'Meaning?'

'Meaning there were things he didn't want to get into.'

'Such as?'

'Trafficking, people . . .' Dino looked up and down the hallway. 'And kids.'

Drake didn't need reminding.

'Hamid Balushi.'

Dino nodded. 'He did Goran's dirty work back in the day. He was an animal.'

'According to Donny, Sal Ziyade is going after his business.'

'I always told him that was a mistake.' Dino, the sage advisor. 'You start giving things away and people start to get ideas.'

'Right.' Drake wondered if Dino was getting ideas above his station. 'Still, with this coming after that thing over in Freetown?'

'The kids on the scooter?' Dino was shaking his head. 'They were going into business for themselves, I heard. Some local hotshot. It happens from time to time. Never comes to anything.'

'So it was nothing to do with Ziyade?'

'Not his style.' Dino was adamant. 'Ziyade's too upmarket. Likes selling cocaine to beautiful rich kids up in Knightsbridge.

'Which reminds me, I almost forgot.' Dino reached into his leather jacket and pulled out a fat envelope. 'I was supposed to give you this when Donny took a dive.'

Drake took the envelope and looked inside to find bundles of notes.

'Ten big ones,' said Dino, reading his mind. 'There's more where that came from.' Dino paused. 'He wants you to talk to Sal Ziyade.'

'Why would Ziyade talk to me?'

'Because you're neutral. You don't work for Donny, not directly. I can't do it, because I work for Donny in a certain capacity. Someone should find out what he has to say. It would be better if it was someone neutral.'

'Donny wants to make peace with Ziyade? You're sure about this?'

'It's what he told me before, you know, this . . .' Dino jerked a thumb over his shoulder.

'I'm curious,' Drake said, finally. 'How'd you get that name? You don't look like Dean Martin.'

Dino frowned. 'No. Not Dean Martin. Dino da Laurentis.' The eyebrows tightened further when he saw the incomprehension on Drake's face. 'You know, like the famous movie producer?'

'Doesn't ring any bells.'

'Well, my mum was a big film buff. She knew everything: actors, directors, who won an Oscar, who was nominated, where they came from. A lot of them were Eastern European. Did you know that?'

'No, actually I didn't.'

'Sure.' Dino warmed to his task. 'Take Kirk Douglas, he was Russian. Lauren Bacall was Romanian.'

'I didn't know that.'

'Well, that's the kind of thing Mum loved. She said, it's all show business. Nothing is what it seems. And she was right.' Dino was grinning now. 'Show business.'

'If I agree to speak to Ziyade, maybe you can help me with something? Berat Aslan. What can you tell me about him?'

Dino's smile faded. 'He's a sleaze bag, like a rat. He scurries all over. Why the interest?'

'It's connected to a case I'm working on. Where do I find him?'

'He has a place.' Dino nodded. 'A cheap hotel. The Jonson.'

'The Jonson?'

'Yeah, named after the dick he is.' Dino chuckled at his own humour. 'The Ben Jonson Hotel.'

32

Frodo was hiding something. That much was clear from his fidgeting around the kitchen of the Nest. The more he tried to hide it the more obvious he made it.

'Look,' Crane said. 'I've had a long day, so please, stop wasting my time and tell me where she went.'

Frodo stared at her. He wasn't going to make this easy.

The day had begun with her spending an hour waiting outside the supermarket as agreed only for Selina not to show. No great surprise, but rather something she had been anticipating from the start of their 'collaboration'. Selina had been a reluctant partner at best. True that the animosity towards Magid Bouallem's new young wife had provided some motivation, but Crane's feeling about Selina was that she was the kind of person whose convictions changed according to which way she thought the wind was blowing. She skated through life switching from one lane to another, unable to make up her mind about what she really wanted, which is how she had got herself into all of this in the first place. It wasn't that she felt any great conviction about anything, least of all religion. Islam just happened to come along at the right time. It answered some call to be rebellious, different. Maybe she was inspired by something she read about, or saw on YouTube. To a girl from a conventional, middle-class home, Islam must have seemed about as radical as you could get, along with an added dash of Oriental mystique. Only time and circumstance had changed what looked like a way out into a trap. Now, she was bored of the charade.

Drake called as she was about to start the car.

'How are you getting on?'

'She's a no-show,' Crane sighed. 'I may have lost her. How are things at your end?'

'Hard to tell. I seem to be making progress, but it's slow.'

'Any mention of Jason?'

'Nothing concrete. Bouallem claims not to remember him, but I'm pretty sure he's lying. I'm going to have another crack at him. The key here is Adeeb Akbar. I tried to get Kelly to check if Counter Terrorism has anything on him, but I think she's annoyed with me.'

'It had to happen. Want me to run it by Mason?'

'Why not?' said Drake reluctantly.

Crane pulled out of the supermarket car park and started roaming the streets. She listened to Drake as she drove by the café where she and Selina had sat. She circled the Common. Nothing.

'Also, I was handed a retainer by one of Donny's lieutenants. He says Donny told him to do it before he went for a dive.'

'Money for what?'

'Donny seems to think I can get through to Sal Ziyade.'

'A word to the wise, Cal, don't get yourself into something you can't get out of.'

'Don't worry, I have no intention of doing that. What should I do with the money?'

'Keep it for the moment. We'll figure out how far we want to go with this later on.'

'That's kind of how I see it,' said Drake. 'I want to give it a day or two more with these clowns and then I think we can officially call this a dead end.'

Which would have meshed with Crane's feelings at this point. She had been about to give up, crawling along the High Street ready to call it a day and head over to Shepherd's Bush, when she spotted Selina. It came as a surprise, never having expected to see Selina coming out of a pub. A brief glimpse of the side of her face. Freed of headscarf and wearing a fawn-coloured raincoat and jeans.

'Oh, shit!' Crane had to turn her head to be sure. She stamped on the brakes and pulled around the next corner to park. 'I'm going to have to call you back. I've spotted her.'

'Okay, keep me posted.'

'Likewise.'

In the mirror Crane watched Selina stumble over a kerb and almost come to grief in front of a black cab. Parking on double red lines, Crane jumped out of the car and ran to catch up with her. She put out a hand and Selina spun round, swinging wildly. Her face was almost unrecognisable, her eyes glazed.

'Hey, don't touch me!'

'Selina, it's me!'

The bloodshot eyes struggled to focus, then she swore and turned away. Crane took her by the elbow and led to a nearby café, where she ordered coffee for both of them.

'I think I'm going to be sick.' Selina clutched a hand to her mouth and rushed for the toilet.

'Great,' muttered Crane.

She was gone for a good ten minutes. Crane was worried about the car. She was about to go and drag Selina out when the door opened and she stumbled into view. Her face was ashen and her hair hung in damp strands around her chin, but she seemed to have recovered somewhat. Crane picked up the coffees and led her back out to the car, where a warden was writing up a ticket.

'You're lucky it's still here.'

Crane thanked him profusely and managed to get Selina installed. They drove in silence to a quiet spot next to a large chestnut tree. Crane switched off the engine and turned to her.

'What's going on, Selina?'

'I just . . . I can't deal with this any more.'

'You mean, the situation with Ayesha?'

'I don't care about that stupid bitch. She can have him, as far as I'm concerned.'

Crane handed her the coffee and Selina stopped shaking her head to focus on lifting the cup to her lips without spilling anything. She managed a couple of sips before closing her eyes with a groan. 'How am I going to get out of this mess?'

'That depends on you.'

Selina's eyes snapped opened. 'I shouldn't even be talking to you,' she said. She looked pale and scared. The coffee cup shook in her hands.

'Drink some more. You need to get sober before I can take you home.'

Selina took another sip.

'Listen to me, right now I'm the only person capable of helping you.'

'How do I know I can trust you?'

'You have no choice, Selina.'

'You think I set Jason up, that I sent him to Syria.'

'Didn't you?'

'No!' Selina winced, then took another sip of coffee to calm herself. 'I told him what he wanted to hear,' she said quietly. 'That's the truth of it.'

'How did he get there? Who arranged it?'

'I don't know.'

'Come on, Selina. You can do better than that. No way a small-town boy like Jason could have done it alone. He had to have help.' Selina wiped her eyes with the back of her hand. Her nails were bitten to the quick. Crane reached out to pull her hand away from her mouth. 'You want custody of your son, right? Then you have to give me something.'

'How can I trust you?'

'You don't have a choice.'

'Aren't you required to tell the police everything?'

Crane shook her head. 'My first loyalty is to my clients. The Spencers in this case. Of course, if I learn that somebody's life is endangered then I am obliged to inform the authorities.'

Crane reached over for the other woman's hand. 'I can't help you if you don't level with me.'

'It's not Magid.' Selina pulled her hand free and chewed on the skin of her thumb. 'He talks a big game but at the end of the day he does nothing but distribute money.'

'Whose money?'

'I don't know. It comes from donors, people in the Gulf. Rich Arabs. Pakistanis. That's all he would tell me.'

'So he distributes money, and some of it is used to transport people in and out of the country.'

Selina nodded.

'There's a guy. A real creep. Magid knows him. He brings people in. Magid gets a commission.'

'What kind of people?'

'Women, mostly. From Turkey, I think.'

'And you know this how?'

'I've heard them talking on the phone.'

'And they can get people out as well?'

Selina nodded.

'What did you mean when you said it was mostly women?'

'They make them work for them.' Selina shrugged. 'You know . . .'

'You mean prostitution?' Crane stared out of the window. 'How does that square with spreading Islam?'

'Causing social chaos. Bringing down the kuffars with their own medicine. That's the unbelievers.'

'I know what kuffar means,' said Crane quietly.

'Of course you do.' Selina looked into her cup. 'They have a place. A place they keep them when they first arrive.' She had given up drinking her coffee. Now she just gripped the cup as if it might run away. 'That's where they break them in.'

Crane wondered how long she'd known, been storing this up inside her.

'You know where this place is?'

'Somewhere off the North Circular. A hotel.' Her eyes were fixed on her hands. 'I . . . I think they bring in kids as well.'

Crane felt the air go out of her lungs. 'Okay, I really need you to tell me everything you know.'

'I've already told you everything,' whined Selina.

'Listen to me. If it comes out that you are in any way implicated in all this, you can kiss your son goodbye as he's taken into care.'

'No, don't say that.' Selina began to cry. She rubbed her eyes with her sleeve.

'Tell me about the creep. What's his name?'

'I don't know. I never met him.' Selina rubbed a hand over her face. 'I need more coffee.'

'You can have more coffee as soon as you tell me. Do yourself a favour, Selina. Try to remember.'

'Why is he so important?' Selina asked.

'You've just described a human-trafficking ring that involves prostitution and the abuse of minors. I would be an accessory if I didn't take this to the police.'

'My life is such a fuck-up!' Selina whined softly. Her whole body was trembling so hard Crane could feel it. A part of her felt sorry for the other woman. Another part knew that if she didn't keep the pressure on a lot more people could get hurt.

'I need more, Selina.'

'I've told you, I don't know!' Selina's voice rose.

'Well, start thinking. Anything that will lead me to Jason. If he had come back he would have tried to contact you, right?'

'Maybe.' Selina turned her head to stare out of the window. 'I think he was angry with me.'

'Because you led him on?'

'This was years ago. I thought it was what he wanted.' She corrected herself. 'No, that's not true. I believed I was doing the right thing.'

'For Magid, for Islam?'

'Maybe . . .' She threw up her hands. 'I can't explain it. I wanted to push him.'

'Did you ever hear from him when he was over there?'

'He posted some pictures on Instagram, said he was married.' Selina lifted her shoulders. 'I thought it was to make me jealous. As if I care.'

Crane heard the regret in the other woman's voice and resisted the twinge of sympathy she felt. Everybody was capable of making bad decisions and Selina was going to be living with hers for some time to come.

'Let's go back to this mystery man of yours, Magid's friend, the creep.'

'Yes, but I don't even know his real name.'

'What do you mean, his real name?'

'They call him Aslan. You know, like in the book?'

'That's good.' Crane reached out and placed her hand over Selina's. 'What about Magid's involvement? How does that work?'

'Well, I mean, he's just a front.' Selina tried to gather her thoughts. 'Because he runs the centre. He gets grants and so on. A lot of things are in his name.'

'You mean like cultural centres?'

'Yes, but also other things like . . . I don't know, youth clubs, shelters.'

'Shelters?' asked Crane. 'What shelters?'

Which was how, two hours later, she found herself back in the kitchen of the Nest in Shepherd's Bush. She had delivered Selina home and promised that she would arrange somewhere for her to stay. She suspected Magid Bouallem would not object too strenuously, that he might even be glad to be rid of Selina.

Her immediate problem, however, was to persuade Frodo to cooperate. Unlike Selina, he wasn't scared. On the contrary, he liked his position of authority. A small man in a small office, but for the moment he was in charge. He relished the feeling. Today the shelter was busy with people coming and going. Frodo, with his wispy beard, would break off their conversation from time to time to get up and deal with something. This seemed mostly to involve telling people what not to do. That's not how the toaster works. This one is for the organic, not plastic. Everyone has to tidy up behind them. It was a losing battle. Crane surmised fairly quickly that it wasn't that they didn't understand, it was that they recognised his weakness, even enjoyed winding him up. A small man with no sense of his own limitations. Crane had the sense of him as a moth fluttering about in the grey light surrounding the darkness that was driving all of this. Women

317

like Selina got themselves caught up in these webs of chaos formed by the confusion of such men. She wondered if Nahda was the same.

'You were supposed to be protecting her,' she said when she had his attention again.

'It's not as simple as that.'

'Nothing ever is.'

'What are you saying?' He was trying to roll himself a joint, trying to look cool as he did it and failing.

'I'm asking what you're doing here? You said you took it over because of your mother. Was she one of them? A woman who had nowhere to go? Is that your story?'

'What's your point?' His fingers weren't working today. He threw down the joint in frustration.

'Why work in this place if you don't want to make a difference? You should be protecting women like Nahda.'

'You don't understand.'

'You wouldn't believe the number of times I hear men telling me I don't understand.'

'It's not that easy.' Frodo was adamant. 'What am I supposed to do? I can't stand up to them.'

'Stand up to whom?'

'Them.' Frodo gestured, waving a hand at the window at the world at large.

'Sorry, but you're going to have to do better than that.'

He stared at her dully as he took up the joint again, ran his tongue along the paper and twisted it. The end result looked like a dead, wrinkled worm. His disappointment showed. He couldn't even bring himself to light it.

'Are you telling me that you don't get some kind of kick out of this?'

'How do you mean?' He tried lighting the joint but it wouldn't catch.

'I mean, favours. Do you get favours from them?' Crane held his gaze. 'Is that it? You give them a few scare stories about them being taken away and you get what you want?' Frodo was silent. 'What if we were to get social services in here to conduct a few interviews?'

He got halfway to a grin before it folded on him. 'You wouldn't.'

'Don't bet on it. I've got a lot of contacts. We can do it discreetly, with promises of anonymity.'

Frodo looked unhappy.

'I had no choice. I had to hand her over.' He set down the lighter. 'She owes them money.'

'The people who brought her in?' He gave a reluctant nod. 'And who are they?'

'People. They're just people. Not monsters.'

'People? Like you? I get it, Frodo.' Crane gestured at the joint. 'They get you what you need. Some dope. A few pills to keep you happy, right? And then there are the women . . .' She leaned forward. 'But let's be clear, they are trafficking women and children. These are not people.'

Frodo bowed his head and flicked his lighter a couple of times, without effect. Crane thumped a fist on the table.

'Cut the crap, Frodo. She came here seeking shelter and you called them to let them know.'

'I have a condition,' he stammered. 'I've been in and out of institutions. This is the only stuff that works. Keeps me mellow. I can't go back. I just can't.'

'Well, my heart bleeds. That might lighten your sentence, but you'd still get jail time.'

He lifted the joint and flicked the lighter a couple of times without result. Crane leaned over him.

'Where? Where did they take her?'

Lighter and joint clattered to the table. 'I can't . . . You can't let them know I told you.'

'You don't seem to understand.' Crane looked him in the eye. 'We're way beyond the point where you can try to strike a bargain.'

33

Drake had worked undercover more than once. Experience had taught him that there always came a time when you have to take a chance and step out of your comfort zone. You risked blowing your cover, exposing yourself and others to danger. And you were never really sure you'd made the right move until you saw the results. But there was no other way.

His most extensive period was playing a minor drug dealer trying to infiltrate Goran Malevich's organisation. They had been coming back to him recently, memories of that time, and just how hard it had been to separate his real self from his cover story. To be effective you had to live inside the skin of the identity you were creating, the person you were pretending to be. That time it had come easy to him, maybe because there wasn't all that much in his ordinary life to go back to. Everything lay ahead. This time felt different, perhaps because all of this, the group of disenfranchised young men, the faith, was closer to home, closer to something that he had once held dear. He had gone through his own cycle of radicalisation as a teenager. Back then there was nothing he wanted more than a chance to prove his faith through martyrdom. That felt so far away from where he was now he had trouble believing it had really been him, but it was.

He had warned Crane that Bouallem might turn on Selina. Drake suspected that his digging might have raised doubts in the other man's mind. Not much they could do about that, but better to be ready for whatever might come. After that he poured himself a couple of rums over the usual limit and slept badly. The next morning he was woken early by a call from Bouallem passing on a message. Adeeb was renovating a flat and he had put in a good word. Adeeb had consented to allow him to work.

'I told him you were good with your hands, so you'd better not let me down.'

An hour later found him standing on a street corner in Clapham Junction, when a battered white van pulled up and the side door slid open.

'Salaam aleikum, brother!' A beaming Slimany put out a hand to pull Drake inside. They all sat on the floor with their backs to the walls, separated by boxes of tools and sheets of plywood, pipes and a bathroom sink. He'd expected Adeeb to be in the front, but Kaseem was driving. Drake didn't know him well, had never spoken to him, but knew he was a student in his twenties.

The flat was in Freetown. Drake gave no indication that he knew the area, that he had even lived there for a time, or that his mother had died there. The less everyone knew about him the less chance there was of them uncovering his true identity. The flat itself was on one of the north-west blocks, an area Drake knew well. They parked in one of the tunnel bays between blocks. The kind of spot, Drake knew, that was a magnet for idle kids. This van wouldn't be recognised and certainly wouldn't have the protection of Wynstan's limousine. He said nothing.

Upstairs, Adeeb met them at the door dressed in a set of disposable coveralls and a face mask.

'What's with the outfit, bro?' Kaseem joked. 'You the first Muslim superhero, or what?'

He and Slimany cracked up at that, high fiving and clutching their ribs. It struck Drake again just how immature they were. They were kids at heart. The centre was a progression of sorts from hanging around bus stops catcalling and messing with other kids. A means of trying to make something of themselves. One of the few avenues they saw open to them. Adeeb appeared not to be tickled. It turned out he was quite the hypochondriac. He took off the mask and immediately began sneezing.

'You never know what's in these walls,' he said, wiping plaster from his face. His eyes stood out as dark and bloodshot. He hadn't remembered to get goggles.

'What difference does it make?' Kaseem shot back. 'You'll be the first shaheed to die of abestosis.'

'That's not what it's called,' objected Slimany.

'What are you talking about?'

'The thing, the sickness you're talking about is something else.'

Adeeb finally lost patience and marched off. Drake followed him down the hallway.

The rooms on either side were bare of furniture. They appeared to have been stripped down. The windows were covered with brown paper. Drake was reminded of another flat he'd seen a few years ago. On a couple of doors there were heavy-duty bolts, or hasps. When he reached the end of the hall, Drake found himself in a long room. Adeeb stood in the middle. He was holding a circular buzz saw and was about to cut through another sheet of drywall partition. Catching sight of Drake he lowered the power tool.

'What is this place?' Drake asked casually. It looked as if the room had been divided into little compartments.

'What it is, right, is none of your business. You're only here to help, okay?'

'Sure,' shrugged Drake. He thought about not pressing the point, and then he decided to go ahead anyway. 'I mean, it looks like people were locked up in these rooms.'

'What's the matter with you, bro?' Adeeb demanded angrily. 'Did I not just tell you to mind your own business?'

'Yeah, I mean, I was just asking.'

'Well, do yourself a favour. Don't. Start by clearing this stuff up. There's some old plastic sacks in the hall.'

'Don't I get a mask?'

'Just . . . you know, use your shirt or something.'

Adeeb turned to the partition and squeezed the trigger. The high-pitched whine put paid to any further conversation. The saw's teeth dug in, sending a spray of white gypsum powder into the air. Drake stripped off his T-shirt and tied it round his face before putting his sweatshirt back on. He managed to find a pair of gloves and spent the next hour shovelling debris into the slippery sacks and setting them by the door ready for taking down to the container in the yard. As he moved around the flat Drake wondered who had been kept here and why. He found a blue ribbon choked with grey dust in among the rubble and then a tooth, tucked them both into his pocket.

He went down with a couple of sacks that were heavy and hard to carry. If they had done this properly they would have set up a chute and dropped everything straight off the walkway into the container, but Adeeb wasn't organised that way. This was amateur hour.

When he got back up to the flat he heard a shout coming from the living room. Slimany and Kaseem had found a television set. They had plugged it in and switched it on. Drake leaned in the doorway. On the screen a huge gorilla was holding a blonde woman in his palm, stroking her with the tip of his finger, which conveniently dislodged her top. The woman scrambled to cover herself. Kaseem chuckled quietly to himself. They were eating tortilla chips from a packet they'd brought with them.

'What is this?' Drake asked.

'Old movie,' said Slimany, offering the chips. Drake shook his head.

'It's great,' nodded Kaseem. 'Have you not seen it? It's fab. At the end, right, he climbs the Twin Towers. Prophetic, innit?'

'How's that?' asked Drake.

'Well, it was a sign, like. You know, how the Twin Towers symbolised capitalism?'

Drake looked sceptical. 'Serious? From this film?'

'Yeah, bro. Believe it.' Kaseem spoke with a northern accent. He made everything sound as if it were unquestionable fact.

'A sign,' nodded Slimany. 'Everybody knows that.'

'This was Osama Bin Laden's favourite,' declared Kaseem. 'You din't know that?'

'No,' said Drake. 'I did not know that.'

'Well, it's a fact. I can't believe you din't know that.'

The two men fell silent as the action shifted to New York, and true to Kaseem's account, the gigantic gorilla became transfixed by the full moon in the night sky framed by the silhouette of the two towers.

'The great Sheikh Allah Yarhamu used to love this film,' murmured Kaseem.

Drake would have liked to know exactly how he knew this, but he didn't want to labour the point.

'*King Kong*,' Slimany said.

'You know why they call him that?' Kaseem asked, a leering grin on his face, tortilla chips flaked around the corners of his mouth. 'On account of he's got this huge dick.' That amused both of them no end. They chuckled away like naughty schoolboys. Drake was silent. He recognised the mindset. A direct line connecting immaturity to martrydom by way of devotion. Replace knowledge with superstition, magical thinking. Limited understanding armed with total, unquestioning loyalty. Wasn't that how all fanatics were created? Was that what linked Hitler Youth, the Khmer Rouge, Isis?

'What was this place used for?'

The other two were still staring at the screen. Slimany managed to tear his eyes away.

'It's like a hotel, a hostel. You know, people passing through?'

'What kind of people?' Drake pressed.

'Just, you know, people who have to stay somewhere.'

Kaseem hissed for them to be quiet. The giant ape was scaling the tower. Some creaky old special effects. The blonde woman peered out from inside the hairy fist. Kaseem grunted his approval.

'Who runs this place?'

'What?' Slimany glanced up at Drake.

'You askin a lot of questions, bro,' said Kaseem, without taking his eyes off the screen.

'Does Imam Magid know what happens here?'

'What's going on here?' Adeeb stood in the doorway. 'We're not here to watch pornography.'

'It's *King Kong*,' explained Slimany.

'I don't care what it is. We're here to work, so get to it,' said Adeeb. He kicked a crowbar and a sledgehammer across the floor. 'Switch that shit off.' Kassem and Slimany scrambled to their feet. Drake made to follow but Adeeb put a hand out to stop him.

'Still asking questions?'

'I'm just curious.'

'Stop sticking your nose where it don't belong.' Adeeb held out a hammer and chisel. 'Clear the bathroom tiles.'

Drake was about to respond when the other man's phone rang. Adeeb waved Drake towards the bathroom as he answered.

'Be down in two,' Drake heard him say. Placing hammer and

chisel on the floor, Drake picked up the last sack of debris, then waited thirty seconds before going after him. He followed along the gallery to the stairwell, leaning over the side to see the top of Adeeb's head. The stairs came out on the connecting walkway that led across the east side of the building and another stairwell. Drake stayed on the same floor and made his way out to the rear gallery. From there he had a good view of Adeeb coming out at the bottom, walking into the open. The plastic boiler suit and mask were gone. He was wearing a green bomber jacket with a kick-boxer on the back.

A large black BMW was parked in the middle of the forecourt. Drake didn't recognise the short man in the tan leather jacket who climbed out. Together the two men went behind the car, where the smaller man opened the boot. When Adeeb reappeared he was carrying a rucksack over one shoulder. Drake memorised the plate number. He wondered if this was Berat Aslan.

'Where you bin?' Kaseem asked when Drake pushed open the door to the flat.

'Just taking the last of it down before I start on the bathroom.'

'Yeah, sooner you than me, mate!' Kaseem grinned. He went off whistling tunelessly.

In the bathroom Drake set himself to work, hammering and scraping loudly, working his way round the little room. It did stink. He wasn't exaggerating on that score.

Adeeb didn't come straight back to the flat. He returned over an hour later, dropping off a bag of takeaway for their lunch before disappearing again.

'He's a busy man,' Drake mumbled, as the three of them sat around a cardboard box for a table.

'Why you so nosy?' Kaseem asked.

'I just like to know what's going on.'

'Yeah, well, drop it, right? It's not our place to ask questions.'

'Right,' Drake nodded as he reached for one of the foil wraps, which turned out to be a kebab.

'He was in the army, you know,' Slimany said.

'Fighting for the infidel. Man, that's evil.' Kaseem tutted loudly while chewing. 'You go straight to hell for that.'

'Maybe. I was a kid. It was either that or wind up in prison.'

'Which you did anyway, right?' Kaseem followed up. 'Don't make a lot of sense, if you ask me.'

'Nobody did ask you,' said Slimany.

'What?' echoed Kaseem, shocked at this comeback.

'Prison was after I came back from the war.' Drake examined the inside of his kebab before putting it aside. 'I had trouble settling down.'

'You fought in Iraq, yeah? Killing Muslims?'

'Insurgents.' Drake looked Kaseem in the eye. 'It was either us or them.'

'What kind of gun did you have?' Slimany wanted to know.

'It was something called an L85A2.'

'Fuck off!' said Kaseem. 'Why're you asking about that?'

'You ever fired a gun?' Slimany turned on him.

'No, course I haven't.'

'Well then, shut up and learn. So, what's it like?' Slimany's eyes were lit up.

'Well, the A2 had a number of problems.' Drake paused, noting that Kaseem was paying attention. 'But it's different. When you're carrying an assault rifle you feel you can do anything.'

'Fuck!' said Kaseem, as he was drawn in.

Slimany was lapping it up. 'I'd love to train with guns, but Adeeb says we're not going to need them.'

'Not going to need them for what?' asked Drake.

'Shut up!' Kaseem punched Slimany's arm. 'You stupid, or what?'

'What?' Slimany looked offended.

'Always talking. You're like an old woman.'

'I didn't say anything.'

Kaseem glowered at him. For a time they ate in silence.

'I don't see why you get angry with me,' Slimany whined. 'I just asked a question.'

'Well, don't. Just . . .' Kaseem gestured wordlessly. 'Just don't.'

'Thing is, I know I did wrong,' said Drake after a beat. 'That's why I'd like to make amends.'

'How do you mean?' Kaseem asked.

'He means jihad, don't you?'

Drake nodded at Slimany. 'That's right. Imam Magid said maybe he can connect me.'

'Are you fucking kidding me?' Kaseem was taken aback. 'He said that?'

'That's what he told me. Why, you think he doesn't have connections?'

'I dunno,' Kaseem shrugged.

They finished their lunch in silence and went back to work.

Drake spent the next couple of hours chipping away with a hammer and chisel. They only had rudimentary tools. His arms were aching and his face was covered in a film of plaster dust and sweat. It was when he reached the rear wall, behind the toilet cistern, that he found it. A sheet of rotten plywood needed pulling away. The acrid stench of it made him gag. He was in a hurry to get this over and get out of here. So much so that he almost didn't get what he was seeing when it fell out at his feet. He picked it up. Blackened by rot and mould. He brushed it off and held it up to the light. A child's rag doll.

34

I van Hedley was a twenty-eight-year-old white male. Marsh didn't have to dig far to find that he already had a fairly busy history on record. Two counts of Grievous Bodily Harm and one for possession of stolen goods. This did not seem to have posed an obstacle to his being hired by DKGS. She was glad to see that at least it raised an eyebrow as far as DS Chiang was concerned.

'Funny they never flagged any of this,' he said, glancing over the sheet she handed him.

'Well, either they are not fussy, or . . .' said Marsh as she steered.

'Or what?' Chiang looked up from Hedley's record. His hair was more unruly tonight, as if it needed washing.

'Or he's exactly the kind of person they are looking for.' She still didn't feel entirely comfortable sharing information with DS Chiang, but there didn't seem to be any other way. She'd have liked to have known more about his proximity to Pryce, about the old days when they worked vice together in Chinatown, but this was the only way forward as far as she could tell. Probably just Drake's paranoia rubbing off.

'You're talking about one of the leading security firms in the country.'

'Hey, don't shoot the messenger. I'm just laying out the facts as I see them.'

'You're doing more than that.' Chiang stared grimly out of the window at the strip of shops and takeaway joints. 'Okay, so what more do we know about DKGS? What's the connection to Zoë Helms?'

'They run security on her house.' Marsh wanted to throw in the connection to Mourad's DNA and Katy Gardiner, but she thought maybe she ought to save that for later.

'So Hedley was personally involved in her home security?'

'I'm surprised you don't recognise the name. Didn't you check them out?'

'Don't rub it in, okay?' Chiang lit a cigarette, ignoring her pleas not to do so in the car.

'He was part of a team. It means he would have had access to alarm codes and so forth.'

'Exactly, then why would he break the glass in the kitchen door?'

'Misdirection,' said Marsh. 'Throw us off the scent. If he had used the codes it would have given him away.'

Chiang swore quietly under his breath.

'In her statement,' Marsh went on, 'Helms stated that she suspected a couple of times that somebody had been in the house. Things had been moved.'

'Why did this guy Hedley not come up before?' The question seemed to be directed at himself.

Marsh was beginning to feel sorry for him. 'We were focussed on Mourad, remember?' She might have said 'you', but didn't want to rub it in. Chiang was working it out for himself. 'It still ties into the idea of Helms being the target,' she offered.

'I thought you didn't buy that theory?'

Marsh shrugged. 'It's still possible that he killed Perkins intentionally. Either way, we need to speak to him.'

'Fair enough.'

Marsh had considered this eventuality and decided she could not ignore it. If Hedley had killed Perkins by accident then she could drop the theory about her book. If, on the other hand, Perkins had been the intended target this was the quickest way of making that case. Persuading Chiang to come along was a hassle, but she knew she had to have him there, whichever way it worked out.

Marsh had to admit she was impressed at how quickly he had changed his tune. If Mourad's death was due to his haste, it would not look good on his record.

Chiang was looking at her again, which made her nervous for a different reason. 'I wouldn't push your luck, Marsh. Let's talk to this guy first and see where it gets us.'

The White Lion was a dingy-looking red-brick building on a forgotten corner off the Cromwell Road. Most of the windows had been bricked in or blacked out. A flag of St George, dyed grey from years of passing traffic, was draped limply across the wall over the door. They crossed the road, damp from the rain that had been pelting down all afternoon but had now stopped.

'Looks like an interesting place,' said Marsh.

'Definitely has character,' conceded Chiang, giving the exterior the once-over.

'Perhaps it would be better if I went in first.'

'Seriously? You think I can't handle it?' He sounded more surprised than offended.

'I'm just saying.' Marsh didn't quite know how else to put it.

Chiang pushed the door open. 'I've been dealing with this lot for years, Sergeant. A sight longer than you, I imagine.'

'All right, no need to get your knickers in a twist.'

'Fine.' He let go of the door and stepped back. 'I'll tell you what. We'll play it your way. Give the woman's touch a chance. You have ten minutes, then I'm coming in.'

It was better than nothing, but it meant at least that he trusted her.

The interior of the pub was relatively quiet. The clientele were by and large male. She counted two women. One of them behind the counter, a collection of tattoos showing on her shoulders and arms through the tank top she was wearing. She looked Marsh over with a wary eye, immediately spotting her as an outsider.

'You lost, darling?'

'I was looking for someone. Ivan? Do you know him?'

'Ivan? You mean, Hedder?' The woman carried on wiping down the counter. 'You a friend of his, then?'

Most people in the White Lion were dressed informally.

Jeans, sports clothing, trainers off a market stall. In her off-the-rack suit Marsh looked out of place.

'Oh, yeah . . .' Marsh looked down at her clothes as if she'd just noticed. 'I just came from work.'

'Been working his magic, has he?'

The woman in the tank top grinned at her own joke. She sniffed as if something was off, but she couldn't decide. Finally, she tilted her head to the left.

'Try downstairs.'

Marsh had already spotted the top of a staircase in the right corner of the room against the yellowed wallpaper. She could feel the vibrations of heavy bass coming through her feet and knew that it was coming from below. Nodding her thanks, she went over. An open doorway at the bottom of the stairs was dark, lit by the regular pulse of red and blue strobes coming from within. When she got down there Marsh could see that it was a kind of club room, with a smaller bar counter and a row of little semi-circular booths along the wall. The walls were painted black and the music was loud metal. Whatever was planned for this evening, it was clearly still too early. The room was empty but for a small group of men who sat in one of the booths against the far wall. Four of them. All bore the same style. Short hair, T-shirts, jeans and boots. They were in their late twenties or early thirties. Marsh walked over to the bar on the right. A large Confederate flag was pinned up on the wall. Left of this a poster of Pepe the Frog. On the other side another flag, green with a black cross and the words 'Republic of Kekistan' written on it.

Eventually one of the men in the booth got up and came over.

'Looking for a bit of rough stuff, are we, darling?'

He wore a smug grin and had a hummingbird with an arrow through it tattooed on his neck. The music was so loud he had to lean in and yell for Marsh to hear. He smelled of beer and mothballs.

'Ivan?' Marsh asked. 'Hedder?'

'Why, you his mother?' He threw back his head and laughed. Then his eyes darted left towards the doorway she had just come through. Marsh noted the change in him and turned. DS Chiang had decided that ten minutes was way too long. He must have come in and seen she wasn't upstairs and decided to come straight down. The man with the hummingbird let out a whistle as he pushed her aside.

'Oi, you can't come in here. It's members only, mate.'

DS Chiang smiled as the man came towards him. 'I just came to collect my friend.'

Hummingbird looked back and forth between Chiang and Marsh. 'Yeah, well, she's welcome to stay, but you can hop it.' As he drew closer, the man squinted at him. 'Hold on, you a chink?'

'Chink?' Chiang looked amused. 'Isn't that a little dated?'

'That's me, mate, old-fashioned, traditional. I like things to stay the way they are.'

'The way they were, you mean, surely?' Chiang smiled.

The man frowned. He waved a hand over his shoulder at the others. Two of the men got up and came over. 'Look at what the world is coming to, boys.'

'Where'd you get that coat, then?' one of the newcomers asked.

Marsh could see that the last of the group had remained where he was, seated in the booth with his back to them.

'This?' Chiang held out the sides of his long leather coat. 'I bought it. Why?'

'Because it's mine now, hand it over.' The man held out his hand. Hummingbird grinned.

'You'd better do what he says, chink, or else.'

'Or else what?' Chiang asked.

Marsh stepped forward. 'Listen, we're just looking for Ivan Hedley.'

'Like I said, bitch, you can stay,' said Hummingbird. 'But he goes.'

'Without the coat,' added the second. He stepped towards Chiang and put out a hand to grab the jacket. Chiang moved without haste. With one hand he pinned the man's grip to his lapel. The other hand came up. It was hard to see that he had even hit him. He seemed to reach out gently and touch the man's throat. The effect was immediate. The man broke off and stumbled backwards, his free hand clutching his throat. Chiang let go of his hand. The other two men watched him disbelievingly.

'It's fucking Jackie Chan!' Hummingbird laughed.

By now Marsh had her warrant card out.

'Police! Now step out of the way.'

'Bitch! I knew it!' spat Hummingbird. But then the unexpected happened. The third man, who was the smallest of them, darted forward. There was the flash of a short blade and he let out a loud cackle.

'Got the bastard!'

Chiang stared at Marsh in disbelief before staggering backwards, one hand to his side. Even in the gloom she could see the slickness seeping through his fingers. She stretched a hand out for him as he fell away, barely aware that the men were pushing her aside. Kneeling down she tried to call for help. She looked up as the fourth man went by, the one who had remained in the booth with his back to her. Ivan Hedley. The phone kept slipping out of her hands, which she realised were covered in blood. She put down the phone, wiped her hands on her jacket and tried again, putting the phone on speaker as she tried to apply pressure to the wound.

'Officer down, request urgent medical assistance.'

'What is the condition of the officer?'

'Stab wound. Abdomen, front left side. He's losing a lot of blood.'

'Okay, I'm passing you to a medical officer. Ambulance is on the way.'

Marsh was no longer listening. She had the jacket off and was rolling it, pressing it against the wound. Chiang was lying back.

'This is not how I expected this to go,' he gasped.

'You should have stayed in the car and kept the Bruce Lee stuff for another time.'

Chiang spoke through gritted teeth. 'Is that a veiled racial slur, or is it just me?'

'Try to be still.' Over her shoulder, Marsh saw the woman from the bar upstairs standing in the doorway. 'Hey, do you have a first aid kit?'

'What the fuck is going on here?'

'We're police officers. Bring me the first aid kit.'

The woman stared at her uncomprehendingly, then finally swore and sprinted up the stairs.

'You're not so bad, Marsh,' said Chiang.

'You're delirious. It's the loss of blood.'

'No, I mean it,' he gasped. 'I . . . underestimated you.'

'Save your energy. You're going to need it.' Marsh was struggling to keep the pressure on the wound.

'Did you see him?'

'Hedley?' Marsh nodded. 'He ducked out with the rest of them.'

'Find him.' Chiang winced. He put his hand over hers. 'Do it for me.'

'What are you talking about? You can do it yourself.'

'Not sure about that.' Chiang's smile wavered, his eyes rolling back in his head.

Half an hour later, Marsh was sitting in the car. Her hands were sticky with blood. It was all over her clothes and the steering wheel. She had tried washing it off with the remains of a bottle of water she had, but it was everywhere. She realised she was shaking. Not just her hands, but her whole body.

Ahead of her through the windscreen she could see lights flashing. The ambulance had headed off but the uniforms were milling around. DS Bishop was in there with his men taking statements. She had been staring at the lights for ten minutes without moving. She was remembering the time she was stabbed. Some two years ago now, with Cal, in pursuit of a suspect in the Magnolia Quays case. Everything seemed to lead back to there. She would wind up like him if she didn't watch it.

There was a knock at the window and Marsh turned to find the last person she wanted to see: DCI Pryce. He stepped away and waited for her to push the door open and climb out. She stood there swaying in front of him.

'DS Marsh, would you mind explaining to me what the hell is going on?'

'It's my fault, sir. I persuaded DS Chiang to accompany me.'

'I gather that, but accompany you in what exactly?'

'Following up on a hunch, sir.' She didn't even have the strength to argue her case. Pryce was already shaking his head before she had finished speaking.

'I don't know what it is with you, Marsh. You have the makings of a fine career ahead of you yet you persist in pissing it away.' Pryce heaved himself up to full height. 'I have no choice but to put you on suspension.'

'I understand, sir.' Marsh felt a mixture of dismay and relief.

Pryce started to turn away and then stopped. 'I don't get it. The case is closed. The suspect died. Why were you here?'

'It was a follow-up. I thought it was important. I persuaded DS Chiang to come with me.'

Pryce made a sucking sound of impatience. 'The case is closed, Marsh. We're still dealing with the fallout from Mourad's death. Accident or not, the press still blames us. Can you imagine how it'll look if we turn around and say he was innocent?'

'All due respect, sir, but our job is to find out who murdered Cathy Perkins, not to worry about the optics.'

'Thank you, sergeant, but I'm well aware of what our duty is. I might add that in your position adding insolence to misconduct doesn't seem like a wise move.'

'Yes, sir, I mean, no, sir.' Marsh saw the upraised hand.

'I have no choice in the matter. Consider yourself on indefinite suspension, pending the investigation into what the hell happened here. Thanks to you, a fine officer is in critical condition. You'd better pray that DS Chiang pulls through.'

'Sir, I . . .'

'I'm sorry to say this, Marsh, but perhaps your promotion was a little premature.' Pryce was starting to move off, but he had more to say. 'I really hoped that you would avoid falling under Drake's influence, but it appears I was wrong.'

Marsh watched him walk away. The suspension seemed unfair. But that wasn't what annoyed her the most. What bothered her was that Pryce had made no mention of getting the people who'd done this. All he seemed to care about was their public image.

Through the windscreen Marsh saw another figure step into the alley and start walking towards her. Head down with a leather biker's jacket over her tank top, she recognised the tattooed bartender. Marsh lowered the window on the passenger side as the woman leaned down.

'Can you give me a lift? I just don't think I can stand waiting for the bus tonight.'

'Hop in,' nodded Marsh.

They drove in silence for a time. Marsh had the feeling she just had to wait. And she was right. They were stopped at a traffic light when the other woman began.

'I hate them. I mean, they come in making the same stupid jokes, laughing at people.'

'Why do you let them?'

'Not my call. I need the job. The owner is in with them. White pride, and all that crap.'

'Right. So they meet there regularly?'

The other woman wasn't really listening. She seemed to have crossed a line and wasn't planning on going back anytime soon.

'I had to make a statement. One of the officers. Young guy with acne on his face. I didn't tell him.'

'Tell him?'

'I mean, I don't have an address, but I have a telephone number.' She was holding out a scrap of paper. Marsh took it. There was a number and the word Hedder. 'They shouldn't have done that. Do you think he's going to die?'

'I hope not,' said Marsh, realising that it would be a shame for a number of reasons.

'Have you ever been stabbed?'

The question surprised Marsh. 'Actually, yes,' she said. 'It hurts like hell.'

'Just up here is fine. I can catch the Tube.' She leaned in the window as she got out, pushing her tangled hair out of her face. 'Just get the bastard.'

35

Max Stafford-Bryce was holding a stalk about two feet long that appeared to have Brussels sprouts attached to it. Drake wondered if this was some kind of hipster packaging deal. Not that he would have ever described the rotund journalist as a hipster, more like an ageing hippy.

'I've never seen them like that,' said Drake.

'It's the way nature makes them,' Stafford-Bryce explained with a withering look. He moved on, with Drake falling in behind him.

'I've never really taken a good look at these places,' Drake said, indicating the stalls around them. 'Very interesting.'

'You sound like David Attenborough. It's a farmers' market. Nothing special about it.'

'Well, maybe for you, but I don't come this way all that often. Would you mind? Only I missed breakfast.'

Stafford-Bryce looked round to see Drake making a beeline

for a falafel stall. Made with only the best organic ingredients, according to the sign, but Drake wasn't fussy.

'You're no longer with the Met,' said Stafford-Bryce while they waited.

'You've been checking up on me.'

'Seemed wise.'

'Well, you're right. A parting of the ways. Like everything else in this country, I've passed on to the private sector.'

'Shame. You were a credit to the service. That investigation in Matlock would have gone nowhere without you.'

'Kind of you to say so,' said Drake. 'Not everyone was as appreciative of my efforts.'

'So, why are you here?' Stafford-Bryce asked while they waited.

'The list I showed you.'

'Ah.' Stafford-Bryce winced as Drake reached for the hot sauce and squirted it liberally over the outsized sandwich he'd just been handed.

'I really have to start being more choosy about what I eat,' said Drake, as he paused to sink his teeth into the whole mess. 'What was I saying?'

'The list of names. Where did you get them?'

'I've been doing some digging.' Drake wiped his mouth with a napkin. 'Which one did you recognise?'

'Who says I recognised any of them?'

'Come on, Max.' Drake grinned. 'You've just been waxing lyrical about my abilities as an investigator.'

'Okay.' Stafford-Bryce came to a halt. He looked back down

the street the way they had come. 'Do you have any idea what you are dealing with?'

'That's why I came to you. I thought maybe we could help each other.'

'I don't see that happening,' said Stafford-Bryce, brusquely, before turning away.

'There's a reason you didn't let on,' said Drake, stepping in front of the other man. 'I think that you feel responsible in some way, for Cathy's death.'

'You have no idea what you are talking about.'

'Then enlighten me. Tell me why you didn't say anything. Is it because you want the story for yourself?' Drake nodded. 'That would be about right, wouldn't it? Profit from your friend's death?'

'That's unfair.'

'Humour me, Max. If Cathy was killed in a clumsy attempt to silence her, then the key lies in that book.'

'The book doesn't exist. Whoever took her laptop has it.'

'Yes, and you being her mentor would be the obvious choice.'

'We've been over this.'

'Supposing a copy were to show up.'

'Then anyone would have to be a damn fool to try and finish it.' Stafford-Bryce shoved his glasses back up his nose. 'I'm not a damn fool.'

'Perhaps not, but you are bitter.'

'You've lost me again,' said Stafford-Bryce.

'You lost your job because you were pushing a certain story.' Drake trailed after him, as the other man walked on. 'I made some calls.'

'That's what you came here to tell me?' The journalist tossed his head. 'Jesus, what a monumental waste of time.'

'Look, Max, we can't get to the bottom of this if you don't tell us what you know.'

Stafford-Bryce rounded on Drake. 'What do you think this is all about? Why do you think she was killed? There are powerful people behind this.'

'I thought you wanted to bring them to justice.'

'Oh, for god's sake, don't be so naive! These people don't get brought to justice. They slip through the bars like smoke and reappear somewhere else with another name and another company to safeguard their fortune.' Stafford-Bryce cast around. 'I need a drink.' With that he headed straight across the street at full tilt. Drake took one last bite before jettisoning the remainder of his breakfast into a bin. He watched Stafford-Bryce disappear through the entrance to a pub. By the time he'd got inside, the burly journalist had fought his way to the bar and ordered himself a pint of Guinness. He looked round as Drake joined him.

'Better make that two,' he said to the bartender.

They took the drinks to a corner. Stafford-Bryce took a long draught of beer, belching quietly.

'Everyone assumes that because I speak with a posh accent I come from a wealthy background. I don't. My father was a train driver. He and my mother worked hard and made sacrifices to send me to a fancy school so that I could talk like this.'

'So what's with the double-barrelled name?'

'I created that. Thought it would help me get ahead.'

'How did that work out?'

'The newspaper world is full of middle-class yobs who want to be treated like gentlemen. A club in St James, invitations to Royal Ascot and so forth.'

'That's what drives you?'

'Let me ask you a question.' Stafford-Bryce set down his glass. 'You were demoted and sent north to the wilds of Derbyshire because you screwed up a case and someone got killed.'

'I don't hear a question in there.'

'Don't you think that was a little over the top?'

'Maybe.'

'But you carried on. You took your punishment. You went north and came home in triumph, one serial killer under your belt, and you went back to work for them again.'

'What are you getting at?'

'It sounds foolish, I know,' Stafford-Bryce nodded. 'But I've devoted my life to exposing the hypocrisy at the heart of our society. Sometimes you have to make sacrifices for what you believe in.'

Drake studied the burly man. 'You really see yourself on some kind of crusade, don't you?'

'I wouldn't go that far.'

'You were let go because you wrote something that you shouldn't have. Something that annoyed the people upstairs, the ones who owned the paper – Jarvis Barron.'

'Barron. That's a laugh. His real name is Baranov, Yasha Baranov. Born in St Petersburg, family left for Paris during the anti-Jewish pogroms of the 1950s. Dropped out of school, went into business. He has a wide range of interests, but his main sphere is the media, a handful of papers and more recently television.' Stafford-Bryce ran a hand over his shiny head. 'The only way of holding these people to account is through exposure.'

'I assume Cathy would agree with you.'

'She believed in holding people accountable.' The journalist gazed into his glass, searching for wisdom. 'It never sticks. These people are connected. They have money, they have politicians in the palm of their hand. Those are the ones you have to go after. Bring them down and the big dogs will fall.'

'Why don't we start with you telling me what exactly you think you know?'

Stafford-Bryce looked away for a moment. 'All right. Alex Hatton. Zoë Helms's former husband. Years ago he had a drug problem and got himself into a position where he owed money to some nasty people.'

'What people?'

'The criminal kind. I'll come to that.' Stafford-Bryce swatted the question away impatiently. 'Hatton was obliged to do them favours. He became involved in pushing drug money through property purchases so that it came up clean.'

'Money laundering. This was when he was working for Clayton Navarro?'

Stafford-Bryce nodded. 'He made a tidy packet for himself in the process, and his wife. He also found himself some powerful friends, including Jarvis Barron.'

'This is what Perkins had on Zoë Helms? This is what she was writing about?'

'Among other things.'

'Where is Hatton now?'

'Drying out on some Caribbean island, I imagine. Or not.'

'How deeply was Helms involved in all this?'

'Maybe not in the actual mechanics of it, but she knew and she certainly took advantage.' A smile spread on Stafford-Bryce's face. 'She loved it. Like all small-minded people with political ambitions.' He waved an arm expansively. 'They come from little places. They have no imagination. Suddenly, they were moving up, drinking cocktails on the deck of a fancy yacht. That was the name that caught my eye on your list, by the way. Novo Elysium.'

'I thought that was the name of a company.'

'Also. One of his slip-ups, or just a touch of vanity.'

'He used the same name twice.'

'Arrogance is Jarvis Barron's modus operandi, and his Achilles heel.'

'What did Barron do for Helms?'

'The sky's the limit. He set her up, made sure the publicity was there for her. A few good articles in prime Sunday papers. A nice spin on her work. Keep her in the limelight.' Stafford-Bryce grinned. 'Control the media and you control the message.'

'How would Helms have returned the favour?' Drake asked.

'A word in the right ear. Leaning a committee his way. You don't have to go as far as putting forward bills, but that would have been the next level. Meanwhile, Helms and her ex-husband were regulars on the Barrons' social circuit. They would hobnob

350

with newspaper editors, spin doctors, lawyers and, of course, the odd visiting prime minister or president.'

'Barnaby Nathanson. Does that ring any bells?'

'Sure.' Stafford-Bryce frowned. 'Nathanson worked with Alex Hatton at Clayton Navarro. He was less discreet than Hatton and left in disgrace. Is that where you got the list from?'

'I've been trying to make sense of this for months,' said Drake. 'I thought it was tied in to Magnolia Quays and the death of my witness.'

'The business that sent you to Matlock,' nodded Stafford-Bryce. 'Well, you're right about Magnolia Quays. That whole development was riddled with inconsistencies.' Stafford-Bryce rubbed a line of sweat off his upper lip. 'What do you know about Panama?'

'The silly hat, or the funny place down in South America?'

'It's in Central America and there's nothing funny about it.'

'I'll take your word for it.'

'Panama was set up by the American banks back in 1903. Before that it belonged to Colombia. It became a focal point for financial transactions that could take place beyond the scrutiny of the law. Do you know what a shelf company is?'

'Something like a shell company?'

'No flies on you.' Stafford-Bryce drained the remainder of his pint. 'A shelf company is like a respectable old whore, if such an anachronism exists. These are companies that have been around for centuries. Old colonial entities, like the East India Company, were very much of the same ilk. They lent respectability to the plunder of countries that fell under the sway of the empire.'

351

Drake reached for his glass. He wasn't really in the mood for drinking but pretended to take a sip before putting it back on the table. Stafford-Bryce rolled his eyes.

'For christ's sake, you're going to have to do better than that.' He held out his glass. 'The next round is on you.'

Drake fetched the drinks and returned to find Stafford-Bryce muttering to himself. He had the sense that the man was in a spiral and he need to get as much as he could out of him before he went down for the count.

'We used to produce things in this country, as a nation. Nowadays everything is global. Politics is steered by the economists, not the other way around. Try to impose conditions on a company and they skip across the nearest border. So the problem facing any politician today is, how do I improve the economy when I don't control it, and the answer is, you can't. All you can do is suck up to the money men, bow to their every wish. Thatcher through Blair down to this shower of jumped-up schoolboys. We're already a long way down that road, but it's going to get a lot worse.'

'You were talking about Magnolia Quays.'

'Well, that project was a test case. You probably didn't even know that.' There was an animated tone to the journalist's voice, a rising note that could have been excitement, or hysteria.

'How do you mean, a test case?' Drake glanced around him. The pub was crowded with noisy Saturday afternoon punters, all out to alleviate the weekend boredom. For some reason his hands felt itchy, which usually meant he could feel someone watching him. The journalist's paranoia rubbing off on him perhaps.

'Questions were being asked in parliament. They were passing legislation about foreign investment in construction. Magnolia Quays was just the kind of project they were looking for. Zoë Helms was chairing a parliamentary committee. You can guess how that turned out.' Stafford-Bryce was breathing hard.

'You're saying she scuppered the committee?'

'Oh, they went through all the motions, called witnesses and examined documents, but in the end nothing came of it.' Stafford-Bryce laughed. 'Magnolia Quays was founded on dodgy money and should have been stopped in its tracks. It wasn't.'

'Can you prove that Helms benefitted personally?'

'No, of course not. Not directly, not without evidence.'

'But you think Cathy Perkins had evidence?'

'It's possible. She was tying all the threads together.' Stafford-Bryce rubbed his face. He looked exhausted. The drink probably wasn't helping. 'Now that we're clear of the EU we are no longer subject to the same scrutiny as before. We'll be free to make up our own rules, which is what they want.'

'Isn't it the job of the media, to inform people?'

'Used to be.' Stafford-Bryce's rounded bear-like shoulders gave something like a boxer's shrug. 'I'm old enough to remember the eighties, when the media barons were allowed to get away with murder. That's when it began. It's not so much a message nowadays as a wall of lies that you can't get through. Outside the EU, we no longer have access to the Europol Information System. That means we won't be notified about money being transferred across borders. Money flows by with no questions asked. A Singapore-style model for open investments and free ports would play straight into the hands of the criminal syndicates. We'll become a haven for organised crime. Hell, we already are. It's going to get worse.'

'And you're saying Zoë Helms is part of that?'

'Cathy was intrigued by Zoë for a number of reasons. One thing led to another. I don't think she knew that much about her in the beginning, but she started discovering things. About six months ago she called me up. She was very upset. She wanted to talk. Not over the phone, of course. Neither of us trusted phones. She came over and we talked long into the night.' He smiled at the memory. 'We managed to get through a couple of good bottles of red wine.' Stafford-Bryce heaved a sigh that might have been nostalgia, or regret. 'She believed that Zoë Helms was deeply involved in this whole business. A chameleon, she called her. Helms had started out as a Conservative, then switched to the Lib Dems, and then went back to the Conservatives. Her values changed. Nowadays she's blocking financial regulation and supporting the sale of arms to Saudi Arabia.' Stafford-Bryce squinted at Drake. 'The war in Yemen?'

'What about it?'

'We're selling them weapons to use on civilians, but since nine out of ten people couldn't find Yemen on a map, who cares, right?'

'How bad would the exposure be for Helms?'

'Nowadays? Who knows? It should ruin her, but people are not as outraged about politicians' misdemeanors as they once were.'

'So what's the point of all this?'

'The point is that somebody has to try.' The journalist tilted his head to one side to squint at Drake. 'Somebody has to care. We shouldn't be talking about this here.'

Drake took a sip of his beer and glanced casually over his shoulder. His feeling that someone was watching them. He saw a man, wearing a flat cap. Around forty years old, greying hair poking out from under the sides. When Drake caught his eye the man turned away.

'I'm just kicking myself for starting the ball rolling.'

'How so?' asked Drake, turning back.

'I was the one who put Cathy onto Zoë Helms.'

'When was this?'

'Six or seven years ago. She was on the rise and people were keen to court her. She was getting a lot of media exposure. Someone was clearly pushing her into the limelight.'

'Jarvis Barron?'

'He would be the obvious candidate. I mentioned it to Cathy.' He stared into his glass. 'If I'd never said anything she might be alive today.'

Drake noticed the dark discolourations spreading under the arms of the journalist's shirt. This was not just a story for him.

'What would Helms do if she found out Cathy was about to publish an exposé about her?'

'She would tell someone,' shrugged Stafford-Bryce. He thought for a second. 'Her husband.'

'Alex Hatton.'

'She goes crying to him. I made a mistake. You have to help

355

me. Alex Hatton would tell her not to worry. He would take care of everything, make a few calls.'

'He would take the story to someone else.'

'Someone who could help with these matters. With an understanding of the media and of politics, someone whose business or reputation might be harmed.'

'Someone who could arrange a killing,' said Drake.

'That too.'

Drake heaved a deep breath. 'This is where you tell me you have a copy of her book.'

Stafford-Bryce lowered his head. 'Sorry.'

'All of this is going to be hard to prove without it.'

'I'm going to find that book and I'm going to publish it. Not in my name but in hers.' Stafford-Bryce wiped a hand across his brow. 'Cathy died for this. She believed in this story.' Beads of sweat popped on the veteran journalist's forehead. It was a big forehead and he was a big man, overweight, out of breath. He was on a marathon and he seemed close to the finishing line.

'Careful there, you're starting to sound like a man with a mission.'

'I'm no idealist,' said Stafford-Bryce. 'I just can't stand the idea of the bastards getting away with it.'

'You really believe a book can bring people down?'

'Of course it can. Look at Wikileaks. Look at Snowden. People are brave. They come out and risk their lives. Cathy wanted to do something good.' Stafford-Bryce ran dry and reached for his glass only to find it empty. 'They are killing people, with their money. The wars out there. Syria, Yemen,

Libya. They allow the circumstances to move in their favour and they profit.'

'They? Who is they?'

'The rich. The oligarchs and oil princes. The criminals and the politicians who enable them, all rubbing elbows. They have to maintain the system.' Stafford-Bryce grinned. Not a happy grin. The grin of a man on the brink. 'Complete anarchy would not work in their favour. Keep the masses too busy to revolt. So they let women drive in Saudi. They give away money on game shows. They keep arms manufacturers in business. Panama was just the beginning. There are dozens more offshore locations. Dubai, the Cayman Islands, Jersey. Places that are just out of reach of our jurisdiction. Money moves through them, just as it moves through this city. It's like a well-oiled snake gliding beneath the surface. Every now and then you catch a glimpse of a shadow, or a flick of its tail, and then it's gone.' Stafford-Bryce snapped his fingers in the air.

36

Marsh's warrant card got her past the uniform at the bottom of the steps. She sprang lightly up and rang the bell, part of her suddenly wanting to get this over and done with. The door was answered by Helms herself, wearing a fancy kitchen apron with a dinner jacket ensemble printed on the front. Marsh began to explain who she was but the politician cut her off.

'Of course I know who you are. I never forget a face. You'll have to come in.'

Marsh followed her through the front room, shaking the rain from her coat and realising she was leaving wet footprints on the floorboards behind her. The desk by the window had disappeared and the rest of the furniture was covered with clear plastic sheeting.

'I'm afraid it's a terrible mess,' said Helms over her shoulder as she led the way through to the kitchen. 'I've decided to redecorate. I couldn't stand to see it.'

'I'm sure it's been a terrible shock.'

'I can't offer you a glass of wine, I suppose?' Helms asked as she went round the kitchen island. Marsh shook her head, pushing a hand through her wet hair to try and restore some dignity. To her right was a long table set with plates, glasses and candle holders. Helms read her mind. 'I know it might strike you as odd that I should be entertaining so soon after Cathy's death, but it's work. Life goes on and all that. There are people who depend on me.'

Marsh held up a hand. 'No need to explain.'

'So, how can I help you?' Helms lifted her glass of white wine. 'I assume this is to do with the investigation?'

'I'm not sure if you heard, but DS Chiang has been stabbed.'

'What?' Helms set down her glass. 'No, I didn't know. My god. That's terrible.'

'We were trying to apprehend a possible suspect. It went sideways.'

'They didn't tell me.' Helms frowned. 'When I didn't see him, I just assumed he was on leave.'

'Probably they didn't want to alarm you.'

'But I don't understand. I thought the person who killed Cathy had been apprehended, or rather there was an accident, wasn't there?'

'Yes, ma'am.' Marsh knew that she was taking a risk just by coming here, but she'd decided that time was running out for her and she didn't have a whole lot of options left. 'The death of the suspect left us with some unanswered questions.'

'Unanswered questions?'

'Yes, ma'am. In terms of motive.'

'Now I'm curious.' Helms narrowed her eyes as she took up her glass again. 'I thought it was established that I was the intended victim. He mistook Cathy for me, didn't he?'

'That is what we believed, yes.'

'Believed? As in, you no longer think that's the case?'

'I would just like to be sure.'

'But this man, the one who died, you had DNA evidence. That's what I understood, at least.'

'That is correct.' Again, Marsh found herself hesitating, suddenly wary of giving too much away. 'It's not clear how that DNA came to be in this house.'

Helms frowned, setting down the glass again and folding her arms. 'I'm afraid I don't understand. Where else could it have come from?'

'That's what I'm trying to get to the bottom of.' Marsh produced her notebook from her coat pocket. A droplet of water fell from her hair onto the page, blurring the ink, dissolving her words. 'We still haven't managed to recover Ms Perkins laptop or a copy of her work.'

'Her work?' Helms said slowly. 'Is that what you are suggesting, that Cathy was silenced because of her book?'

'We're looking into that possibility,' Marsh sniffed, looking Helms in the eye. 'Right now, we really don't know.'

'But why? Why would anyone do that?'

'The thing is, without the book we can't really say.'

'But this is absurd. You must have some idea?'

'The person we were trying to apprehend last night has links to right-wing extremists.'

Helms nodded. 'There's nothing strange about that. I get threats from right-wing nuts all the time. Comes with the territory.' Helms started to reach for her glass and then stopped herself. 'Why exactly are you here?'

'This may seem a little far-fetched and I apologise for barging in like this, but I just need some idea what she was working on.'

'I understand,' Helms smiled. 'Sticking your neck out, are you? Well, no need to apologise. I know how hard it is for a woman to get ahead. Sure you won't have that glass of wine?'

'Well, maybe just a tiny one.'

'That's more like it.' Helms reached for another glass and poured.

'So, ask away,' she said.

'You and Cathy were together. She must have talked about her work. Did she give you any idea what the book was about?'

'Nothing beyond the vague outlines, I'm afraid,' said Helms. 'Cathy was secretive about her work, always afraid someone would steal her ideas.'

'So you weren't involved in what she was writing? She never consulted you.'

'I'm not sure where you are going with this.' Helms tossed her hair. There was something sensual about her anger. It hinted at hidden depths. The carelessly untidy hair, the sharp, flashing eyes. Marsh could see how she might be seen as seductive. 'What was your name again?'

'DS Marsh, ma'am.'

'No, I mean your first name, and please stop calling me ma'am.'

'Kelly, ma— Sorry.'

Helms reached for the bottle to refill her glass, adding a drop to Marsh's on the way.

'All right, listen to me, Kelly. I am surrounded by people who are paid to do my bidding. I have personal assistants and secretaries. I spend my life listening to councillors and enterprise initiative leaders and what have you. They all tell me what they think I want to hear. I look at you and I see a woman who is not afraid of telling the truth. You must tell me what you know.'

'Fair enough.'

'That's the spirit. Have a seat and let's get to the bottom of this.' She slipped her apron off and draped it over the counter. 'My dinner guests are going to have to wait,' she smiled. 'So, how long have you been a detective?'

'Well, to be honest, this is my first big murder case.'

'Ah, well, then it's important we get this right.' Helms raised her glass. 'Here's to success.'

Marsh returned the toast, then said, 'Would it be all right to use your bathroom?'

Helms waved down the stairs behind her. 'Along the corridor to the left.'

Marsh knew exactly where it was. She walked down the five steps to the tiled floor and the narrow corridor that ran back past the utilities cupboard and the shelf with the VHS video collection. She walked slowly, her eye flitting across the titles quickly until she came to what she was looking for. *Black Narcissus.* She pulled it down and opened the box. It was empty, of course. The tape was lying in an evidence box beside her desk at Raven Hill. She tried to ignore the disappointment and made to return it to its place when she felt something move.

The flashdrive was small, flat and red, the size of a postage stamp and the thickness of a slip of cardboard. It was tucked into the spine of the box, between the plastic cover and the paper insert. She tapped the box against the side of her hand and it fell into her palm. She slipped it into her back pocket and replaced the box on the shelf. When she got back up to the kitchen Helms was sitting at the kitchen counter looking at her phone.

'I can't find anything about Officer Chiang.'

'We're keeping a media blackout on it. We didn't get the suspect, Hedley, last night.' Marsh picked up her wine glass. 'You could still be in danger.'

'I'm sure my security detail has been alerted,' Helms said, folding her arms. 'You have protocols. So tell me, why exactly did you come here? You want to know if I am in her book. Is that it?'

Marsh took a sip of wine. It was rich and fruity and didn't come out of any bargain bin.

'Are you?'

'If I am, does that make me a suspect?' Helms tilted her head to one side, peering at Marsh from under her lashes.

'I forgot that you studied law.'

'So you have been looking into me.' Helms smiled. 'Yes, I studied law. I also practiced for a number of years. I certainly know my rights.'

'I didn't come here to accuse you of anything.'

'No? But you have doubts. Do you really think I could have her killed?'

'Do you mind if I ask you a personal question?'

'Why not?' Helms leaned over to top up Marsh's glass.

'Were you in love with her?'

'In love?' Helms peered into space. 'I don't know if that's what it was. We enjoyed each other's company. We cared for one another. Isn't that enough?'

'I'm not an expert. So, convenience, but no real commitment?'

Helms threw back her head and laughed. 'You're forthright, I'll give you that.'

'Cathy was staying here, so I assume you supported her work in some way. Writing a book takes time.'

'That's true. I think both of us were clear from the outset that our first commitment was to our careers. Neither of us would expect the other to sacrifice opportunity for the other.' Helms ran a finger around the rim of her glass. 'Maybe I'm not very good at handling relationships. Cathy meant a lot to me, probably more than I told her.'

'Isn't that always the case?'

'I thought you weren't an expert?' Marsh made a throwaway gesture. Helms continued. 'I could have said more, been more. Work. It takes you away from the things you really should care about.' Her eyes lifted. 'Who have you spoken to, any of her colleagues?'

'A couple of them.' Marsh tipped her head. 'Not much help, I'm afraid. She kept it all under close wraps as far as everyone is concerned.'

'I understand. Well, if you want to know the truth, I was helping her, but only in the sense of answering her questions.' Helms gave a deep sigh. 'The fact of the matter is that the only person who really knew what the book was going to be about was Cathy herself. I'm sorry I can't be more help.'

Before Marsh could reply they heard the sound of a key in the front door. A tall, neatly dressed man wearing a raincoat over his suit came in shaking an umbrella. Under his arm he carried a case of wine. Helms laid a hand briefly on Marsh's, where it rested on the counter, as if to say we will continue this at some other time. Then she got to her feet and became business-like.

'Oh, thank you, dear,' she breezed. The transformation was instant. 'You are truly a lifesaver.'

Her laughter left the man unmoved. He was staring at Marsh. Helms said, 'Oh, this is DS Marsh. My new body-guard, DS Barnes.'

'I know who it is,' the newcomer said coldly. 'DS Marsh should not be here.'

'Whyever not? She's investigating the murder.'

'No,' Barnes shook his head. 'She's not. DS Marsh has been suspended.'

'What?' echoed Helms, turning to stare at Marsh.

'You'll have to leave,' said Barnes.

'It's okay, I'm going.' Marsh raised her hands in a gesture of surrender. She turned to Helms, an apology forming on her lips before realising the futility of it. She turned and headed for the door, with Barnes right behind her. Outside on the front step she heard Helms inside demanding answers. The rain was coming down now, cold and dark. Marsh didn't care. She walked down the steps feeling the water hitting her face. At the bottom, she turned to look back up the steps at the house and smiled to herself. It hadn't been a complete waste of time.

37

Amaia was waiting for Drake outside the Tube station in Knightsbridge. He spent twenty minutes trying to find her. The station concourse was crowded with people moving in every direction at once. He'd only ever seen her wearing an apron and here she was wearing a dress. Not just any old dress either, but something dark blue and stylish that left him feeling decidedly shabby. She'd also done something with her hair, which had been let loose into a magnificent tangle of dark curls.

'Are you still there?' Crane had been talking to him as he wandered up and down, looking for Amaia, increasingly convinced that this whole date thing was a bad idea.

'Sorry, what was that last bit?'

'Why do I get the feeling you're not really listening to me?'

'I'm supposed to be meeting someone. Only, now I'm not sure I'll recognise her.'

'Sounds like you're out of practice,' laughed Crane. 'Did you join Tinder without telling me?'

'I wouldn't dare.'

'Well, don't panic. She'll find you.'

The crowd rushed by him and Drake was forced to step aside. He pressed himself back against the wall. Drake filled Crane in on his conversation with Stafford-Bryce in the pub.

'According to him, Cathy Perkins was on the verge of exposing a number of politicians, including Helms. There seems to have been a whole lot of trading political favours for lucrative property deals and luxury holidays in exotic places going on.'

'But he says he doesn't have a copy of her book. You believe him?'

'I think so. He's suffering from a guilty conscience. Thinks it was all his fault.'

'And no news from Kelly on Adeeb and the number plate you gave her?'

'Nothing so far.'

'Well, Mason ran the name. Adeeb Akbar was on the watch list, apparently, but he was taken off. Lack of manpower.'

'So far, so familiar. How are you getting on with Selina?'

'She had a bit of a meltdown today. One thing that did help is she mentioned Aslan as the one running the sleazy side of things for Magid.'

'Okay, well, that's something. Jason hasn't made contact?'

'She claims Jason wouldn't try to reach her even if he was back in this country. According to her, the last thing she heard from him was that he had got married.'

'In Syria? A jihadi bride?' Drake was bobbing and weaving as he spoke, scanning the crowd. 'Our mystery woman with the child?'

'It's possible. It would explain her approaching the Spencers' house.'

'What if he came back before her? That might explain why she would go back to the traffickers. To find her husband.'

'Could be. I went back to our friend in Shepherd's Bush. Turns out he's been doing favours for some people.'

'The women in the shelters?'

'It's all a set-up. They use them as a way of getting people into the benefits system. Frodo would fiddle the papers and not ask any questions. He gave me an address of a hotel that I think Selina was referring to over in Romford. I'm going there tomorrow. You never know.'

'I'll come with you.'

'That might blow your cover.'

'Consider it blown. I think we're beyond that now.' Drake suddenly caught sight of Amaia. He couldn't understand why he hadn't spotted her before. She was lingering close to the wall on the other side. The way she looked around her suggested that she too was having second thoughts. As he pushed through the crowd towards her, Drake saw her turn and start moving towards the station exit.

'Either way,' Crane was saying, 'it might make sense for you to steer clear of Bouallem for the time being.'

Drake told her about the flat he'd been clearing. 'I found a child's doll.'

'Selina mentioned children,' sighed Crane. 'We really have to see this through, Cal.'

'I agree. It's more than just about finding Jason now.' Drake had lost sight of Amaia again and wanted to hang up before he lost her completely.

'Where are you exactly?'

'I'm following up on something.' Drake bumped a woman with his elbow and received an obscenity in return for his apology. 'I'm not sure where it leads.'

'Don't make this about unfinished business, Cal. That's a bad road to take.'

'Too late I'm afraid. That's where it's all leading,' said Drake, speeding up. 'Unfinished business. Zelda. Magnolia Quays. I can tie this thing up. I know it.'

'Sounds like your old obsession is back.'

'You can't solve one thing without another. There's one more thread I want to explore. I'll tell you how it goes later.'

'Listen to me, Cal. Cal?'

But he had gone. Amaia had disappeared. He looked left and right but she was nowhere to be seen. He turned back towards the lighted interior.

'There you are.'

Drake spun round to find her standing right behind him.

'I thought maybe you'd changed your mind.' She looked worried.

'No, not at all. I was just' – he held up his phone – 'my partner. I mean, work, business partner. Whatever. Shall we?'

Amaia still seemed uncertain about whether this whole date thing was a good idea. Drake was asking himself the same question. Seemed like a good idea at the time. Which they could probably carve onto his headstone.

The ground floor of the Zugag Shisha Bar & Restaurant was occupied by fashionable young things tilting their heads back for an aromatic hit from waterpipes that had lava lamps built into their base. Swirling coloured wax and low lighting gave the place a psychedelic texture. Amaia's eyes lit up.

'Wow! This place looks expensive.'

She was right; it did. A waitress with a Spanish accent appeared and within seconds she and Amaia were hitting it off like long-lost cousins. Drake trailed behind them to a booth at the back. Their table was being prepared upstairs.

'I love this place,' laughed Amaia. She aimed a quizzical look at him. 'Somehow this is really not what I expected from you.'

'What can I say?'

Not a lot really. It wasn't the kind of place Drake would ever have thought of going. Way too upmarket for him. And on a normal day he would run a mile to avoid the fashion-conscious and clearly wealthy crowd who were packed in wall to wall. Amaia didn't care. She was amused and clearly had smoked a shisha before.

'It's very popular in Spain,' she shouted, bringing her mouth close to his ear. You had to shout to be heard in this place, but it gave him a lungful of hair and perfume, which wasn't bad.

The waitress eventually arrived to show them upstairs to the restaurant, which was more upbeat in decór, with long crimson drapes over the door in the glass wall that soundproofed them from the ground floor café. A trapeze artist swung gracefully back and forth over the middle of the room, trailing long crimson ribbons. They were given a table by the wall with a view over the café below. They barely had time to look at the menu before a stern-looking man in a tuxedo appeared at their table and gave a little bow.

'Mr Ziyade would like to speak with you,' he said with a heavy accent.

'With me? Now?'

'Now.' The man nodded towards the rear of the room, where a doorway appeared to lead to the kitchen. Drake wondered how Ziyade had known he was here. He got to his feet slowly.

'I'm sorry about this. Go ahead and order some wine, I'll be right back.'

Amaia didn't seem too bothered.

'Take your time,' she said. The waitress had appeared with a tray of dips and she was examining them with a professional eye. 'I'll be fine.' She waved him off.

Drake followed the man across the room, surprised at how quickly they had spotted him. A glance up at the security cameras that were tucked high in every corner told him somebody was on their game.

A set of swing doors opened to reveal an extensive kitchen area in full motion. Drake followed the man away from the main action, slipping between rows of stainless-steel worktops and shelves, hanging pots and pans. All around orders were being shouted. Raw flame flared. Sizzling oil hissed.

Sal Ziyade was in the far corner. A broad-shouldered man of around sixty, with a hard, square face. Handsome, the way a rock is handsome. The cold angularity of his face softened by age and a scruffy beard turning grey. The salt and pepper hair was pulled back tightly from his face in a ponytail. He was busy removing the rings from his fingers. Maybe a dozen in all. Setting each one carefully next to the other in a row on the steel shelf in front of him. Drake saw a skull and cross-bones along with precious stones, ruby and turquoise, a crescent moon of silver. He looked up as Drake approached.

'We've never met before, right?'

'As far as I know.'

'Yet you know who I am.' Ziyade's accent betrayed traces of Arabic and London. 'And I you.'

'I'm honoured.'

Ziyade gave a slight bow. 'Your reputation precedes you. You speak Arabic? *Bitahky araby?*'

'Only a little, I'm afraid.' Drake shook his head. 'Very basic.'

'A shame, but no problem. We speak English, unless you prefer French?'

'English will do fine.'

Sal Ziyade slipped off his jacket and began rolling up the sleeves of his white shirt.

'Are you hungry?' he asked before answering his own question. 'I'm always hungry and I hate people cooking for me.'

'That must kill the joy of owning a restaurant,' said Drake, glancing round and meeting the flat-eyed stare of the man to his left, his face as expressionless as a dead fish on a cold slab.

'In the olden days, kings and queens had food tasters to avoid being poisoned.' Ziyade wagged a finger in the air. 'We would be wise to learn from the past.'

'Personally, I think the past is overrated.'

The man in the tuxedo disappeared silently. At the far end of the room two heavies had assumed the position, hands clasped in front of them, their backs to a big metal cabinet door. They seemed calm, as if they had witnessed this scene before. Drake wondered how it ended.

'Well, I'm afraid you are wrong, my friend. There is a lot to learn from the past.'

'Such as?'

Ziyade was moving about, gathering items up from shelves and drawers. The whole room was bright with white neon light that gleamed off stainless-steel surfaces.

'I don't have to tell you about the Middle East.' Ziyade came to a halt, his eyes fixed on Drake. 'War there has become a way of life. Twenty years it's been going on. Generations have seen nothing more than destruction. You saw it. You were there.'

'I was there.'

'Things might have turned out differently if we had paid heed to the past, don't you think?'

'I don't know. Politicians do what they think is best for them. They don't listen to much else.'

Ziyade flipped over the large slab of raw beef he was holding and sliced it dexterously with a long-bladed steel knife. He worked the blade with precision, suggesting that he had some training and not a little experience.

'I've been running restaurants for thirty years,' he said, glancing up and apparently reading Drake's mind. 'This is where I began.'

'You were talking about war,' Drake reminded him.

Ziyade nodded. 'The wars I remember from my childhood.'

He poured a stream of oil into a pan. 'Beirut in the 1970s. The Israeli invasion in 1982. Those wars somehow made sense. Old hatreds working themselves out. Nowadays war is its own logic. Nobody remembers what it's about. There's no end game, no outcome. It's as if we need to have this endless war.' He pointed the knife at the doors Drake had just come through. 'You think most people out there know what is going on in Yemen?'

'Probably not.'

'Yet this country is exporting weapons worth billions which are killing innocent people.' Ziyade shrugged. 'Tell me how that makes sense.'

'There's only so much bad news people can take.'

'War is what makes the world turn. You lost friends in Iraq, I take it?'

'Some.'

'You believe one of them killed your informant. Brodie.'

Drake felt his spine stiffen. 'How would you know about that?'

'It is my business to know things.' Ziyade beamed as he tossed chopped garlic in after the oil and rattled the pan around noisily. 'Remember, the reason we are having this chat is to avoid another war.' Resting his hands on the counter, Ziyade said, 'Donny's brother is married to my sister. If you knew my sister you would understand why I'm not interested in starting a war with her, Calil.'

'Contrary to popular belief, most murders happen within families. How do you know about Brodie and Zelda?'

'Like I said, it's my business to know things.'

'Sorry.' Drake shook his head. 'That's not going to wash. You've been in this for a while now. You and Donny, trying to outplay each other.'

'We're business rivals.'

'Tell me about that. You worked together to get rid of Goran Malevich.' Drake waited and got a shrug from Ziyade. Neither a yes nor no, more like a heavy lean towards maybe.

'Zelda was your informant.'

'She was helping me get Goran, but she must have found something else, something that somebody saw as a threat. So she was killed.'

'Seems a reasonable assumption. Like I said,' Ziyade shook the pan a little, then threw in a couple of pinches of ground pepper and salt, 'you have no real idea what you are dealing with.'

'I have a fair idea. Someone cut off her head.'

'I understand, but you are still looking too closely. You're missing the big picture.'

Ziyade reached for a bottle of expensive-looking cognac on the table behind him. He poured a liberal dose into the pan and leaned back as a thick gout of flame shot up. Then he took a long swig from the bottle. Nothing wrong with that. It was his kitchen after all. He could do what he liked.

'So, tell me, what am I doing here?'

'I thought we could help each other,' Ziyade said without looking up. 'You're no longer a cop, right?'

'What difference does that make?'

'Maybe none, maybe a lot. Once you're outside the law the lines get a little hard to see.'

Drake glanced about him. Over on the other side people were busy, moving around, calling out orders, preparing dishes. The two heavies were still leaning against the steel doors. Nobody paid any attention to Drake and Ziyade. Nobody even looked in their direction.

'You're talking in riddles.'

'I'm saying that you need to take a step back, to see all the pieces.'

'Well, the way I see it right now one of those pieces happens to be Donny Apostolis taking a dive off his balcony.'

Ziyade studied him for a long moment. 'Hand me one of those peppers, would you?'

Drake plucked a red bell pepper from the rack next him and tossed it over.

'What difference does it make who threw him off?' Ziyade shrugged. 'Donny's been looking for a reason to retire for some time now. It's what he's always wanted.'

'I'm not sure intensive care is what he had in mind.'

'Probably not.' Ziyade swept the sliced meat into the pan, tipping it to light the oil. A gout of flame shot upwards. It was warm enough for Drake to feel the heat on his face. 'Do you have children?'

'None that I'm aware of.'

That drew a faint smile. Drake regretted the comment almost as soon as he made it. It brought unwanted flippancy to the exchange.

'My wife,' Ziyade went on, 'she cares more about these things than I do. She wants our daughters to go to the best schools. To make their way through the British system.' Ziyade shrugged.

'What do I know? I do what she tells me. If she says this school is the best I don't look at the price, I say to myself, this is what we must do. You understand?'

'It's not my world.'

'For you it is different. You were born in this country. Maybe you think you belong, maybe not. Either way, for us, the ones who come from outside, these things matter.' He leaned his hands on the counter. 'The old world is gone. Nobody survives by themselves. Nowadays everything is politics. Some people don't understand that. Donny doesn't understand.' Ziyade reached up to the shelf and produced two plates. He shared the food onto them and placed one in front of Drake.

'Please, you have to try this.' Ziyade handed Drake a fork. 'All this nationalist bluster. Immigrants out. They talk as if we are still in the nineteenth century, as if the world wants to invite them back, to colonise them all over again. They sing it in their national anthem. Never be slaves, yet they expect the world to want to serve them. I've tried to make a home for myself and my family in this country. You understand?'

'If it's a refund you're after, you're talking to the wrong man,' said Drake.

'My point is that this is no longer the country they think it is. It doesn't exist. Maybe it never did. It's a fantasy built from fairy-tale books about knights and princesses in castle towers.'

'So,' Drake gestured around them, 'all of this . . .?'

'A means to an end. Respectability. I want my children to have that.'

'Take it from me, class doesn't matter so much any more.'

'It matters. In the right circles, it is everything. You have to talk the right way, dress the right way, go to the right schools, have the right friends.'

'I still don't see what any of this has to do with why you threw Donny off the balcony.'

'Please, it's my mother's recipe.' Drake obliged and picked at the food. It was good. Tender and tasty, but he had no appetite. 'You know what the spice is that I used?'

Drake tossed his fork on the counter. 'I think I've had enough of this game.'

Ziyade lowered his head and sighed, then he snapped his fingers impatiently.

Across the room the two heavies heaved their combined weight upwards and stepped away from the door they were leaning on. The one on the right snapped open the big lever. There was a hiss of air as the door opened. Ziyade gestured and the heavies stood aside. Drake followed him over. The figure hanging inside there was barely recognisable as Dino. He'd been stripped and beaten. The blood ran down over his skin in rivulets.

'In this game, as you call it,' Ziyade said, 'you always need to have one eye over your shoulder. Never trust anyone completely. Sooner or later, everyone starts to get ideas. The clever resist the temptation. The less clever don't.'

Drake couldn't tell whether Dino was still alive. His feet weren't touching the floor. His considerable weight was hanging from his wrists, which were chained to an overhead railing. But then Drake saw him twitch as Ziyade came near. His breathing started up in panic and his chest began to heave. Drake realised that Ziyade was still holding the knife. Dino tried to scream but the gag was pretty effective. Ziyade pushed the point of the blade into his shoulder. It was very sharp and went in easily. Drake watched a line turn red and start to seep down over his chest. That's where the blood was coming from, a thousand tiny cuts all over his body.

'Is this really necessary?'

Ziyade turned to look at him. 'You don't like?'

'I'm having trouble believing Dino would turn on Donny.'

'Every dog dreams of one day becoming his master.' Ziyade smiled. 'Dino has been playing his own game. Dino serves a new master.'

'What new master?'

'A man named Berat Aslan.' Ziyade tapped a finger on the point of the knife. 'Sometimes people look around them and think it's theirs for the taking. Sometimes they have to be put in their place.'

'The two cops who ran down the boys. Warren and Taylor. I thought they were working for you.'

'They were, but they got greedy. I shall deal with them.' Ziyade paused as a thought occurred to him. 'Or perhaps you would like to see them face justice?'

'I can't prove anything.'

'I have evidence. I can give it to you. Everybody wins.'

'What are you trying to prove?'

'Calil, you have to trust me.' Returning to the sink, Ziyade ran his hands and the knife under the water to wash them. He handed the knife to one of his goons in exchange for a towel that he used to wipe his hands. 'You want justice for the death of your informant. I can give you that too.'

Behind him, Drake heard Dino give a whimper as the heavy steel door swung closed again.

'I don't work for you,' said Drake.

'Not yet, perhaps, but one day, who knows?' Ziyade opened his hands skywards. 'Look around. What do you see? A nice place. We have wealthy clients. Regulars who ask me for favours. It's the way of the world. We all need help sometime.'

'Why bother about people like Dino, or any of the others?'

'I have a reputation. A man loses his reputation, he never gets it back.' Sal Ziyade tilted his head. 'This is about putting an end to the war before it gets out of hand. War can be good for business, but not this kind of war. Tell that to Donny. Now please, Calil, enjoy your evening. Order whatever you like, on the house.' Ziyade held out his hand. 'I think you will soon see that I can be a useful contact to have.'

'I wouldn't count on it,' said Drake, ignoring the hand.

Back at the table, the party was in full swing. Amaia was drinking champagne. A bottle stood in an ice bucket.

'I didn't order it,' she giggled. 'They just brought it. Compliments of the house. It seemed a shame to waste it.'

'Don't worry about it, but maybe we should leave, if you don't mind?'

Amaia was already on her feet. 'I couldn't understand what was taking you so long.'

'I know, I'm sorry. A business acquaintance. It went on longer than I thought.'

She turned on him, clearly disappointed. 'That's why we came here, is it, so you could meet someone?' She didn't wait for a reply, but was already through the door on her way downstairs. They didn't speak on the way back to south London. As he was parking the car he tried again.

'I'll make it up to you. I promise. We'll do this properly.'

'I'm not sure that's such a great idea.'

Amaia jumped out of the car and disappeared without a word.

'Nice one, Cal,' he muttered to himself as he put the car in gear and turned towards home.

He was walking up towards the front of his building when a shadow stepped out from behind the large plane tree opposite the entrance. Drake turned to see Adeeb coming towards him, pointing a finger.

'I knew there was something off about you!' he said.

Drake had barely opened his mouth to speak when he heard the screech of brakes in the road behind him. As he started to turn, someone grabbed him from behind, pinning his arms to his sides. There were three of them. They dragged Drake to the kerb, towards a dirty white van. The side door slid open and a hood was pulled down over his head. Then he was bundled inside.

38

The Ben Jonson Hotel had seen better days. It was located on a dead stretch near the aptly named Gallows Corner. The building was set back from a grey trunk road that spewed exhaust fumes as thick as fog. The white facade had turned a grubby shade of shale and the forecourt was cluttered by a logjam of plastic containers overflowing with rubbish. The sharp stench of urine hit Crane as she climbed from the car. She probably should have parked further away. Too late now.

The lobby was in a similar state of decay. Islands of concrete poked through the thinning blue carpet. The furniture was sparse. In one corner, a woman in a short purple dress and rainbow-coloured leggings sat hunched over, a phone pressed to her ear. Her eyes lifted to size up Crane as she came in before returning to her call, one hand covering her mouth as she whispered.

Behind the reception desk sat a man with a sharply receding hairline and bulging eyes, which attached themselves to Crane's breasts as she walked towards him. The lopsided tag pinned to his shirt said his name was Warsame. He was alone. She knew that because she'd seen two other men heading out to fetch lunch, just as they had the previous day.

'Help you?'

'I'm here to see Nahda.'

'No one here by that name,' Warsame said, sucking his teeth. 'You want room?' he asked hopefully.

'I don't think so. She has a small child with her.'

'Like I say, no one here like that.' He turned the broken biro he was holding over in his hands.

'That's not what Aslan told me.'

'Aslan?' Warsame sniffed. He didn't know if she was bluffing, but he wasn't going to take any chances. Aslan was not the kind of person you wanted to be on the wrong side of. 'Aslan send you?'

'Would I be here if he hadn't?'

This didn't help Warsame's confusion. The woman on the sofa over in the corner muttered something that Crane didn't catch in a language she didn't speak. Warsame responded under his breath, but the doubt was written clearly on his face.

'Room sixteen, up the stairs.' He reached under the counter to press a button to release the door. 'I call Aslan to check.'

'Tell him I said "Hi".'

'Hey, what's your name?'

The door slammed shut behind her, cutting off his protest. At this point she had to admit it would have been nice to have had Drake along, but she'd waited long enough and he wasn't answering his phone, which she imagined meant that the date had gone well last night and he had other things on his mind.

The hallway behind the reinforced firedoor was narrow and dark. The only light came through the wired glass in the door behind her and a green emergency light on the staircase to the left. It was an old building. The stairs creaked. The hall smelled musty and damp, like something had died. On the first floor a corridor led left and right. Crane followed the numbers on the right-hand side down to the end. The door was simple. Cheap plywood, grubby paint. No handle and a cheap lock that looked as though it had been fitted by the guy on the front desk. Crane knocked. There was no reply but she could hear someone moving around inside.

'Nahda?'

Whoever was inside stopped moving.

'Nahda, I'm a friend,' Crane said, switching to Arabic. 'We don't have much time. I'm here to help you.'

She waited. She wasn't sure who Warsame would be able to reach. He might, after all, have been bluffing, but if it was anyone close to Aslan she was pretty sure it wouldn't take long for them to realise something was wrong. Crane pressed her ear to the door. She could hear the sound of a garment rustling and sensed that Nahda was close.

'I'm here to help you and the boy.'

'Who are you?' came an uncertain voice.

'My name is Rayhana. The people here mean you harm. You need to trust me.'

'How can I be sure?' cried Nahda with a sob. 'I don't want to be here.'

Now, Crane could hear the sound of the child crying.

'You can come with me. But you must hurry.'

Another long silence. Crane heard the footsteps withdrawing. Another sound made her turn. The fire door slamming shut down below and now the sound of someone coming up the stairs. She rapped on the wood urgently.

'Nahda, we have to move now!'

'I can't open the door.'

'Just get ready.' Crane looked around for something to open the door with.

'Hey!'

Crane turned to face Warsame as he came up to her. He looked her up and down again.

'You cannot be here. You must leave.'

'I am leaving, but I'm taking her with me.'

'No, no.' Warsame wagged a finger in her face. 'You leave. She stays here.'

'Maybe we should ask her.'

'Ehh! You have no permission to be here. Mr Aslan is coming.'

'This woman is being held against her will. Maybe we should involve the police?' Crane reached into her pocket for her phone.

'No, no police.' Warsame put out his hand to stop her.

'Don't touch me.'

'Why?' The receptionist licked his lips. 'What will you do?'

'Just give me the keys.' Crane held out her hand. Warsame grabbed her wrist.

'I told you not to touch me,' said Crane, spinning round. She wrenched upwards and over, holding his hand in place and twisting the palm backwards. Warsame gave a squeal of pain as she forced him down. He swore. Crane kept the pressure on until he was on his back on the floor.

'The keys.'

'Let go!' yelled Warsame, clawing with his other arm to grab her.

'Sorry, but I did ask nicely.' Crane wrenched the man's wrist until she felt it snap. Warsame howled. With his other hand he held up a ring of keys. It took a moment for Crane to find the right one. By now she could hear banging from other doors in the corridor. She found the right key and opened it quickly before going for the door opposite. A girl of about fifteen appeared. Crane handed her the keys and gestured at the corridor.

'Open the rest of them.'

Behind her Nahda appeared. She was wearing a coat and holding a supermarket carrier bag. In her other arm she cradled the little boy. She was younger than Crane had expected. Crane saw the horror on her face as she grabbed the bag from her.

'Let's go,' she said.

The two of them made their way back to the stairs and down, Warsame's screams following them. The commotion was growing behind them as others were shouting and banging on the doors. Remarkably, the baby was silent now. Crane went first, leading the way. She carried the plastic bag and dragged Nahda along with her. When they reached the fire door, Crane peered through the glass. The reception area was still deserted apart from the woman in the purple dress who was staring at her. Pulling open the door, Crane pushed Nahda through.

'What are you doing?' the woman asked, getting to her feet. Crane held up a hand.

'Don't get involved.'

The woman looked towards the stairs where Warsame was screaming something from above.

'No! You cannot take her!'

Crane urged Nahda in the direction of the front door. They were almost there when the woman ran at them. Crane felt long fingernails digging into her neck. She dropped and stepped in, hitting the woman in the kidneys with her elbow.

'Bitch!' the woman screamed. Crane sent her staggering back across the floor and into the wall. There was a splintering of glass as a picture frame shattered. By then they were out through the door. Crane bundled Nahda and the little boy into the back seat and started the engine. They spun into the road, narrowly missing hitting a van and then they were on their way, the Ben Jonson Hotel just a memory shrinking in the rear-view mirror. Crane punched the redial on her phone and listened to it going to voicemail. Where was Cal?

39

When the hood was wrenched off his head, Drake found himself in a darkened room with no windows. There was no furniture other than the chair he was sitting on. The only light came through the open doorway. It took a moment, but he recognised it as the room at the end of the hallway in the flat they had been renovating. His arms ached from the position they were in and his neck hurt. Slimany stood holding the hood.

'What's going on?' Drake asked.

'Why didn't you say you was a copper?'

'I don't know, maybe because I'm not,' said Drake.

The other man stared at him open-mouthed. 'You was drinking, in a bar.'

'You saw me drinking?'

'We followed you there. How could you do that?'

'I was there to meet someone. I wasn't drinking.' Which

was technically true. Amaia had been drinking the champagne. 'It was business.'

'You was with a woman.'

'That's not haram. I did nothing wrong.' There seemed little point in keeping up the act, except that it was buying him time. Slimany was confused.

'Adeeb said—'

Drake cut him off. 'Adeeb doesn't know what he's talking about.' He tried pulling his hands apart and felt the electric flex dig into his wrists. They had left the plastic sheath on the wire, which was a blessing, but whoever had tied him up had done a thorough job. 'Come on, akhi, get me out of this.'

'No, man. This is well fucked up.' Slimany was shaking his head.

'Listen to me, okay? Adeeb is a bad person. He's had it in for me from the start. You know why?' Drake searched Slimany's face for some sign of sympathy. 'Because he's pushing drugs.'

'What you talkin about? What drugs?'

'I'm telling you. He's using you.'

'No man.' Slimany's head rocked from side to side. 'He's our murshid, our guide.'

'Your guide?' Drake was confused. 'Guide to what?'

'Jannah,' Slimany smiled. Paradise. Drake looked at him.

'He's going to get you all in trouble, Slimany. Untie me and I can explain.'

'I can't do that.' He was backing towards the door. 'It's too late. It is written.'

'You don't know what you're mixed up in. Please, listen to me.'

'Yeah, go ahead, listen to him.' Adeeb appeared in the doorway. He was wearing a grey uniform with the familiar blue and red patch on the shoulder. .

'What's this all about, Adeeb?' Drake asked.

'What it's about?' Adeeb took the hood from Slimany as he moved past him into the dark room, wrapping it around his right hand as he walked. 'It's about you, kaffir.' He spat in Drake's face. 'Traitor! Who're you working for?'

'What are you talking about?'

'That place you was at, in Knightsbridge, you know who owns that?'

'Why would I care?'

'Stop lyin!' yelled Adeeb. He stabbed a finger at Drake. 'You're working for him, yeah?'

'Working for who?'

Adeeb swore and spun in a circle before punching Drake hard across the mouth. Drake saw it coming and rolled with it. Even so, it still hurt.

'You're a copper, right?'

'Make your mind up.'

'You fucking kaffir!' Adeeb screamed, jabbing a finger at his face. Drake felt blood from his split lip running down his chin.

Slimany finally found his voice. 'Maybe we should listen to him . . .'

'Shut up!' Adeeb rounded on him. 'You're as stupid as he is! Either he's working for those Arabs, or he's a copper.'

'How . . .?' Slimany was lost. Adeeb swore again as he rounded on him.

'Why aren't you in your uniform?'

391

'I was just checking on him,' mumbled Slimany.

'I'm not police,' Drake said quietly. Adeeb turned back to him.

'I knew, I knew there was something about you. Right from the start.' Adeeb thumped a fist into his palm, getting worked up again. Turning in circles, he swung round and hit Drake again. This time on the side of his head, almost casually. It was still a hard blow.

'You're going to fucking pay for this, kaffir. You hear me!'

'I don't work for anyone.'

'You'll be begging to tell me the truth, but it'll be too late then.'

With that, Adeeb disappeared out of the room.

Alone, Drake was left to his own thoughts. He wondered what time it was. From the sounds he could make out, he estimated it was still the early hours of the morning. The uniforms worried him. He'd never heard anything about Adeeb working for DKGS, so the outfits were borrowed or stolen. The question was, what did they need them for? He had a headache and there was a constant ringing in his ear where Adeeb had hit him. He struggled with the wire that bound his wrists until he realised he was just tiring himself out and decided to save his strength.

Time went slowly. The light on the window began to change as night gave way to dawn. He closed his eyes and tried to breathe calmly, to rest. When he opened them again he could hear voices out in the hallway. Then footsteps. A man filled the doorway. Drake had seen him before. Close up, Berat Aslan was less impressive than he was ugly. He had a black scar on the right side of his face that was the size and shape of a bullet. He was short and muscular, wearing a cheap white polo shirt with a blue collar and yellow stains under a cheap leather jacket.

'What the fuck?'

'I told you,' said Adeeb. 'He's a snitch.'

'I don't care if he's the fuckin' emperor of China, he shouldn't be here!'

'He's been spying on us.'

'Hey, Bin Laden, listen to me, okay? Doesn't matter what you think you know. You get rid of him, and I mean fast. I don't want this blowin' back on me. Do I make myself clear?'

Adeeb put up a wavering smile. 'Don't worry about it. I'm going to cut him to pieces and feed him to the fish.'

'I don't care if you fuckin' stick him on a grill and eat him with hot sauce, just get rid of 'im.' Berat Aslan bit his thumbnail and spat it on the floor.

'I'm not police,' murmured Drake.

'You see?' Berat Aslan rolled his eyes. 'Even he knows this is fucked up.'

'Shut up!' Adeeb shouted.

'I wasn't talking to you.'

'Hey, fuck you!' Adeeb drew back his fist to hit him again, but Aslan stepped in.

Drake licked his lips. 'Water . . .?'

'He wants water,' Aslan chuckled. 'I'll give you water.' He reached into his pocket and produced a Stanley knife. Stepping forward he grabbed Drake's chin tightly in his left hand and twisted, pressing the thin blade to his cheek.

'How about I carve a slice out of you right here?' He held the position for a moment and then pushed Drake away and stepped back.

Slimany appeared carrying a bottle. Aslan knocked it out of his hands.

'You get one chance, then I'm cutting you. Is you or is you not police?'

'Not.'

'He's lying!' Adeeb hissed. 'He's been spying on us.'

'Just calm down, will you? I can't hear myself think,' said Aslan, turning back to Drake. 'You're working for the Arabs, is it? Ziyade, right?'

'I don't work for anyone,' muttered Drake.

'He's lyin!' Adeeb surged forward but Aslan held him back.

'Course he is. He's lying because he's more scared of them than he is of us.'

'What are we going to do with him?'

'Nothing.' Aslan had a nasty smirk on his face. 'We go ahead just as planned. After it's done, it'll be too late for anyone to stop us.' He was still chuckling to himself as he headed for the door.

Adeeb kicked Drake's leg and smiled. His eyes were glistening with excitement. 'You can't hide the truth from Allah, bro. He sees into your heart.'

'Give it a rest, will you?' Drake felt nauseous. He was afraid he was going to pass out. He felt suddenly weary, tired of people making speeches. Tired of this whole mess. Out of the corner of his eye he saw Slimany appear in the doorway, shifting from one foot to the other. Adeeb turned.

'Stop fidgetin', man. Like a little girl, you are. How can I be sure of you in the operation?'

'You know I'm true, bro.' Slimany thumped a hand to his chest in a gesture of commitment.

'Yeah? Just be sure about that.'

'You don't have to worry about me.'

'Whatever,' said Adeeb.

'What operation?' asked Drake.

Adeeb turned back to him. 'Don't worry about it, bro. Seriously. It'll all be over before you know it.' He said the words as if he'd been rehearsing them for a long time. Then smiled and hit him again and this time Drake passed out.

M arsh made her way through the high glass front of the new entrance. Ahead of her wide steps rose up to the main concourse. She recognised two of the security guards in grey DKGS uniforms standing there. Warren and Taylor. The two officers who had run down the kids on the scooter. She didn't know if they had been suspended, or if they were just moonlighting. They looked her over, but if they recognised her neither showed any sign of it.

Inside, the high roof had been partly replaced with glass sheets to bring in more light. It was busy. Over the heads of the crowd she glimpsed a golden dragon twisting in the air. Someone had decided to include Chinese New Year in today's celebrations, regardless of the fact that Marsh didn't recall there being any historical link to the Chinese community around here. Maybe that no longer mattered. She pushed her way through, edging along close to the wall. She was still hoping that Drake would show, but unless he called now she couldn't see much chance of finding him in here.

She'd lost count of the number of times she'd tried to call Cal over the last twenty-four hours. Finding Cathy Perkins' flash drive had given her new insight into Zoë Helms involvement. The book clearly wasn't complete, but there was enough there for Marsh to know that Helms was going to be badly exposed if and when it was ever published. The personal nature of the material suggested that much of the information could only have come from the intimate relationship that had sprung up between Perkins and Helms. Marsh would even go so far as to suggest that Perkins had played Helms, if not from the start, then certainly from soon after they had become romantically involved. There were details about the business connections Helms and her then husband, Alex Hatton, had cultivated over the years. Power enables power, Cathy Perkins wrote, just as surely as it corrupts. It was an acid portrayal of a woman who was drawn to power and willing to do just about anything to get ahead. It was fairly safe to say that if Helms knew what was in the book she would be furious, to put it mildly. It was a betrayal. The question remained as to whether it was enough for her to arrange to have Perkins killed. It seemed extreme. Surely someone in Helms's position could have found a more elegant way, an easier way, to short-circuit the book's publication?

In the book, Perkins outlined how close the relationship was between Zoë Helms, Alex Hatton and media mogul Jarvis Barron. If Helms had suspected that her lover was working on a book to undermine her, where would she have gone? Barron was the obvious choice. Barron could lean on the publishers directly. More to the point, he could use the outlets he owned – papers, television and talk radio – to discredit Perkins' book before it even saw the light of day.

Barron was as rich and powerful as they come. Friend and mentor to prime ministers going back to Thatcher's day. He was also around thirty years older than Helms. According to Perkins, Barron had formed an attachment to the young, rising barrister long before her political career took off. She hinted that they had had some kind of sexual relationship, at least in the beginning. Helms was not even married then. Barron had a long-standing wife who later died. In exchange for sex, Perkins explained, Barron became her mentor and Helms found her career gliding smoothly into high gear. She was fast-tracked onto advisory commissions and given a place on a government think tank. Naturally, her name appeared in a number of newspaper articles through Barron's media machine. He was always in the shadows, preferring to propel others into the limelight.

As Helms grew in stature and reputation, so did Barron's hold on her. After she married, the sexual favours apparently stopped, although that was not entirely clear. In any case, now there were other ways she could repay him. She helped pass a number of bills into law that directly aided his businesses and banking arrangements. Both she and her husband became regular guests on Barron's private yacht, as well as his various estates, in the Caribbean, the Maldives, the Côte D'Azur. It was no coincidence when Alex Hatton took over some of Barron's legal work. Eventually, though, it seems Hatton was not happy with the hold Barron had over his wife. There was a suggestion that the breakdown of the marriage owed something to Hatton's disapproval of how close Helms was to the magnate.

All of that was supposed to have changed when she met Cathy Perkins. At this point the book veered into highly personal territory, as Perkins described the disappointment she felt when she discovered that Helms was not really finished with Barron at all, but was still very much connected to him. Specifically, there was talk of an arms deal to Saudi Arabia that Helms was helping to push through. At this point the book descended into disordered notes and paragraphs that Marsh had no way of unravelling. One read: 'How much did she know?' Another: 'Check bank accounts for outgoing transfers. Cross ref/Panama Papers?' Perkins was a woman with a mission. The tone of the writing also suggested some bitterness. Maybe she had gone into the relationship with an open mind, only to discover later that Helms had not changed. Still, allegations in an unpublished book were one thing, but they were a long way from making a solid case. Marsh had a lot of questions, like how much did Helms know about the contents of Perkins' book and did she have the break-in staged to get rid of her? Marsh intended to confront Helms. She certainly didn't expect Helms to break down and confess all, but a public confrontation would certainly rattle her and oblige her to agree to a formal interview.

That, at least, was the plan. But things did not work out that way.

There was a substantial milling about in the main area of the mall. Crowd marshals and private security in DKGS uniforms were holding people back. Marsh was a little surprised to see how many were there. Marsh checked her phone again. Still no word from Drake. Where was he?

She was edging towards the far end of the central space. It was all very nice, but a shopping mall was just that and this was nothing special. Sure, they'd made an effort with the Victorian iron work on the gallery fittings from the old baths. It was a nice touch, but the whole thing had lost something, trading in authenticity for gimmickry.

At the back of her mind a little voice that sounded a lot like Milo was asking her what the hell she thought she was doing. Why was she sticking her neck out? She was still suspended and in enough trouble with Pryce to know better than to push him further. Somehow, none of that mattered to Marsh. She wished Cal was here. He would understand. Some things don't leave you alone. You don't stop thinking about a case just because you've been taken off it. Why did this one sting her so much? She knew it had something to do with blaming herself for Mark Chiang getting stabbed. If she hadn't insisted they follow up on her hunch he would be fine right now, walking along in his fancy coat.

A man coming the other way bumped into her, paused to look back, but then walked on without a word. Marsh was still staring after him when she spotted Ivan Hedley. He was on the other side of the mall, within a moving crowd.

She was confused at first. Why would he be here? She knew the answer almost before the question had finished forming itself in her mind. He was here because of Helms. To speak to her? To harm her? Now that he was on the run it might occur to him that she could help him. Whatever his intentions, Hedley was moving and Marsh forced her way through the crowd now with increased urgency. He vanished again, further towards the front where the stage had been set up.

The dragon was writhing its way sinuously through the crowd to her right. There were drums and cymbals banging somewhere up there. Hedley wasn't supposed to be here. It upturned everything.

As she tried not to lose sight of him while moving through the crowd, she worked out how Hedley had known Zoë Helms would be here today. No doubt his access to the DKGS operation would have told him that the politician would be opening the centre. The question of why remained unresolved. If Helms, or someone connected to her, had set up the break-in to get rid of Perkins, then why would he risk approaching her now? Could Marsh be wrong after all? Had Helms been the target all along? Or was this about something else? Could Hedley be just a loose cannon and whoever hired him had made a fatal miscalculation.

The crowds swelled around the bright crimson dragon writhing in the air, its golden tail whipping overhead. Someone was lowering a red packet of money down on a string from the first-floor gallery. They were going all out with the show. Cheering onlookers oohed and aahed, held up their phones to take pictures. There were rows of paper lanterns strung across the main hall. She caught another brief glimpse of Ivan Hedley, still moving towards the stage at the far end of the mall.

Marsh considered her options. She wasn't on the job, wasn't carrying handcuffs or a retractable baton. A situation like this could easily get out of hand. The crowd around her cheered their appreciation as the dragon swallowed up the packet of money. There were no uniforms in sight. The opening was entirely in the hands of private security.

Gathering around the stage was a group of official-looking men and women. Businessmen and local councillors. Marsh spotted Chiang's replacement in the same instant as he saw her. DS Barnes looked at her for a long moment before deciding either he was mistaken or it didn't matter. He was edging around Zoë Helms, who was smiling and talking to a tall, slim woman wearing a smart white trouser suit. The delegation moved up the steps onto the stage.

'What are you doing here?'

Marsh whipped round, as DS Barnes grabbed her arm.

'Ivan Hedley is here. You need to move her. I think she's in danger.'

Barnes smiled. 'Come on, Marsh, pull the other one.'

'I'm not joking, get her out!'

But Barnes wasn't buying it. 'Get out of here before I arrest you for interfering in security operations.'

'Look, maybe I was wrong,' Marsh said. 'Or maybe he's just got a grudge. Either way, I think he's here to finish her off.'

Barnes didn't seem to hear what she was saying. 'This can go one of two ways, Marsh.'

She pulled her arm free and darted left, hearing him curse behind her as she ducked in front of the dragon approaching the steps to the stage. She elbowed one of the onlookers aside, disturbing his camera angle and drawing more curses. A skinny little guy in a shiny suit stepped into her path. Some kind of bodyguard, she guessed, for one of the local entrepreneurs. He had a hard face and sharp cheekbones. Marsh held up a hand.

'Police. Get out of my way.'

He didn't understand, or maybe he didn't care. Either way, he didn't move. Over his shoulder she caught a glimpse of Hedley. Marsh rushed the goon, thumping him in the shoulder.

'Move! Now!'

Instead, he grabbed a hold of her, pinning her arms from behind with both of his. He was a weedy little runt but strong nevertheless. Marsh struggled for a moment then lifted her boot and stamped down on his instep. The man gave a squeal and let go of her to clutch his fancy shoe. She threw off his arms and started forward again. She could see Zoë Helms staring at her, the fixed smile on her face turning to a look of confusion. There were more arms trying to grab Marsh now; she felt as if she was fighting her way through thick forest.

Hedley had disappeared behind the stage. An area that everybody seemed to have overlooked. There were carpeted runways leading to and from the steps, back to a reception area that had been set up in one of the shop spaces off to the side. Tables covered with white paper. Serving staff pouring drinks into trays of plastic glasses. The place still looked bare, as though nobody was expected to spend long there. Just in and a few handshakes and then leave.

Marsh ducked behind the curtains and found Hedley crouched down, reaching into a sports bag on the floor.

'It's over, Hedley. Give yourself up!'

With a cry of rage he turned and threw the bag at her, spraying out a cloud of paper flyers. She ducked to see him disappearing through the curtains on the other side. Marsh went after him. She burst out to find the world in chaos. Everyone was screaming and running in all directions at once.

Something terrible had begun.

Through the melée she saw DS Barnes dragging Zoë Helms towards the rear exit, yelling into the radio mike in his sleeve. Marsh saw the fear on her face. She reached out a hand towards her and said something that Marsh couldn't catch.

Instead, Marsh turned and began pushing the other way, moving against the stream, fighting her way through the panicked crowds. She had no idea what she was moving towards, but whatever it was, a feeling in her gut told her it was bad.

41

The van door slid open with a screech. The hood was wrenched from his head as Drake was pushed out, something sharp in the canvas scratching his ear. Drake blinked, looking around, trying to get his bearings, squinting against the sudden light. For a moment he didn't know where he was. The steps leading up to the front entrance were unfamiliar, even though he knew the place, had known it for longer than he cared to remember. He saw the bright red letters curling over the glass portico that stretched across the front of the building. It looked like a weird Disneyfied version of a nightmare he had once had. He remembered hanging by his fingertips. Rats scurrying around the bottom of the pool below. Freetown. Seemed he could never get away from this place.

A hand at his back shoved him forward so that he had to stumble onto the steps and up to avoid falling over. The others were packed tightly around him. Another thump in his back. The three of them were there. Adeeb ahead, Kaseem on the right, Slimany to his left. Each had a firm hold of the oversized parka he was zipped into. It looked weird but everybody around them was too busy doing their own thing to notice. He was the only one not wearing a uniform.

They reached the top of the steps and one of the guards there started moving towards them. Drake recognised him from the other day. Heavily built, muscle turning to fat and the tattoos on his forearms. Drake saw the confusion on the man's face.

'Hey, what's going on here?'

'Allahu Akbar!'

The man seemed to lean into Adeeb and then stagger backwards. He twisted away and then spiralled, falling heavily, tumbling past them down the steps. Drake heard cries of alarm and caught a glimpse of the dark stain spreading over the front of the grey uniform but then he was being propelled upwards in through the wide doorway.

Underneath the parka he had been zipped into a vest that had been duct taped around his chest. At a distance, a crude attempt at a suicide vest. Close up, Drake could see sticks of plasticine and lengths of wire connected to an old phone. Kids could have done a better job, but he knew that from a distance it would be enough to buy him a shot in the head from an Armed Response Unit. The zipped-up parka pinned his upper arms to his body. Effectively, he was immobilised. Also, his hands were rigid. Something was fixed to them, something bulky and heavy. They felt as if they were wrapped in tape. He could move the tips of his fingers but nothing else. The tape was so tight the circulation had been partially cut off. He wriggled his shoulders to loosen it, opening and closing his fingers as much as he could to get the blood moving. He felt something hard and sharp dig into his thigh and a shudder ran down his spine: they had strapped knives to his hands.

'Stop this,' Drake whispered urgently, leaning into Slimany, the weakest of the three. 'You don't have to do this.'

'Be happy, bro.' Slimany smiled at him. 'You're going to become a shaheed. Very soon.'

'Don't throw your life away.' Drake was out of breath, talking as he stumbled up the steps, holding back, so that Kaseem had to work hard at keeping him moving. 'You still have time to change.'

'No, you don't understand.' Slimany's eyes were shining and Drake realised he was on something. Amphetamines, benzocaine or some kind of upper. He was high.

'Keep moving!' Kaseem hissed at him.

There was a shout from behind them, as someone saw the security guard whom Adeeb had stabbed. The doors ahead of them opened and Adeeb addressed two other DKGS guards.

'He just collapsed,' he said, pointing down. The guards looked at him, not recognising him, but seeing the uniform. They could see something wasn't right, but they couldn't work out what. One of them reached for the radio on his belt. Adeeb stepped in and thrust his knife into the man's ribs before pushing him into the other one. The two of them tumbled down the steps.

Then they were through the doors.

Adeeb was carrying what looked like a machete in one hand and a hunting knife in the other. He raised both above his head, clashing the blades together.

'Allahu Akbar!' he yelled.

By now they were all through the front doors and inside the main hall. Drake could see there was no police presence. No need. Security had been handed to the grey uniforms of DKGS, and already he could see a few of them scurrying along the upper galleries, running where it wasn't clear. Chaos. Their training probably hadn't covered this.

One group of people were standing frozen, staring at these new arrivals. Like rabbits caught in the headlights. Drake flung himself left and right, managing to confuse Slimany and then slamming into Kaseem to send him staggering off to the side.

'Run!' he yelled to the people who were staring at him in disbelief. 'All of you, run!'

They didn't run. They stood and stared with perplexed looks on their faces. Rabbits caught in the headlights. Twisting round, Drake managed to get an elbow up through the opening in the parka and forced the cheap zip. Slimany grabbed hold of him, allowing Drake to pull his shoulder free. The parka began to slip down. Ahead of him Adeeb was preoccupied with choosing his targets. He ran towards a group and they broke like balls on a pool table, splintering in every direction. A man in his thirties stopped and turned to face Adeeb.

'No!' Drake tried to yell. 'Just get away from him!'

Slimany was still trying to hold on to Drake. He turned and headbutted him, feeling the other man's nose breaking. Slimany staggered back, his hands trying to stem the blood pouring down his face. The parka was loose now and Drake kicked it to the ground and stepped out of it. He raised his arms to wave people back, realising that having a kitchen knife strapped to each hand wasn't helping. Over to his right he saw a blonde woman standing alone. She was backed against the glass of a shop window, trying to film everything on her phone. Kaseem decided to add some theatrics for the camera. Raising his hands high, he moved towards her, yelling 'Allah Akbar', brandishing his knives. Drake stepped in and hit him sharply in the throat with the bottom of his fist, using the hilt of the knife strapped to his right hand. Kaseem dropped with a gurgling sound. The woman came to life and was now running towards the entrance.

'Make your peace with Allah, kaffir,' Kaseem spluttered, hands to his throat. 'Today you will die.'

'We'll see about that,' said Drake, giving him a kick in the ribs for good measure. In the distance, he could hear sirens. Far too late. It was only a matter of minutes, but right now every second counted. He also knew that once the armed units arrived things would not look good for him with knives strapped to his hands.

Up ahead, a young man with a backpack stood facing Adeeb as he got up off the ground. He pulled off the rucksack from his back and held it in front of him in defence.

'No!' yelled Drake. 'Don't!'

The young man didn't stand a chance as Adeeb came at him, hitting him with a flurry of blows, stabbing him left and right. The man went down. There were screams all around them now, as people started running in all directions. Some were picking up their children, others were yelling for help.

Still no sign of the security guards trying to intervene. Drake started off in pursuit of Adeeb. The duct tape on his right hand was coming free. He ripped at it, using his teeth. As it started to unravel he jabbed the tip of the blade deep into the wood panelling of a seating island. The flimsy wood splintered as he wrenched hard but he managed to work the thick hilt out of the tape.

With a loud cry, Kaseem slammed into his right side and the two of them went down, sliding along the polished floor. Drake twisted over, blocking a blow that would have killed him. He kicked away Kaseem's right knee and rolled him off to one side. Throwing himself onto Kaseem's back, Drake managed to get a stranglehold around the man's neck. Normally, after fifteen to twenty seconds unconsciousness ensures. It took a little longer this time, but when Drake felt Kaseem slump in his arms, he pushed him aside and got up to go after Adeeb.

He ran, tearing at the last pieces of tape holding the second knife to his left hand as he went. Adeeb had been busy. Drake counted three victims lying on the ground. When he reached him, he had cornered a group of teenagers. They were huddled together. One of them pointed. Some of the men were trying to man up, getting ready to have a go at him. Drake knew then that Adeeb planned to escape. If all went according to plan, three of them would be taken down with a killshot straight to the head. Standard procedure when faced with assailants who are strapped with what looked like suicide vests. Kaseem and Slimany had always been expendable. Drake himself was just a convenient prop. With Slimany, Kaseem and Drake

410

out of the way there would be no witnesses to his involvement. Drake came to a halt as he saw another figure step out in front of Adeeb. He was about to yell a warning when he saw who it was.

From the expression on her face, Marsh was equally surprised to see Drake. There wasn't time for anything more. Throwing an arm around her throat, Adeeb pulled her tight to him, pointing the hunting knife at Drake.

'Back off!'

Drake was raising his arms. 'It's all right, take it easy.'

'You stay!' Adeeb yelled. 'You don't move.'

'Okay, okay. Just don't hurt her.'

Adeeb had other ideas. He dragged her backwards. They went by the stage, now littered with debris from the panic, the planned reception space where glasses and bowls had been overturned, bottles of champagne rolled on the floor. The curtain behind the stage hung in tatters. Adeeb was backing past this when he suddenly stopped. A baseball bat touching his arm made him jump as if it was a snake.

'What kind of wickedness you bringing here?' drawled a familiar voice.

Adeeb's face clouded in confusion as Wynstan stepped out from behind the curtains. He was not alone. Two others appeared on the other side. Drake recognised the Maori tattoo and the satin jacket. Adeeb licked his lips. He still made the mistake of thinking he could take them on, hopped up on adrenaline and whatever else was in his bloodstream. Either way, he let go of Marsh and went for Wynstan. He'd taken two steps before the Rock stepped in and laid him flat with one swing of his bat. He made it look effortless. Adeeb's feet lifted from the floor and he was out for the count before he hit the ground. They each took hold of one foot and dragged the unconscious man down the main hall towards where two others had Slimany and Kaseem under control. Marsh was shaking with shock. The sirens were close now and the air pulsated to the flare of flashing blue lights. Wynstan ran a critical eye over Drake.

'Man, they done you up like a turkey,' he chuckled. 'You'd better make yourself scarce. We'll take care of this.' He nodded towards the rear.

'Thanks, Wynstan,' said Drake, looking back at the mayhem.

'Don't mention it, man. Just sweepin' the neighbourhood clean.'

42

Crane was driving. She hated being in a car with anyone else behind the wheel so Drake had to settle for riding shotgun. Marsh was in the back with Nahda, who sat in silence. The child on her lap, half sleeping, half watching Marsh on the sly.

'They picked up Ivan Hedley at his mother's place,' Marsh was saying. It was four days after the events in Freetown and things seemed to be settling. Facing charges of attacking a police officer and inflicting grievous bodily harm, Hedley had come clean, giving them the names of all his accomplices, including the man who had stabbed DS Chiang.

'How's he doing, by the way?' Drake twisted round to see a wistful smile on Marsh's face as she stared out of the window. 'What's that about?'

'Nothing,' she said too quickly, which clearly meant there was something. 'He's not so bad once you get to know him.'

'I see,' said Drake, exchanging looks with Crane.

413

In medical terms, Mark Chiang was out of danger and well on the road to recovery. He would be back on light duties in about a month. Marsh had been asked to take some time off before being fully reinstated with a commendation for bravery from Superintendent Wheeler that had overridden any misgivings Pryce might have had.

'So what's Hedley saying about the Perkins murder?' Drake asked.

'Well, so far he's sticking to his story that it was an accident,' Marsh sighed. 'He didn't intend to kill anyone. He just panicked.'

'Do you believe him?' asked Crane.

'Not for a second. I think he was paid to kill Perkins, but he's more afraid of whoever paid him than he is of us.'

'What about the framing of the other guy, Mourad?' Drake continued.

'Yeah, he admits that. He said it was too easy. He got the DNA evidence from Mourad's previous case with the help of a couple of DKGS colleagues.'

'Warren and Taylor?' said Drake.

'Exactly.' Marsh shook her head. 'Those two are up to their ears in it.'

'They were being paid off by Aslan, right?' Drake asked. 'You have enough to prove it?'

'We've got plenty. Adeeb was singing like the proverbial canary,' said Marsh. Adeeb, Slimany and Kaseem would be going to prison for a long time. Thankfully nobody was killed, but there were some serious injuries, with two people still in critical condition. 'I still don't get why they did it.'

Drake had a theory about that. This was Aslan's grand plan. He thought letting Adeeb and his boys carry out their attack would hit the Freetown Arena hard, maybe even force it to close. In particular, he was hoping it would hit Ziyade and Donny, giving him a better chance of muscling in on their territory. It was an ambitious, not to mention reckless, plan and Drake was not convinced it would ever have worked, but when did that ever dissuade anyone?

'Has Aslan been picked up?' Crane asked, glancing in the mirror at Marsh.

'He's disappeared,' said Marsh.

'My feeling is that we're not going to see him again, not alive at least.' Drake looked over at Crane.

'Sal Ziyade?'

'He's not the forgiving type,' said Drake.

'We're lucky your friend Wynstan showed up,' Marsh said, leaning over the front seat.

'I know. I owe him one.'

'So what about Helms?' Crane asked.

'Perkins paints a not-too-flattering portrait of her,' Marsh said. 'I think if and when the book comes out she's going to have a lot of explaining to do. It'll be the end of her political career for sure.'

Drake wasn't as convinced. 'These people have more lives than a witch's cat. She'll move into the private sector for a while and when it's all blown over she'll reinvent herself. Just wait and see.'

'Would she really have gone that far?' said Crane. 'I mean, contracting someone to kill her lover is pretty far out.'

'She was probably not alone on that decision,' said Drake. 'Stafford-Bryce is busy working on knocking the book into shape. According to him, there are a lot of people implicated. It could be, it just got out of hand.'

Sitting alongside Marsh in the back, Nahda and her little boy were silent for most of the way. They had arrived back at Balfour Mews exhausted and terrified. Nahda was afraid the traffickers would come after her. Crane assured her they wouldn't. She gave mother and child time to settle down and take a long bath. She had to go and buy her fresh clothes because what Nahda had in her carrier bag was dirty and worn. She had shed the black ebaya and was now wearing jeans and a down jacket. It took a while for the young woman to relax enough to trust Crane. Leaving her alone at home had given Nahda some much needed breathing space. When she got back, Crane found mother and child playing on the Persian rug on the floor in the main room. Nahda clutched her child to her when Crane opened the door, but within minutes had started to relax.

It took time, but over the next few evenings, Nahda had told Crane her story. She was nineteen years old. When she was barely fifteen Daesh had come to her home village near Raqqa. Her brothers felt it was best to join, in order to avoid trouble. Her father refused and was hanged from a lamppost outside their house. They were not allowed to take him down for days.

'All the men were killed and the women were taken prisoner.'

'That's when you met Jason.'

Nahda shook her head. 'First there was another man.' She closed her eyes. 'I don't want to remember him. Later, he died in an air raid. Then they told me I was to become the bride of another fighter. Abu Hamra, they called him. The red one, on account of his hair. At first I was scared of him, this man with a big red beard, but he was always very kind to me.'

The faint trace of a smile appeared and then vanished again. After a couple of days of decent food and rest, she looked better. Her hair was washed and hanging loose. Sitting cross-legged on the floor, she gazed down at her baby, who lay gurgling contentedly before her. Crane guessed that whatever happy memories she might have had, they had long since been snuffed out by the sadness that had followed.

'In the beginning, he would not touch me. I was very young. I thought he did not like me.' Nahda gave a sniff. 'He said only when I was ready.'

'It must have been a difficult time.'

'You never knew when the bombs would come. Every day when he took his gun and went out, I thought I would never see him again.'

Crane waited and then, very gently, asked, 'What happened to him?'

'One day, he just never came back.' Nahda was shaking her head at the memory. 'By then the Americans were bombing very hard. We had to move. The city was in ruins.'

'What happened then?'

Nahda shrugged. 'I don't know. I asked about him. I went to their offices and they told me he was a shaheed and I should be proud of him.' She looked down at her child. 'I knew then that I had to leave.'

Crane recounted the story as she drove. Marsh had not heard the whole thing before. Nahda seemed to understand enough to know they were talking about her. She turned her head away to stare out of the window at the landscape passing by. However hard it was for her to talk about her time under Islamic State, it was even harder for her to describe her ordeal in the camps. She couldn't bring herself to speak in any detail. It would take time. Crane understood that Jason had arranged safe passage for her back to Britain in the event of anything happening to him. He used the same network he had used to get out to Syria in the first place. But things had changed and a woman travelling alone with a small child was easy prey. The gang had decided she was worth more under their control, and so she was passed along the chain until she wound up in their little brothel at the Ben Jonson Hotel. It was hard to imagine a more sordid ending to her story. It would take time for all the details to emerge, but in the meantime what mattered was finding somewhere she could be safe for now.

It was the second time in a week that Crane had driven this stretch of road. Today it felt a little more relaxed. She'd managed to get the hard part over with two days ago, when she had sped up on the bike alone. She knew that what she had to tell Mrs Spencer couldn't be done on the phone. It had to come from her in person. In the end she had taken it well. She sat quietly for a moment on the sofa in the living room and then she took a deep breath and let the air slowly out of her lungs.

'It's what I've been expecting,' she said quietly. 'It's what we've

418

both been expecting for a long time. In a way it's a bit of a relief to know.'

'I'm sorry it couldn't have been better news.'

'What will happen to her now?' Mrs Spencer had been staring out of the window at the garden. She turned round to face Crane. 'I mean, will she be allowed to stay in this country?'

'It's not clear. The law is quite tricky. They keep moving the goalposts.'

'I understand. But surely, the boy?'

'There are no legal grounds for establishing that Jason is actually the father.'

'Couldn't we do a DNA test. Wouldn't that prove it?'

'It's possible. I'm not sure that would be enough to satisfy the authorities.'

Mrs Spencer stared at her. 'But you believe her?'

'I do, yes.'

'If we did the tests and recognised him as our son's child?'

'That would help, of course. For her, too.'

Mrs Spencer was silent for a moment, looking down at her hands. Then she said, 'I'd like to meet him. Them. I'd like to see them. Could that be arranged?'

'Of course. And your husband, will he be all right with it?'

'I'll speak to him before you come.' Mrs Spencer nodded, before adding, 'I'll know. When I see him, I'll know if he's my grandson.'

In the mirror, Crane could see Nahda staring out of the window at the green, unfamiliar world she was now living in. She wondered what the young woman was thinking. If she was imagining a life for herself here, for her son. Up ahead, Crane could see the sign marking the turn they needed to take. She smiled to herself as she swung the wheel. She had a feeling it was going to be all right. Everything was going to be all right.